SECRET VOWS

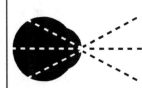

This Large Print Book carries the
Seal of Approval of N.A.V.H.

SECRET VOWS

ROCHELLE ALERS

THORNDIKE PRESS
A part of Gale, Cengage Learning

GALE
CENGAGE Learning·

Detroit • New York • San Francisco • New Haven, Conn • Waterville, Maine • London

GALE
CENGAGE Learning

Copyright © 2013 by Rochelle Alers.
A Hideaway Novel Series #3.
Thorndike Press, a part of Gale, Cengage Learning.

Thorndike Press® Large Print African-American.
The text of this Large Print edition is unabridged.
Other aspects of the book may vary from the original edition.
Set in 16 pt. Plantin.

LIBRARY OF CONGRESS CATALOGING-IN-PUBLICATION DATA

Alers, Rochelle.
    Secret Vows / By Rochelle Alers.
        pages cm. — (A Hideaway Novel Series ; 3)
    ISBN-13: 978-1-4104-6228-2 (hardcover)
    ISBN-10: 1-4104-6228-5 (hardcover)
        1. Cousins—Fiction. 2. Wagers—Fiction. 3. Families—Fiction. 4. Large type books. I. Title.
    PS3551.L3477S425 2013
    813'.54—dc23   2013029159

Published in 2013 by arrangement with Harlequin Books S.A.

Printed in Mexico
1 2 3 4 5 6 7 17 16 15 14 13

HIDEAWAY WEDDING SERIES

Good-natured boasting raises its multimillion-dollar head at the Cole family compound during a New Year's Eve celebration. Family patriarch Martin Cole proposes each man in attendance place a one-million-dollar wager to the winner's alma mater as an endowment in their name. The terms: predicting who among Nicholas, Jason and Ana will marry before the next New Year's Eve.

Twins Jason and Ana Cole have given no indication they are even remotely thinking of tying the knot. Both claim they are too busy signing new talent to their record label. Former naval officer Nicholas Cole-Thomas has also been dragging his feet when it comes to the opposite sex. However, within the next six months Ana, Nicholas and Jason will encounter a very special person who will not only change them, but change their lives forever.

In *Summer Vows,* when CEO of Serenity Records Ana Cole signs a recording phenom to her label, she ignites a rivalry that targets her for death. Her safety and well-being are then entrusted to family friend U.S. Marshal Jacob Jones, and Ana is forced to step away from the spotlight and her pampered lifestyle. She unwillingly follows Jacob to his vacation home in the Florida Keys until those responsible for the hit on her life are apprehended. Once Ana gets past Jacob's rigid rules, she finds herself surrendering to the glorious sunsets and the man willing to risk everything, including his heart, to keep her safe and make her his own.

Nicholas Cole-Thomas's entry into the world of horse breeding has caused quite a stir in Virginia's horse country. Not only is he quite the eligible bachelor, but there is also a lot of gossip about his prized Arabian breeding stock. In *Eternal Vows,* Nicholas meets Peyton Blackstone, the neighboring farm's veterinarian intern. He is instantly drawn to her intelligence, but recognizes the vulnerability she attempts to mask with indifference. Nicholas offers Peyton a position to work on his farm, and when they step in as best man and maid of honor at his sister's spur-of-the-moment wedding, he tries to imagine how different his life would be with a wife of his own. Just when he opens his heart to love again, someone from Peyton's past resurfaces to shatter their newfound happiness, and now Nicholas must decide whether their love is worth fighting for.

Record executive Jason Cole will admit to anyone that he has a jealous mistress: music. As the artistic director for Serenity Records Jason is laid-back, easygoing and a musical genius. His brief tenure running the company is over and he's heading to his recording studio in a small remote Oregon mountain town to indulge in his obsession. But all that changes in *Secret Vows,* when Jason hears restaurant waitress Greer Evans singing backup with a local band. As they become more than friends, he is unaware of the secret she jealously guards with her life. And when he finds himself falling in love with Greer, Jason is stunned to find she is the only one who stands between him and certain death, at the same time realizing love is the most desperate risk of all.

Don't forget to read, love and live romance.

Rochelle Alers

HIDEAWAY SERIES

Everett Kirkland - Teresa Maldanado* - Samuel Cole -

Martin Cole -Parris Simmons[1]   Josephine

Oscar Spencer- Regina Cole - Aaron Spencer[5]   Tyler Cole - Dana Nichols[9]   Arianna   Gisela   E

Clayborne   Eden   Martin, II   Astra   Samuel II

Nancy Cole - Noah Thomas

Timothy Cole-Thomas - Nichola Bennett   Ynez   Grace   Mali

Diego Cole-Thomas - Vivienne Neal[13]   Celia Cole-Thomas - Gavin Faulkner[14]

Samuel   Isabella   Nicholas -

Matthew Sterling - Eve Blackwell - Alejandro Delgado[2]   Joshua K

Sara Sterling - Salem Lassiter [6]   Christopher Delgado - Emily Kirkland[7]

Isaiah   Eve/Nona (twins)   Alejandro   Esperanza   Mateo

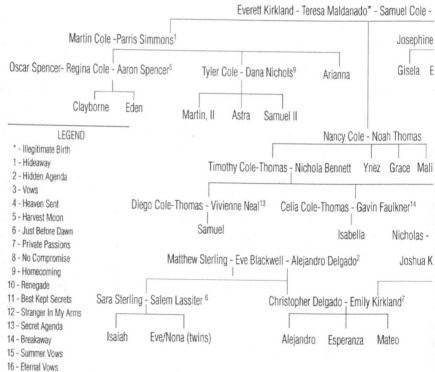

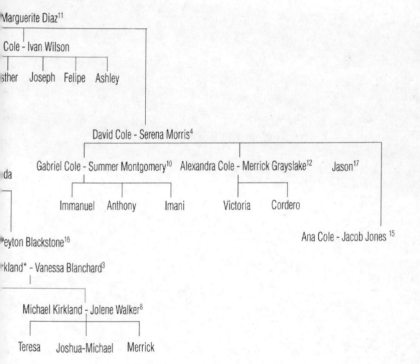

Marguerite Diaz[11]

Cole - Ivan Wilson

sther   Joseph   Felipe   Ashley

David Cole - Serena Morris[4]

da

Gabriel Cole - Summer Montgomery[10]   Alexandra Cole - Merrick Grayslake[12]   Jason[17]

Immanuel   Anthony   Imani   Victoria   Cordero

Ana Cole - Jacob Jones [15]

eyton Blackstone[16]

kland* - Vanessa Blanchard[3]

Michael Kirkland - Jolene Walker[8]

Teresa   Joshua-Michael   Merrick

Happy the husband of a good wife,
twice-lengthened are his days;
a worthy wife brings joy to her husband,
peaceful and full is his life.
— *Sirach* 26:1, 2

PROLOGUE

West Palm Beach, Florida

Timothy Cole-Thomas felt his cell phone vibrate. Reaching into the pocket of his shirt, he stared at the display, smiled and tapped a button. "Hello, Nicholas."

"Hello, Dad. I just called to let you know I'm getting married."

Low-key, soft-spoken Timothy cut a step, spun around and bellowed at the top of his lungs. "Yes!" Everyone standing or lounging around the pool at the West Palm Beach family compound turned to stare at him as if he'd completely lost his mind. "Who is she?" he whispered conspiratorially, walking a short distance away so he wouldn't be overheard by four generations of Coles who'd gotten together for the Labor Day weekend. He listened as Nicholas told him about the veterinarian with whom he'd fallen in love. "When are we going to meet her?" he asked his youngest son.

"That's not going to be for a while," Nicholas said.

Timothy felt a shiver eddy its way up his back when his son explained why Peyton Blackstone wouldn't be able to travel for at least two months. She'd been stabbed by her ex-husband before the man was shot by a member of her cousin's horse farm's security team.

"If the farm has optimum security measures in place, then how did her ex-husband bypass it?"

"We discovered he had paid a member of the catering staff to let him use his uniform to surprise his girlfriend with an engagement ring. The poor man had no way of knowing he was being set up as an accomplice to an attempted murder. This is a reminder that anyone can breach the best protected property."

Timothy was aware that his son's horse farm used the most sophisticated electronic equipment available, and he'd also hired highly trained security personnel to protect his investment, but there were those willing to risk life and limb to steal his prized Arabians.

"I want you to be careful, Nicky."

"I will."

"Shall I give the rest of the family the

good news?" he asked.

"Sure. As soon as Peyton's up to receiving visitors, I want you and Mom to come and stay for a few weeks. Peyton's mother is here, and I know she would like to discuss wedding plans with Mom. Peyton wants a simple church wedding at the chapel on Blackstone Farms, and she's agreed to repeat her vows on New Year's Eve along with Ana and Jacob in West Palm. I already called Ana and asked if she wouldn't mind sharing her wedding celebration with us, and she said yes. I'd asked her not to say anything to you or Mom until I told you myself."

Timothy nodded even though his son couldn't see him. It was obvious Nicholas was either nervous or excited because he was talking nonstop. "So, that's why Ana's been giving me strange looks ever since she got here. I'll be certain to let her know you told me. If you guys want to take a honeymoon, then renovations to the house in Venice should be ready by the end of the year. Your mother and I are going back next year for Carnival, and you and Peyton are more than welcome to join us. The villa has three apartments, so there's plenty of space where we won't have to run into one another."

"I'll tell her, and then I'll let you know.

15

I'm sorry to ring off, Dad, but I have to meet with someone at three."

"Thanks for calling, and congratulations."

"Thanks. Love you, Dad."

"I love you, too, son."

Timothy ended the call, and then approached his uncles who were engaged in a heated discussion about the upcoming football season. "*Mis estimado tíos,* I'd like to speak to you in the library."

Martin Cole rested an arm on his nephew's shoulder. "Since when did we become esteemed uncles? I've always been *Martin.*"

David Cole flashed a matched set of dimples. The bright Florida sun glinted off his cropped silver hair. "The only one who has ever been *uncle anything* is Josh."

Joshua Kirkland smiled behind the lenses of his sunglasses. "That's because I've always struck fear in the heart of this pup."

Timothy laughed again. "I'm over sixty and much too old to be a pup. Even Diego — who'll be forty in a couple years — can't be considered a pup. Now, Martin's grandson Clayborne is definitely in the pup category."

Martin nodded. "Let's go inside so we can find out what Timothy has been sniggling about."

Timothy waited until everyone was seated

in the library, its shelves lined with first edition classic bestsellers, antiques and reproductions. "Nicholas just called me to say he's getting married." A couple groans followed his announcement. "Hold up," he said, when the three men started talking at once. "He's having a small church wedding at the chapel on the neighboring farm, and then he and his wife plan to repeat their vows here on New Year's Eve. And before you ask, David, Ana and Jacob have agreed to a double wedding ceremony."

David ran long brown fingers over his face. "Why didn't Ana say anything to me about this?"

"She didn't because Nicholas had asked her not to," Timothy explained.

Martin laced his fingers together and slumped farther down in his favorite leather chair. "I guess you're done with the wager, Timothy. And this only leaves David's Jason. What do you think, Josh?"

It was early in the morning of the past New Year's Day when the four men had wagered whose single thirty-something children would marry before the end of the year. Each man had put up a million dollars, the winner setting up an endowment in their name to their alma mater. David was the exception when he had to wager two million because his unmarried twin son and daughter were two of the three targets reluctant to change their marital status. That had all changed when Ana had married U.S. Marshal Jacob Jones. Those who'd selected Ana to marry first, and then Nicholas, were certain to win the wager.

David frowned. "Martin, why are you asking him about my boy?"

"Because Joshua is impartial, David," Martin countered. "None of his kids are involved in this wager."

Joshua, having removed his sunglasses, massaged the bridge of his nose. His light green eyes shifted from his brothers to his nephew. "I don't think Jason's going to remain single much longer."

"Why would you say that?" Timothy asked.

Looping one leg over the opposite knee, Joshua met David's eyes. "Jason and Ana are twins who've done everything together. They never had to look for a date for red carpet events because they always had each other. Since Ana is married and has hinted she wants a baby, Jason is almost forced to find someone to step in and replace her. Up until now his life has been rather safe. He'll date a woman for a little while, but then he'll drop her because he claims she doesn't measure up. No woman will ever measure up because my nephew doesn't know what he wants."

David's frown deepened. "You guys have a nasty habit of psychoanalyzing my kids."

"Josh is right," Martin concurred. "You and Serena have provided safety nets for your children that Josh and Timothy haven't. You built a house with enough room for your kids to live there for the rest of their lives. Correct me if I'm wrong, brother. Doesn't Jason still live at home?"

David crossed his arms over his chest. "Yes. But he's moving out when —"

Martin put up a hand. "No buts, David. I know Jason plans to move into Ana's condo when she and Jacob buy a house, and that Jason built a place in Oregon, but he's still living at home. If your thirty-three-year-old son proves me wrong, then I'll be the first to apologize, but only after Joshua apologizes," he teased.

Joshua placed both feet on the priceless rug, rising from his seat. "Oh, hell no. I'm not apologizing. We'll see come New Year's who's right and who's wrong." He extended his hand, palm down, and individually each man stood, placing his hand on the top one; then they took turns pounding Timothy's back, while congratulating him on his son's upcoming nuptials.

Two down and one to go, and then the winner of the wedding wager would be revealed.

CHAPTER 1

Phoenix, Arizona

The intercom on Greer Evans's desk buzzed softly. Unconsciously she reached for the receiver, while at the same time her gaze was fixed on the internal report she'd spent the past hour perusing. "Evans," she said in her usual greeting.

"The director would like you to come to his office."

Her eyes shifted to the telephone display. She and the others assigned to the Bureau of Alcohol, Tobacco, Firearms and Explosives' Phoenix, Arizona, field office attended biweekly meetings in the director's office where they were brought up-to-date on regional operations. It wasn't often she was singularly summoned.

"When, Miss Kelly?" she asked the woman who monitored everyone and everything going on at the site.

"He wants to see you *now.*"

21

"I'm on my way."

Greer hung up, coming to her feet and exiting the cubicle where she had spent countless hours since being reassigned to the southwest region. The adjustment hadn't been an easy one for her. The first thing she'd had to get used to was living in the desert. The dry heat, smog and occasional monsoon were a far cry from the change of seasons she'd experienced in Chicago and Washington, D.C. During the summer months she went directly from the air-conditioned office to the air-conditioned car and then drove to her artificially cooled one-bedroom furnished apartment with picturesque mountain views.

Plus she had to adjust to sitting at a desk. At first it had been difficult but, as the months passed, Greer had come to look forward to not going undercover; she was content to spend the rest of her professional career office-bound until it came time for her to collect her government pension. Why, she mused, was she thinking about retiring when that wouldn't become a reality for at least another thirty years? At thirty-two, it should be the last thing on her mind.

Greer didn't want to become cynical about her chosen career path because, after all, her mother had warned her of the pitfalls of undercover work. Her parents had met when both were recruits at the Quantico training facility. Her mother had joined the FBI, and her father had chosen the DEA. Then there was her twin brother. He'd followed in the family tradition of law enforcement when he also had joined the FBI.

She knew her mother, a retired FBI forensic technician, was uneasy each time Greer was selected for an undercover assignment, but she'd sworn an oath to uphold the Constitution of the United States against all enemies, foreign and domestic, and those dealing in the sale and transportation of illegal explosives and firearms were enemies. She barely glanced at Sheila Kelly sitting in an alcove outside the field director's office as she pushed open the door and walked in, realizing Roland wasn't alone.

"You wanted to see me, Roland?"

Roland Peña's head popped up. "Yes." Rays of sunlight coming through windows bathed him in a halo of gold. Smiling, he rose to his feet, indicating the chair facing a sofa. "Please sit down."

Pushing off a worn leather sofa was a tall pale man in an ill-fitting black suit. Her gaze shifted from the stranger to the man whom she'd grown to respect — unlike her former supervisor who wasn't above using his power to intimidate his subordinates. Roland was soft-spoken, approachable and well liked by everyone in the regional office.

Her supervisor walked over to the sofa and sat down. "I'd like you to meet special agent Bradley Plimpton. He's the assistant director of the Seattle Field Division."

Greer nodded. "Special Agent Plimpton," she said in acknowledgment. Once she was seated, he sat back down on the couch, one ankle propped on the opposing knee.

Bradley's coal-black eyes narrowed. Greer didn't know why, but there was something about the man's emaciated appearance, black suit and straight raven hair brushed off his forehead that reminded her of caricatures of undertakers.

"I'm sorry to spring this on you without warning, Evans. Your supervisor just approved your transfer to my division."

She hadn't realized she'd been holding her breath as she mentally repeated his last statement. What was Bradley talking about? She hadn't spoken to Roland about a transfer. Not once since she'd come to Arizona had Greer mentioned to anyone that she didn't want to live in the desert, that she preferred to see an actual change of seasons. Yet, if she was going to be transferred to the

Seattle Field Division, then that meant she would become part of the ATF's largest geographic division in the country. This transfer could have her living and working anywhere in Washington, Idaho, Alaska, Hawaii, Guam or Oregon.

"Why?"

"We need you to go undercover in Mission Grove."

Greer leaned forward, the motion seemingly robotic. "Mission Grove?" she repeated.

"Yes, Agent Evans. Mission Grove," Bradley said, placing both feet on the floor. Clasping his hands together, he sandwiched them between his knees. "We know you spent your childhood summers there with your aunt and uncle. We also know that you still keep in contact with your uncle even though your mother's sister passed away three years ago."

"What does that have to do with me going undercover in Mission Grove, Agent Plimpton?" she asked when he paused and stared at the floor.

A beat passed before Plimpton raised his head. "One of our agents was shot near the Mexico-Arizona border during a confrontation with drug smugglers. He managed to kill one of them, and when we recovered their weapons, we were able to trace them back to a man living in the Hood River Valley."

"Did you interrogate him?" Greer asked, her voice barely a whisper.

"We couldn't."

"And why not?" She'd asked yet another question.

"We couldn't because he died four years ago. What we did find out was that he'd had a break-in at his home the year before he passed away, yet reported nothing missing. We figured whoever broke into his house wasn't looking to steal money or valuables but his identity. When I ran his name through the federal firearms database, I discovered hundreds of semiautomatic pistols and assault rifles purchased from gun shops in Vancouver, L.A., and as far east as Texas and Tennessee. We also traced at least a half dozen pistols used by several Seattle gangs back to a gun shop burglary in the Hood River Valley. There have also been a string of similar break-ins ranging from Portland to Mission Grove. Whoever is spear-heading this operation has probably amassed an enormous arsenal, selling these illegal firearms to drug dealers. The DEA is dealing with the drug problem, but the sale of illegal firearms falls under our jurisdiction. We've selected you to identify the person or persons behind this because you're familiar with the region."

"What I don't understand," Greer said, "is why break into someone's home to steal their personal information? Why not do it electronically? Cybercriminals do it every day."

Plimpton shifted slightly when his right hand twitched noticeably. "The man wasn't online. Whoever stole his identity must have known the victim personally."

She knew the states that didn't require a permit to purchase firearms, although many required licenses needed to carry a concealed firearm. Oregon was one of those states. But if someone was buying guns legally, afterward reselling them to those who couldn't pass background checks, then that had raised a red flag with the ATF.

Greer listened intently when briefed about her new assignment. She would become a waitress at Stella's. Her uncle, former Special Forces Robert "Bobby" Henry knew she and her brother were federal officers. "Have you told my uncle that I'll be working at his restaurant?"

Bradley gave her a subtle nod. "Yes. We had to give him clearance because we're going to use his place for your base of operation."

Greer exhaled an audible breath. It made her feel better knowing that she didn't have to lie to her uncle as to why she'd come back to Mission Grove for an extended stay. "When do I leave?"

Roland crossed his arms over his chest. "You'll have tonight to pack and clean out your apartment. A team of agents from the bureau are flying up to Portland tomorrow morning to join in the search for the three missing kids from a nearby campground. They'll pick you up at four in the morning for a six o'clock liftoff. Don't worry about your vehicle. I'll have one of the agents retrieve it from your apartment building's parking lot."

Pushing to her feet, she nodded like a bobble head doll. "I guess I'd better start packing."

Roland stood and extended his hand, smiling. "You take care of yourself out there."

She took his hand. "I will." Walking out of the director's office, Greer returned to her cubicle. It took fewer than two minutes to fill a cardboard box with her meager accumulation of personal items: a coffee cup, several paperback novels, a crystal heart-shaped paperweight and a miniature cactus plant.

"Going somewhere, Evans?"

Greer nodded. The auditor peering over her partition had a problem processing the word no when she'd told him she didn't believing in dating her coworkers. But that hadn't stopped him from seeking her out whenever she ate in the employee lunchroom. "I'm being transferred."

Harold Browning approached her, his hazel eyes widening in surprise. "When did you find out?"

"Just a few minutes ago."

Harold's sandy-brown eyebrows lifted. "You're kidding, aren't you?"

She shifted the box to a more comfortable position as she picked up her handbag. "No, I'm not."

"Where are you going?"

Greer wanted to tell Harold that she was going far enough away so she wouldn't have to be annoyed by his persistence. "Portland," she said instead of Mission Grove. "I have to go."

Harold looked as if he was going to burst into tears. He ran both hands over his thinning blond hair. "I'm going to miss you, Evans."

"I'm going to miss you, too, Browning."

She would miss seeing him leaning over the partition to her cubicle to greet her every morning and his puppy-dog expression whenever she chided Harold for asking her out. The CPA was as brilliant as he was annoying. He'd pursued her when he should've focused his attention on some of the other single women who'd made it known they were interested in him. Why, she thought, did people always want what they couldn't have?

Turning on the heels of her rubber-soled shoes, Greer headed for the exit, ignoring curious glances from special agents, investigators, technicians and support staff as they watched her departing figure.

When she stepped outside, the summer heat hit her like opening the door to a blast furnace, making it difficult for her to draw a normal breath. It was mid-August, and the afternoon temperature was over one hundred degrees. She was going to Oregon, a place where she didn't have to contend with triple-digit summer heat and hardly a drop of precipitation. Oregon — a spot where all she had to deal with were moderating temperatures and the invigorating feel of rain on her face.

Even without asking, her prayer had been answered. Greer didn't want to think about her next assignment once she identified who'd stolen identities to buy and sell firearms to criminals. It was always easier to think about the present, while concentrating on not blowing her cover. Working at her uncle's restaurant would be like attending a kiddie birthday party. No pressure, no having to look over her shoulder or worry about her backup. All she had to do was keep her eyes and ears open.

Getting into her compact car, Greer started up the engine. She waited for the vents to blow cooling air over her face before she shifted into gear and maneuvered out of the parking lot. She wasn't given much time to pack; however, living in a furnished apartment definitely had its advantages. All she had to do was clean out her closets, dresser drawers, put up several loads of laundry and then pack everything in two large rolling duffel bags, one containing her service revolver, bulletproof vest, government-issue laptop, a case with an assault rifle and clips of ammunition. She'd learned to travel light with what she deemed the essentials. If it didn't fit into the duffel bags, then she could do without it.

Early the next morning Greer turned off the air-conditioner. She took one last look around the apartment where she'd spent the past five months of her life, then walked into the bathroom. When her former supervisor had initiated her transfer with a recommendation to desk duty, he'd claimed she was close to burnout, and the department couldn't afford to lose one of their best undercover special agents.

She'd agreed and was grateful for the respite; there were occasions when she had a problem remembering who she actually was because she'd been so deep undercover. Looking at her reflection in the mirror over the vanity, Greer brushed her hair and secured it in a ponytail. The purplish tint had faded completely. She'd been tempted to dye it back to its natural shade, but her hair had undergone so many colors and styles during the years she'd been undercover as a special agent for the ATF, she was surprised it would grow to any appreciable length. There was a time when she'd shaved one side of her head. Then she'd affected twists, braids and extensions.

The sound of the doorbell echoed in the apartment, and Greer left the bathroom to answer the intercom. She punched a button. "Yes?"

"I have a four o'clock pickup for Ms. Evans."

"Come on up." They'd sent a woman to meet her.

She punched the button to disengage the lock on the downstairs door. Opening the door to her apartment, Greer stood off to the side. When she saw the man coming up the staircase, she launched herself at him. He wore khakis, a black golf shirt with the FBI logo over the breast pocket and black hiking boots. It was apparent her twin brother had been selected as a member of the team of agents going up to Portland to search for the three boys who'd vanished without a trace.

"Cooper!"

Cooper Evans caught his sister in midair, holding her against his chest. There was no mistaking they were related. They shared the same golden-brown complexion and slanting light brown eyes; however, Cooper was taller, a more masculine version of his twin sister. He kissed her cheek. Her bare face made her appear much younger than a woman in her early thirties. The desert sun had darkened her complexion to a rich cinnamon-brown.

"You seem to have fared well for a desk jockey."

Looping her arms around Cooper's neck,

Greer pressed her forehead to her brother's. "Jealous, bro?"

"Heck, no. I love being in the field." He tugged playfully on her ponytail. "Let's go. The others are waiting for us. During the flight, you can catch me up on what's been going on since we last spoke to each other."

Although she and Cooper exchanged texts a couple times each week, it was a rare occasion when they were able to talk on the phone, but never about their jobs. Greer again glanced around the living/dining area, then grasped the handle to one of her bags, but Cooper usurped her when he lifted both effortlessly. She left the keys to the apartment on the table in the dining area and walked out, closing the self-locking door behind her. A black Suburban with heavily tinted windows sat idling in the parking lot. Cooper opened the hatch, placing her bags in the cargo area.

She opened the rear door, slipping onto the third row of seats beside a young attractive brunette who wore a wind-breaker stamped with the letters identifying her as a special agent with the FBI. Other than the driver and their lone female agent, two other agents were fast asleep, soft snores echoing in the vehicle's interior.

The woman flashed a friendly smile. "Allison Singer."

Greer returned her smile. "Jane Evans," she whispered, introducing herself, while not wishing to wake the other sleeping passengers. Legally she was Jane Greer Evans, but her father insisted on calling her Greer.

Cooper got in beside Allison and settled back against the leather seat. The driver maneuvered out of the parking lot, accelerating and following the signs to the Sky Harbor International Airport.

The Learjet had lifted off at six, and Greer was rendered speechless when her brother revealed that in another three months he'd become a permanent member of the FBI's Hostage Rescue Team. This meant he would have to deploy on short notice to any location in the United States or internationally. Although she didn't see Cooper as often as she would've liked, the thought of him leaving the country to confront the most complex threats was chilling.

"Have you told Mom and Dad about this?" she asked him. Their parents had relocated from D.C. to a retirement community in Ashburn, Virginia.

Cooper nodded. "I discussed it with Dad before submitting my application. He wasn't overjoyed, but he did give me his blessing. What's up with your transfer?"

She told him about the illegal gun sales. Her voice rose in excitement when talking about working at Stella's. The year they had celebrated their eighth birthday, their parents had sent them to Mission Grove to spend the summer months. They had learned to fly-fish, swim in the ice-cold lake, pick berries for the pies their aunt Stella made for the restaurant and, when they were older, how to hunt and survive in the woods. Greer and Cooper waited anxiously for the end of the school year to board a plane for the cross-country flight. They would always return counting down the months when they would again enjoy a short summer where they existed like wood sprites.

Pressing his head to the back of his seat, Cooper closed his eyes. "You be careful. I don't want anything to happen to you where you can't marry or make me an uncle."

Greer landed a soft punch on her brother's rock-hard shoulder. "I didn't know you were a comedian. And you of all people should know I don't want another husband. Been there, done that. Now it's your turn."

"What about making me an uncle?"

"There's no way I'd bring a child into this

world given my career. What about that nice artist you were dating?" she asked, steering the attention away from her.

"We still see each other every once in a while."

"And?"

"And nothing. We've decided not to be exclusive because I can't commit when I don't know where I'm going to be next year."

"She wants marriage?"

Cooper stared out the window of the sleek aircraft. "She wants marriage *and* kids. She claims her biological clock is ticking, and she doesn't want to wait too much longer before starting a family."

"Do you love her?" Greer asked.

His head came around and he stared at his sister. "Not enough to propose marriage."

"Then let her go, so she can find someone else willing to commit to a future with her."

"You're probably right."

Greer's eyes met Cooper's. "I know I'm right. No woman wants to be strung along wishing and praying her man will step up and do the right thing."

Cooper and Greer continued their whispered conversation until the jet touched down on a private Portland airstrip. He

37

kissed her goodbye, then followed the other agents to a Suburban, while Greer was escorted to a Ford SUV.

The last time she'd seen her uncle was before her final undercover assignment. It was as if the light had gone out behind his bright blue eyes. It had been her aunt Stella who had helped Bobby adjust to civilian life, had encouraged him to open the restaurant and had taught him to cook the dishes that made Stella's a favorite restaurant among locals and tourists.

Waiting until the driver stored her luggage in the cargo area of the SUV, Greer slipped onto the rear seat. Opening her handbag, she took out her cell phone, scrolled through her contacts and punched the number to Stella's. It rang twice before she heard a familiar gravelly voice.

"Stella's."

"Uncle Bobby, this is Greer."

"Where are you?"

"We touched down few minutes ago. I should be there in an hour." It was about fifty-five miles between Portland and the Hood River Valley.

"Did you eat?"

"I had a little breakfast." Her *little breakfast* was a cellophane-wrapped sweet bun and a cup of coffee.

"I'll fix something special to welcome you back."

Greer smiled. "I'd like that, Uncle Bobby."

Ending the call and slumping lower in her seat, she closed her eyes and did what she should've done during the flight: sleep.

CHAPTER 2

Mission Grove, Oregon

The flight attendant leaned over her lone sleeping passenger. "Wake up, Jason. We'll be descending soon."

Jason opened his eyes, sat up and peered out the oval window. "Thank you, Carrie-Ann."

He'd asked the attendant to wake him a half hour before they landed so he could shower and change clothes. He'd flown over three thousand miles and not once had he looked out the window. When the Gulfstream G550 became airborne and the seat belt light extinguished, he'd reclined the seat into a queen-size bed. It'd become customary for him to sleep during the flight from Florida to Oregon. The three-hour time difference played havoc with his body's circadian rhythm for several days, but sleeping around the clock the first day was the trick in keeping the effects of jet lag at bay.

Coming to his feet, he walked into the bathroom, stripped bare and stepped into the shower stall. Turning on the faucets and adjusting the water temperature, he soaped his body with a shower gel anchored on a built-in shelf. Jason had surprised his parents when he'd announced that he'd bought property in Oregon near the Cascades on which he'd built a sprawling house he dubbed Serenity West. It was where he spent four to six months each year writing and recording new music. This year was different because he'd delayed traveling to the Pacific Northwest for two months.

Once his father had relinquished the day-to-day operation of Serenity Records, an independent recording label, to Jason and his twin sister, he and Ana had continued the trend of discovering new and innovative musical talent. Ana handled contracts and all legal negotiations, while he worked behind the scenes as the artistic musical director writing, recording and editing music.

Usually he left Florida the beginning of June, but when Ana had gone into hiding, it had become Jason's responsibility to run the company. Once they had discovered there was a mole at Serenity passing information to a rival record company, he'd closed the office, relocating it from a high-rise office building to a freestanding structure outfitted with the latest high-tech surveillance equipment. He'd contracted with a security company to install cameras inside and around the perimeter of the building to monitor everyone coming and/or leaving. All employees were vetted, given electronic badges to swipe in and out, even if they went to their cars in the parking lot for any reason. The tight security was necessary to ensure the safety of everyone associated with the company.

Jason wanted to believe the threat against Ana and Serenity Records ended with Basil Irvine's untimely death from a massive heart attack, but something wouldn't permit him to relax completely. The public was led to believe the CEO of Slow Wyne Records was only thirty-nine, but his death certificate indicated he was forty-three. If he'd hidden his age, then what else had the deceased concealed?

Jason raised his head, allowing the water to flow over his face and body. The gurgling sound coming from his belly reminded him that it had been more than twelve hours since his last meal. As soon as the jet landed, he planned to eat, then go directly to sleep. Turning off the shower, he opened the shower door and reached for a thick towel from a supply on a nearby table. By the time he'd changed into a pair of laundered jeans and a long-sleeved black T-shirt, matching thick cotton socks and Timberland boots, the Fasten Seat Belt light chimed throughout the aircraft.

Jason made his way back to the main cabin. The flight attendant had repositioned the bed into a seat. He sat, fastened his seat belt and shared a smile with Carrie-Ann who'd taken her seat outside the cockpit door. She was one of two permanent flight attendants on the ColeDiz International Ltd. payroll, along with three full-time pilots. There was an unwritten rule that anyone claiming Cole blood was forbidden to fly commercial carriers. The edict was instituted more than forty years ago when, as a child, Regina Cole Spencer had been kidnapped and held for ransom, before she was rescued and found unharmed by her uncle and a close family friend.

Flying in the corporate jet suited Jason's laid-back persona. He abhorred crowds or being jostled as passengers crowded around the gate once their flight was announced. He also liked the fact that he could travel light and didn't have to go through airport screening. All he needed was a carry-on with toiletries and a change of clothes. The closets in his Serenity West home were filled with everything he would need to dress casually, attend a formal affair or a sporting event.

Whenever he settled into a routine at Serenity West, Jason loathed returning to Florida. He was more than content to live in Oregon writing and recording music, while someone else assumed the role as musical director for Serenity Records. He'd spoken to one of his cousins about coming to work for the record company, but Graham had yet to make a decision whether he would leave ColeDiz International Ltd., the privately-held, family-owned conglomerate. Graham had complained to Jason that Diego, CEO of ColeDiz, was a hard task-master and he preferred a more relaxing workplace atmosphere.

The sound that the landing gear was activated echoed throughout the cabin as the jet began its landing. Jason smiled when he caught a glimpse of Mount Hood's snow-covered peaks, and he chided himself for not learning to ski. However, growing up in the Sunshine State didn't lend itself to cold-weather sports. Within minutes the plane touched down smoothly on a private runway, coming to a stop several hundred feet from a gated area with parked vehicles. Waiting until Carrie-Ann opened the hatch and pressed a button for the stairs to descend, Jason unbuckled his seat belt, reached for his carry-on and prepared to disembark. He thanked the flight crew, took the stairs and walked across the tarmac to where the rental company had parked the Range Rover he'd requested.

He didn't own a car outright, preferring instead to rent whether in Florida or Oregon. His family teased him constantly about his unpretentious lifestyle. He had his own apartment in the expansive Boca Raton mansion where he'd grown up; preferred jeans, T-shirts and running shoes for his work attire; and spent most of his free time either in the recording studio at the record company or in his parents' home-based recording studio. He dated occasionally, but hadn't had a serious relationship in more than two years. Jason was comfortable with his lifestyle because he was in complete control of his own destiny; he was independently wealthy and that was something the majority of those in their early thirties weren't able to claim. He made his way over to a booth where a man sat watching his approach. Reaching into the back pocket of his jeans, he handed the stoic-looking armed guard his driver's license. After typing his name and license number into a computer, the man handed him a set of keys to the Range Rover.

Jason's belly made rumbling noises again as he maneuvered out of the parking area, following the signs indicating the airport exit. Glancing at the dashboard, he noted the time. It was 3:55 p.m. Pacific Time, while his body was still in the Eastern Time Zone. Accelerating into the flow of traffic along the interstate, Jason realized he would make it to Mission Grove in time for the start of Stella's dinner hour.

Touching a button on the steering wheel, he turned on the satellite radio, tuning it to a station featuring blues. His fingertips kept tempo on the leather-wrapped steering wheel as the gravelly voiced vocalist belted out a rousing rendition of "Sweet Home Chicago." Driving along the Columbia River highway, Jason lost himself in the music as the landscape changed from skyscrapers to scenic towns nestled in valleys with dense forests making a continuous curtain of green. There were magnificent gorges and breathtaking views of mountain lakes. The sight of Mount Hood never failed to make him catch his breath.

There was something about the natural

untamed beauty of this part of the country that made Jason feel as if he'd been reborn, a blank slate where he could selectively choose what he wanted to do, remember or avoid.

The road sign for Mission Grove came into view and within minutes he drove over the single lane road and into the town with a population of 3,956. There had been a time when the population boasted nearly six thousand inhabitants when logging camps sprang up at the height of the logging boom. Now it had become a haven for fishermen, hikers, skiers and retirees and those whose European ancestors came to the Pacific Northwest as traders and settlers in the late-eighteenth century.

Stella's, an enormous log-hewed building, was erected in a clearing with parking for at least sixty vehicles and overlooked a lake bordered by towering pine trees. Picnic tables and benches were set on a grassy area for those wishing to eat outdoors. There were a number of signs warning diners not to leave food on the tables or on the ground because it would attract bears and other woodland creatures.

Jason pulled into a space between two pickup trucks and cut off the engine. It was a few minutes after five and the lot was half-filled. He walked into Stella's and was met with a plethora of mouthwatering aromas. He hadn't taken more than three steps when he stopped short, staring at a young woman in jeans, running shoes, white shirt and matching apron tied around her waist as she leaned over a man seated at a table, her face pressed close to his. At first Jason thought she was going to kiss the diner until he noticed the color of his face. It had gone from bright red to purple. The three other men sharing the table stared mutely, their eyes widening in shock.

It ended when she stood up straight, glaring at him. "Touch me again and I'll castrate you." Her voice carried easily in the expansive space. She turned on her heel and walked away with a sensual sway of slender hips. Guffaws of laughter followed her retreat, while the seemingly hapless victim's chest rose and fell as he struggled to regain what was left of his dignity.

Jason couldn't stop the smile stealing its way over his features when he realized what had just occurred. Some men had to learn the hard way that women didn't like to be touched without permission. His gaze swept around the restaurant for an empty table, then spied one with a lone diner. He was fewer than five feet away when the deeply tanned man with shaggy gray-flecked brown hair stood up, hoary-gray eyes widening in surprise.

"I see you haven't lost your edge," Jason said quietly.

Chase Bromleigh pulled Jason into a bear hug that threatened to bruise his ribs. "How the hell are you? You told me you were coming two months ago. What did you do? Walk from Florida?"

Attractive lines fanned out around Jason's gold-flecked eyes as he smiled. "I had a family situation."

Chase dropped his arms. "And we're about to have another situation. Bobby doesn't look too happy."

A deafening silence descended over Stella's as six-foot-four, two-hundred-fifty-pound Bobby Henry made a beeline to the table where the customer had harassed his waitress. First the man was sitting, then he was up and running, heading for the door before Bobby could reach him.

The ex–Green Beret folded huge arms over his chest, blue eyes flashing dangerously as lights from hanging fixtures reflected off his shaved pate. "I've said it once and I'll just say it one more time." His baritone voice carried easily in the hushed silence. "Anyone harassing my niece will have to deal with me. And I promise to tune you up where you wish you'd never taken your first breath." Reaching behind his back, he pulled out an expandable baton, tapping it against the palm of his large hand. "Do I make myself understood?" There were nods and a few whispered yeses. "Good. Now enjoy your dinner."

Jason sat down across from Chase. "It looks as if Bobby's niece can take care of herself."

Chase nodded. "I'm certain she can if she threatened to castrate the poor man."

Jason's gaze shifted to the woman in question when she returned with a tray hoisted on her right shoulder. He didn't know why, but there was something about her that reminded him of his mother. Perhaps it was the color of her hair or the shape of her eyes. That's where the similarities ended because she was at least four or five inches taller than Serena Cole.

"When did she start working here?" he asked Chase.

"I assume you're talking about Greer."

"If that's her name, then of course I'm talking about her."

Chase leaned closer, studying the expression of the talented musician and record producer. "Her name is Greer Evans and she's just getting over a rather nasty divorce, so if I were you, I'd keep my distance."

Jason met Chase's eyes. "I came here to write music not get involved with a woman."

"Isn't it time you get involved with a woman?"

"I'll get involved with one when you do the same, friend."

Slumping back in his chair, Chase held his head at an angle. "I'm not the marrying kind. Women have accused me of being too moody, and I happen to like coming and going without having to check in with someone."

Jason stared at the man who owned a home in the same gated community where he'd built Serenity West. Charles, or Chase as he preferred to distinguish himself from his father, was the first to welcome him to the exclusive neighborhood in the Hood River Valley. Like Jason, Chase was born into wealth, but kept a low profile when he'd disappear for months and then reappear as if time had stood still. Although two years his senior, it was difficult to pinpoint Chase's actual age by looking at him. Tall, rawboned with a network of fine lines around his gray eyes and with finely honed reflexes, he projected an air of danger that kept most people at a distance.

Jason nodded in agreement. "I hear you. Speaking hypothetically. Suppose I had a girlfriend in Florida. Do you think she would go along with me living three thousand miles away for months at a time?"

"She would if she loved you enough."

"Yeah, right," Jason quipped, smiling. "Maybe it would work a couple times, but after a while she'd probably accuse me of having another woman to keep me company when I'm not with her."

Chase picked up a glass of beer, draining it. "Women. We can't live with them, and we can't live without them."

Jason wanted to tell his friend to speak for himself. It wasn't that he didn't like women because he did. He didn't have a steady girlfriend, but what he did have was a very jealous mistress: music and the two were like oil and water. They did not mix.

CHAPTER 3

Greer spooned a generous portion of fluffy mashed potatoes onto a heavy cafeteria-style dinner plate. She added two thick slices of meat loaf, along with peas and carrots, and then ladled au jus gravy over the meat and potatoes. Reaching for a pair of tongs, she placed a generous serving of corn bread on a separate dish. It had been exactly two weeks since she'd come to Mission Grove to work in her uncle's restaurant. During that time, she'd learned to ignore the gawking, and occasional crude overtures from some of the men, but what she refused to ignore was being groped. She gave her uncle a sidelong glance as he carved a golden-brown turkey.

"You've posted signs warning your customers about carrying concealed handguns, bringing in open bottles of beer and liquor, and not serving alcohol to anyone under the age of twenty-three. What you also need

is a sign prohibiting customers from groping the help."

"It's not going to happen again." Bobby's
voice had taken on a hard edge. "The next
man who puts his hands on you will be
barred from coming here, but that's only
after I kick his ass."

Greer rested the warmed plate on the
towel looped over her forearm. "I don't
need you getting arrested for assault."

Bobby snorted loudly. "The sheriff and I
were in Nam together, so I doubt if I'll get
arrested."

"So it's like that, Uncle Bobby?"

He winked at her. "You've got that right.
Folks around here have asked me to run for
mayor, but I have no patience for politics —
or should I say *poli-tricks.*"

She returned the wink. "I'll be back for
the turkey."

Greer shouldered her way through the
swinging door, heading for the table with
Chase Bromleigh's order. She had come to
know many of the regulars and Chase was
one. He came to Stella's Tuesday and
Wednesday for dinner, always ordering the
day's special.

Chase was one of two men she'd placed
on her mental watch list; the night before
when she'd stepped out to get some air,

Greer had observed Chase exchanging a package with a biker in the parking lot. It had been too dark to see what he'd given the other person. She didn't want to jump to conclusions and say either he or the man were dealing guns or drugs. Even if she couldn't recognize the biker's face, she was more than familiar with the make and model of his bike. Unfortunately she hadn't seen it again parked in the lot. At no time could she forget that she was on the job. The only difference was, this time, it would be as an observer. Becoming an observer was akin to a civilian informant. She would observe, while eavesdropping and gathering information, which data she would eventually pass along to the Seattle office.

She was relieved not to have to go undercover in Mission Grove. After her involvement with a group purchasing guns in Virginia and transporting them along I-95 to gangs and drug dealers in Philadelphia, New Jersey and New York, Greer didn't want to repeat that scene less than a year later. Then, she'd been Jaylee Roseboro, supposed stepdaughter of undercover DEA drug trafficker Malcolm Kelly. She had made the drive once a week, each time in a different car, the stash of weapons hidden in a compartment under the trunk. If she'd been stopped by turnpike police, she would've given them her boss's name and number, but that wasn't possible because at no time had she ever been in the vehicle by herself. The man supplying the guns always had one of his men accompany her as insurance so she wouldn't be tempted to take off with his merchandise. She delivered the guns, while her tagalong partner picked up the money. It was the supplier's way of having them watch one another. His mantra was "Deliver the goods and come back with my money or else I'll hunt you down and kill you, but not before I kill someone in your family."

It had taken Greer nearly two years to gather enough information for the U.S. Attorney to issue warrants for the gun smuggling ring that netted six men and two women. She was rounded up with the others, processed and held without bond in protective custody for several days. The day before she and the others were scheduled for arraignment, jail officials announced she'd hung herself in her cell. Greer was whisked away under the cover of darkness to a safe house; she removed the contact lenses, false teeth, braided extensions and began a strict diet to lose the twenty pounds she'd gained while undercover. Indulging in a spree of eating fast food had wrecked her regimen of healthy eating. She was re-assigned to a desk in a field office in Phoenix, becoming a glorified clerk.

Relocating to the Pacific Northwest was as different as night was from day when she compared the geography of the Southwest to the rugged untamed forests and the majestic splendor of Mount Hood. Waking up in the bedroom she'd occupied during her childhood summer vacations was like stepping back in time when she'd slept with the windows open because there was hardly ever a need for air-conditioning.

She had the entire two-story house to herself. Bobby claimed he could no longer stay there since losing his wife of nearly forty years. He now lived in one of the two apartments above Stella's. The other apartment was occupied by an Iraq War veteran recovering from post-traumatic stress disorder. Bobby had hired Danny Poe to clean the restaurant and stock the bar and kitchen pantry. Danny, who was undergoing counseling, usually kept to himself, spoke when spoken to and accomplished his chores in record time.

Stella's had begun as a family restaurant, but over the years it was also a sports bar and a favorite hangout for locals, college students and tourists. It opened six days a week from noon to three for lunch and five to nine for dinner; buffet-style dining was available only on Thursday, Friday and Saturday, with the kitchen closing at midnight. Sundays from ten to three featured a country-style buffet and table-service dinner until eight.

Thursday nights were set aside for karaoke when the number of customers increased appreciably with those wanting to showcase their vocal talent, while a live band provided entertainment on Friday and Saturday nights. If Greer had grown bored sitting at a desk, the same couldn't be said when she found herself on her feet waitressing.

Maggie Shepherd, a single mother with two school-age children, worked the lunch shift, while Greer assumed the responsibility for serving dinner along with two college students who came in Thursday, Friday and Saturday.

Greer set the plates down in front of Chase, her eyes meeting those of the man seated opposite him. A slight frown creased her smooth forehead before she caught herself staring. She'd recognized Chase's dining partner. *What is Jason Cole doing in Stella's?* she mused.

She'd seen enough photographs and television footage of the recording executive to recognize him immediately. Although he'd been identified as a music industry celebrity, he'd managed to maintain a low profile without hordes of paparazzi shadowing his every move. Questions swirled inside Greer's head as she wondered what was his connection to the man she had on her mental radar?

Forcing a smile, she angled her head. "Is there anything else I can get for you, Chase?" she asked the taciturn man who usually dined alone.

Chase stared at the plate of food, then glanced up at Greer. "Nothing for me, but I'd like you to get my friend a beer."

Reaching into the pocket of her apron, she took out a pen and a pad. "Good evening, sir. Would you like to order something to go with the beer?"

A slow smile found its way across Jason's face, dimples deepening in both cheeks. Greer didn't know why, but she found the expression to be more of a leer than a smile. Curbing the urge to roll her eyes at him, she wanted to tell him she wasn't one of his adoring groupies, ready and willing to do anything to get him to spend time with them. What she had to admit was that he was pretty, an adjective she rarely attributed to a man. However, his patrician features, deeply tanned olive complexion and large brown eyes with pinpoints of gold were mesmerizing.

Jason's smile grew wider as he pointed to Chase's plate. "I'll have what he's having, but I don't want the peas and carrots. What other vegetables do you have?"

Greer held his steady gaze. "Beets, spinach, smothered cabbage and —"

"I'll have the spinach," Jason said, interrupting her.

She slipped the pad and pen back into the apron pocket. "Do want corn bread?"

"Yes."

Turning on her heel, Greer walked over to the bar to put in the beverage order. There were only eight patrons at the bar, while the bartender stood motionless watching ESPN. Of the five flat-screen televisions in the restaurant, three were always tuned to sports channels, one to an all-news channel and the remaining on the weather channel. They were muted but displayed closed captions.

"Pepper, I need a tap beer and a glass of water."

Jimmy Pepperdine turned around, reached for a Pilsner glass and filled it with beer from the tap. A self-proclaimed hippie, Jimmy's arms were covered in colorful peace sign tattoos and the names of the musicians who'd performed at Woodstock. He wore his graying hair in a long ponytail, with small gold hoops in his earlobes.

"It looks as if it's going to be a slow night at the bar," Pepper drawled.

"It's still early. By the time we close, they'll be standing two deep."

The bartender nodded. "Yeah, but I get antsy just standing around."

Pepper was antsy but Greer welcomed the lull. Those who sat at the bar didn't yet nibble on pretzels and peanuts usually ordered from the kitchen. She picked up the two glasses, returning to the table and placing them on coasters advertising a popular imported beer. She headed for the kitchen, nearly colliding with the college student who was more than an hour late. Her uncle was usually easygoing with his employees; the exception was lateness. She overheard the young man tell Bobby his brother had taken his car without his knowledge and he'd run out of gas. Greer didn't hear her uncle's response as she busied herself filling orders.

The grandfather clock near the entrance chimed a half hour past ten as Bobby closed and locked the front door after the last two customers were reminded it was after closing time. Greer flopped down at a table, slipped out of her running shoes and wrapped both hands around the mug filled with hazelnut-flavored cappuccino. She took a sip, and wiggled her sock-covered toes. "This is delicious."

Bobby sat down opposite Greer. "Pepper is the best when it comes to mixing drinks and brewing coffee."

Greer peered over the mug, watching Danny as he stacked chairs atop tables before sweeping and mopping the tiled floor. "Did Pepper serve in Vietnam?"

"Why are you asking?"

Her gaze shifted to Bobby. "I figured him for a conscientious objector because of his peace tats."

Bobby ran a forefinger around the rim of a snifter of Jack Daniels. "He went to Nam like most guys our age, but when he came back, he joined Vietnam Veterans Against the War, got arrested a few times, dropped out of sight for at least twenty years, then one day he showed up here looking for work."

Greer laughed softly. "What are you running? A halfway house for wounded veterans?"

"Don't knock the military, kid. It saved

my life. I graduated high school, enrolled in college and started cutting classes. I was ready to drop out when my advisor talked me into joining the ROTC, and as they say, the rest is history. What I needed was structure and discipline, and the military was the answer. I probably would've become a lifer if I hadn't met your aunt. Stella wasn't cut out to be an army wife, so after I finished my last tour, I put in my papers and never looked back. We each worked two jobs for a couple years to save up enough money to buy this restaurant. It was nothing more than a shell, but Stella saw its potential. Every year we put aside half the profits to make renovations, and thankfully she was able to witness what she had envisioned for her namesake before she passed away."

Greer nodded. The restaurant's rustic exterior belied its interior. Track lighting over the raised band area and the bar, hanging Tiffany-style fixtures over each table and a floor-to-ceiling stone fireplace taking up an entire wall invited patrons to come and stay awhile. A large colorful jukebox blared old-school rock-and-roll, blues, country and Pop. A pool table, dartboard and mechanical bull occupied another section of the expansive restaurant/sports bar with a dining capacity for 130.

"You've done well, Uncle Bobby."

Reaching across the table, Bobby held Greer's now-free hand. "This place is going to be yours once I decide to hang up my apron and spatula."

"That's not going to be for a long, long time," she countered. Her aunt had promised Greer that the restaurant would be hers once she and Bobby retired. Every summer Greer watched Stella carefully as she prepared the dishes that perpetuated Stella's reputation of serving the best homemade food in the region. Greer had become a good cook, but it could take years before her skills would come close to matching her uncle and late aunt's.

"It may not be that long, kid. I'd told myself I would retire at seventy, but my knees are telling me they won't last that long." He held up a hand. "I know I need to lose at least fifty pounds but that's not going to happen as long as I hang out in the kitchen."

Greer took another sip of coffee. "I'd love to help you cook, but I have to . . ."

"I know why you're here, Greer, and it's not to be my sous-chef because I already have one," Bobby said when her words trailed off.

"How often does Jason Cole come here?" she asked, deftly changing the topic of conversation.

"He usually hangs out here for several months, then goes back to Florida. Every once in a while he'll sit in with the band playing piano or guitar."

"How tight is he with Chase?"

Bobby shrugged broad shoulders as he tossed back the liquid in his glass. "They both live in Bear Ridge Estates, so that would make them neighbors. Why are you asking?"

It was Greer's turn to shrug her shoulders. "Just asking."

Bobby narrowed his eyes. "You had to have a reason, Greer."

If her uncle had been cleared as to her assignment, then she was somewhat obligated to be forthcoming with him. "There's something about Chase that disturbs me," she whispered.

"I don't think you have to worry about him. He comes from money, so I doubt if he would be involved in anything illegal. Folks say he's angry because he has no purpose or direction in life except to exist."

"Boo hoo," Greer drawled. "We should all have that problem. My heart doesn't bleed for him, Uncle Bobby," she added sarcastically.

"What would you do if you suddenly found you were wealthy beyond your wildest imagination?"

She sobered quickly. "That's not going to happen, and if I did come into a lot of money, I'd put in for a leave of absence, then go to some private tropical island and do absolutely nothing but eat, drink, swim and sleep for at least three months."

Bobby nodded. "That's what I intend to do when I retire. What I have to decide is whether I want Hawaii or the Caribbean. Speaking of Chase, he's an interesting character. And once you get to know Jason, you'll realize he's an all-around nice guy."

"Why did he build a place here in Mission Grove? Wouldn't L.A. be more his style?"

"Jason's the antithesis of Tinseltown. He built a nice little house on an eight-acre parcel that sold for more money than some people make in two or three years. It's not as ostentatious as a few of the others. I overheard someone say it's somewhere around five thousand square feet."

"How large are the others?" Greer asked. In her opinion five thousand square feet was definitely not a little house.

"Anywhere from ten to fifteen thousand."

She scrunched up her nose. "Unless you have a tribe of children, what would you need with fifteen thousand square feet of living space?"

"I wouldn't know. When Stella and I bought our house, we'd planned to have at least two kids, but I suppose the good Lord knew what He was doing when He didn't give us any with both of us working around the clock."

Reaching across the table, Greer patted his forearm. "He did give you kids, even if it was only part-time. You have me and Cooper."

Bobby grasped her hand, pressing a kiss on her knuckles. "That He did." A wry grin twisted his mouth. "I loved taking you and your brother camping in the woods, teaching you guys how to fly-fish and shoot. Cooper was always pissed off because you were a better shot."

"He eventually got over it after he joined the bureau."

Greer's thoughts drifted back to Jason. She wanted to ask her uncle, if Jason was really a nice guy, then what was his connection to Chase? She found it odd that Chase never shared his table, and only on a rare occasion did he sit and talk with anyone for any appreciable length of time.

"I'm going to call it a night. After I soak my feet, I'm going straight to bed," Greer said.

Standing up, she kissed Bobby's cheek, and then walked on sock-covered feet to the kitchen, leaving the mug in the stainless-steel sink for Danny to put in the dish-washer.

Returning to the table to put her shoes back on with a groan, she exited the building and headed to Bobby's vehicle, on loan to her for as long as she was here.

All thoughts, of Chase, Jason and why she was working in Stella's, faded as she started up the ancient truck. The engine to Johnny B. Goode II roared to life, shattering the quiet of the night. The year she had turned fifteen, Bobby had taught her to drive. He'd bought the 1956 Ford F-100 from a farmer and named it after his favorite Chuck Berry song. Greer had stalled out a number of times until learning to ease off the clutch slowly while depressing the gas pedal. The classic truck had a rebuilt engine and was fitted with power disc brakes. It sported a new coat of red paint, and black leather seats had replaced the tattered cloth ones.

She preferred a standard shift car to an automatic because it forced her to concentrate on the narrow road winding around the lake. Several times each year a motorist would speed, fall asleep or miss a sharp turn and end up in the lake. Fortunately there were few that drowned. She passed the sign leading to Bear Ridge Estates, noting the gatehouse and towering massive iron gates protecting the residents living in the exclusive community with multimillion-dollar homes.

She still couldn't shake her nagging suspicion that Charles "Chase" Bromleigh was more than a ne'er-do-well that didn't have to concern himself working as a nine-to-five. He wouldn't be the first wealthy psychopath that embarked on a life of crime, and if her instincts were right, then Greer knew — in order to get close to Chase — she would have to befriend Jason. And she had the perfect secret that was certain to get Jason's attention.

Maneuvering into the driveway of the house that had become her temporary home, Greer punched a button on the visor of the pickup and the automatic door to the two-car garage slid up. She parked beside an outboard motor boat resting on a trailer. The boat, also named Johnny B. Goode, was several years older than the pickup, and she had lost track of the number of times she and Cooper would take the boat across the lake to Stella's before either of them had driver's licenses. Bobby had issued a firm mandate that they wear life vests when riding in the boat although they'd become proficient swimmers.

She unlocked the door leading from the garage into a mudroom, disarmed the security system, then activated it again before slipping out of her running shoes and leaving them on a thick straw mat. It was time she traded the running shoes for a pair of shoes that gave her legs the support needed for her to be on her feet for hours at a time.

The moment Greer climbed the staircase to the second floor, she knew why her uncle had decided not to continue to live at the house with awesome views of the lake and valley. It was too quiet. Even now that her aunt was gone, her presence lingered along with the scent of her favorite perfume.

Greer had programmed the lights in the house to come on and go off at different intervals, giving the appearance that it wasn't unoccupied. The crime rate in Mission Grove wasn't what it would be in a more densely populated area, but there was enough criminal activity to warrant having a four-man police force. There had been a time when the small town was patrolled by the county sheriff, but that had changed once the residents of Bear Ridge demanded more of a police presence and were willing to underwrite the cost of having around-the-clock police protection beyond what they paid for private security. Anyone, other than residents, entering or leaving was subject to go through a security checkpoint.

Greer turned on the water in the bathroom, added a generous amount of scented bath salts and stripped off her clothes, leaving them in a large wicker hamper. By the time she'd brushed her teeth and washed her face, the water had reached the level she needed for a leisurely soak. Removing the elastic band holding her hair in a ponytail, she combed it out and secured the chemically relaxed strands in a topknot.

All thoughts of why she was in a small Oregon town faded when she stepped into the warm water, sat down and closed her eyes. The water cooled and Greer still did not stir. It was when she found herself falling asleep that she picked up a sponge and a bottle of bath gel and soaped her neck and shoulders.

Her movements were slow, mechanical, when she finished bathing. Wrapping a thick bath sheet around her body, she returned to her bedroom and fell across the bed. Within minutes she'd fallen into a deep, dreamless slumber.

Chapter 4

Jason woke at three the following morning, but forced himself to remain in bed. He fell asleep once more and didn't wake again until daylight came in through the bedroom skylights. He knew his first day would be spent settling into Serenity West. He had to be up and dressed by nine. He'd contacted a cleaning service before leaving Florida to send a team to dust and air out the entire house.

His to-do list also included shopping for groceries to stock the refrigerator/freezer and pantry. Jason was as deficient when it came to housecleaning as he was proficient in writing music. He'd continued the tradition of Cole men whose mothers had taught them to cook so they wouldn't have to rely on a woman to feed them. He knew it would take another day before he'd get into the routine of rising and going into the studio.

Going up on an elbow, he glanced around

the bedroom. He'd lingered long enough the night before to remove dust-covers from tables, chairs, the armoire, triple dresser and highboy. Jason had worked closely with the architect that his interior decorator aunt had recommended, and it'd taken more than three months before he had finally approved the house's design.

He wanted a house that would fit into the forest setting. It was to be constructed from a log-timber frame, with a broad sheltering roof and using lots of natural materials. The design brought the upper and lower decks close to a forested area, and the generous overhangs kept rain off the windows while protecting the siding and foundation. The lower level was an open gallery of rooms, the media center separate from the primary family living space and the recording studio accessible by a stairway leading to the basement level.

His cell chimed a familiar ring tone. Reaching across his body, Jason picked up the phone. "Good morning, Mrs. Jones."

Ana's giggles came through the earpiece. "Good morning, Jay. How are you?"

Jason smiled. "Wonderful."

"I'm calling because Mom claims she hasn't heard from you."

His smile vanished quickly. "Tell *your*

mother that I'm okay."

"I'm not going to act as a go-between —"

"But you are, Ana," Jason accused his twin sister, "when you accuse me of not checking in. I shouldn't have to tell you how old I am because we share the same birthday, and at thirty-three, I don't believe I should have to check in with my mother. You never did when you went away."

There came a beat of silence. "It's because I didn't live at home at thirty-three. Within months of graduating law school, I moved out and got my own place, while you're still living at home. It's about respect, Jason. Mom didn't even know you were gone until she spoke to Diego who told her that you'd made arrangements with him to fly to the west coast. You could've left a note."

Jason ran a hand over his cropped hair. He knew Ana was right. And it was because he still lived under his parents' roof that his mother felt he was obligated to let her know if he planned to be away for a while. All of his siblings had moved out in their twenties, and he'd stayed much too long. Recalling what Chase had said the night before — about not having a wife monitoring his coming and going — brought everything into focus.

"I'll call her, Ana, and let her know that

I'm okay."

Jason knew his mother's apprehension came from the alleged feud between Serenity and Slow Wyne Records because Ana had won the bidding war to sign singing phenom Justin Glover. Basil Irvine, humiliated because he'd lost to a woman, had taken a contract out on his rival. The assassin hired to kill Ana had missed his target. Tyler Cole had taken a bullet to the head intended for Ana. Fortunately Tyler recovered, and Ana had gone into hiding where she'd married her protector.

"Thanks, Jay. Mom hasn't been herself since we discovered one of our employees was spying for Slow Wyne Records."

Jason nodded although Ana couldn't see him. "That's over, Ana."

"Is it really?"

He heard the apprehension in her voice. "Of course it is. Basil's six feet under, so he can't bother anyone again."

The carefully orchestrated plan to take out the CEO of the L.A.-based record label was reminiscent of a plot from a cold war spy novel. The operative was in and out of Basil's palatial Beverly Hills mansion in fewer than twenty minutes, having never been seen. Basil's houseboy discovered his boss's lifeless body. He called Basil's brother and then the LAPD. The medical examiner's report confirmed Basil had died from a massive coronary, attributing it to a combination of alcohol and antianxiety medication. Basil's younger brother Webb had assumed control of the label and, unlike the deceased CEO, had elected to stay out of the spotlight.

Jason chatted with Ana for another two minutes before ending the call. He touched the cell's screen for his mother's number, holding the phone away from his ear when she launched into a tirade about how his disappearing act was hastening her demise.

Waiting for a pause in the ranting on the other end of the line, he said in a calming voice, "Mom. I've never known you to be so melodramatic." His attempt to placate Serena backfired when she switched from English to Spanish, the words tumbling over one another. His mother was born in the States, but raised in Costa Rica after her mother had married a Costa Rican government official. Jason heard his father in the background asking his wife to calm down. Jason was tempted to hang up when David's voice came through the earpiece.

"What did you say that set your mother off? She's hysterical."

"Dad, come on. You know how she is

nowadays."

"No, I don't know *how she is,*" David countered defensively. "All I know is *my* wife and *your* mother is having an emotional meltdown."

Jason repeated the conversation he'd had with Ana. "It's apparent *your* wife and *my* mother is under the impression that I'm a child who has to check in as if I were on work release. Would it make her feel better if I wore an ankle monitor?"

There came a beat. "Jason, I want you to try and understand where your mother is coming from. We came very close to losing Tyler, when we all know that bullet was meant for Ana. This is the second time Martin and Parris have found their children's lives at risk, and that is a situation no parent should have to experience."

"What does this have to do with me, Dad?"

"I want you to be careful, son. We may have chopped off the head of the snake, but this snake is different because it has the uncanny ability to grow another head. One that belongs to Webb Irvine. One of Simon's investigators found a witness who claims it was Basil and not Webb who'd stomped a man to death. Meanwhile Webb did a term for his older brother because, as a fifteen-year-old, he knew he would be sent to a juvenile facility rather than jail."

"But Webb did go to jail," Jason argued. The man had spent ten years in a California minimum security prison.

"That was only after he'd turned eighteen. There had been bad blood between Basil and Leon Burke because Leon owed him money, but the situation got worse when Webb got Leon's thirteen-year-old sister pregnant, then denied the baby was his. Leon extracted revenge when he cut up Webb's face. Basil retaliated by kicking him to death."

"Why are you telling me this?" Jason asked his father. "Basil's dead and I doubt if Webb is going to follow in his brother's footsteps."

"I doubt it, too. But this is not about Slow Wyne Records. It's about your mother. She's earned the right to worry about you because she *is* your mother."

Jason exhaled an audible breath. "Okay. I'll give her that, but she can't expect —"

"I know what you're going to say," David interrupted, "and I agree with you. You're an adult, and you shouldn't have to check in. Just promise me you'll be careful, and I'll make things right on this end."

"I'll be careful, Dad." He'd say anything not to prolong the conversation.

Jason wasn't argumentative by nature, eschewed confrontation and occasionally stepped in as the mediator during a family conflict. Unlike his older brother Gabriel, Jason never ingratiated himself into his sisters' romantic relationships. The only love-related advice he'd given his siblings was not to get involved with anyone in the music business. Fortunately they'd heeded his warning. Alexandra had married a man who worked for the CIA, and Ana had recently married a U.S. marshal.

"Thanks, Jason."

"No problem, Dad."

He ended the call, shaking his head. Jason could not have imagined his day would begin with family drama. After all, it wasn't the first time he'd taken off without letting his parents know where he was going. If they'd wanted to know his whereabouts, then they only had to ask Ana. But things had changed because Ana and her husband divided their weekends between Boca Raton and the Keys.

Jason had come to Mission Grove to get away from the chaos, madness and mayhem that had everyone in his family on edge for the past three months. All he wanted to do was go into the studio and write the music that had haunted him for more than a year.

Swinging his legs over the side of the bed, he headed for the bathroom. He planned to be dressed by the time the cleaning service arrived.

Los Angeles, California
Webb Irvine came to his feet when the man he'd waited days to see was ushered into his home office. He hadn't known what to expect but it wasn't the pale, slightly built, seemingly emaciated man wearing small oval sunglasses, making it impossible to discern the color of his eyes. His gaze went from the shaved head, narrow face and down to an ill-fitting black suit. It was impossible to pinpoint his age. He could've been anywhere between thirty and fifty. Webb smiled and the network of scar tissue along his left cheek was reminiscent of blisters. What had been a shockingly handsome face was now hideously deformed.

He nodded to the woman whom he'd come to depend upon to keep his household running smoothly and to covet his innermost secrets; she was his mother. "Thank you, Donna," he said softly. "And will you please close the door."

It wasn't until after the death of his brother that Webb had asked her to come and live with him. At first she'd balked, then relented. After all there was more than enough room in the Hollywood Hills mansion for them not to run into each other. Webb had fired his former housekeeper because she was a snoop. The woman didn't know he'd installed cameras throughout the house, and every night before retiring for bed, he'd view the footage. At first he'd believed it was a fluke and that she was just straightening up his desk, but when he saw her attempting to open the wall safe behind a painting, he knew he had to fire her. His mother could care less about his business dealings. She was grateful he'd moved her out of Watts to an upscale community where the price for homes started at seven figures.

Webb took his visitor's extended hand and then gestured to two facing off-white leather love seats. "Please sit down, Mr. Monk."

"It's just Monk, Mr. Irvine."

Waiting until the man was seated, he walked over to a well-stocked bar. "Would you like something to drink, Monk?"

"No, thank you. I just celebrated my sixteenth year of sobriety." He lifted a frightfully thin hand. "It won't bother me if you have something."

Webb smiled again. "Congratulations on your sobriety."

He hadn't outlined what he wanted from

Monk, but the fact that the man had agreed to meet with him would warrant a celebratory cocktail after he left. Opening the built-in refrigerator, he took out a bottle of sparkling water and poured it into a crystal glass. Sitting opposite Monk, he raised the glass in a salute. "I want to thank you for agreeing to meet with me."

Monk wanted to tell the man with the scarred face that he'd only agreed to come in person because Webb Irvine had been recommended by a mutual friend. "Tell me what you need, and I'll let you know whether it can be done."

"Are you familiar with Serenity Records?"

Monk nodded. "I've heard of them."

Putting the glass to his mouth, Webb took a deep swallow. "They're my direct competition and . . ."

"And you want them eliminated," Monk said, reading Webb's mind.

Crossing his legs, the president and CEO of Slow Wyne Records stared at the toe of his imported slip-on. "I think I better give you some background information on my dilemma. My late brother hired someone to eliminate Ana Cole. She's responsible for the day-to-day operation of Serenity." He paused long enough to take another sip of water. "Basil hired a sniper to take her out, but they missed and shot one of her relatives."

"That was his first dumb mistake," Monk drawled. "If you want to eliminate someone, you get up real close and personal and put a bullet in her head."

Webb gritted his teeth. He wanted to tell the man in black that he shouldn't speak ill of the dead but he didn't want to alienate him. Not when he was prepared to pay him an obscene amount of money to give Basil in death what he wasn't able to obtain in life.

"You can't go after her again," Monk continued.

"I know. That's why we've shifted our attention to her brother. His name is Jason Cole."

"Where does he live?"

"Boca Raton, Florida. We had someone on the inside at Serenity that told us he still lives in his parents' home, but mentioned he may have a place in either Washington or Oregon."

"Did this person tell you which city?"

Webb shook his head. "No. She's no longer working there."

Monk rested his hands on his knees. "Tell me about this Jason. Is he married? Does he have a girlfriend or children?"

"I believe he's single. I'm not certain whether he has a girlfriend, and I doubt if he has children."

"That doesn't matter. It's easy enough to find out about his kids."

"If he has kids, then I don't want them touched." Webb didn't know how, but he could feel the heat of Monk's gaze behind the dark lenses.

"I don't know what you've heard about me, Mr. Irvine, but I don't kill children. If Jason has children, then it would make him more visible. After all, children have to go to school. I will eliminate your Mr. Cole using my own methods. You've been told that my fee is half down and the other half when the job is completed. Once I pick up my final payment, you will never see me again."

The sweep hand on Webb's gold timepiece made a full revolution before he asked, "What if you don't complete the job?"

Bloodless thin lips parted in a feral grin. "I've never started something I didn't finish. But if I don't, barring divine intervention, then you'll be out a half million dollars." Reaching into the pocket of his jacket, Monk took out a cell phone, placing it on the love seat cushion. "This phone will be our only contact until the job is done. I'll call to give you updates. If you don't pick up, then I'll call again because I don't believe in leaving voice mails or texting."

"If I miss the call, then I'll just call you back," Webb said.

Monk shook his head. "You won't be able to call me because I've blocked all outgoing calls. Once we conclude our business arrangement, the phone will be deactivated. You're in security, so I know you're familiar with burn phones." Monk flicked his wrist, glancing at his watch. "I don't want to be rude but I must leave. My taxi is waiting and the meter is running."

Webb stood and walked over to his desk. He picked up a large expandable pleated envelope, handing it to Monk. Earlier that afternoon he'd opened the safe and counted out five hundred thousand dollars in hundreds and fifties. He normally wouldn't have had more than ten thousand dollars in the safe, but that was before Basil passed away.

When Basil's houseboy had called to say he'd discovered the lifeless body of his boss sitting in a chair in his home office, Webb had rushed to the Beverly Hills' mansion and emptied the safe. He didn't own a counting machine, so it'd taken him almost three days to tally more than six million dollars in cash. Basil had drawn up a will, leaving Webb everything: house, cars, jewelry, money in several personal bank accounts and Slow Wyne Records. He now was the head of two companies. Slow Wyne and a security company selling high-tech surveillance equipment.

Webb had contacted his former cellmate to ask if he knew someone to help him with a personal problem. Ian Scott had spoken to his father, a shadowy man with ties to organized crime. Mr. Scott had quoted a figure and Webb had agreed. He would've paid any amount of money in order to bring down Serenity Records.

Monk gave him a warm smile for the first time. "Thank you. There's no need for your mother to see me out. I know the way."

"How did you —"

"How do I know that your housekeeper is your mother?" Monk asked, reading Webb's mind.

He nodded numbly. "Yes."

"Do you actually believe I'd meet with you in person if I didn't check you out, Mr. Irvine? I know everything about you, and I do mean *everything*. You have a good evening."

Webb waited a full five minutes and then returned to the refrigerator for a split of champagne. The pop of the cork echoed softly in the meticulously furnished home office. He'd spared no expense when it came to decorating his home. For Webb the house, personal tailor and on-call driver were surrogates for what he reviled most. He hated the opposite sex. It was because of a girl's lie and his denial that her brother had disfigured his face. It was Basil who'd exacted revenge for the mutilation, and Webb had repaid him by Webb confessing that he'd killed his assailant, pleading self-defense when Basil would've been charged with second-degree murder.

He heard movement and turned to find his mother staring at him. Donna Gibson hadn't passed her surname or any of her physical characteristics along to her sons. Both looked like the men who'd gotten her pregnant.

"How did it go?" Donna asked.

Webb filled two flutes with the bubbly liquid. "Good." He handed her a flute, smiling when their eyes met. "Now we wait."

Chapter 5

Mission Grove

Jason knew he'd remained cloistered much too long when he opened the refrigerator to discover he'd run out of milk. It was apparent he'd drunk more *café con leche* than usual. He glanced at the clock on the microwave. Where had the day gone? It was after seven.

Scratching his bearded cheeks, he decided he was ready to leave the house. He didn't want to believe he'd been in Mission Grove for ten days, and in all that time, he'd ventured out once. He'd driven into town to shop for enough groceries to stock the freezer and pantry for at least a month, and it was time he replenish the perishables.

Time had stood still for him once he descended the staircase to the studio. He'd spent hours writing music, stopping only to take power naps, eat, drink copious cups of coffee liberally laced with milk and sugar, return emails, shower and change his clothes. He'd been in the zone composing pieces that were different from what he'd written before. They weren't for the artists signed to Serenity Records or any other producer wishing to pick them up for their label. It was for himself. The instrumental reflected his present state of mind. It was moody, atmospheric, otherworldly. His bare feet were silent as he walked across the kitchen to the staircase at the rear of the house. It was time to shave off the beard and end his self-isolation.

Jason found enough space in the parking lot to park the Range Rover next to a Volkswagen Beetle. It was Thursday and Stella's would probably be filled to capacity. An unlimited buffet and karaoke drew regulars and wannabe singers like bees to flowers.

He preferred eating at Stella's rather than many of the up-scale Portland restaurants. He liked the home-style dishes and the laid-back atmosphere that beckoned customers to come in and stay for leisurely casual dining. Tuesday and Wednesdays catered to family dining with table service and the rest of the week offered a buffet with choices of main dishes, soups, salads and desserts.

He was always a curious spectator on

Karaoke Night. Some of the performers could barely carry a tune, and those who could occasionally flubbed the lyrics. There had been a young teenage boy with an amazing vocal range, but when Jason had approached him asking him to make a demo tape for Serenity, the kid had claimed his parents were totally against him singing secular music. He'd been one of the rare finds whose talent would thrive in the Christian music market.

Jason waited in line to pay the fixed price for the all-you-can-eat buffet first. Drinks from the bar were not included in the price. Thereafter he wended his way through the throng, while searching the crowd for Chase. Smiling, he spied his friend at a table with several members of the house band. The drummer waved him over. Jason shook hands with each of the men at the table. They were a motley-looking group, having unkempt beards and eschewed haircuts, and favored multiple piercings and tattoos. However, their appearance did little to belie their talent.

"Where the hell have you been?" asked Doug, the lead vocalist and guitarist.

Jason's dimples deepened in his clean-shaven face when he flashed a broad smile.

91

"Sorry about that, but I got caught up writing."

Doug waved to a waiter, pointing to the empty pitcher on the table, then putting up two fingers. "Can you pull yourself away for a few hours on Fridays and Saturdays?" he asked Jason. "The band needs you because we just lost our keyboard player and female vocalist. They ran off to Vegas and got married because she got tired of being his baby mama."

"It's about time he did something noble," Chase mumbled under his breath.

"Ladies and gentlemen, we're about to begin Karaoke Night," boomed the MC's voice through the speakers set up around the restaurant. All conversations halted. Dressed in a red top hat, matching silk shirt with checkerboard suspenders, black knickers, argyle knee socks and a pair of oversize bright yellow shoes, he strutted across the stage like an inebriated clown. He stopped, reached into the pocket of his knickers and put on a large red clown nose. The restaurant exploded in laughter. "For those of you who are here for the first time, let me to introduce myself. I'm MC Oakie. If I look different tonight, it is because I'm going to change it up a bit. We'll have singing, and maybe we'll be able to get in a little dancing. Right now I'm going to ask the wait-staff to stop what they're doing and come up on the stage." He beckoned to Greer. "Come on up, Greer. Your uncle will not fire you if you take a five-minute break."

Jason couldn't pull his gaze off Greer as she walked up the steps to the stage, the other waiters following. She looked different tonight. Her hair was a mass of tiny curls that bounced around her shoulders and framed her incredibly beautiful brown face. He was sitting close enough to notice the light cover of makeup that accentuated her eyes and lush mouth. Chase had mentioned she'd gone through a contentious divorce yet, looking at her, she radiated poise and confidence. Jason smiled. She'd changed her running shoes for a pair of red clogs.

MC Oakie took off his hat, cradling it against his chest. "Every week I watch you guys lip-synching with your customers. Tonight I'm going to flip the script because it's your turn to entertain everyone and no lip-synching." Hooting and whistling followed the announcement. He bowed low. "Ladies, you'll be first. Think about what you'd like to sing because you're not going to know when I'm going to call your name. You may leave the stage now."

The increasing heat in Greer's face had nothing to do with the overhead spotlights. She wanted to pull off MC Oakie's red nose for putting her and the others on the spot. He was right about lip-synching because she was guilty as charged. She enjoyed singing in the shower and also when cooking and cleaning the house. She'd been one of those little girls that used a hairbrush as her microphone. She'd also sung in the school choir from grade school through college. Her mother had accused her of choosing the wrong career path but Greer knew she didn't have the temperament to go into the music business.

Walking off the stage, she returned to the bar to fill beverage orders. Immediately after her aunt had passed away, business at the restaurant had decreased appreciably because there were days when Bobby refused to get out of bed. Greer had taken time off to fly to the West Coast and have an indepth conversation with Bobby, pleading with him not to let Stella's dream die with her. His comeback was that there was no Stella's without his wife. It took a while, but Greer had convinced her uncle to restructure, incorporating family-style dining with activities that would attract a more diverse crowd. The result was two days for table service and four days for buffet dining.

Also her uncle had resisted raising his prices when everything was going up. Thankfully he owned the building outright so, instead of mortgage payments, he only had to pay property taxes. Karaoke night always brought in new customers who would eventually become regulars, and hiring the live band had reestablished Stella's popularity. Greer picked up two pitchers of beer, mulling over which song she would sing.

Jason really didn't want to commit to sitting in with the band because it meant rehearsals and playing four-hour sets on Fridays and Saturdays, but the band had willingly performed as session players whenever he had needed driving, funky baseline tracks.

"I . . ." His words trailed off when he saw Bobby's niece approach their table with a pitcher of beer in each hand. Their eyes met when she set them on the table. Reaching into the pocket of his slacks, he withdrew a money clip and handed her a large bill.

"Put your money away, Jason," Chase

ordered. "I've got this round."

Grasping Greer's hand, Jason gently squeezed her fingers. "Take it and keep the change." Pushing back his chair, he stood. "Excuse me, gentlemen. I'm going to get something to eat. And, Doug, you've got yourself a keyboard player." Agreeing to sit in with the band was a no-brainer, but getting to see Bobby's niece two nights a week was an added bonus. He wasn't certain what it was about her that drew him, but he wasn't going to dwell on that.

There hadn't been so many women in his life that he hadn't been able to recall their names or faces. However, none of them were willing to take a backseat to his music. His last relationship had ended when a woman he really liked had complained that she didn't see him enough. Writing and editing music and working long hours with temperamental singers didn't lend itself to a nine-to-five workday.

Jason likened his lifestyle to the wind. It could change direction at any time. There was no pressure for him to marry and give his parents grandchildren. His brother, Gabriel, and sister Alexandra had fulfilled that obligation. Ana and Jacob had decided to wait until their six-month anniversary before starting a family. No one was more surprised than Jason once his twin announced she didn't want to end her marriage of convenience to Jacob Jones. The man who'd appointed himself her protector had become her lover, husband and life partner.

Picking up a plate, Jason moved along the buffet station, selecting baked chicken, dirty rice and collard greens with pieces of smoked turkey. He viewed the dessert section, eying a sweet potato casserole with a pecan crust. He'd never been one to favor dessert, but as a born and bred Southern man, he loved sweet potatoes. Moving over to the beverage section, he filled a glass with sweet tea.

By the time Jason returned to his table, karaoke had begun in earnest. One young woman with waist-length extensions belted out "Proud Mary," while her two backup dancers gyrated as Ikettes. He enjoyed the dance moves more than the vocals. An elderly man, supporting himself on a cane, had to be lifted onto the stage. He sang an incredible rendition of Louis Armstrong's version of "Hello Dolly." Everyone stood and applauded him as he bowed before someone physically lifted him off the stage.

MC Oakie applauded along with the others. "Good people, I'd like to call Stella's own Greer Evans to the stage." An eerie hush fell over the assembly as she made her way to the stage. Oakie dropped an arm over her shoulders. "Have you selected your song?"

She nodded. "I'm going to sing 'And I Am Telling You I'm Not Going' from *Dreamgirls.*" She took the microphone and waited for the musical lead-in and lyrics to appear on the screen.

Jason felt the hairs on the back of his neck stand up the moment Greer opened her mouth. If he hadn't been there in person, he would've sworn it was Jennifer Hudson singing the heartfelt torch song, along with superb acting that had earned her an Oscar.

Doug whispered a curse under his breath. "I had no idea she could blow like that. I'm going to ask her to sing with the band."

Doug wanted Greer to sing with a local band of musicians who, although extremely talented, still hadn't made it big. Their only recording credits were on records produced by Serenity. Jason witnessed in Greer what he and Ana had recognized in Justin Glover. It was untapped raw talent. The song ended to stunned silence. Seconds later Jason found himself on his feet, applauding and whistling through his teeth. She was magnificent!

Greer stepped off the stage, eyes downcast as she walked quickly in the direction of the kitchen. She smiled at Bobby who shook his head in amazement. He extended his arms, and she moved into his strong embrace. "You were great."

She wrapped her arms around his waist and laid her cheek against his chest, listening to the slow, steady beats of his heart. "You're biased."

Bobby dropped a kiss on her hair. "Damn straight. You sing as well as my Stella. I used to love to listen to the two of you singing whenever you cooked together."

"Do you know that I still cook and sing?" Greer had stopped trying to understand why her aunt's quirks and idiosyncrasies had influenced her more than her mother's. Perhaps it was because her mother was a scientist and only dealt in what could be proven so that Greer had found her aunt's lifestyle much more off beat and exciting.

Easing back, Bobby cradled her face. "I'm so glad you're here."

Going on tiptoe, she kissed his cheek. "So am I."

At no time since she'd come to Mission Grove had Greer forgotten why she was working at the restaurant. She wasn't here to reconnect with her uncle or old-timers who'd watched her grow up. Someone was selling guns to those who couldn't pass the background check. Every two hours she took a break, lingering in the parking lot to observe those coming and going. Charles Bromleigh was still the only name on her list of suspects. He came to Stella's a minimum of four of the six days they were open for business. Chase always sat at the same table, ordered the day's special or took advantage of the buffet Thursdays through Saturday. Tap beer was his drink of choice, with never more than two glasses on any given day. Despite his taciturn demeanor he was generous when it came to tipping. Most of the restaurant patrons avoided him as if he carried a communicable disease. The exception was Jason Cole.

She patted Bobby's shoulder. "I better check the buffet trays. It looks as if the dim sum, pot sticker dumplings, spring rolls and barbecue spareribs are a big hit tonight." Greer's favorite was the steamed dumplings filled with chicken, pork or prawns.

Her uncle had hired an assistant cook whose mother's ancestry was traced back several generations to Western China. Although they'd intermarried and assimilated, the women in Andrew's family continued to prepare the dishes that had been passed down from great-grandmother to grand-mother to mother to daughter.

Greer walked out of the kitchen as Andrew walked in through the opposite swinging door carrying an empty tray. He winked at her. "Great job."

She smiled at the slender blond man with sparkling hazel eyes who had legions of young women chasing him. What they hadn't known was Andrew was in a com-mitted relationship with a much older woman.

"Thank you. What needs replenishing?"

"Nothing right now."

She returned to the dining floor, picking up discarded plates and flatware, and stack-ing them in a large plastic bin for the wait-ers who did double duty as busboys and dishwashers on buffet nights. Greer ac-knowledged those with a smile and a nod whenever they complimented her singing.

"Yo, miss. Over here!"

She turned and made her way to a table with six young men, some who didn't look old enough to shave. "Yes."

One with a five-o'clock shadow held a twenty dollar bill between his fingers. "I'd like to order a pitcher of beer."

Resting her hands at her waist, Greer gave him a direct stare. "I have to see some ID.

You must be twenty-three to be served alcohol."

"Isn't the legal drinking age twenty-one?"

"It is."

"Then what's the deal?" he asked.

"The deal is I can't serve you alcohol unless you're twenty-three." She smiled when he tucked the bill into his shirt pocket. "There is unlimited soda, tea and fruit punch." Greer turned around so they wouldn't see her smile, running headlong into Jason. She almost lost her balance but he managed to steady her, his hands going to her shoulders. Standing so close to him made her aware that he was very tall. She was five-seven but he had to be at least three or four inches over the six-foot mark. "I'm sorry," she whispered.

"I should be the one apologizing," Jason countered.

Why, Greer thought, hadn't she noticed his slow, drawling speech pattern that identified him as someone who'd grown up in the South? His voice was deep and soothing at the same time. He also smelled wonderful. His cologne was a combination of musk, sandalwood and a hint of bergamot. It was as intoxicating as its wearer.

"Is there something I can get you?" she asked quickly, recovering her physical and emotional equilibrium.

Jason handed her a folded napkin. "I'd like you to call me."

Greer glanced at his name and a number on the paper, recognizing the Florida area code. She continued to stare at the napkin rather than let him see the delight shimmering in her eyes. Jason had made the first overture, which eliminated her need to concoct a ruse to come on to him.

"Why?" she asked, not wanting to appear *too* eager that the record producer had approached her.

"I'd like to discuss some business with you."

She looked up at him. "You want to talk business? What happened to your business card, Mr. Cole?"

Jason looked sheepish. "I didn't think I'd need them tonight. I could always go home and bring some back with me."

Greer saw people watching them instead of directing their attention to the stage where a quartet harmonized a Boyz II Men classic. "Please follow me." She led him down a narrow hallway to an Employees Only door, stepping out into the cool late-summer night. Stopping, she turned to face Jason. The light over the door illuminated the area where Dumpsters were labeled

Garbage, Paper, Plastic and Glass. Bobby was pedantic when it came to recycling.

Crossing her arms under her breasts, Greer angled her head. "What type of business did you want to discuss?"

Jason didn't want to believe Greer wanted to carry on a conversation surrounded by Dumpsters. He wrinkled his nose. "Is there someplace else we can talk without smelling garbage?"

Greer shook her head. "I'm sorry, but this is the only place where we can talk without someone eavesdropping."

"Okay, then I'll make this quick. I'd like to make a tape of you singing several songs."

"As in a record?"

He nodded.

"Why?"

Pushing both hands into the pockets of his slacks, Jason gave her an incredible stare. "Has anyone told you that you have a remarkable voice?"

Greer shook her head. "No," she admitted truthfully. She'd been told she had a good voice, but not a remarkable one.

"Well, you do."

"Because you say so?" she asked.

"No," Jason countered. "Because *I* know so. You have perfect pitch."

Greer paused, stalling for time because

104

she had to make him believe she was wary that he'd approached her. "How do I know if I can trust you? I've heard too many stories about men offering women —"

"Stop it, Greer," he interrupted. "I've never taken advantage of any woman *and* I happen to have too much respect for Bobby to mess over you."

She decided on another approach. "Let me think about it, and then I'll call you."

Jason smiled. "Thank you."

She returned his smile, silently admiring the dimples creasing his cheeks. "You're welcome. Hold on," Greer urged when Jason reached for the door handle. "I have to unlock it." She hadn't yet put the key into the lock when the door opened. Danny stood in the doorway gripping a black plastic bag.

He stared at her. "Sorry. I didn't know you . . ."

"It's all right, Danny. We were just coming in." Jason's arm circled her waist as the ex-Marine continued to stare at her.

"Is he your man?"

A beat passed as she replayed the totally unexpected question in her head. Jason wasn't her *man,* and if he was, then what was it to Danny? Something about the way he was looking at her was off-putting, and

Greer wondered if he was experiencing a flashback.

Jason didn't know if Greer and the man she'd called Danny were previously involved with each other, then remembered Chase's comment about her going through a nasty divorce; he doubted whether she would continue to work with a man to whom she'd once been married.

"Yes, I am her man," he stated firmly.

The tension-filled moment passed as a half smile lifted a corner of Danny's mouth. "That's good. She needs someone to take care of her."

"Thank you," Jason drawled. "I'll make certain to always take care of her."

Danny extended his free hand. "Danny Poe."

Jason had to drop his arm to shake hands. "Jason Cole."

Greer rested her hand on Jason's back, feeling his body's warmth through the cotton shirt. "I have to get back before Bobby comes looking for me." The mention of her uncle's name galvanized Danny into action as he headed for the Dumpsters.

"Is he all right?" Jason whispered in her ear as they reentered the restaurant.

Going on tiptoe, Greer pressed her mouth

to his ear. "Iraq."

He laced their fingers together. "Is he in therapy?"

She nodded. "I really have to get back. And I promise to call you."

Jason leaned against the wall, watching the seductive sway of Greer's hips in a pair of fitted jeans as she walked away. He didn't know why he'd admitted to Danny he would take care of Greer because that wasn't even a remote possibility. She didn't need a protector when she had Bobby Henry.

He followed Greer, losing sight of her in the crowded restaurant. People were up on their feet singing and fist pumping to Flo Rida's megahit "Wild One." A woman grabbed his hand, leading him to a space where the tables were pushed back. Jason found himself caught up in the infectious rhythm as he danced with the petite buxom blonde. Dancing had reminded Jason of how long it'd been since he'd been to a club. Earlier that year he'd dated a woman living in Miami. She had professed to be a certified party girl, and after two months of nonstop partying, Jason was forced to break it off. Their weekends began Friday nights and didn't end until Sunday morning. He'd been so sleep deprived it had taken several months for him to reestablish a normal sleep pattern.

The song ended and he managed to escape the woman's clutches, making a beeline toward the exit. He left Stella's, driving to an all-night mini-mart where he bought milk, eggs, butter and bread. As he drove back home, he thought about how his best-laid plans had suddenly changed. He was now a member of a local band, and he hoped Greer would honor her promise and call him.

CHAPTER 6

Greer sat on the porch in the cushioned rocker as she stared out at the lake. The cries of a hawk had awakened her and she hadn't been able to go back to sleep. She had left her bed, showered, washed her hair and pulled on a sweatshirt and pants over her underwear. At dawn the mid-September air was cool and crisp. The smell of pine wafted to her nose as a gentle breeze rustled the branches of massive trees growing around the lake like ramrod-straight soldiers at a military parade.

She'd forgotten the number of times when she got up early, put on a swimsuit and raced out of the house to the lake as if something in there was calling her. The water was cold enough to make her teeth chatter, but after a while she didn't feel it. Swimming, boating and fishing had become the highlight of her summers, times filled with childlike abandon.

The word *abandon* conjured up images of Karaoke Night. It had become New Year's Eve with everyone singing, dancing, eating and drinking. She'd caught a glimpse of Jason dancing with a curvaceous woman. After the song had ended, she looked for him but he'd disappeared.

Greer had promised him she would call him, and she intended to keep her promise. Picking up her cell phone, she scrolled through her contacts and punched Jason's number. If he was serious about recording her voice, then he would not get upset if she called him at sunrise.

"Jason."

She smiled. He didn't sound as if he'd been asleep. "This is Greer," she crooned.

His soft chuckle caressed her ear. "Good morning."

"That it is."

"What are you doing up so early?"

"I could say the same about you," Greer countered. "I thought musicians stayed up all night and slept all day."

"Not this one. In fact I don't get enough sleep."

Greer had no comeback. She didn't want to ask if it was music or women that kept him up. "You wanted me to call you," she said instead.

"Yes, I did. I want to know if you're willing to block out some time for me to record your voice."

"What do you intend to do with the demo?"

"That's something we will have to talk about."

Shifting on the rocker, Greer pulled her legs up into a yoga position. "I'm free this morning."

"Are you working tonight?"

"Yes. I have to be at the restaurant between four and four-thirty." She went in early to set up the buffet station.

"I can pick you up in thirty minutes. Does that give you enough time to be ready?"

Greer wanted to tell Jason that she was more than ready — ready to find out all she could about his friend and neighbor. If Chase hadn't been so shadowy or standoffish, she would've attempted to get close to him directly.

"Yes. Do you know where my uncle's house is?"

"Yes. I'll see you later."

Disconnecting the call, Greer felt as if she'd scaled one hurtle. The next one would be to uncover who Chase was, what did he do and where did he go whenever he disappeared for weeks at a time.

Jason maneuvered up the paved driveway to Bobby's house, slowed and parked next to a classic red pickup truck. He turned off the engine and got out of the Range Rover, unable to take his eyes off the restored vehicle. He heard the sound of a door opening and glanced up to see Greer come out of the house. She looked deliciously alluring in a white man-tailored shirt, low-rise black jeans and matching high-heeled leather booties that made her legs appear even longer. He stood there, unable to move, tongue-tied. Slowly, seductively, his gaze slid downward from her face to the sensual curve of womanly hips before reversing itself.

She rested a hip against the porch column. "Beautiful, isn't it?"

The dulcet sound of Greer's voice shattered his entrancement. "Yes."

"Johnny B. Goode II is my uncle's pride and joy."

Jason frowned in confusion before he realized Greer was talking about the truck. "It's exquisite. Nineteen fifties?"

She smiled and nodded. "A 1956 model to be exact. Uncle Bobby bought it from a farmer who'd shattered his leg and couldn't depress the clutch. It took my uncle more than ten years to restore it."

"I've never seen him drive it."

Greer came down off the porch, while he openly stared at her approach. He repressed the urge to reach out and run the back of his hand over her face to see if it was as velvety as it appeared. He'd admitted to Danny that he was Greer's man but that was a lie. A falsehood. If circumstances were different, that could possibly become a truth. Jason had worked with a number of female artists since taking over as Serenity's musical director, but he'd never crossed the line with any of them to mix business and pleasure.

"That's because he usually keeps it garaged." She touched the hood. "I learned to drive on this baby."

"So you like driving a vehicle with a manual transmission."

"I like control."

Her statement told Jason everything he needed to know about Greer Evans. "Control," he repeated softly. "What about compromise, Greer?"

She blinked. "What about it, Jason?"

He leaned closer, their noses nearly touching. "Do you ever compromise?"

Greer smiled, bringing his gaze to linger

on her lips. "Only when I'm not offered an alternative."

Jason didn't know her age, but she looked incredibly young with her scrubbed face and ponytail. His mouth curved into an unconscious smile. "Then I must make certain to offer you an alternative to what I've planned for our future venture."

"You've already planned my future when I'm not sure where I'll be or what I'll be doing three months from now?"

He inclined his head. "I apologize for being presumptuous. Now, let's leave."

Greer went completely still. She did not want to believe Jason had offered a backhanded apology while issuing an order in the same breath. Exhaling an inaudible breath, she had to remind herself that she had been given a directive to identify those buying and selling illegal firearms, and that she'd become an actress in a role wherein she could not afford to break character.

Earlier this morning after logging on to the government-issued laptop, she'd typed Jason's name into a classified database and had come up with hundreds of Jason Coles. She'd narrowed the search with Serenity Records, transfixed with the data. Greer knew his date of birth, middle name, the schools he'd attended and net worth. She also had to remember, whatever role she assumed, Greer couldn't afford to succumb to what she knew was the total package for any normal woman. Jason was tall, dark, handsome, sensual and charming, and a few other adjectives she wouldn't permit herself to acknowledge.

Gathering information on Charles Bromleigh had proved less fruitful. There were other Bromleighs who had a penchant for naming their sons Charles. However, the Charles she sought did not exist. It was as if he were a ghost, a specter. He was there, yet he wasn't. It would've made Greer less suspicious if she'd found a file or fingerprints on him that were classified. The fact that he presumably didn't exist had only strengthened her resolve to go after him.

Turning to Jason, she forced a smile. "I just have to get my bag and car keys, and I'll be right back."

Jason caught her wrist. "We're going to take my truck."

Greer stared up at him through her lashes, garnering the reaction she sought when his jaw dropped. Yes, she was flirting with him. "I don't want to put you out when you have to drive me back."

Jason shook his head. "Greer," he said

softly. "Remember I'm the one asking you to do me a favor, not the other way around."

Whenever he said her name, it came out like a sensual growl. The first two letters began in the back of his throat while the next three were barely audible. "You're right. I still have to get the keys to put the truck in the garage." Even when she drove the truck to Stella's, she parked it in the garage on the premises. "May I have my hand back?" she asked him. Instead of letting go of her wrist, Jason raised her hand, dropping a kiss on her knuckles.

"Of course you may." His fingers slipped away, releasing her delicate wrist. He winked at her, and she returned it with a sassy smile.

Jason leaned against the bumper of the pickup emblazoned with black letters from the song title of one of his favorite rock-and-roll artists, watching Greer walk back to the house. He doubted if she knew just how sexy she actually was. It wasn't just her face and body but also her body language. It was why the men at Stella's couldn't stop themselves from touching or brushing up against her.

He'd known many and dated one very beautiful woman. The difference was their beauty was only skin-deep. A few had him looking for the nearest exit when he had discovered they couldn't carry on a simple conversation. Usually all they wanted to talk about was themselves or name-drop as to who'd asked them to model or appear in music videos. It had reached a point in his life where Jason much preferred his own company to the opposite sex. He was very comfortable spending time alone in the studio experimenting with different music genres or losing track of time when he put on a playlist of his favorite songs spanning six decades.

Several of his single male cousins were forthcoming when they had asked if he was gay because they rarely saw him with a woman, but he reassured them that he liked women. It was just that he was very discriminating when it came to sharing time and space with the opposite sex. Hanging out with a group of men was very different from interacting one-on-one with a woman. Not only was he expected to show her a good time, but there was also the question of whether he wanted to sleep with her. Once he committed to taking a woman to bed, it translated into being in a committed relationship. It wasn't just physical. It was also emotional.

He stood up straight when Greer re-emerged with a black leather tote slung over her shoulder. She locked the front door, and he approached her and took the keys to the pickup. "I'll put it in the garage."

"You can drive it to your place if you want."

Jason's smile was sheepish. "How did you know?"

Greer rolled her eyes upward. "Duh. I saw your eyes light up when you first looked at it."

His teeth flashed whitely in his sun-browned face. "Was it that obvious?"

"Sometimes your face is an open book, Jason. You're not that hard to read."

He sobered. "Is that so?"

Greer nodded.

"What am I thinking about now?"

Her somber expression mirrored his. "I don't read minds, just faces." She didn't add body language because that would give too much of herself away. Dangling the keys to the pickup, she dropped them into Jason's outstretched hand. "Do you want me to pull your truck into the garage?" she asked him.

"No. It can stay here." Cupping her elbow, he led her around the pickup to the passenger side, opening the door and assisting her onto the seat.

Greer felt like a small creature unable to

move for fear of attracting the attention of a predator when her eyes met Jason's. She opened her mouth to tell him that he could close the door now, but the words were locked in the back of her throat as she found herself caught in a trance from which she did not want to escape. His large expressive brown eyes were framed by long black lashes better suited on a woman. Her gaze went to the short black strands on his head and lower to the emerging stubble. There was something about Jason that was quietly dangerous, and she knew she had to be careful or she would find herself emotionally in over her head. She'd known special agents who'd become involved with their targets because it had been the only way they could secure the evidence needed for an arrest. Fortunately it wasn't Jason but Chase who'd become her person of interest. The soporific spell was shattered when Jason finally closed the door.

It was in a moment of absurdity that Jason had imagined what it would be like to make love to Greer. He didn't know whether the thought had come from prolonged periods of isolation, celibacy or the sacrifices he'd made for his jealous mistress.

He slipped behind the wheel and started

up the truck. The engine roared to life, then purred like a contented cat. Shifting into Reverse, he backed out of the driveway. The gears shifted smoothly as he maneuvered onto the local road.

"This baby is sweet." Jason gave Greer a quick glance. "Do you think Bobby would be willing to sell it to me?"

Greer gave him a stunned look. "Why would you want this when you have a top-of-the-line SUV?"

Jason shifted into a higher gear. "I don't own a vehicle. I'm renting the Range Rover."

"What about your car or cars in Florida?"

"I rent there, too."

A slight frown formed between her eyes. "Why don't you own a car?"

Lifting his shoulders under a white cotton pullover, Jason concentrated on the narrow winding road. "I don't know. Owning a car isn't something that turns me on. I merely view them to get me from point A to B."

"If that's the case, then why would you want to buy this one?"

"Because it's a classic. There's a lot of history in old cars."

Shifting slightly on the seat, Greer stared at his distinctive profile. "Do you feel the same about music?"

"Yes and no. I'm somewhat partial to the music from the '50s, '60s, '70s and '90s."

"What about rap and hip-hop?"

Jason shifted again when he came to a steep hill. "I like both. There's something about old-school music that connects and reflects the sign of those times. If you sit and listen to the protest songs from the '60s, it's like a referendum on change in order for the country to move in another direction."

"Protest music and old cars. Did anyone ever tell you that you were born too late?" Greer asked, smiling.

Jason laughed softly. "I hear it all the time."

"Does it bother you?"

"Not in the least." He downshifted as he turned off to the private road bordered on both sides with towering trees and up a steep hill to Bear Ridge Estates. Slowing, Jason stopped at the gatehouse because he'd left his remote sensor to open the gate in the Range Rover.

The armed guard leaned out the window, smiling. "Nice truck, Mr. Cole. What year is it?"

"Nineteen fifty-six."

The guard pushed a button on a console, activating an eight-foot electronic gate.

"Have you thought about selling it?"

"No," Jason and Greer chorused, and then shared a smile. The gate opened and he drove through. "You see I'm not the only one who wants to buy Johnny B. Goode II."

Greer stared out the side window at the sprawling Colonial with meticulously landscaped lawns and gardens. It was minutes before she saw another house, this one with a five-car garage. The Georgian-style mansion boasted eight chimneys. Bear Ridge Estates overlooked the Hood River Valley and she tried imagining waking up year-round to the lush views of the beautiful fertile valley with fruit trees and the magnificence of Mount Hood.

She didn't know what to expect Jason's home to look like when seeing the others they'd passed, but it wasn't the three-and four-story ostentatious residences which were more a showplace than a home for family living. It sat in a sunny knoll amid the fragrant pine forest. Its design was reminiscent of a hunting lodge. The attached three-car garage was constructed in the same design as the main house.

"Don't move," Jason said when she made the motion to open her door. "I'll help you down."

Well all right, she thought, waiting as he

got out and came around the truck. Finally she'd met a man who'd help a woman in and out of a vehicle without her asking. It was a pet peeve of hers, and she and her ex had argued constantly about it when dating, yet she'd foolishly married him because the sex was good.

Jason extended his arms and she slid off the seat, her hands on his shoulders as he lowered her effortlessly to the ground. She hadn't missed the flexing of his solid muscles under her fingertips when she held on to him. His clothes had artfully concealed a well-conditioned physique. She reached for her tote. Resting a hand at the small of her back, he escorted her to a side entrance. Lifting the door handle, Jason punched in a code.

Greer smiled up at him when he pushed open the door. "It's nice not having to use a key." She followed him into a mud/laundry room with a slate floor. There were built-in shelves filled with red, white and blue canvas bins.

"I have an unfortunate habit of misplacing my keys." He sat down on a bench and removed his shoes. "I have socks that will fit you if you want to take off your boots."

"Thank you."

She sat on the bench, unzipped the four-inch booties, wiggling her toes. The polish on her left big toe had chipped. She'd set aside Mondays to drive into town for a day of beauty that included hair and a mani-pedi. Jason pulled out a bin labeled Socks and handed her a pair of white golf socks.

"Have you had breakfast?"

Her head popped up. "No."

Jason held out his hand, pulling her to her feet. "Neither have I. We'll talk while I cook."

"You cook?"

He narrowed his eyes at her. "Of course I can cook. Who do you think feeds me?"

Greer made a face. "There's no need to get so snippy, Jason. You could have a girlfriend who comes to cook for you."

He angled his head. "Is that your way of being subtle?"

"Being subtle about what?"

"To find out whether I'm involved with a woman."

Throwing back her head, Greer laughed until tears filled her eyes. "Sure . . . surely you jest," she sputtered, touching the corners of her eyes with a forefinger. "I don't know what you've heard about me, but I'm not ready to become involved with a man."

"Is it because of your divorce?"

A beat passed, while she stared at Jason.

His question had caught her completely by surprise. "Who told you I was divorced?"

Jason wanted to lie and say he'd overheard someone talking about her, but he'd never perfected lying. "It was Chase."

Her heart pounded painfully against her ribs. "You and Chase were discussing me?"

"He said Bobby told him about your divorce because he'd asked about you."

"Why would he ask about me?" Greer wasn't paranoid, plus she knew her uncle would never tell anyone she was a special agent for the ATF. However, there was a remote possibility Chase could've gained access to her classified file while she wasn't able to come up with anything verifying his existence.

Jason tugged on her ponytail. "Come on, Greer. You can't be that naive. You have to know what you look like. Only a man who isn't normal wouldn't give you a first, second *and* a third look."

Greer wished she'd had this information before today. She would've approached Chase directly instead of trying to make nice with his friend. It was too late for her to change her plan of action in midstream without arousing suspicion.

"I suppose I should be flattered, but I've never been drawn to the brooding type."

"Chase is rather laid-back once you get to know him," Jason said in defense of his friend.

He draped an arm over her shoulders. "What do you feel like eating?"

Tilting her chin, she smiled up at him. "It's been a while since I've had French toast."

Lowering his head, Jason kissed her hair. "You're in luck because I went to the supermarket last night, and I have all the ingredients to make your French toast."

"I'm going to like hanging out with you. You cook *and* shop."

"I can also do laundry," he boasted proudly.

"Now I know you're a keeper."

Jason laughed. "You may change your mind once you discover I don't know how to clean."

"That's why people hire housekeepers."

The smile that brightened Jason's expression made him look boyish. "A cleaning company comes twice a week. They're under contract to service all the residences in this community."

Greer filed away this piece of information. That meant the company probably cleaned Chase's house. Wrapping her arm around Jason's waist, she leaned in closer. "Would you like some help in the kitchen?"

"No. Today you're my guest."

"What about the next time, Jason?"

"Will there be a next time?" he asked, answering her question with one of his own.

"After we talk, if we can come to an agreement, then there will definitely be a next time."

CHAPTER 7

Greer's eyes were drawn to a magnificent black concert piano as she followed Jason into what was an open gallery of rooms on the first floor level. The kitchen, dining and living rooms flowed seamlessly into the great room. Natural wood, stone, hardwood floors and leather furniture created a warm and personal family space.

The media center — with a large wall-mounted flat screen and audio components which were separate from the primary living space — and the massive rock-faced fireplace provided a cool contrast to the warmth of the wood's crooks and the support beams' arches.

"How many bedrooms do you have?"

Standing behind Greer, Jason rested his hands on her shoulders. "Five and a half."

She gave him a skeptical look. "How can you have half a bedroom?"

"I'll show you. Would you like a quick tour

of the house?"

She wondered how many other women he'd invited to take a tour of his house, then chided herself for entertaining the thought. Again she was forced to remind herself why she'd agreed to come to Bear Ridge Estates. It wasn't because she had romantic notions or wanted a record deal. It was to gain access to the guarded, gated community and Chase Bromleigh.

"Sure."

Jason reached for her hand. "We'll start upstairs, then I'll take you downstairs to the studio."

Greer climbed the carpeted winding staircase, stepping off onto a corridor wide enough for two or three to walk abreast. Lamps with crystal bases sat on a mahogany drop leaf halfway down the hall. Jason touched a wall switch and recessed lighting brightened the space, and the floor shimmered with a reddish patina. She sucked in her breath.

"The floor."

Jason gave her a sidelong look. "What about it?"

"It's beautiful."

"I didn't want the same type of wood throughout the house, so my aunt suggested Brazilian cherrywood."

"Was she the architect?"

He gave Greer's fingers a gentle squeeze. "No. She's an interior decorator who recommended the architect."

"She has exquisite taste."

Jason grasped Greer's free hand and pressed his back to the wall covered with a wheat-colored fabric. His eyes lingered on her upturned face, marveling at the perfect texture of her skin. He wanted to tell her she was flawless, that everything about her appeared young, fresh and natural. The natural look was something he'd found missing in so many high-maintenance women he had come into contact with. Many in their attempt to *enhance* their looks had standing appointments with plastic surgeons. Even women under thirty were injecting their faces with fillers. He'd seen Greer three times and each time she looked different. He found himself as transfixed with her voice as much as he'd been with the lights over the stage illuminating her hair and face. Chase may not have been her type, but Jason realized Greer was definitely his.

"Before I show you the bedrooms, I want you to know that it took longer for me to approve the plans for this house than it did to build it."

Greer freed her hands, resting them on Jason's chest over his heart. "Are you always so indecisive?"

His eyes under lowered lids lingered on her mouth. "No. It was my first time buying property, so I didn't want to invest in a house, then end up selling it a few years down the road."

Her eyebrows lifted a fraction. "You don't own property in Florida?"

"I don't know how to say this."

"Say what, Jason?"

He glanced over her head. "I still live at home."

"And . . ."

"And what?" he retorted. "Don't you think it's weird that a thirty-three-year-old solvent man still lives at home with his parents?"

"No more weird that a thirty-two-year-old college grad waiting tables and living in her uncle's house."

Jason stared, complete surprise freezing his features. "You're thirty-two?"

"Yes. How old did you think I am?"

"Twenty-five. Maybe twenty-six."

Going on tiptoe, Greer kissed his stubble. "Thanks for the compliment."

He went still. "You think I said that just to flatter you?"

"I don't know, Jason. I've discovered men say a lot of things they really don't mean to flatter a woman."

The seconds ticked as he glared at her. "I'm not a lot of men, Greer. I don't know anything about your marriage or why you're divorced, but I'd like to remind you that I am not your ex. And there is one thing I want you to know about me if we're going to have a business relationship, and that is, I'll never lie to you. The recording industry — like any other competitive business — is fraught with pitfalls wherein behemoths lie in wait to take advantage of those responsible for putting them in their mansions, Bentleys, underwriting the cost for their diamonds, yachts and private jets. And they do this by lying, cheating and stealing from the innocent and unsuspecting."

Greer struggled not to lose her temper. "Why are you bringing up my divorce?"

"Because it seems as if you lump all men in the same category as your ex."

"Are you married or were you ever married?" she countered.

"No. And even if I was, I don't think I'd paint all women with the same broad brush. I've had some real crazy girlfriends and a few who were wonderful, but I didn't distrust or mistreat the nice ones because of the crazies."

She took a deep breath to calm her quaking innards. "Why are we arguing, Jason? You're supposed to be giving me a tour of your house."

"We weren't arguing," Jason said in a quiet voice. "We were having a minor difference of opinion." Wrapping both arms around her shoulders, he pulled her close and kissed her hair. "As I was saying — I still live at home, not because I can't afford to live elsewhere, but because I have my own apartment there and easy access to my father's recording studio."

"That's a whole lot better than sleeping on your mama's couch or on a blow-up mattress on the basement floor."

Jason smiled, dimples winking. "Damn-m-m," he drawled.

Ditto, she thought. That's exactly what her ex was doing. He'd had so much potential but squandered it when he was unable to separate fantasy from reality. "Where's your bedroom?"

"It's the first one on the left." He opened the first door on the right. "We'll start with the guest rooms."

Greer entered, feeling as if she'd walked into a suite at a four-star hotel. A king-size bed with a white leather headboard was the room's focal point. Her gaze shifted to a matching footstool and a corner chaise. The chocolate-brown-and-white bed dressing, sheer wall-to-wall cream-colored silk drapes and modern furniture in gleaming mahogany provided an inviting space to sleep for hours. The bed faced a wall with a large flat screen and built-in electric fireplace. One other wall held walk-in closets. Further examination of the bedroom revealed an Asian-inspired bathroom-spa with twin vanities, a free-standing tub equipped with a Jacuzzi, shower, glass-enclosed sauna and dressing area.

The other three guest rooms were similar to the first with the exception of the color schemes. One had a king-size bed. Another held a queen-size bed and the last one was furnished with two full beds. This one was obviously decorated for children. There was no television on the wall opposite the beds. All of the furniture was white as was the comforters. Throw pillows in blues, pinks, yellow and mint green provided a riot of color in the otherwise pristine space. It contained an alcove with a cushioned window seat and an entertainment unit with a television, a Wii gaming system, book shelves, 3-D glasses and DVDs.

Greer ran her fingertips over the spines of

nursery rhymes and chapter books. "I really like this room."

Crossing his arms over his chest, Jason angled his head. "Once I marry and start a family, it will become a nursery and later a bedroom for a teenager. Speaking of teenagers, every year the entire clan gets together for a family reunion in West Palm Beach. Everyone comes in for Christmas Eve and stays the entire week. New Year's Eve is traditionally for weddings."

"There is a wedding every New Year's Eve?" she asked, pleasantly surprised by this revelation.

"Not every year, but this year we'll definitely have two. My twin sister will renew her vows, and I just got an email from a cousin that he's getting married in Virginia at the end of October, but will renew his vows for the entire family on New Year's Eve. Thanksgiving is different because my father, his brothers and sisters, their wives and husbands celebrate the holiday together, while my generation celebrates separately. Initially our parents thought we were rebelling, but after a while, they were okay with it as long as we joined everyone for the week between Christmas and New Year."

"Where are you spending Thanksgiving

this year?"

"We don't know yet. It was supposed to be in Mississippi, but my cousin canceled it because he had an accident earlier this summer. My cousin Regina wants us to come to Brazil, but the family in New Mexico doesn't want to travel that far just for a four-day weekend. They have school-age kids, and if they decide to stay longer, then that would mean the kids missing classes."

"Have you ever hosted it here?"

Jason shook his head.

"Why not?" Greer asked. "It's not as if you don't have enough room."

"I usually come out here in June and leave around Halloween. However, this year is different because I probably won't leave until just before Christmas."

"Then you should host Thanksgiving."

Greer had given him an idea. He'd planned to stay in Oregon until the end of the year, and celebrating Thanksgiving and having children running in and out of the rooms at Serenity West was something he'd welcome. Jason made a mental note to contact his first cousins to let them know he was willing to open his home for this year's Thanksgiving gathering.

"It's something I'll definitely consider."

Greer affected a sexy moue. "You and I

have something in common."

"What's that?"

"I'm also a twin."

"Sister or brother?"

"Brother. He always says he's the prettier twin."

"I doubt that, but I tell Ana the same thing," Jason teased.

She made a sucking sound with her tongue and teeth. "That has to be a male twin thing. Do you and your sister look alike?"

Jason nodded. "More or less. We have our dad's black hair and dimples, but our mother's eyes. I'm also a lot taller than she is." He didn't want to tell Greer that her hair and eye color were similar to his mother's.

"Cooper and I definitely look alike. But he's got a good six inches on me." Greer glanced around the proposed nursery-to-teen bedroom. "That's four bedrooms down and one to go."

He steered her across the bedroom to a narrow hallway. "This is a shortcut into my bedroom. I'm surprised your parents didn't give you names like Daniel and Danielle."

"When told she was having twins, my mom decided to treat us like brother and sister instead of twins. She never referred to us as *the twins.* It was her son and daughter, or Cooper and Greer. Cooper is my mother's maiden name. My dad is Gregory so I became Greer."

"People probably believe you were named after Greer Garson and Gary Cooper."

"Folks who are movie buffs have asked me that."

Greer was intrigued by Jason. If he'd been born in the '40s or '50s, there is no doubt he would exhibit the sensibilities and norms from those decades. But for someone born in the 1980s, she found him to be an enigma. From what he'd shown her, he did not appear to be self-centered, boastful or arrogant like some of the kids from well-to-do families she'd attended school with, dated and eventually married. He was one of the music industry's more successful young writers/producers, preferring to stay out of the limelight and therefore out of the tabloids.

She liked watching major awards shows not just to find out the winners, but who were the movers and shakers. Although Serenity Records was a small independent record label, their artists' successes were anything but small. The songs from their latest crossover singing sensation were played on every major radio station. Even she'd downloaded Justin Glover's album to her iPod.

Jason opened the door, and she preceded him into the master bedroom suite. It was twice the size of the one they'd just left. The khaki, cinnamon and paprika-red tones in the expansive bedroom paired with furnishings that recreated British campaign furniture — made popular in eighteenth-century India, Africa, West Indies or even the South Sea — exuded sophisticated elegance. It was the same with the dressing stand and bureau and carried over into the carvings in the posts of the large bed. Two neatly folded throws in khaki and maroon lay on the bench covered in natural suede at the foot of the bed. She glanced up at the trio of skylights, then to the wall-to-wall walk-in closets and the stone fireplace.

Greer made her way across the room to windows overlooking a garden with a water-fall and wildflowers growing in abandon. A short distance away was an inground pool, tennis and basketball courts, gazebo and hot tub. Jason had spared no expense to construct and decorate a home designed for ultimate family living, recreation and relaxation.

The adjoining bathroom bordered on decadence with walls of frosted glass that let light in while keeping prying eyes out, a white stone floor, a black marble sunken tub, a free-standing shower and built-in sauna. She left the bathroom, walked into an antechamber and found Jason lounging on an off-white English-style sofa lined with throw pillows in shades from beige to maroon. A glass-topped caned coffee table evoked a Caribbean feel. A stack of coffee table books occupied the corner of the table set on an area rug. The doors to a mahogany armoire were open to reveal a television and audio components, while bundles of dried herbs lay on the fireplace grate behind a decorative screen.

She sat down next to him, picking up a cream-and-red silk striped pillow. "Do you sleep in your bedroom?"

"I did the first day I arrived, but not since. Why?"

"It looks so sterile. Everything is in its place."

"I only come up here to shower and change my clothes."

"Where do you sleep?"

"In the downstairs studio."

There came a beat as Greer measured her words carefully. "Why didn't you build a bedroom in your studio if you spend so much time there?"

Jason ran a hand over his face. "I don't

intend to spend that much time there, but once I get into a piece, I lose track of time."

"Do you use blank sheet music or a computer program?"

"Both. I begin writing on blank sheets, then I play it on the piano. If I need to change a note or chord, it's easy because I can just erase it. I use this method for every instrument I want to use in a composition. Once I complete the composition, I go to the synthesizer and computer for the first draft."

"How many drafts do you go through before you settle on a final?"

"It all depends on if I'm really into it. There are days when I feel as if I'm just going through the motions and start writing notes that don't work or play well with one another."

Greer stared into eyes so much like her own. "What do you do then?"

"Scrap it and start over."

"That must be frustrating."

"It is," Jason admitted, "but I try and not let it get to me."

"What about lyrics?" she asked.

"They're easy. Once I listen to the music track, the words just come." He patted her knee over the denim fabric. "Let's go downstairs and eat." He pushed off the sofa, extending his hand. He wasn't disappointed when Greer took it. Tucking her hand into the crook of his elbow, they retraced their steps to the first floor.

"Are you certain I can't help with something?" she asked when he seated her on a stool at the cooking island.

"No. I've got everything under control."

Resting her elbows on the granite countertop, Greer watched Jason as he opened the door to the built-in refrigerator/freezer gathering the ingredients he needed for the French toast after he'd washed his hands in a half bath off the kitchen. "Would you like bacon or sausage with your toast?" he asked, peering at her over his shoulder.

"I'll have whatever you have," she said.

He narrowed his eyes at her. "I'll make both." Jason had to make two trips to the cooking island as he gathered eggs, a loaf of challah bread, milk and packages of sausage and bacon. Picking up a remote device, he aimed it a cabinet and music filled the kitchen.

Greer smiled when she recognized the song, and joined in singing Sade's "Diamond Life."

Jason stopped to listen to Greer singing. She was no fluke. Greer really did have an incredible voice. It was warm, smoky and undeniably sexy. Taking down a mixing bowl from an overhead cabinet, he cracked several eggs and beat them with a whisk.

There was so much he wanted to ask her, but he didn't want Greer to stop singing. The next twenty minutes passed as she continued to entertain him with her singing as he grilled sausage and bacon on the stovetop grill, placing them in a warming drawer while he measured flour into a large mixing bowl, slowly whisking in milk, eggs, cinnamon, vanilla extract, sugar and a pinch of salt. He soaked slices of bread in the mixture until saturated.

Multitasking, Jason set the corner of the island with two place settings, and filled goblets with orange juice as he reheated the lightly oiled grill. The tantalizing aroma of cinnamon and vanilla wafted throughout the kitchen when the battered toast was placed on the grill.

Greer watched in awe as the toast fluffed, as the edges became a golden brown before Jason flipped them over. He'd fixed a sumptuous breakfast within thirty minutes. "I can see why you didn't need my help."

Bending slightly, Jason removed the platter of bacon and sausage from the warming drawer. "I find breakfast the most challenging because it's not a one- or two-pot meal.

Most people wake up hungry, and they don't want to wait hours to eat. When my brother and sisters were still living at home, I would get up and make breakfast for everyone." He ladled two slices of toast onto a plate for Greer. "Do you want fruit on your toast?"

She shook her head. "No, thank you."

He placed a dish of butter and a bottle of maple syrup on the countertop. "Coffee or tea?"

"Coffee, please. Sit down and eat, Jason," Greer urged when he walked over to a coffeemaker. "I'll have coffee later."

Jason complied, raising his goblet. *"¡Bueno apetito!"*

Greer touched her goblet to his. "Same to you." She took a sip of the cold orange juice, peering at him over the rim. "Do you speak fluent Spanish?"

He nodded, swallowing a mouthful of juice. "Both my parents are fluent in the language. What about you, Greer?"

"What about me?" she asked.

"Do you speak any other language?"

"No. I had four years of French in high school and another year in college, and I can remember enough to order a few dishes at a French restaurant. Other than that, I'm stuck with English." It was a lie because she

144

was fluent in the language.

Over a leisurely breakfast Jason told Greer about his Cuban-born grandmother marrying U.S. businessman Samuel Cole and their marriage that had lasted seventy-five years. "My grandfather was one hundred three when he passed away, and my *abuela* died several years ago at the incredible age of one hundred six."

Totally enthralled, Greer asked, "How did they meet?"

Jason got up to get their coffee. "That's a long story. I'll tell you at another time. Meanwhile I'd like to talk about making you a tentative offer for a recording contract."

Greer's serene expression successfully concealed the riot of emotions going on inside her. If Jason had offered to sign her to his record label before she had joined the ATF or even before she had married Larry, she would've jumped at the idea even if she never made it big.

"I can't accept it."

Jason's hand stopped as he attempted to bring the coffee cup to his mouth. "Why not?"

"It's personal."

He lowered the cup. "If it's so personal, why then did you call me this morning?"

"It was to talk."

Jason's expression changed from shock to anger.

"I can't accept a contract but I am willing to . . ."

"To what, Greer?" he asked when her words trailed off.

"Let you record me, but that's it."

Reaching across the small space separating him from Greer, Jason took her left hand, increasing the pressure when she tried pulling away. "Who are you hiding from?"

"What makes you think I'm hiding from someone?"

"Why else would a thirty-something woman with a college degree wait tables in a restaurant in a town that's a blip on the map? Does your decision have something to do with your ex?" he asked when she averted her eyes.

If Jason believed her decision had something to do with her ex-husband, then Larry would become the perfect alibi for her reluctance to reject an offer that was certain not only to change her life but also her future.

Greer lowered her eyes. "Okay." She sighed. "It does have something to do with my ex-husband. I'm not going to go into detail about my marriage, but it's something I don't want to ever relive. I'll make the tape for you, and if you believe I'm that good, then I will record your songs. I will not accept payment and nowhere will I allow my name to appear in the credits or I'll sue you and your label."

Jason knew he was between the proverbial rock and a hard place. He and Ana had the uncanny ability to recognize an exceptional vocal talent within seconds of hearing the first note. It'd been that way with Ana when she'd heard Justin Glover's tape, and she'd managed to sign him by default.

Basil Webb had been the first to hear Justin's demo record, but after Slow Wyne offered the young twenty-year-old a deal that had him indebted to the company for the first two years of his contract, Justin's agent went to Serenity. Basil knew he had to change the terms of the contract or he would lose Justin. Then it had become a bidding war with Serenity as the winner even though their last bid was lower than Slow Wyne's.

His sister's skill was negotiating, but Ana wasn't in Mission Grove sitting across from Greer Evans. He was. They hadn't lost Justin and Jason had no intention of losing Greer. He exhaled an audible breath, releasing her hand. "Okay. No contract, no credit."

Greer nodded. "I'd like that in writing." She wanted to cover all her bases.

He felt as if he'd won. Albeit a small victory, but nonetheless a victory. "I'll call my sister and have her draw up an agreement as to what we just discussed."

"Have her address it to J. Greer Evans."

The Greer he'd first witnessed — when he had walked into Stella's to find her threatening to castrate a man who'd made the mistake of groping her — was back. Under the delicate exterior was a woman whose protective instincts were on high alert. His respect for her had increased appreciably. "I'll let her know. Are you ready to see the studio?"

She took a quick glance at the clock on the microwave. "I'll see it the next time I come. I need to get back and put up several loads of laundry before I go to work."

Jason swung his leg over the stool. "I'll drive you back now."

The return drive was completed in silence. He parked the pickup in the garage, then came around to assist Greer. Cradling her face, he kissed her forehead. "I'll see you tonight."

CHAPTER 8

I'll see you tonight. Greer didn't know why Jason made it sound as if they were dating because it wasn't like that. She was working at Stella's, and Jason, instead of sharing a table with Chase, was on the stage playing guitar with the house band.

She and Bobby had come outside the kitchen to listen to the music. Doug, playing the lead-in guitar riff to The Rolling Stones' "I Can't Get No Satisfaction," was greeted with rousing applause from those in the crowded restaurant. She felt electricity in the air, and Greer wasn't certain whether it was from the music or because the Seattle Mariners had taken over first place in the American League Western Division in what had become the best season since they were enfranchised in 1977. Every television was tuned to the sports channel.

"The music's good tonight," she said to her uncle. The band performed hits by

Earth, Wind & Fire, plus The Rolling Stones, Maroon 5, Nirvana, Kool & the Gang, The Black Eyed Peas, Los Lonely Boys and U2.

Bobby crossed massive arms over the bibbed apron stretched over his broad chest. "It's always good when Jason sits in with the band. I don't know what it is, but they seem to have a little more swagger —"

"Swagger, Uncle Bobby?"

"Maybe swagger isn't the right word. It's more like the other guys are freer, willing to take more risks." He pushed out his lips. "Doug asked me if I could spare you for a few sets on Fridays and Saturdays because they lost their female singer."

Greer stood up straight. "He wants me to sing with the band?"

"Yep."

"Why didn't he ask me, Uncle Bobby?"

Bobby shifted to his right as the swinging door opened, and Andrew emerged from the kitchen with a tray of stuffed shells. "He figured, because I'm your boss, he'd ask me first. And if I said yes, then he'd come and ask you."

"And what did *my boss* tell him?"

"Don't get your nose out of joint before you hear what I told him."

Greer registered the censure in Bobby's

voice. "I'm sorry."

When she wound her arm around his waist, Bobby rested a large hand on her shoulder. "There's no need to apologize. I know what you're going to say. 'Uncle Bobby, you can't afford to forget why I'm working here,' " he mimicked in falsetto, repeating what she'd told him a few times when he'd suggested she take a day off and have some fun.

Even if her uncle had forgotten, Greer couldn't. "Doug isn't the only one who wants me to sing for him." She told him about her meeting with Jason. "Why couldn't I have met Jason before I got involved with Larry?"

"Are you talking a singing career or something more . . . romantic?"

She rolled her eyes upward. "Don't even go there, Uncle Bobby. I don't have time for a man."

"When are you going to have time, Greer?"

"I can't have a normal relationship given what I do for a living."

"Yes you can, honey bunny."

She rested her head on his shoulder. It'd been years since he'd called her that. "It would take a very secure man to deal with me being reassigned every couple years."

"Once you finish what you're here to do, I want you to hand in your resignation and begin to live for yourself. You don't have to worry about where your next dollar is coming from because this place is yours."

"It's not mine."

Bobby frowned. "Why are you being so pigheaded? You know your aunt wanted you to take over after we retired. I also revised my will after Stella died leaving you everything I own. This restaurant, the house on the lake, the pickup and the boat. I also plan to make you a signatory on the business and my personal accounts so if anything happens to me —"

"Nothing's going to happen to you, so stop the drama."

"Don't interrupt me!" Bobby snapped angrily. "You're in denial if you believe I'm going to be sweating over a stove when I'm ninety. Don't get me wrong, baby. I love cooking, but standing up for hours and carrying this weight is taking its toll on my knees, legs and feet. My doctor has been telling me to lose weight, and I've turned a deaf ear because it never bothered me before. Now it is."

Greer couldn't ignore the flutters in the pit of her belly. Even though she and Bobby Henry didn't share DNA, she'd always thought of him as a member of her family. "What are you going to do?"

"I'm going to take off a couple days a week and work with a personal trainer. I already have a special diet I'm supposed to follow. It just means I'll have to stick to it."

"What is it you need me to do?" Greer asked.

"I want you to manage the place and assume some of the cooking duties."

She nodded. "What about Andrew?"

"He'll run the kitchen, and you'll assist him until we get another cook. I'll ask Andrew if he knows someone who went to culinary school with him and needs work."

"You're going to have to hire someone to wait tables on Tuesday and Wednesday if I'm going to work in the kitchen." Greer preferred waiting tables because it gave her the opportunity to eavesdrop on conversations. She'd learned many people ignored the waitstaff, continuing with their conversations even if she lingered to set down or remove a plate, or came over to ask if they were enjoying their meal.

"That's easy enough. I'll put an ad in some of the local newspapers. You and I will have to talk about going completely buffet-style on those days."

"In other words Stella's will become a buffet restaurant." Her question was a statement.

"That's what I'm counting on. What do you think about doing away with Sunday dinner table service?"

Greer chewed her lower lip as she thought about Bobby's suggestion. After serving Sunday brunch, the number of patrons who came into Stella's for dinner didn't actually warrant table service. There were some Sunday nights when she was able to cover all of the tables, including those who preferred eating at the bar.

"I like that idea."

"Then that does it. We go fully buffet Tuesday through Sunday, and no more Sunday dinner table service."

Greer nodded. Not having to wait tables would give her more time to observe the goings-on in the restaurant. She'd come in earlier to help in the kitchen, then it would be up to her to keep the buffet replenished. "I'll make up flyers and pass them out so everybody will know of the changes. When do you want them to go into effect?" she asked Bobby.

He shifted his weight from one foot to the other. "We'll start Tuesday. That will give our regulars the weekend to get used to the new hours and service." Lowering his head, he pressed a kiss to Greer's hair. "You see? That was easy. Now, tell me what you're going to do with Doug?"

"I guess it wouldn't hurt to sing a couple sets for him."

Bobby's blue eyes sparkled when he smiled. "I'm certain he'll be glad to hear that."

"I hope I'm not making a mistake, Uncle Bobby. Singing on stage in front of an audience makes me more conspicuous than waiting tables."

"I wouldn't worry too much about that. When I saw footage of you being rounded up with those others, I couldn't recognize you," Bobby said sotto voce. "Between the weight, hair, contacts — and what the hell you did to give yourself the nastiest overbite I'd ever seen on a woman — your change in appearance was ingenious."

Greer laughed under her breath. A technician had fashioned a dental prosthesis she could slip on over her own teeth to make her the poster child for acute orthodontia care. "The only thing I could eat with those choppers was burgers and fries, and that's why I blew up like a blimp."

"At least it didn't take you that long to lose it." Bobby patted his belly. "This time next year I hope to be lean and mean."

Tilting her head, Greer met the winking blue eyes. "You're already mean."

"That's only for show. The only time I lose it is when someone messes with you."

"You know I can take of myself."

After a childhood and her teen years spent on homework, piano, ballet and karate lessons, Greer was more than ready to spend the summer months in Mission Grove. She'd excelled in karate and earned her black belt the year she turned sixteen. Although she no longer competed, she'd continued to train with a karate master up until she became a special agent.

"I know you can, but it would look better if I kicked a dude's ass than if you did. If men know that a woman can put a hurtin' on them, then they'll avoid them like the plague."

"That's not such a bad idea."

"Come on, Greer. You can't let one idiot turn you off on the entire male gender."

Greer wondered what had gotten into her uncle where he insisted on talking about her and other men. He was like a dog with a bone, refusing to let it go. "I'm not turned off. I'm just not willing to walk down that road again."

"Are you telling me you don't want to get married again and have children?"

"I would like to have a child, but I don't have to be married."

Bobby patted his bald pate. "Please don't tell me that you're going to be one of those women who claim she can raise a child on her own?"

"Women do it every day."

"And that's why kids are so screwed up nowadays. It is one thing if a father or mother is widowed, but it's entirely different when women absolve men of their responsibility for raising their son or daughter. I don't care what Larry Hill tried to do to you, you still came out the winner. And if you let him sour you on men, then he's won. Is that what you want, Greer?"

"No. It's not want I want, Uncle Bobby."

"Good. Now maybe you'll take some time off and have a little fun."

"What do you call fun?"

"Flirt. Dance. When someone asks to take you to the movies, you say yes instead of giving them the screw face."

"I'll try."

"Don't try, honey bunny. Just do it."

"I better go and see who needs more liquid refreshment."

The band had taken a break, and Greer approached a table asking if anyone wanted something from the bar. She took several orders, headed in the direction of the bar when she came face-to-face with Jason. He'd shaved and was dressed entirely in black.

"You were great," she said softly.

Jason inclined his head. "Thanks. It feels good to play in front of an audience."

"I'm going to the bar. Would you like something? There's no charge for band members."

He wanted to tell Greer what he wanted wasn't at the bar. He wanted to spend more time with her. Everything about her had lingered even hours after he'd taken her home. The scent of her perfume on the sofa in the bedroom's antechamber, the sound of her voice he could recall in vivid clarity and the silken feel of her skin whenever he had touched her.

Jason had told himself he'd come to Oregon to write new music and not become involved with a woman. Especially not one who lived so far away from his home base. His relationships with women who lived in Florida hadn't worked out, and there was no reason for him to believe he could maintain one with a woman living thirty-three-hundred miles away.

And if he were truly honest with himself, Jason would have to admit it wasn't merely

Greer's voice that had initially attracted him to her. It was the whole package — face, body, voice and the spunk she'd shown when the man at Stella's had sought to grope her. It was obvious Greer was confident enough to stand up for herself.

He smiled. "Thanks for the offer, but I'm drinking water tonight. May I ask you something?"

"Sure. What is it?"

"Do you have any days off?"

She angled her head. "Yes. I'm off on Mondays."

He leaned closer, his mouth pressed to her ear. "What are you doing Monday night?"

Greer closed her eyes. Jason smelled so good she likened him to a decadent dessert that she wanted to savor for hours instead of minutes. Pinpoints of heat pricked her cheeks when she realized her thoughts had taken an erotic route.

"I don't have anything planned. Why?"

"I'd like you to go out with me."

She went completely still. "Out, as in a date?" she whispered.

"Yes. What time can I pick you up?"

"Hey, Mr. Piano Man. Stop flirting with the lady waitress, and let her bring us our drinks!" shouted a man at the table where

Greer had taken orders. Heads turned, necks craned and an eerie silence descended on the restaurant like a shroud. The sound of pool balls connecting echoed abnormally loud in the quiet.

Jason stood up straight, an arm going protectively around Greer's waist. "You should have more respect for yourself to know when you've had too much to drink." The man half rose from his chair. "Don't do it." Jason's warning, though spoken softly, carried easily across the space, and the two men flanking the obviously inebriated man pulled him back to sit.

Greer felt the tension in Jason's arm as he stood his ground. The last thing she wanted was a confrontation. Occasionally when someone couldn't handle their alcohol, an argument would ensue, but between Bobby and Pepper, they were able to stop it before it escalated into something physical.

The crowd parted when Pepper walked over, while Bobby came from the opposite direction. "What's up?" asked the bartender.

"What the hell is going on?" Bobby shouted.

"Marvin's upset 'cause that guy's flirting with Greer," volunteered one of the men who'd stopped his friend from doing something he would regret. He pointed to Jason, who had a six-inch height advantage and was at least twenty years younger than Marvin.

Bobby rested his fists at his sides. He saw Jason with his arm around Greer's waist. "Who she flirts with is *her* business. And you know what I've said over and over about disrespecting my niece. You dodged a bullet tonight, Marvin, because it's obvious you've had too much to drink. You guys better take him home before I call the sheriff and have him thrown in jail for disorderly conduct. And, Marvin, the next time you come in here, you will have a two-drink limit, or you will not be served at all. Don't worry about the tab," he continued when one of the men reached into his pocket to pay for their drinks. "Now get him out of here."

Waiting until the trio left, Pepper nodded to Bobby. The bartender held up his hands to the rest of the diners. "Sorry for the interruption, but the next round is on the house."

Greer felt herself relax against Jason. She hadn't realized how tense she'd been. The drawback of working in an establishment selling alcohol was the risk of serving someone with a low tolerance. Pepper usually monitored the number of drinks he served to any particular person at the bar but it was different with table service.

Jason dropped his arm. "Are you all right?"

She forced a smile she didn't feel. "I'm good. How about you?"

"I'm okay." He would've been better if the scene hadn't occurred. What, he mused, was there about Greer that brought out the worst in some men? He'd watched her while he was on stage and, at no time, had he observed her flirting or being overly friendly with any of the male patrons. Although he'd never been involved in a bar fight, Jason knew he wouldn't back down if confronted.

Greer patted his shoulder. "Thanks for sticking up for me. I'll see you later."

The rest of the night went smoothly for Greer. She got word to Doug that she would sing with the band, but no more than two songs each night, and he would have to let her know when and where they would rehearse. The members of the band had packed up their instruments and sound equipment, Danny was stacking chairs in a corner, when Jason walked over to where she and Bobby sat.

"May I sit down?" he asked.

Bobby waved a hand. "Of course."

Greer noticed he'd slipped on a black leather jacket over his cotton sweater. Light from the overhead slanted across his face, and she caught her breath. He'd become a bust of black and gold. His short raven hair shimmered like a sleek fur pelt. Initially she had thought the flecks of gold in his large brown eyes were similar to tortoiseshell, but upon closer inspection, they were more similar to polished amber.

Placing his hands on the table, Jason gave Bobby a long penetrating stare. "I'm sorry about what happened earlier. I never would do anything to put Greer's reputation at risk."

Bobby covered one of Jason's long slender hands with his much larger one. "Come on, son. You did nothing wrong. If you'd thumped his ass, I would've extended you complimentary food and drinks for a year."

Jason looked directly at Greer. "I'm not one for violence, but I won't walk away if I feel threatened."

Bobby removed his hand, picking up the snifter filled with Jack Daniels. "I like you, Cole. There's something about you that reminds me of myself back in the day. I wouldn't let anyone look at my woman wrong or I'd —"

"I'm not Jason's woman, Uncle Bobby," Greer said in protest.

Bobby took a sip of his drink, then blew out a breath. "Either Mr. Daniels is getting stronger or I'm getting too old to drink the hard stuff." He gestured to Jason. "Can Pepper get you something from the bar before he closes down completely?"

"No thanks. I have to drive home."

"Good for you. Now I know I can trust you with Greer. You have my permission to ask her out."

Attractive slashes appeared in Jason's lean cheeks when he smiled. "You're a little late because I've already asked her out."

"And what did she say, son?"

Jason's smile grew wider. "She didn't say no."

"Bobby! Jason! Don't y'all talk about me as if I'm not here."

Leaning back in his chair, Jason winked at Greer. "You can join the conversation at any time you want."

"Hey, Cole!" Doug shouted. "We're going into Portland to visit a few clubs. You coming?"

Jason shook his head. "Nah. I'm going to hang out here for a while."

"Next time maybe. And thanks, Greer, for agreeing to sing with us."

She smiled. "No problem."

It was no problem when Jason had just told Bobby their business. She didn't have a curfew or need to report her whereabouts to her uncle, but she didn't want to advertise that she had a date. Pushing back her chair, she stood up. "Tonight I think I'm going to have something stronger than coffee."

Jason popped up. "What do you want? I'll get it for you."

"I don't know what I want until I get there. What are you doing?" She practically hissed at him when he followed her.

"Getting something from the bar." She stopped and he bumped into her, his hands going to her shoulders. "Careful, darling. I wouldn't want you to fall on that beautiful face."

"I'm not your darling just because I agreed to go out with you."

"You deserve to be a man's darling."

Turning slowly she faced him. There was an arrogant tilt to her chin. "What if I was your darling, Jason? What could I expect from you?"

Jason studied the delicate face with the wide-set eyes, stubborn little chin and nose that turned up slightly at the end. "You would never want for anything."

"I'm not talking about material things."

"If I were in love with you, then I would protect you at the risk of giving up my own life. And if you loved me enough to marry me, then I would spend the rest of my life making you as happy as I'm certain you'd make me. My family would become your family and your family mine. Our children would be heirs to a dynasty that spans generations. A dynasty that is ever expanding to even greater heights than what my grandfather could or would have ever dreamed. Does that answer your question, *darling*?"

Greer felt as if the very oxygen had been sucked out of her lungs. Self-confidence radiated off Jason in waves she couldn't see but feel. Was it because he was *that* certain of his rightful place in the world? He'd been born into wealth, did not have to concern himself about what he wanted to do or be. When his father had relinquished control of his company, Jason had taken his place in what had been a smooth and uneventful transition.

"Yes it does, *dah-lin'*."

Taking her hand, Jason led her to the bar where Pepper was busy stacking empty bottles in plastic crates. "You sound just like a Southern girl."

"That's because I am a Southern girl."

"It looks as if I have to get to know you better."

Pepper stopped what he was doing and

approached them. "What can I get for you folks?"

Jason bowed low. "Ladies first."

She studied the bottles. "I'll have a martini."

Pepper shared a look with Jason, their eyebrows lifting a fraction. "Don't you mean a Cosmo?"

"No. I want a martini with Bombay Sapphire. Extra dry *and* extra dirty."

"Damn-m-m," the two men chorused, drawing out the word.

Greer called on all her self-control not to laugh. She'd never been much of a drinker, nursing a beer for an hour while her friends were drinking margaritas, Jack and Coke and doing shots. Once she had joined the male-dominated ATF, she had graduated from beer to gin.

Pepper ladled ice into a shaker. "What can I get for you, Jason?"

"Cîroc, straight up."

Greer nudged him. "You go, playa."

Jason winked at her. "I could say the same thing about you. Somehow I figured you for a fine wine woman."

"The only time I drink wine is with dinner."

He ducked his head, the gesture so endearing Greer wanted to hold him close.

"I'll be certain to remember that whenever we share dinner."

Pepper shook the shaker with the ingredients for the martini. "You kids go and sit down with Bobby, and I'll bring your drinks."

Resting his hand at the small of Greer's back, Jason escorted her to the table. "I'll follow you when you leave to make certain you get home all right."

"Who's going to make certain you get home in one piece?" she teased.

"Come home with me and find out. And it's not what you think, Greer," Jason said quickly when she frowned at him.

"What am I thinking, Jason?"

"That I'm going to try and get you to sleep with me." He shook his head. "It's not about that. I thought, if you don't have to go to work until the afternoon, then I could test your voice and go over possible songs for the mixed tape. I could also help you rehearse the songs for tomorrow's playlist."

"If I rehearse with you, will I still have to rehearse with the band?"

"No. I'll let them know I went over everything with you."

She stopped before they were within earshot of her uncle. Getting close to Jason was progressing faster than she'd planned.

If Chase proved not to be a person of interest, then she would have to redirect her focus.

"Do I get to choose my own bedroom?"

Jason's smile was dazzling. "But of course."

"If that's the case, then you've got yourself a houseguest."

CHAPTER 9

Los Angeles

Webb Irvine walked into his bedroom, towel tucked around his waist and droplets of water glistening on his sable skin from an ice-cold shower. It was as if nothing was going well for him. He hated anything and everything to do with Slow Wyne Records. He didn't like the employees, the artists signed to the label, and he loathed rap and hip-hop.

He still didn't understand how Basil had put up with the antics of street thugs who really believed their own hype. Webb felt few, if any, of them had any talent. What they had were hard bodies covered with so much ink they could double for a collage. And then there were the women who followed them blindly, hoping for a piece of their stardom while attempting to lure them into bed where they would become their baby mama.

He hadn't had a woman in twenty years, and it would be another twenty years plus twenty more after that before he'd want one. He didn't trust himself around women; his hatred for the opposite sex ran so deep, he feared any contact with them would send him back to prison. Occasionally he dreamed he'd slashed the face of every woman he'd met or seen. And he didn't need a psychiatrist to tell him that he was internalizing what had happened to him as a teen. Spending his adolescence and early twenties locked up with other men had taught him to take care of his own sexual needs in private.

Webb knew his frustration had come from spending more time at Slow Wyne than at his own security firm. His interest in computers had begun while incarcerated. He'd learned to take them apart and reassemble them in record time. He was proud that he'd made good use of the thirteen years he'd spent behind bars. He had earned a high school diploma, and once paroled, he'd enrolled in college and graduated with a degree in computer science. Basil had given him the money he had needed to set up his own security firm, designing and selling state-of-the-art surveillance equipment.

Removing the towel, he dropped it over a

valet stand. One of the three cells phones on the bedside table rang, garnering his attention. It was the phone Monk had given him. Taking two long strides, he picked it up.

"Irvine," he said in greeting.

"Found him."

Webb smiled. "Where?"

"Just verified he does have a place in Oregon. Still don't know what city."

"How long do you think that's going to take?"

"Hopefully, not too long. And when I do find him, I'll let you know."

"Thank you, Monk."

There was no response on the other end, and Webb knew the man had hung up. The call had lasted exactly fifteen seconds. He set the phone down next to the other two. Once he gave Monk his final payment, he would begin the process of dismantling Slow Wyne. Then he and Basil would be even.

Mission Grove

Greer slipped into bed, sighing softly when the mattress enveloped her like a comforting embrace. She hadn't taken more than two sips of the martini before setting it aside. Pepper had made it much too strong.

172

When Greer had told Bobby she was leaving the pickup in the garage behind the restaurant because Jason was driving her home, Bobby had warned the younger man to drive carefully because he was carrying precious cargo.

Jason heeded Bobby's warning, maintaining the twenty-mile-an-hour speed limit; they stopped at her house where she packed a bag. The drive to Bear Ridge Estates was even slower, given the lateness of the hour and the fog coming off the lake that made visibility nearly impossible. Instead of stopping at the gatehouse, Jason continued along a private road for residents with remote devices that activated the electronic gates.

Once inside, she reminded Jason — because it was her second visit to his home — that she was no longer a stranger and could find the bedroom without his assistance. Greer had chosen a suite decorated in the style she recognized as Colonial American, and as soon as she closed the door, she stripped off her clothes and headed for the bathroom. Turning on the faucets in the bathtub, she added several capfuls of foaming bath oil; she cleansed the makeup off her face, brushed her teeth and then slipped into the sunken bathtub while emitting an audible sigh. The Jacuzzi worked its magic. After a leisurely bath, it was with a great deal of reluctance that she climbed out, patted herself dry and liberally lathered her body with a scented body cream. Her eyelids were drooping when she pulled on a cotton nightgown and got into bed. She hadn't quite dozed off when something startled her. Sitting up, she stared at the door.

"Jason?"

"Are you in bed?" he asked on the other side of the door.

"Yes."

"May I come in?"

Reaching, Greer turned on the bedside lamp, while pulling the sheet and blanket up to her chest. "Come in, Jason."

The door opened and he walked in with a mug of steaming liquid in each hand. He'd changed into a pair of blue pinstriped pajama pants and a white T-shirt. His biceps were firm, muscled. Jason had a swimmer's physique. Broad shoulders, muscled upper arms, flat middle.

"I brought you something that'll help you to sleep."

Greer wanted to tell him she had been falling asleep already. Then she remembered he was a musician and two in the morning was much too early for him to retire for bed. Maybe, she thought, he should've joined Doug and the other bands members who'd gone to Portland.

"Thank you," she said instead.

Jason handed her one of the mugs topped with whipped cream. "Do you mind if I join you?"

Smiling, she patted the bed with her free hand. "Please." She was now wide awake.

Jason got into bed, lying on the comforter instead of under it. He kissed Greer's cheek. "You smell wonderful."

She kissed him on his cheek, as well. "So do you. What cologne are you wearing?"

Gripping the handle of his cup, he supported his back against the headboard. "It's a special blend."

"A blend made especially for you?"

Jason nodded. "There's a shop in Palm Beach where a family of chemists have been blending perfumes and colognes for at least seventy-five years. My uncle turned me on to them. I don't know how it's done, but they're able to match certain oils and notes with your body's pheromones and the result is extraordinary. I've worn the same cologne and aftershave since I started shaving."

"It must be nice to have a personal perfumer."

"It has its advantages. Take a sip of your coffee — decaf — to see if you like it."

Greer did, moaning softly. "It's delicious." She had drunk cappuccino many times, but this taste was slightly different — sweeter. "What did you put in it?"

"Take a guess." She took another sip, and then attempted to lick the cream off her lips. Jason angled his head, pressed his mouth to hers and his tongue flicked over her parted lips. "You missed a spot."

With wide eyes, Greer stared at the man sitting so close she could feel his breath on her cheek, while her heart beat a runaway rhythm against her ribs. Her lips burned as if someone had touched them with heated metal. She wondered if he was aware of the effect he had on women. Whenever she had circulated throughout Stella's, she had overheard women telling one another as to what they wanted to do *to* Jason and *with* him. There weren't too many things she'd seen or heard when undercover that could shock her, yet she had found herself blushing at their vulgarity.

"You didn't bring napkins."

Jason stared at Greer under lowered lids. He hadn't planned to lick her lips, but he hadn't been able to resist tasting her lush mouth. "I'll go downstairs and get some now."

Greer stopped him when she rested a hand on his arm. "Why don't you get some tissues from the bathroom?"

"Hold my cup. I'll be right back."

A minute later he returned with handful of tissues. It looked as if he'd emptied the box.

Biting on her lower lip, she shook her head. "We don't need that many, Jason. I'm going to have to teach you how to eat in bed."

He got back into bed, dropping the tissues in her lap. "Which type of eating are you referring to? Because there's one technique I believe I've perfected."

Her jaw dropped when she realized what he was referring to. "I was talking about food."

Throwing back his head, Jason roared with laughter.

His laugh was so infectious that Greer laughed in spite of herself.

He sobered, dimples winking at her. He pressed his shoulder to Greer's bare one. He'd been forthcoming when he had told her that he wasn't trying to get her to sleep with him, but that didn't belie the fact she was in a bed under his roof, and he was reclining in *her* bed. Jason knew nothing was going to happen only because he didn't want to do anything to derail their easygoing friendship.

"To answer your question as to how I made the cappuccino, actually it's caffé mocha. It's one-third espresso, one-third hot chocolate and one-third steamed milk, added to the cup in that order. Tonight I added mocha syrup, enough to coat the bottom of the cup before adding the espresso. I topped it with whipped cream and ground sweet cocoa."

"Did you ever work as a barista?"

"No. Regina me taught how to make caffé mocha."

"Isn't she the cousin who lives in Brazil?"

Jason gave her an incredulous look. "You remembered."

Greer wanted to tell him that she'd been trained to remember whatever she heard or saw. Like when she observed Chase in the parking lot giving a package to the biker. She reminded herself to talk to Bobby about installing closed-circuit cameras in and around the restaurant property. No one had complained about their vehicles being vandalized or stolen, but if someone was dealing drugs or selling illegal guns out of Stella's, then they would be caught on film.

"I remember because you'd mentioned she wanted you to come to Brazil for Thanksgiving."

"Speaking of Thanksgiving, I took your suggestion and sent out a mass email inviting everyone to come here for the holiday."

She smiled. "Did you get any responses?"

Jason nodded. "So far the New Mexico folks are coming."

"They're not that far away."

"Word," he drawled. "Tyler's wife just gave birth to a baby girl last week, so by that time, she'll be okay to travel."

"Where do they live?"

"Mississippi."

"That's not too far, either," Greer said. "How many are you expecting, and do you have enough room to put everyone up?"

"I'll find out once I get a final head count. If not, then I'll ask Chase if some of them can stay at his place."

"How many bedrooms does he have?"

"Four. He usually goes to Hawaii to spend the Thanksgiving holiday with his parents."

Jason mentioning Chase gave Greer the opening she needed to ask him about his elusive friend. "Does he work?"

"Why don't you ask him?"

"I'm asking you, Jason."

"Chase and I have remained friends because I don't get into his business. If he doesn't disclose, then I don't ask. The only thing I'm going to tell you is that he has a weakness for beautiful women. I'm certain if you ask him, he just might tell you."

Greer successfully schooled her disappointment behind an expression of indifference. "I told you before, he's not my type."

"I thought most women liked the strong, silent type."

"I'm not most women."

Dropping his arm over her shoulders, Jason pulled her closer. "I guess that's why I like you because you're not like most women."

She shivered, hoping he wouldn't notice. "Because you like the way I sing?"

"It's more than that. You're incredibly feminine and natural. I don't like women with embellishments."

"Don't you mean enhancements?"

"No. Embellishments, like exaggerated breasts and over-the-top hair extensions that I'm not allowed to touch. Nothing turns me off more than a woman who tells me I can't touch her hair or her breasts."

"What if she has short hair? There's more upkeep in maintaining a short style than one that's longer." It was easy for Greer to fix her shoulder-length hair in different styles even when she didn't visit a salon.

"I've paid for women to have standing appointments to get their hair done, so that's no excuse."

Greer took another sip of the coffee. "Then that means you're a very generous boyfriend."

"It has nothing to do with generosity, Greer. It's about making her happy. If she's happy, then I'm happy."

"You must be very easy to please."

Jason chuckled softly. Either Greer was extremely perceptive or he was that transparent. "Somewhat," he drawled.

She folded several tissues, using them as a coaster when she set her cup on the table on her side of the bed. Sliding down to the mound of pillows cradling her shoulders, she stared up at the reflection of the light on the ceiling. "Tell me what makes you happy."

"Music."

"That's a given."

Jason handed his cup to Greer, who placed it beside hers. Shifting slightly, he pulled her close until her head rested on his shoulder. "Silence. It is when I'm surrounded by nothing but silence that I'm able to hear the music in my head. Sometimes it's loud and raucous like rush-hour traffic, and sometimes it's soft and melodic as the trilling of a canary. There are times when I'm happiest when I'm alone. My mother claims I'm selfish, but maybe it's because, as a twin, I was forced to share the same space with another human being for nine months.

"Don't get me wrong. I love Ana, yet there are times when we both decide we need our own personal space. Ana was sixteen when she told me she was leaving home to live the bohemian life in Key West. She'd saved some money, and I gave her what I had, then she made me promise not to tell anyone where she was going. When Ana didn't show up for dinner and my father asked where she was, I told him I didn't know."

Greer heard the slow, strong, steady beating of Jason's heart under her ear. She didn't want to believe she was sharing a bed with him as if it was something they'd done many times before. "Did he believe you?"

"Hell, no. My folks knew Ana never went anywhere without telling me and vice versa. He issued a litany of threats — from withholding my trust fund until I was thirty to grounding me until it was time for me to leave for college — but I continued to deny that I knew where she was."

"You are very loyal."

"I am not a snitch."

"Now you sound like people who witness a murder, then claim they saw nothing."

"I wasn't giving up my twin sister."

"What did your father do?" Greer questioned.

"When he discovered her car missing, he called the police and told them she'd stolen it. He could do that because it was registered in his name. The Miami-Dade P.D. held her until Dad drove down to get her. He paid someone to drive the car back to Boca Raton. She had to give him her driver's license, and he treated her like a stranger for at least a month. Ana said the alienation was worse than if he'd grounded her."

"Did she ever get her license back?"

Jason nodded. "Eventually. I had to drive her everywhere when she was on lockdown. One day I confronted Dad after Ana came to me crying hysterically that her father hated her, and I got to see another side of my father that I don't want to ever see again. He went off, warning me never to question his authority again when it came to raising his children. He still wasn't talking to Ana, and after that, I refused to talk to him. To say there was a lot of tension in the house is an understatement."

"How did your mother react to the drama?"

"She refused to take sides. Thankfully our apartments were in another wing of the house, so we didn't get to see or hear what went on between our parents."

Greer didn't know why, but she was intrigued by the story. "I have to assume you guys reconciled."

"It was *Abuela* who ended the stalemate. She claimed Ana was a lot like her when she was a young woman in Cuba. My grandmother permitted an artist to take photographs of her wearing next to nothing, and because she was born into a very proper upper-class family, it proved to be quite scandalous in 1920s Havana. Her father threatened to marry her off to the first man in their social class who would have her, regardless of his age. She countered saying she was going to become a courtesan, but my grandfather salvaged her family's reputation and *Abuela* from an arranged marriage when he married her and brought her back to Florida."

"That is so romantic. Do you have photographs of them?"

"I have an office in my studio where I keep family photos. You'll see them tomorrow —"

"It's already tomorrow, Jason," Greer said

teasingly.

"You're right, and I'm keeping you from going to sleep." Jason sat up, swinging his legs over the side of the bed. "What time do you have to leave?"

"I don't need to be at Stella's until four. I brought the clothes I plan to wear with me."

"Good. That means we can spend the day together." Pushing off the bed, he rounded it, picking up the mugs. Leaning over he kissed her forehead. "Sleep well."

She smiled up at him. "You, too."

"Do you want me to close the door?"

Greer smothered a yawn with her hand. "Yes, please." She reached over and turned off the lamp at the same time Jason closed the door. Her eyelids fluttered, her breathing deepened as she expelled a soft sigh.

In talking to Jason, he'd revealed a lot about himself. He'd admitted to being solitary and uncompromisingly loyal. He'd sworn an oath to his sister that he wouldn't reveal her whereabouts, and he hadn't even under the threat of losing his trust fund.

If Jason had been born too late, then it was Greer who'd met him too late. She thought about his relationship with women when he had professed: *it's about making her happy. If she's happy, then I'm happy.* Her uncle may have been right when he had said, once she got to know Jason, she'd realize he's an all-around nice guy.

Nice or not, she was still wary of men. She'd believed Larry was a nice guy until she had become Mrs. Lawrence Hill. He'd changed from the wonderful boy next door into something and someone she didn't recognize. She wasn't his wife but a possession. Someone he put on display for his friends and business associates. It had reached a point when she'd had enough and, a week past her second anniversary, she had left the man with whom she believed she would spend her life. As soon as she'd received a copy of her divorce, Greer vowed she would never marry again.

CHAPTER 10

When Greer left her bedroom, the door to Jason's suite of rooms was open. She didn't know whether he was still in bed or if he'd gotten up early to go into the studio. Her sock-covered feet were silent as she descended the staircase and headed for the kitchen. It was eerie because the house was as silent as a tomb.

Greer opened the refrigerator and freezer, taking inventory of its contents. "Bless you, Jason," she whispered. The refrigerator was stocked with what she needed to make omelets and parmesan steak fries. She made two trips from the fridge to the cooking island, gathering potatoes, eggs, butter, pepper and onions, a carton of crumbled feta cheese and a plastic bag with fresh spinach leaves.

Opening and closing drawers under the countertop, she found a cutting board and knives. Overhead cabinets held spice racks, dishes, cups and saucers, and another with mixing bowls. Jason had installed an audio unit in one of the cabinets, but Greer hesitated turning it on because she wasn't certain whether he was still asleep.

Humming softly, she preheated the oven, then sliced the potatoes into wedges, adding ground garlic powder and dried parsley. Greer had forgotten how much she enjoyed prepping a meal as she sliced, chopped and diced. For all her pleasant memories of cooking, and singing while cooking, still Bobby's revelation that he was going into semi-retirement had been totally expected. Her uncle had accused her of being in denial if she believed he would continue running the restaurant for the next ten years. Last night, while soaking in the Jacuzzi, she'd thought about the possibility of owning and managing Stella's.

Bobby was offering an alternative to the undercover work that had been so much a part of her life for the past six years. She smiled. Every summer her aunt would remind her that someday the restaurant would be hers. But at that time Greer hadn't thought about becoming a businessperson. She'd loved watching Stella prepare dishes before attempting them herself, but it was swimming and boating, hunting and hiking that had become a priority for her.

How, she mused, had she gone from teaching first and second graders to becoming a special agent for the ATF to contemplating taking over a family-owned restaurant?

As she cut the potatoes into wedges, Greer found herself warming to the idea of running Stella's. The landmark eating establishment had survived competition from fast-food restaurants popping up all over the region. The quality of the food had remained consistent for three decades, Pepper's skill as a mixologist had become legendary, and the appeal of Karaoke Nights each Thursday and the live band on Fridays and Saturdays offered something for everyone from teens to seniors.

Converting Stella's into an all-you-can-eat buffet restaurant was certain to bring in even more families. When Bobby had first introduced buffet dining, he'd believed people would fill their plates with food, then Bobby would have to throw away their leftovers. Wasting food was a pet peeve for her uncle because he'd grown up in Appalachia where many nights he and his sisters had gone to bed hungry. The posted sign, Take What You Want, But Eat All That You Take, was a constant reminder for the loyal patrons and those coming for the first time.

One more time, she tossed the potatoes in the bowl with parsley and garlic power and olive oil, before placing them on a parchment-lined baking sheet, finally dusting them with grated parmesan cheese. Greer then turned her attention to the omelets. Seeing movement out the side of her eye, she turned to see Jason in a pair of wet swim trunks and flip-flops.

She smiled. "Good morning."

Jason's teeth shone whitely in his stubbly face.

Jason hadn't known what to expect, but it was a pleasant surprise to find a woman in his kitchen. Especially if that woman was Greer Evans. His gaze moved leisurely from the hair pinned haphazardly atop her head, down to the black tank top outlining the thrust of her firm breasts and lower to a pair of denim shorts displaying her long, slender legs to their best advantage and stopping at a pair of ankle socks.

Jason had slept fitfully, his dreams filled with erotic images of him making love to her. At first he'd believed it was because it'd been a while since he'd slept with a woman, then realized it was *the woman* sleeping in a bedroom across the hall from his. And when he got up earlier that morning, he chided himself for getting into bed with Greer the evening before. It was something he would make certain not to repeat if he wanted a restful night's sleep.

"Good morning. I didn't know you were up. Otherwise I would've invited you to join me in the pool."

Greer continued chopping spinach. She didn't trust herself not to gawk at the mat of chest hair tapering down to a narrow line and disappearing under the waistband of his trunks. "I didn't bring a suit."

"You don't need a suit. Either you can swim in your underwear or in the buff."

Her hand halted. "You swim nude?"

Jason nodded. "Only at night. The pool is lit and heated."

"Aren't you concerned about someone seeing you?"

He came closer, leaning his chest against her back.

Greer held her breath.

"No." He pressed a kiss to the side of her neck. She smelled delicious. "You smell wonderful."

Greer smiled. "And you smell like chlorine." Her voice trembled with laughter.

"I'm going upstairs to take a shower."

"I'll hold breakfast until you are ready."

"What's on the menu?"

"Feta and spinach omelets, parmesan steak fries, sliced fruit and coffee or tea."

Jason kissed her neck again. "You definitely are a keeper," he said, repeating what she'd told him — what now seemed so long ago. Why, he mused, did it feel as if he'd known Greer for several months when it'd only been weeks?

Greer swatted at him with a dish towel. "Go shower."

"Yes, darling." She gave him an eye roll and Jason put up his hands. "I'm going."

Greer was hard-pressed not to smile when he executed a snappy salute, then turned on his heels and marched out of the kitchen. But she did smile when she realized how comfortable she felt around Jason. She'd slept in his house without the pressure of having to lock her bedroom door to keep him out. Even before she'd married Larry, Greer had dated men who'd expected her to sleep with them because they'd taken her to dinner. She forgotten how many times she'd said she wasn't any man's dessert.

Bobby had urged her to go out, date and have some fun. Not only had she taken his advice but, fortunately, she was able to combine business with pleasure. Jason had talked about having some of his family members sleep over at Chase's house if he ran out of room at his home. If she hadn't identified the person or persons responsible for illegal gun sales by then, it would present the perfect opportunity for Greer to gain access to Chase's home if he was in Hawaii.

Her smile grew wider. Jason Cole was the perfect conduit through which she could get close to Chase. Although she'd professed Chase wasn't her type, there was nothing stopping her from befriending him without arousing his suspicions. After all, she was dating one of his best friends.

Dating. The word sounded strange to Greer because it had been a very long time since she'd had a date. She and Larry had dated off and on for years before he had finally proposed marriage. Then it was another eighteen months before they had tied the knot, and nothing could have ever prepared her for what was to come. Initially she had believed he was being protective. Protectiveness became overprotectiveness, then she began to feel as if she was being smothered. That escalated until Greer knew, if she didn't end her sham of a marriage then, like a lot of emotionally abused women, she would never get out. It had ended with one act that had left her stunned and close to contemplating murdering her husband. She had called Cooper, and he had come to get her. It took all her strength to beg and plead with her brother not to kill his brother-in-law, and Cooper made her promise that she would never reconcile with Larry or he *would* kill him.

Knowing her brother wasn't issuing an idle threat was another key to her not reconciling with Larry even when he had told her that he was seeing a therapist. Larry hadn't made it easy when she had filed for divorce. He'd manufactured illnesses and scheduled hospital stays wherein he wasn't able to meet with Greer's attorney or keep his court appointments. The entire process dragged on for nearly two years, but in the end, she had won. She was granted a divorce and the only thing she wanted was to revert to using her maiden name.

Picking up the baking sheet, she placed it in the oven, then concentrated on slicing strawberries for a fruit cup. She added blueberries and blackberries, creating a colorful mix. The potatoes were turning a light golden brown when Jason entered the kitchen in a T-shirt with a faded college logo, ripped jeans and socks. Droplets of water clung to his hair. His straight, white teeth were a sensual contrast to his deeply tanned olive-brown face.

"You didn't leave anything for me to do," Jason said when he saw that Greer had put out place settings at the dining table instead of at the breakfast bar.

Greer looked at him over her shoulder. "You can make the coffee."

He walked over to the industrial-type coffee machine. "What do you want?"

"Surprise me."

Jason closed the distance between them and stood behind her. There was something in the way Greer looked that reminded him of seductive perfume ads. The just-made-love-to mussed hair, parted lips and the expression of wide-eyed innocence created a quiet storm in his loins.

Instead of taking a step backward, he pressed his groin to her hips.

"Please don't move," he pleaded helplessly.

Greer had to feel the pulsing flesh against her buttocks, and she gripped the edge of the countertop to keep her balance. Her breathing was coming fast. "What are you doing?" she whispered.

Jason responded by wrapping his arms around her waist. "I just want to hold you."

"You can't do that," she protested. "Not when you're aroused."

He smiled, burying his face between her scented neck and shoulders. "I can't help it. Just looking at you makes me aroused."

Greer swallowed. "This isn't just about you, Jason."

"Then what is it about?" he whispered in her ear.

"It's about us."

"What about us, darling?"

Greer's shaking knees gave way, and Greer found herself slumping into Jason's hard body. Being in his arms reminded her of how much she had missed being with a man. His erection throbbing against her was a blatant reminder of how much she'd missed the intimacy of joining her body with a man's.

"Is this the ploy you use to get women to sleep with you?" Jason's arms tightened around her waist until she found drawing a breath difficult.

"What the hell are you talking about?"

"You're squeezing me too tight." His hold eased and Greer exhaled audibly. "You offer them a recording contract as a ruse to get them into bed with you?"

The chuckle that began in Jason's throat

escalated to unrestrained laughter. "Is that what you believe? For your information, you're the first woman, other than the women in my family, to ever come here. And if I'd wanted to sleep with you within minutes of meeting you, I definitely would've let you know that. I told you before that I have too much respect for Bobby to mess over you. I like to think of myself as a normal man with normal sexual urges. The problem is that you are unable to accept that you are a very sexy woman. Why do you think the men at Stella's are drawn to you?"

"You included?"

"Yes. Me included. But for a different reason. Do I want to make love to you? Yes," he said, answering his own question. "But it would have to be on your terms, Greer. If you say never, then I'll accept it and withdraw honorably. What say you?"

Greer felt as if Jason had put her on the spot. That the final decision had to be hers. Then she wondered how many men were willing to give a woman the advantage of determining when they wanted to take their relationship to another level? None of the men in her past had offered her that choice.

She had to acknowledge that she liked Jason. Probably enough to sleep with him because the physical attraction was undeniable. "I'm not going to say never, but I'm not willing to say yes at this time."

Jason turned Greer around to face him.

He must have known she was conflicted because of her failed marriage, but still she felt she could trust him enough to know that he wouldn't do anything to exacerbate the emotional turmoil she'd endured with her ex-husband.

Cradling her face in his hands, he pressed a soft, healing kiss to her mouth. "Take all the time you need," he whispered. "I'm not going anywhere and neither are you."

Greer wanted to tell him that he was wrong. As soon as she finished her assignment, she would leave him and Mission Grove. And if he left before she did, then she would have her memories of a man who was not like any other she'd met.

"Please let me go so I can take the potatoes out of the oven before they burn."

Jason kissed her again. This time at the corners of her mouth. "I'll take them out."

Smiling, Jason released Greer, picked up a remote device and turned on the radio. The distinctive voice of Bonnie Raitt singing "I Can't Make You Love Me" came from the speakers. Picking up a pot holder, he took the baking sheet from the oven, the delicious aroma of garlic and cheese wafting to his nose.

The hair on the back of his neck stood when he heard Greer singing the hauntingly beautiful song of unrequited love. He stood, transfixed, listening as she cracked eggs in a bowl and mixed them with a whisk before ladling a portion into a heated omelet pan. She then added the spinach and cheese, testing the underside for doneness.

"Please bring me a plate, Jason."

It took a full twenty seconds for him to force his legs to move. He handed her the plate, smiling when she folded the omelet in half and slid it onto the plate.

"You do that like a pro."

She practically beamed with the compliment. "I've had enough practice. And I had the best cook to teach me everything she knew. My aunt Stella," she added when Jason gave her a puzzled look. "My uncle could barely boil water before they met, but look at him now. Please sit down, Jason. I'll be joining you as soon as I make my omelet. Oh, I have a plate in the warming drawer. Could you please put the potatoes on it?"

"Of course, baby."

Greer didn't know how to react to Jason's

endearments. First she was *darling* and now *baby.* Even before their first date together, she'd become his darling. His claim that, if his girlfriend was happy, then he was happy was more than apparent. And Greer had to admit that she hadn't felt this relaxed in a very long time, and she knew it had something to do with Jason.

"You set a nice table," Jason said, pulling out a chair at the table and seating Greer.

She nodded. "Thank you. The only thing missing is flowers."

Jason sat opposite Greer, knowing this was something he wanted to do — and often. He'd never slept with a woman under his parents' roof, despite having his own suite of rooms in the Boca Raton mansion. That was something he didn't feel comfortable doing. If a woman didn't have her own house or apartment, then he paid for a suite at a hotel. But that would change once Ana moved into a house with her husband. He planned to move out of his parents' home and buy the condo in the exclusive gated community from his sister. The amenities included 24/7 property security and concierge services. He didn't have to leave to shop for groceries if he didn't want, and the spectacular views of the ocean from expansive windows and balconies would be all the inspiration he would need to compose new music.

"I'll make certain to pick some flowers for the next time," he said, spreading a napkin over his lap.

"Who designed your garden?"

"Regina."

Greer's eyebrows lifted slightly. "She came from Brazil to design your garden?"

"She and her husband divide their time between Bahia and their second home near Mexico City. She and Aaron spent a few days here while she drafted the layout for the garden."

"It looks as if you have one-stop shopping among your relatives with an interior decorator aunt and landscape architect cousin. Should I assume you also have family members who are doctors, nurses and pilots?"

Jason swallowed a mouthful of fluffy eggs, savoring the lingering taste of the feta and spinach on his tongue. It appeared as if Greer was multitalented. She could cook *and* sing. "You assume correctly. By the way, this omelet is delicious. My mother is a nurse, Regina's husband Aaron is a pediatrician, their son is also a doctor and my cousin Tyler is an ob-gyn. Tyler bears the distinction of delivering a lot of the babies in the family." He paused, seemingly in thought. "There are a few lawyers. We have a federal judge and a veterinarian who's also a licensed pilot. Nicholas is engaged to a vet, so that'll make two. However those who are in law enforcement are marrying into the family so fast I can't keep up with who's CIA, DEA or with the U.S. Marshals Service."

A whisper of a smile trembled over Greer's lips as she affected a smile she didn't feel. She wondered how Jason would react if she revealed she was also law enforcement? And that her brother was active FBI? She doubted whether it would make a difference to him because she had no intention of marrying Jason.

"At least you know you're protected," she quipped.

"That's what I tell my sisters. Alexandra's husband is CIA, and Ana just married her U.S. marshal boyfriend. And my brother Gabriel is married to a former DEA agent."

"What's up with that?"

Jason speared a potato wedge. "Beats me," he answered. "I know I wouldn't feel comfortable being married to a woman who has to carry a gun. It would always be in the back of my mind that she might get involved in a shoot-out and could possibly lose her life."

"Do you have something against guns?"

He blinked as he slowly chewed and swallowed the potato with obvious delight. "No."

"Do you know how to use one?"

Propping his elbow on the table, Jason gave Greer a lengthy stare. "Yes. Why are you asking me about guns?"

"I just need to know if you've got my back in case of an emergency."

He chuckled. "I don't need a gun to protect you, unless the other person has a firearm and I don't."

"Please don't tell me I'm dating a superhero."

"Close enough," Jason countered with a broad grin.

"Are you Bruce Wayne masquerading as Batman?"

"I wish. I have to admit wearing black leather is the ultimate fantasy."

Greer scrunched up her nose. "That sounds kinky." Jason winked at her while at the same time flashing a wolfish grin. Whenever he smiled at her like that, he reminded her of a powerful predator intent on making her his next meal.

"Don't knock kinky until you've tried it."

She flashed a sexy moue. "How do you know I haven't?"

Jason's smiled vanished. "Are you talking BDSM?"

Greer's jaw dropped, her mouth forming a perfect *O.* "No! That goes beyond kinky."

He managed to look sheepish. "I had to ask."

Bracing an elbow on the table, Greer cupped her chin on the heel of her hand. "Tell me about your grandmother. Is she still alive?"

Jason leaned back in his chair, his gaze fixed on the woman sitting across from him. He found it odd she knew more about him than he did her. He'd been more than forthcoming about himself and his family; he knew her age, that she was divorced, had graduated college, her uncle owned Stella's and she'd admitted to being a Southerner.

"I'll tell you everything I know about Marguerite-Joséfina Diaz Cole if you tell me who Greer Evans is."

Greer seemed more than ready to respond to Jason's request. "You know my age and that I'm a twin."

"What does your brother do?"

"He's a cop."

"You're kidding?"

"No. He *is* a cop. We grew up in Silver Spring, Maryland, because Mom and Dad worked for the government. Last year they sold their condo and moved to a retirement community in Virginia. My brother and I attended private schools, and we spent our summers here until our last year in high school. I went to Georgetown University while Cooper was accepted into Brown."

"How did you meet your ex-husband?"

Greer compressed her lips into a hard line. She looked like she was regurgitating bile. "Are you familiar with the name Lawrence Hill?"

Jason shook his head. "No. I can't say I am."

"He's the senator who resigned last year when he was caught on tape attempting to seduce his opponent's wife."

"I remember reading something about that," Jason confirmed.

"Well, I had the misfortune of marrying his son."

"Are you saying like father like son?"

"I wish. If my ex had been unfaithful, I would've been able to deal with it and move on, but Larry was a closet psycho. We dated a few times in high school, but our relationship never progressed beyond the platonic stage. I graduated college and got a teaching position in a D.C. middle school. I'd gone out one night with several teachers to celebrate the engagement of a colleague and ran into him. We reconnected and married a year and a half later in a small private ceremony.

"At that time his father was beginning to dabble in politics, so there were a number of parties and fundraisers that required our attendance. My father-in-law counted on the African-American vote because his son had married a black woman. I was expected to go on the campaign trail with the Hills, so I took a leave from my job, subjected myself to a complete makeover and became a puppet with Larry as the master puppeteer pulling the strings. He selected what he wanted me to wear, and we traveled with a stylist and makeup person. Whenever I looked in the mirror I didn't recognize myself and I loathed waking up because I knew the day would become a repeat of the one before."

"How long were you campaigning?"

"Fourteen months. We must have stopped in every town, city, hamlet and village in Maryland. Lawrence beat the incumbent in a landslide victory, and I thought it was over. Unfortunately the circus started up again with smaller dinner parties. I wasn't a wife, but a possession or trophy to put out on display. One day I'd had enough and told Larry I was leaving him." Greer covered her face with her hands, but not before Jason saw all manner of emotions expressed there.

Pushing back his chair, Jason came around the table and pulled her to stand. Bending slightly, he picked her up and carried her into the living room. He sat, settling Greer on his lap. She was shaking uncontrollably. "What did he do to you, sweetheart?"

Greer sank into Jason's body, feeding off his strength. He was the first man she'd allowed to touch and kiss her in seven years. *If you let him sour you on men, then he's won.* Bobby's sage advice had come back in vivid clarity. Larry lost. He had lost her and then he had lost himself.

"He tried to kill me."

Jason smothered a curse under his breath. "How?"

"He waited until I'd turned my back, and he hit me in the head with the fireplace poker. The first blow stunned me and, when I turned around to defend myself, he hit me again. This time across my chest. I couldn't breathe, and then I blacked out. I woke up in the hospital with a concussion, broken ribs and a collapsed lung. My mother told me someone had broken into the house and attacked me and Larry. I tried to tell her it was Larry who'd assaulted me, but she told me I was mistaken because Larry had been seriously injured, and he was also in the hospital. The lying slug must have called his mother and father, and together they concocted a story to keep Larry from being arrested. When my in-laws came to see me, they said Larry had been airlifted to a private hospital in Virginia that specialized in head trauma. Supposedly the neurosurgeon had placed him into a medically induced coma to reduce the swelling in his brain."

"Did you get to see him?"

"No."

"Why not, Greer?"

"I didn't want to see him. His father told the press he'd hired private security to protect his son because Larry had had an altercation with the nephew of an alleged mobster, and the attack was in retaliation for the kid's arrest. Unfortunately I'd become collateral damage."

"Did he have an alteration?"

She nodded. "A seventeen-year-old kid was pulling out of a parking spot and accidentally scraped the bumper of Larry's car. Larry got in the kid's face and he pushed back. Someone called the police, and when they discovered who Larry was, they arrested the boy who ended up losing his license for six months."

"Did anyone believe your story?"

"My parents did, eventually, but that's about it. I knew what had happened, and after a while, I was tired of trying to convince someone — anyone — that I was telling the truth, and my father-in-law had lied. Once I was discharged, I went back to the house to get my personal papers, and the housekeeper looked at me as if she'd seen a ghost. It was apparent she hadn't expected me to return. She pleaded with me not to go upstairs, but I ignored her. When I went into the bedroom, I knew why she was so anxious to me keep out. Larry had been hiding there. Apparently he'd had a miraculous recovery or the man in ICU wasn't my husband. He said he was sorry and pleaded for me not to leave him."

Greer's voice dropped to a whisper when she told Jason that she had decided to try another tactic to get away from him. She promised Larry she wasn't going to leave if he agreed to them having separate bedrooms. He agreed and she moved her things into a spare bedroom. Meanwhile she'd placed a call to her brother to come and get her. When Cooper got to the house and saw for himself that Larry had lied about being attacked, he threatened to kill him.

"Cooper held his gun on Larry, while I got my passport, birth certificate and social security card out of the safe. My brother made me promise that, if I ever considered reconciling with Larry, that Cooper *would* kill him. It took months before I could get an attorney to handle my divorce. Once they heard the name Hill, I was persona non grata. Larry stonewalled me every chance he got. He paid a psychiatrist to sign off that he needed to be hospitalized for an emotional breakdown. If he wasn't playing crazy, then it was chronic back pain where he couldn't walk without a cane or walker. It was close to three years before he realized I wasn't coming back. Meanwhile I'd moved in with my parents and went back to school to get a graduate degree. Instead of returning to the classroom, I volunteered as a tutor at a community center. When Larry's attorney finally contacted mine for a settlement, I told him all I wanted was my freedom and my maiden name. Five months later the divorce was finalized."

She didn't tell Jason that she'd applied to the ATF, and her graduate degree wasn't in education but criminal justice. She had to undergo an extensive background check, psychological testing and physical training. Her swearing-in as a special agent came a week after her divorce, and she had signed on for undercover assignments.

Her supervisor had been reluctant to approve the request. After all, she was the former daughter-in-law of a member of congress, but Greer convinced him that she wouldn't compromise her identity when she showed him photos of herself with the Hills. Frightfully thin with a very short haircut, she looked nothing like the woman sitting in front of him. Then she'd been Jane Hill not J. Greer Evans.

When Larry had attacked her from behind, she hadn't been able to fight back. If she had, there was no doubt her years of martial arts training would've kicked in and Larry would not have had to fake being injured.

It had taken a while, but when Senator Hill resigned before he was to appear before the ethics committee, Greer felt a measure of redemption. And Larry — who'd played the crazy card once too often — had a psychotic breakdown, rarely venturing out of the basement in his parents' home because he believed aliens were watching him. He preferred sleeping on an air mattress because there was no place for the aliens to hide inside as they'd done with a regular mattress.

Jason pressed his mouth to Greer's hair. "Karma is a bitch, isn't it?"

She smiled. "Yes, it is."

"Not all men are like your ex," he whispered in the fragrant strands. "Men who claim they love a woman don't hurt them."

"That's what I keep telling myself. But it's hard for me to trust a man because I never know when Dr. Henry Jekyll will turn into Mr. Edward Hyde."

Jason had no comeback for Greer. He'd had a few quirky girlfriends, but fortunately hadn't had to contend with stalkers or those who behaved badly in public. He'd dated a woman who was insanely jealous, and he had ended the relationship before he found himself in too deep. Another wanted him to promise never to leave her because all her boyfriends in the past broke up with her after a few weeks. What had saved him from public humiliation or scandal was that he never took any of them to award or red carpet events. He was always photographed with Ana on his arm. It was a win-win for him and Ana. She tended to keep her private life very private.

Greer stirred and Jason dropped his arms. "Stay here while I clean up the kitchen."

"I'll help you."

"That's all right. You cooked, so I'll clean. Sit and relax."

Pushing off the sofa, he smiled down at her. He was surprised that she could still smile after all she'd gone through with her ex. Jason usually didn't make promises because he wasn't certain whether he'd be able to keep them. However, he made himself a promise to help Greer overcome her distrust so she could possibly have a healthy relationship with a man. What he didn't want to acknowledge was he wanted to be that man.

CHAPTER 11

Greer sat on a stool staring at the filter covering the microphone in the sound booth. Jason had selected Bonnie Raitt's "I Can't Make You Love Me" to sing with the band later on that night. To say she'd been overwhelmed by the size and scope of Jason's recording studio was an understatement. He'd explained the walls and floors of the basement were constructed with poured concrete, which provided excellent sound isolation. Insulation and interior walls and ceilings ensured that the noise from above would not intrude into the studio. A wall of sliding doors exposed shelves with every instrument in an orchestra, while a bass violin rested on a stand in a corner. Sophisticated sound equipment, two pianos, a computer and synthesizer provided Jason with everything he needed to compose and record his music.

Jason had also given her a quick tour of

his home/office. A massive slab of beveled glass supported by twin wrought-iron sawhorses doubled as a desk. The colors of white, black and gray predominated. A black leather sofa converted into a queen-size bed, and two white leather love seats also converted into single beds. Now Greer understood what Jason meant when he said he had a half bedroom.

He claimed he'd had the band over for several rehearsals, but they didn't like having to surrender their driver's licenses at the gatehouse. So Doug paid a retired farmer a nominal fee to use his barn for band rehearsal sessions instead. Jason's studio had a bathroom with a shower, a water cooler, minifridge and built-in shelves that were lined with family photos. He'd shown her the restored photograph of his grandparents on their wedding day. The woman Jason had referred to as *Abuela* was stunningly beautiful, and it was apparent she'd passed her black hair and dimpled smile down to her grandson.

Her eyes met Jason's. "This song is as beautiful as it is sad."

"It's perfect for your vocal range. This is one of the two songs I want you to sing tonight."

"What's the other?"

"It's another Bonnie Raitt favorite of mine. 'Silver Lining.' "

A slight frown furrowed Greer's smooth forehead. "I'm not familiar with that one."

Taking her hand, he helped her off the stool. "Come with me." Jason led her out of the sound booth and over to the computer where he typed in the name of the song and the artist. He adjusted the volume on a receiver.

Greer felt as if someone had open a chapter in her book of life to witness the madness that nearly destroyed Mrs. Jane Hill. The lyrics spoke of redemption and a renewal. A sadness filled her chest, and she struggled not to break down. She wondered if Jason had chosen the song because he felt it suited her voice, or was he trying to send her message. The song ended and she couldn't get out of her head the line about being born with eyes open and now filled with hope.

She'd been raised both loved and pampered, yet somehow along the way, she'd permitted someone with whom she fallen in love to determine not only her future but also her destiny.

Being married to the son of a politician wasn't glamorous nor was it fun. It had been pure torture for Greer. Meanwhile she'd fooled everyone, including her parents, brother, aunt and uncle into believing she was living a fairy-tale life.

"What do you think?" Jason asked, interrupting her thoughts.

"I'll try it."

"Let's do this one first because you're familiar with 'I Can't Make You Love Me.' "

Jason knew the song was perfect for Greer because she was still carrying enough pain to connect with David Gray's poignant lyrics. He programmed the words to appear on the screen in the sound booth, waited for Greer to return to the stool as he took his seat at the synthesizer. All he needed was a guitar, drum and piano. He programmed the track, raised his left hand, then she inserted the earpiece in her ears.

Greer's vocal register was lower than Bonnie Raitt's and more soulful, and he knew she'd been born to sing blues. She'd admitted to being able to read music because of years of piano lessons, and that was one obstacle neither had to deal with. "I'll play it through once for you," he said into the microphone. Greer gave him a thumbs-up sign.

A chill washed over Jason when Greer sang the opening four words. He hadn't realized he was holding his breath until he felt the constriction in his chest. Ana had her Justin Glover aka O'Quan Gee aka OG, and Jason had his J. Greer Evans. Justin had the ability to become a crossover artist, singing pop, R&B, rap and hip-hop, while he hadn't yet explored Greer's versatility. If she was as good with blues as with R&B, then he had a winner.

Jason didn't know whether she would ever allow him to promote her as a result of her psycho ex who may once again try to kill her. With her particular history, he understood her aversion to being in the public eye; yet all his life, he'd been in the spotlight because of his musician father. David Cole had put together a band in his twenties, and Night Mood had played every major U.S. venue before going abroad and touring for months.

David had finally left the band at twenty-seven to take over as CEO of Cole-Diz International Ltd. when his older brother Martin had run for governor of Florida. Martin had lost the election, but David continued running the company until their nephew Timothy Cole-Thomas assumed control of the family-run, privately-held conglomerate. Jason's father had set up Serenity Records, an independent label with a focus on discovering new talent. David and his former band mates got together at least once a year to jam and reminiscence about back in the day.

Jason loved every aspect of music. Listening to it. Playing it. Writing it. Music was a drug — a very addictive drug he never wanted to tire of. There were occasions when he woke to music and went to sleep with it playing softly in his bedroom. Every room in Serenity West was wired for sound. Then there were the times when he wanted absolute silence, just like in the song lyrics in "Silver Lining." He'd chosen the song not only for Greer but also for himself. It ended and he raised his fisted hand, smiling. He'd recorded the song in one take.

Greer opened the door to the booth, grinning from ear to ear, and walked into Jason's outstretched arms. His smile spoke volumes. He liked it. What shocked her was she liked it, too. Yes, the song was evocative and moving, but it was as if she was born to sing it.

She felt sheltered, protected in his strong embrace. Her arms tightened around his trim waist. "How did I sound?"

Jason cradled the back of her head. "Incredible. Do you want me to play it back for you?"

Easing back, she met his glowing eyes. "I don't know."

His expressive eyebrows lifted a fraction. "What don't you know?"

"I'm always my harshest critic. I always sang in the school choir, but never as a soloist."

Jason resisted the burning urge to kiss Greer because he didn't trust himself not to stop, especially if she'd pleaded with him to continue. "Well, J. Greer Evans, get used to being a soloist because once you step on stage tonight, everything changes. By the way, how do you want Doug to introduce you?"

"Greer will do."

He nodded. "Come, baby, and listen to your debut effort. What you're going to hear is the unedited version without the added electronic accoutrements we sometimes use to enhance and refine a singer's voice. There aren't too many Whitney Houstons, Mariah Careys, Christina Aguileras, Beyoncés or Kelly Clarksons who sound the same whether live or on a CD."

"Which female singers do you really admire?"

"I can never get enough of Gladys Knight,

Aretha Franklin, Celine Dion and Lisa Fischer. Her 'How Can I Ease the Pain' is one of greatest recordings of all time."

"I love that song." Greer sighed.

"Do you want to try it?"

She shook her head. "No, no, no. I don't have her octave range."

"That's where I can make the synthesizer sound as if your voice is hitting the higher notes."

"That's cheating."

"No, it isn't. We're living in the wonderful age of electronics."

Greer rested a hand in the middle of Jason's back as they sat down together. "Let me hear how I sound on this one, and I'll let you know if I'm willing to make a feeble attempt to sing diva-extraordinaire Lisa Fischer's Grammy-award-winning masterpiece."

"Self-deprecation doesn't suit you."

Her gaze moved slowly over his face. "This is very new for me."

Jason saw indecision in Greer's eyes. "I understand that, but you should get used to it. You don't want to be front and center, but as a backup vocalist or session singer, you're going to be magnificent. Everyone's going to want to know who is that girl blowing like that? And I'm going to plead the

221

fifth because that's what you want."

Greer rested her head on his shoulder. "That's what I *need,*" she said, correcting him. Even though Bobby had talked about her taking over the restaurant there was still the matter of her day job. She may have worked for tips at Stella's but it was the feds that direct deposited her paycheck like clockwork. The ATF would remain her priority until she resigned or retired.

Greer felt a rush of butterflies in the pit of her stomach as she waited to take the stage. Her confidence at singing to a live audience had escalated once she had heard Jason's playback. After rehearsing the Lisa Fischer classic megahit with Jason, he'd decided to postpone her singing "I Can't Make You Love Me" to the following week. He'd made slight alterations to the song to fit her tonality, and the result was amazing.

It was Saturday and date night at Stella's. The eating establishment and sports bar was filled with couples of all ages, and for the first two hours, ladies were offered half-price Cosmos and margaritas. Greer was shocked when Jason and the band filed into the restaurant. She knew something was different about them — they'd cleaned up. The regulars had trimmed their hair and beards.

Tonight they were featuring country, and it had become a sing-along as they played popular hits by Joe Nichols, Keith Urban, Tim McGraw, Chris Young, Darius Rucker and Rascal Flatts. They ended their first set with Kid Rock's "All Summer Long," and Greer found herself singing along with the others. Doug sang lead, while Jason and the drummer backed up on the vocals.

Greer smoothed back her hair for what seemed like the umpteenth time. She had brushed it off her face, pinning it in a twist at the nape of her neck. She'd replaced tiny gold studs with large silver hoops. She was dressed in black: stretch pants, matching long-sleeved T-shirt and four-inch black patent leather and suede booties. Her makeup was more dramatic: smoky eyes and shimmering vermillion lip gloss.

"Stop fidgeting, honey bunny," Bobby admonished. "You look beautiful."

"I'm not worried about how I look, but how I'm going to sound."

"You'll sound great."

She smiled at her uncle. "You're biased."

"Hell, yeah! I have a right to be. I'm so proud of you that I could pop the buttons on my vest."

Smiling, Greer shook her head. She doubted her uncle could find a vest large enough to close around his massive chest. She rested an arm on his shoulder, recalling what he'd said about going on a diet. Ever since she could remember, Bobby had been literally and figuratively larger than life. His effusive personality coupled with his height and bulk made him a standout. She used to squeal in delight when he picked her up and benched pressed her until her aunt ordered him to "Put that child down before you drop her."

"Your boyfriend is like a blood transfusion," Bobby remarked. "It's been a long time since folks have packed this place on a Saturday night."

Greer didn't know what the other Saturdays were like, but she had to admit that, since Jason alternated playing guitar and keyboards, the band was definitely more upbeat. Even the selections were more eclectic, effortlessly crossing genres.

Whistling, applause and stomping followed as the song ended. Doug wiped his face with a towel. He tapped the microphone. "Ladies and gents, we will play one more set before we take a short break. I don't know how many of you were here for Karaoke Night, but we discovered a diamond in the rough when this pretty lady stepped up to show us what she'd been keeping from everyone. Not only does she have the face of an angel, but a voice to match. It took a little cajoling, but she finally came around and agreed to sing two songs for us tonight. As soon as I introduce her, I plan to turn off the mic because you don't need to hear what she's going to say me. I want to end this set with her singing a song that crossed over from country to pop for Lee Ann Womack, 'I Hope You Dance.' Ladies and gentlemen, put your hands together for Stella's songbird, Miss Greer Evans."

Greer's hands curled into tight fists as she glared at Doug. How could Jason let him set her up when they hadn't rehearsed the song?

"Get going, honey bunny," Bobby urged, giving her a slight shove.

She affected a facetious grin as she wended her way through tables to the stage, wolf whistles following her. She felt the heat of hundreds of pairs of eyes on her as Doug approached her, extended his hand and helped her up the four stairs. Leaning into him, she whispered ribald words for his ears only.

Doug flicked on the microphone. "Y'all wanna know what she just said to me?" Doug shook his head, straight black hair swaying with the motion.

The crowd roared a resounding, "Yes!"

"I can't tell you," he drawled teasingly. Resting a hand in the small of Greer's back, he said in her ear, "The lyrics are on the monitor to the right of the amplifier."

Greer knew, if she didn't unclench her teeth, she'd end up with an aching jaw. "Thanks." She took the hand mic, tapping it softly. Counting slowly to ten, she stared at the crowd staring back at her. Even those playing pool and darts had stopped to watch.

"Lookin' good, baby!" a man sitting at the bar shouted.

Greer flashed a smile and lowered her eyes. "Thank you. Is everyone having a good time?" The crowd responded with cheers. "Isn't this band incredible?" More cheering ensued. She was stalling as much to engage the crowd as to calm her nerves. Walking over the corner of the stage, she pulled the stool closer to the center. She draped her body on the edge, one foot resting on the rung, the other on the stage.

Waiting for the intro to the song, Greer felt herself relax. She knew she wouldn't be able to reproduce Lee Ann's distinctive twang so she did the next best thing. Blend country with gospel. The flutters disappeared as did the tightness in her jaw, and her expression softened noticeably.

A shiver raced up her spine when Jason, Doug and the drummer harmonized backup vocals as she sang the hook. Closing her eyes, Greer was swept along with the fluid rhythm and hypnotic, infectious lyrics. It ended; she slipped off the stool and applauded the band. Everyone was on their feet, clapping and whistling.

Jason came over and hugged her. "You were incredible."

"And I'm going to get you guys for springing this on me."

"You're a pro, Greer. You stepped up and killed it."

"I should kill you and Doug for putting me on the spot with something I hadn't rehearsed," she whispered. He flashed his wolfish grin that never failed to make her feel warm all over.

"I knew you could do it." He kissed her cheek. "You're beyond anything I could've ever imagined."

Handing him the microphone, she walked off the stage, smiling at those who were still standing and applauding. She slowed when approaching Chase's table, meeting his eyes when he stood up and clapped with the others.

"Nice job, Greer."

"Thank you, Chase." He'd complimented her on her singing while she wanted to tell him she had her eyes on him.

The band took a twenty-minute break, and she retreated to the door leading out to the Dumpsters. Greer had to get away from the frivolity and Jason to clear her head. Every time he smiled, touched or kissed her, she had to call on all of her self-control not to beg him to make love to her. She knew for certain it wasn't just his celebrity status that drew her to him like sunflowers turning their face to the sun. It was so much more than admiring his musical genius, when he'd easily reproduced any instrument in an orchestra with the synthesizer. She'd spent the night in his house, shared the morning and early afternoon with him, and Greer felt as if she'd known him forever.

What had made her an exceptional special agent was the gift of total recall. If she heard it, she retained it. It'd been her observational skill that she'd needed to hone. There were times when she had believed he was sending her double messages, but it was one statement that had been so profound it was branded in her head like a permanent tattoo: *if I were in love with you, then I would protect you at the risk of giving up my own life. And if you loved me enough to marry me, then I would spend the rest of my life making you as happy as I'm certain you'd make me. My family would become your family and your family mine. Our children would be heirs to a dynasty that spans generations. A dynasty that is ever expanding to even greater heights than what my grandfather could or would have ever dreamed.*

Greer wondered how many other women he'd told the same thing. How many other women had tried and failed to get him to marry them? What had surprised her was his revelation that she was the first woman, other than female family members, who'd toured, much less slept in, the home he'd proudly dubbed Serenity West. What she couldn't deny was her attraction to the talented musician. And the attraction was more than admiration. It was physical.

Picking up a block of wood, Greer opened the door, wedging the wood between the door and frame to keep it from self-locking because she didn't have the key for reentry on her. A small reddish flame caught her attention, and it was then she saw Danny sitting on a wooden box, smoking a cigarette. He jumped up when he saw her.

"Did . . . did Bob . . . Bobby send you to look for me?"

"No, Danny. Please sit down and finish your cigarette." It was the first time Greer heard Danny stutter. Was he uncomfortable being alone with her? "I just came out to get some air." She inhaled a lungful of crisp, cool nighttime air for affect. "I'm going back inside now."

Danny dropped the cigarette and stepped on it. "I'm finished." He bent down, picked up the butt and waited for Greer to precede him.

Greer didn't know why, but she felt vulnerable. Danny was behind her and, for a man his size, his footsteps were remarkably silent. If it hadn't been for the lingering scent of cigarette smoke, she would've believed she was alone in the alleyway. Her sense of hearing and smell intensified as she slowed her pace, forcing Danny to shorten his stride. In what seemed like an eternity, she finally opened the door to the restaurant.

Jason returned from the bar with a glass of sparkling water, sitting down across from Chase. "I'm surprised to find you here this late." It was after ten, and his friend usually departed Stella's around eight, the same time Jason went on stage with the band.

Chase glanced at his watch. "It is a few

hours later than I usually blow this joint, but when I heard that Greer was singing tonight, I decided to hang around." A rare smile parted his lips. "It looks as if your songbird is the real deal."

"She is good, but she's not my songbird, Chase."

Looking down into a glass half-filled with beer, which he should've finished hours ago, Chase stared up at Jason under hooded lids. "You like her, don't you?"

If the question startled Jason, nothing in his impassive expression was evident. "What's not to like? She has a killer voice, face and body. Greer is probably every normal man's ultimate fantasy."

"I'm not talking about other men, Cole, so stop blowing smoke up my ass."

A rush of color darkened Jason's face as he struggled to control his temper. "I told you l like her, so what's the deal?"

"The deal is, my friend, that I've never seen you look at a woman the way you do with Greer."

"How many women have you seen me with — *friend*?"

"Enough. You come here at least twice a year, and women are practically throwing their panties at you, but you act as if they don't exist. You sit in with a band that has too much going for them to play this venue. I've told you before to sign them to your label and —

"Hold up, Chase," Jason interrupted. "Let's get a few things straight. I've recorded Doug and his boys on several of my albums. And I've also offered him a contract, but he claims he doesn't want to be tied down because then he wouldn't be free to play the wedding, sweet-sixteen, and bar and bat mitzvahs' circuit. He's too much like you. Footloose and fancy-free."

"Doug or the band?"

"Doug *is* the band. He put it together, and he's the one who books the gigs. Now back to Greer," he continued. "There's nothing going on between us except music."

"If that's the case, then you won't mind if I ask her out?"

Jason froze as if impaled in the back of the neck with a sharp object. Whenever he was tense, the muscles in his neck tightened. It was apparent Chase had called Jason's bluff. He'd denied there was anything going on between him and Greer, when there was. It had nothing to do with sex, but he knew he was becoming emotionally attached to her. Slumping back in the chair, he regarded the enigmatic man with cold gray eyes. He and Chase had remained friends because

232

Jason respected the other man's need for privacy.

Jason wanted to tell Chase that he was wasting his time asking Greer out because she'd said he wasn't her type. "I don't mind. She's single and not in a relationship, so she's fair game."

A hint of a smile lifted the corners of Chase's mouth. "If you're not doing anything after you finish here, why don't you and Greer come by my place for a couple hours? It'll be a good way for me to break the ice with her."

"The only thing I'm going to promise you is that I'll ask her. If she says no, then you'll have your answer."

Picking up his glass, Chase finished the lukewarm brew. "I'm going to wait to hear her sing again before I leave. If you guys don't make it to my place by two, then I'll know she's not coming."

After taking a generous swallow of his water, Jason stood up. "Let me try and catch her before we go back on stage." He scanned the crowd for Greer, finding her at the buffet station with Bobby's assistant chef. He reached her as Doug and the other band members were returning from their break.

Touching her arm to get her attention, Jason put his mouth to her ear. "Chase wants us to come to his place after closing. Are you all right with that?"

Greer hesitated, not wanting to believe her stroke of good luck. She didn't know why he wanted her and Jason to come to his home, but the reason was of little consequence. The fact remained she would be able to observe him on his home turf. She blinked, feigning confusion. "Do you want to go?"

"It's not about me, Greer. Whenever Chase invites me to his place, I go. It's you who has to decide whether you want to go."

A beat passed. "Okay. Tell him yes. I'll see you later on stage," Greer said, smiling.

Greer stood there, watching Jason walk away. Tall, dark and handsome were the epithets that came to mind. He was all that and more. There were other adjectives Greer could come up with, but those were definitely rated triple X.

Chase inviting them to his house couldn't have come at a better time. She wasn't scheduled to work Sunday brunch and tomorrow would be the last Sunday Stella's would serve dinner. She'd come in earlier today and used the restaurant's computer to make up flyers with the new hours of operation, printing out enough to leave on each table and for the hostess to hand to every customer. Beginning Tuesday, Stella's would become a buffet-only dining establishment.

Picking up a dish towel, Greer wiped up the spillage on the buffet. It was after ten and many of the half-empty trays wouldn't be replenished. Bobby had made it a practice to donate all leftover food to a local soup kitchen. His mother had raised him to waste not and you'll want not.

Greer retreated to the bathroom in the rear of the kitchen to check her face and hair. She was scheduled to go back on stage at ten-thirty. Now she knew why some artists craved the spotlight. Performing live was like a drug. It was captivating and addictive.

Time seemed to accelerate, and she found herself sitting on the stool holding a microphone. A strange calm swept over everyone when all the lights dimmed, and the spotlights shone on Jason and Greer. She turned and stared at him when he began playing the familiar piano introduction to "I Can't Make You Love Me." She was confused because he'd said she wouldn't sing that selection until the following week.

Instead of looking out at the audience,

she sang to him. Their gazes met and held. It was as if an invisible cord held them spellbound as the sound of the acoustic piano floated through the restaurant like ripples on a pond. Jason had become Bruce Hornsby and she Bonnie Raitt, and it felt as if everyone had held their breath until the last note faded away.

Greer finally looked away when the song ended, and she stared at the stage. The words had not come from her mouth but from her heart. She wanted Jason to love her, and she wanted to trust him not to hurt her. *If you loved me enough to marry me, then I would spend the rest of my life making you as happy as I'm certain you'd make me.*

Why, she thought, couldn't she forget his fervent declaration? She was still in the same position when Jason walked over and eased her gently to her feet. Cradling her face in his hands, he brushed his mouth over hers.

"Is she not wonderful?" he asked loudly.

The crowd gave her a standing ovation, while shouting, "More! More! More!"

Jason took the mic from Greer's loose grip. "No worries, good people. There's more. Right now Greer will take a short break, and then she'll be back for your listening enjoyment."

Greer felt like a trusting child as she permitted Jason to lead her off the stage and into the room where Pepper kept kegs of beer and bottles of liquor. Jason closed the door, shutting out all sound. One moment she was staring up at him, and the next, she found herself in his arms, hers going around his back.

Jason buried his face in her hair. "You have to learn not to do that."

"Do what?" she asked.

"Look at me when you sing."

Easing back she met his eyes. "Why not?"

Jason blinked as if coming out of a trance. "Do you know how hard it is for me to keep playing when you do that?"

"I thought I was connecting with you."

He shook his head. "You were doing more than connecting with me."

Greer was totally confused because Jason was talking in riddles. "Please tell me what I was doing if not singing."

Dropping his arms, he stood a step back, putting a modicum of distance between them. "You really don't know, do you?"

"No!"

Massaging his forehead, Jason thought Greer was playing innocent but, when he looked at her, there was genuine confusion on her face. Maybe he'd read more into it because he wanted more from her. "Forget it."

Greer grabbed the front of his sweater, holding him fast. "I'm not going to forget it, Jason. Please tell me what is going on?" she pleaded softly.

Covering her hand with his, he managed to get her to let go of his sweater. "I felt as if you were seducing me."

Wondering if she'd lost her edge, Greer didn't want to believe she'd become that transparent. Or was Jason more attuned to her emotionally than she'd realized? He was the only man outside her family members who knew the details of her marriage. Whenever she went undercover, she'd become an actor in a role giving an award-winning performance. However, Jason was the first man where she didn't have to pretend to be anyone but Greer.

"And that bothers you?"

Jason looked her over seductively. "It would if you were being facetious."

A smile trembled over her lips. "I've been a few things but never facetious."

He angled his head. "So you were?"

"Were what, Jason?"

"Seducing me."

Going on tiptoe, she placed her fingertips over his mouth. "Guilty as charged."

■ ■ ■ ■

Jason stared at the sensual sway of her hips in those body-hugging pants as she walked out of the storeroom, leaving him alone. Jason blew out his breath as he supported his back against a stack of cartons. He'd never met a woman like Greer, someone who had the ability to seduce him with just a glance. There were women who, when they discovered he was the producer for Serenity Records, either knew someone with an allegedly amazing singing talent or they'd try every trick in the book to get him to sleep with them.

Jason had learned how to deal with women from the onset of puberty. His former musician father had sat him down and didn't hold back when his dad had told him about the women he'd met and those he'd slept with before marrying Serena Morris. His advice was to look for a woman who wanted Jason for himself and not for what she wanted him to give her. Every woman Jason had met since becoming sexually active wanted something. It hadn't mattered whether it was money, his family's influence or a chance at stardom.

He'd offered Greer what so many talented

singers wanted — a recording contract — but she'd turned him down.

He walked to the door, opening it. Pepper stood behind the bar, glaring at him. "Is Greer okay?" he growled.

"Why don't you ask her?"

"Look, kid —"

"I'm not a kid," Jason said between clenched teeth. "And if you're not aware that I would never do anything to hurt her, then you're completely clueless."

Pepper beckoned to him. "Come here, Cole." Jason took two steps, and Pepper caught him at the back of the neck. "You're in love with her," he said under his breath.

"What the . . ." The four-letter curse died on his tongue. First it was Chase and now it was Pepper asking him about his feelings toward Greer. Who was next? Bobby?

Pepper gave him a wide grin. "You don't have to answer that, son, because it's as plain as the nose on your face. I know she got to you. And don't worry about Bobby. He likes you a lot so I don't think you're going to have a problem with him."

Jason's impassive expression did not falter. "That's nice to know. Now I'll appreciate it if you let go of my neck."

Pepper dropped his hand. "Sorry about that."

Jason mounted the stage where Doug was playing a guitar riff from John Mayer's "Bold As Love." Greer sat on the stool, keeping time as she patted her thigh. Sitting down at the keyboard, Jason's fingers rippled across the keys, his right foot tapping rhythmically. Doug segued into Mayer's "In Repair." The drummer, sax player and the two other guitarists connected seamlessly in what had become a jam session, while those in the restaurant who were familiar with the song sang along. The Mayer retrospect continued with "Say." Greer lent her voice to the catchy hook.

It took a full two minutes to quiet the crowd, before Greer sang "Silver Lining." The applause hadn't ended when she stood up, returning the stool to the corner. She met Jason's eyes, nodding. He began playing the whistle-sounding notes and a gasp went up.

"Yes!" screamed a woman.

It was the encouragement Greer needed when she held the microphone to her mouth. She began Lisa Fischer's haunting song in a husky whisper. By the time she reached the chorus, she felt free, freer than she'd felt since she was a child swimming in the lake and running through the woods in childish abandon.

She didn't know if Jason had selected the songs to exorcise the demons that wouldn't permit her to trust a man, or if he had felt they would best showcase her vocal range. Singing gave her a sense of freedom, and now she needed Jason to help her trust again.

Greer used the entire stage and her body. She closed her eyes and sang until she felt as if her heart would explode from sheer happiness. She'd become Lee Ann Womack, Bonnie Raitt and Lisa Fischer. Divas in their own right.

The song ended, and she placed the microphone on its stand and blew kisses to the standing crowd. She walked over to each member of the band and hugged them. She felt euphoric, almost high like she'd been injected with a stimulant. Bobby was there to meet her when she walked off the stage, picking her up and swinging her around.

"Oh, if my Stella could be here to see you now," he whispered in her ear.

Greer tightened her hold on his neck. "She is here, Uncle Bobby. She's looking down on us and smiling."

Jason found himself unable to look away from Greer and her uncle. Bobby's expression was that of a proud father. Jason met her tear-filled eyes over Bobby's broad shoulder. Jason smiled and she nodded. Why couldn't he see it when it was so obvious to others? It'd taken him three weeks to discover what he'd avoided for thirty-three years. He'd found a woman he wanted more than music.

CHAPTER 12

Jason touched the button for the wipers as the rain intensified. Despite concentrating on the dark winding road leading to Chase's house, he was ever mindful of the woman sitting next to him. Greer was unusually quiet since they'd left Stella's.

"We really don't have to go if you don't want."

Greer's head came around. "I told you I'd go, so why are you changing your mind?" she asked.

"I haven't changed my mind. It's just that you're so quiet that I thought maybe you're too tired to go out."

Greer stared at Jason's profile, awed by his masculine beauty. When she'd asked him if he looked like his twin sister, his response had been "More or less." In her opinion it was *more*. He truly was a beautiful man; a man she found herself falling madly in love with. Even if they were to have a sexual relationship, she knew it would end here.

Jason had planned to return to Florida just before Christmas, and she wouldn't know where she'd be. One thing she was certain of was that she wasn't going back to Phoenix. She was now an agent with the Seattle Field Division, and that meant she either could continue to work in Oregon or there was the possibility she could be transferred to Washington, Idaho, Alaska, Hawaii or Guam. Greer didn't like extremes when it came to weather, and Alaska wasn't on her favorites list. She didn't mind snow, but not accumulations of biblical proportions.

"I don't think I could sleep even if I want to. I'm really wound rather tight."

Jason gave her a quick glance. "Are you certain you've never sung in front of an audience?"

She shook her head. "Not as a soloist. Why?"

"You have what only a few vocalists have and that's an innate stage presence. It doesn't matter whether you're just sitting and singing or moving across the stage, you're mesmerizing. What you have is the ability to seduce a crowd."

She smiled. "Does that include yours truly?"

His expression grew hard. "You already know about that."

"Why do I get the impression that you're bothered by it? I thought you'd be flattered."

"I'm not bothered."

"Yes, you are, Jason. Why else would you go Neanderthal on me? First you kiss me, then you practically drag me off the stage in front of over a hundred people to a room that is little more than a closet. Can you imagine what they were thinking?"

"No."

"Think, Jason."

He maneuvered around a copse of trees, turning down the road leading to Chase's house. "It definitely wouldn't be a quickie because I prefer long, leisurely lovemaking."

Greer didn't want to talk about lovemaking because it'd been so long since anyone had made love to her that she'd almost forgotten what an orgasm felt like. All the signs were there that her marriage was in trouble when she and Larry had made love on average only three times a month. For most of the campaign trail, she was too tired and him too reticent to make love to her in a hotel room.

"Mission Grove is a small town, and I'm willing to bet there's going to be talk about

Bobby Henry's niece and Stella's house band's piano player."

"If you're that worried about your reputation, then we can always get married," Jason said glibly.

"That's not even funny."

He turned into the circular driveway, stopping in front of a three-car garage attached to a two-story farmhouse with a wraparound porch. "I didn't mean it to be funny." He came to a stop, shifting into Park. "Do you see me laughing?"

The lights from the dashboard threw long and short shadows over his face, making it difficult for Greer to read his expression, and she was at a loss for words. What did he expect her to say? That she was flattered that he wanted her to become Mrs. Jason Cole? Did he believe, if he married her, he could convince her to change her mind about signing a contract rather than an agreement?

"You don't want to marry me," she said in a quiet voice. "What you want is my voice on your terms. But that's not going to happen because I can't sign a contract with Serenity Records."

Resting his right arm over the back of her seat, Jason gave Greer a long, penetrating stare. "I need you to answer one question for me, then I'll never bring it up again."

"What's that?"

"Does your reluctance have anything to do with your ex-husband and his family?"

There was only the sound of their measured breathing and the wipers sluicing rain off the windshield as the seconds ticked by. "No," Greer said after a pregnant silence.

It wasn't the answer Jason was expecting. If it had been her ex, then he would've taken measures to protect Greer. But if she was hiding something, then there was nothing he could do. He'd thrown out marriage just to get her reaction, and he was uncertain of what his own reaction would've been if she'd accepted.

"Let's go inside. I told Chase we'll get here before two."

He tapped lightly on the horn, and the door to one of garages slid up and Jason drove in. By the time he came around to assist Greer down, Chase was standing in the doorway connecting the garages to the main house.

Greer held on to her leather tote as she followed Jason up three steps and into the mudroom. She left her booties on a thick straw mat. She gave Chase a warm smile as he extended his hand.

"Welcome. I'm glad you could come."

She shook the proffered hand. "Thanks for inviting me."

There was something different about the man who came to Stella's for dinner, and then she realized he was wearing glasses. The lenses were slightly tinted. His sun-browned complexion was evidence he spent a lot of time outdoors.

Chase took a quick glance at Greer's bare feet before she slipped on a pair of ballet flats. They were professionally groomed. He usually judged a woman's meticulousness if she took care of her hands and her feet. "Come into the living room where it's warmer." He patted Jason's shoulder. "You guys were *outrageous* tonight. I felt as if I was at a live concert."

Jason left his Doc Martens on the mat beside Greer's booties. "They definitely were on fire." He followed Chase and Greer into the living room where a fire roared behind a decorative screen. Waiting until she sat on a club chair, he took one opposite her.

Chase stood with his back to the fireplace. "Would either of you like something to drink?"

"I'd like some water," Greer said.

Chase smiled. "Wouldn't you like something stronger?"

She shook her head. "Just water, please."

Jason stood up. He knew Chase wanted to be alone with Greer. "I'll get it. Do you want anything, Chase?"

"I'll have a beer."

Greer took in everything about the room in one sweeping glance. It was spacious, uncluttered and decorated for family living, yet she understood that Chase lived alone. Crossing her legs at the ankles she looked directly at him.

"Why did you invite *us* here?"

Chase took three long strides and hunkered down beside her chair. "I wanted to see you."

She blinked once. "You see me at Stella's practically every day."

"What I should've said is I *need* to talk to you."

"What about?"

"When Jason comes back, I want you to ask me to show you the house."

Greer didn't like the direction in which their conversation was going. "I'm not going to ask you to do anything until you give me a good reason why I should."

"We work for the same uncle," Chase whispered. He stood up straight and walked back to the fireplace.

She stared at Charles Bromleigh as if he had a third eye in the middle of his forehead. Greer didn't want to believe they were on the same side. That is, if he was telling the truth. And there was always the possibility that he'd discovered who she was and . . . Her thoughts trailed off. She knew she had to remain calm, in control, until she heard what he had to say. If he knew who she was, then she wanted to know who he was. There was no file on him; no evidence that he had ever existed. Jason had mentioned Chase's parents lived in Hawaii, but she'd checked the name again on her computer and discovered there was no one listed on the state census named Bromleigh. Who was he? CIA? FBI? DEA? ICE? He definitely wasn't ATF.

She engaged him in a stare-down that would've ended in a stalemate if Jason hadn't come back into the room, gripping two longnecks in one hand and a glass of ice water in the other.

"Your fridge needs a serious makeover," he teased, handing Greer the glass of water and Chase a bottle of beer. They touched bottles in a toast.

"I know it's rather bare."

"It's beyond bare," Jason countered. "All you have is bottled water, beer, a single egg and a half stick of butter."

Chase nodded. "Now you see why I eat at Stella's. I'd planned to go the supermarket tomorrow but, about two minutes before you guys drove up, I got a call from a buddy to come and hang out with him for a couple weeks. He has a hunting lodge in Idaho overlooking a lake where we fly-fish, cook our catch over an open fire and watch sports channels 24/7."

"Fishing is something I never got into," Jason admitted.

Greer smiled at him. "I'll have to teach you."

"You fly-fish?" Jason questioned.

"Yes," she said proudly. "My uncle taught me."

Chase angled his head. "Maybe one of these days you'll join us. The lodge sleeps twelve."

Greer studied their host when Chase sat on the sofa, looping one denim-covered leg over the other. His jeans had been washed so much they were threadbare, and his faded navy-blue sweatshirt was equally shabby. Even his footwear had seen better days. The leather moccasins were torn *and* faded. He really intrigued her. He lived in a multimillion-dollar gated community, ate at a local no-frills restaurant and dressed as if he were homeless.

She took a sip of water, then set the glass down on the coaster on a side table. It was time to end the farce. "Chase, I'd love to see your house. Would you mind giving me a tour?"

Chase set down his beer on a matching coaster on the coffee table. "I'd love to, if your boyfriend doesn't mind me monopolizing you for a few minutes."

Nothing in Jason's expression revealed his inner thoughts. "Greer is her own woman, and she doesn't need my permission to do whatever she wants to do."

A smile parted Chase's lips. "That's what I like. A man who is secure enough to trust his woman with another man."

Jason glared at his friend. "It has nothing to do with being secure. It's all about trust."

Greer felt the rising tension and the posturing between the two men. Jason knew how she felt about Chase even if he hadn't known she'd suspected his friend of selling illegal firearms.

"Jason's right," she said in defense of the man with whom she found herself fighting her feelings every second they shared the same space. She didn't want to believe it, had fought the pull, but to no avail. She was falling in love with Jason. "We trust each other unconditionally." She stood up, both men rising with her. "I would like that tour before it gets any later."

Chase offered his arm, and she looped hers through his, feeling the heat of Jason's gaze on her back as they walked out of the living room to a flight of stairs leading to the second level.

"I like that most houses in this development are different architectural styles," she said, climbing the staircase. Greer felt she had to say something, anything to pretend she was interested in seeing Chase's house, which she wasn't in the least. Perhaps she would've been if he hadn't mentioned them working for the same *uncle.* It didn't take the intelligence of a genius to know he was talking about the federal government and perhaps the department of justice.

Chase led Greer down a long hallway to a room at the end. Pushing open the door, he stepped aside to allow her to enter first. She knew instantly it was his bedroom. It was wholly masculine with heavy dark furniture and a leather seating group. He indicated a chair near a window.

"Please sit down." She complied as he sat on a bench at the foot of the large bed. "I'm going to make this quick, so listen carefully. I'm going away tomorrow for at least a month, and I want you to stick close to Jason."

Her brow furrowed in confusion. "What are you talking about?"

"I know who you are and what you do." Chase held up a hand when she opened her mouth. "Don't say anything until I'm finished." It wasn't a request but a directive. "I know why you're in Mission Grove. And please don't ask me how I know."

"Who the hell are you?" Greer asked, disobeying his demand.

"I'm someone who doesn't exist, ATF Special Agent Evans. I'm what is referred to as a ghost."

She closed her eyes, digesting this information. The FBI employed ghost agents whenever they wanted to keep surveillance on other agents they suspected of espionage. "Which agency?"

"It's been eight years since I was connected to an agency. Right now I'm somewhat of a corporate warrior."

Her eyes widened. "You're a professional mercenary."

He smiled and removed the glasses with the tinted lenses. "Actually I prefer the term professional security expert." Chase rubbed his eyes with his fingertips, then replaced the glasses on the bridge of his nose. "Did

Jason tell you about the ongoing feud between Serenity and Slow Wyne Records?"

"No."

"Ana signed Justin Glover to a recording contract in a bidding war with L.A.-based Slow Wyne Records. Although she'd come in with a much lower bid, it was the terms in Serenity's contract that Glover's agent felt were more advantageous to his client's long-term career. Unfortunately Basil Irvine didn't take kindly to being usurped by, what he referred to as, *a little girl.* In the end he was the one who wound up in the ground."

Greer leaned forward. "What does this have to do with Jason?"

"There are people who believe he has replaced his sister as a target for Slow Wyne retaliation."

"Who are these people?"

"I can't tell you that. They've hired me to keep an eye on him. He's safe as long as he's behind the walls at Bear Ridge or at Stella's. Fortunately he spends most of his time at home and the restaurant. But it's when he's out and about that he becomes a sitting duck. I have a few of my people watching him —"

"So you know that he's been to my home," she said, cutting Chase off.

He nodded. "And I know you've spent the

night at his house. I've been paid very well to look after Jason because he's more than a client. He's a friend. I come to Stella's before he arrives, and I always leave before he does. Most times he has no idea that he's under surveillance. Unfortunately I've been called away on another assignment, and that's where you come in."

Greer was still trying to digest what Chase had just revealed. "Are your people still watching him?"

"Yes. I had someone place a tracking device under his Range Rover. What I need is for you to provide additional protection."

Shock after shock slapped Greer. Vendettas, tracking devices and hit men were the elements in a televised movie-of-the-week thriller. "That's not going to be that easy. I'm here on assignment."

"I know that. Hanging out with Jason isn't going to compromise that. If you help me out with this, I'm certain I'll be able to repay the favor. My people are also ghosts, and I'm certain they'll be able to ferret out who has been stealing and selling guns illegally."

"How do you know so much about me when I can't even pull up a file on you?"

"Connections." Chase pushed off the bench. "Let me show you the other rooms before Jason sends out a search party for you. Does he know about your ex-husband?"

Greer rose to her feet. "Yes, I told him."

"He knows about your ex, but not that you're a special agent."

"I can't tell him, even if I want to."

"Be ready for the fallout when he does find out," Chase warned. "If you were any other woman, I don't think it would bother him. But you're different, Greer, because the man's in love with you."

Her jaw dropped. "He can't be."

"Why not? Only a blind person wouldn't see what went on between you and Jason when you're on stage together. More than half the men in Stella's wanted to change places with him. Yours truly included," he added with a sheepish expression. "What shocked me is that he didn't bat an eye when I told him I wanted to ask you out."

Greer laughed, the sound low and throaty. "That's because I told him that you are not my type."

Chase smiled. "So that's why he's so smug. All I can say is you have a good man."

Greer agreed with Chase. Jason was a good man. One she knew she could eventually trust with her secret life. Chase had asked her to look out for his friend and client, a client unaware of his protective surveillance. Jason was also unaware that she never ventured outdoors without her leather tote that contained her badge and a Glock 26, 9 mm Luger semiautomatic handgun with three 10-round magazines. When at Stella's she secured the pistol in her uncle's safe where she kept the government-issued laptop; at home it was locked in a drawer in the cabinet where Bobby stored his rifles. Even if Chase hadn't told her about the probable threat on Jason's life, she knew she would step in to protect him if the occasion arose.

Greer tugged at her left earlobe. "I'd like you to answer two questions for me."

"What is it?" Chase asked, sobering quickly.

"Were you Special Forces?"

Chase shook his head.

"Army Ranger or Navy SEAL?"

"The latter."

"Is Charles Bromleigh Jr. your legal name?"

"No."

"What —"

Chase held up a hand. "You said two questions, not three. Come on, let's finish the tour so you and Jason can go home and do whatever it is you two do together."

Greer was glad the darkness of the hallway hid the flush in her face as she followed Chase out of the master bedroom and into three smaller bedrooms that were twice the size of the one she occupied at her uncle's house. The furnishings were indelibly American eclectic with Chippendale-style beds, chests and chairs. Each room contained an alcove with a sitting area near narrow floor-to-ceiling windows. All of the beds were covered with quilts and mounds of pillows in differing shapes and sizes matching white eyelet dust ruffles. Chase's house did not have the more dramatic flair of Jason's. It was the home of a man which, when he opened the door and walked into the house, was welcoming and cutoff from the world of danger where he floated in and out of like a specter.

She walked into the living room, stopping short. Jason had fallen asleep, his head at an odd angle, the half-empty bottle of beer on the table. It was obvious they were going to spend the night at his house rather than hers.

Shaking him gently, she waited for him to wake up. He opened his eyes, staring at her for several seconds before recognition dawned. "I must have fallen asleep."

"Come on, baby. Give me your keys. We're

going home."

"You're welcome to spend the night here," Chase volunteered.

Greer shook her head. "That's all right. I'll drive. Besides, you're leaving in the morning."

"It's already morning," Jason slurred as he struggled to stand. "Damn! I must be more tired than I thought." Rolling his head on his shoulders, he tried easing the tightness in his neck. He stumbled, but Chase caught him under the shoulder, bearing most of Jason's weight.

"That does it. The two of you are staying over. It's raining too hard for you to try and navigate the roads back to Jason's house. I'll show you to your bedroom. There are towels on a shelf and toothbrushes under the vanity in the bathroom. I'll probably be gone by the time you get up." He stared directly at Greer. "Jason knows where I keep an extra set of keys. Just lock the front door when you leave. The security system will activate automatically within forty-five seconds."

Greer wanted to tell Chase that, although she'd spent the night at Jason's, they hadn't slept together. The only relief tonight was that he was too exhausted to do anything except sleep. He probably didn't average more than four hours of sleep each night.

"Help me get him upstairs and into bed without him falling and cracking his noggin."

Chase's response was to hoist Jason over his shoulder as if he weighed two pounds rather than what she estimated to be two hundred. The *corporate warrior,* or mercenary as she thought of them, was several inches shorter than Jason and wiry. He'd admitted to being former Navy SEAL, and, as one, he had the intelligence, mental and physical toughness to withstand and overcome extreme conditions and situations. Picking up her tote, she followed Chase up the staircase and into the bedroom, pulling back the quilt and top sheet as Chase laid Jason on the crisp sheets.

"I'm sorry about not having anything in the refrigerator."

Greer busied herself removing Jason's socks. "That's okay. Jason needs sleep not food. Tomorrow . . . I mean, today, is Sunday, so that means he can sleep in." Turning she faced Chase, seeing the solitary man in a whole new light. Now she knew why he kept to himself. "Thank you for putting us up."

He waved his hand in dismissal. "There's no need to thank me. Jason would do the same for me." He took a quick glance at his sleeping friend. "I meant what I said about helping you once I get back."

Greer nodded. As soon as she wrapped up this assignment, she had to decide whether or not to take her uncle up on his offer to run Stella's. "Do you have a T-shirt I can use?" She had no intention of sleeping nude.

"Check the chest of drawers. My sister sleeps in this room when she comes to visit. She's about your size, so I'm certain there's something that will fit you."

"Thank you again, Chase."

"No problem." He waved. "See you when I get back."

Waiting until Chase walked out of the room, closing the door behind him, Greer shifted her attention to Jason sprawled on his back, snoring softly. Sleeping with Jason paled in comparison to what Chase had disclosed.

At first she didn't want to believe him, thinking that he'd concocted a story to throw suspicion off himself. But Greer knew unequivocally that Chase was telling the truth. The secure government database — with names, addresses and birth dates of every documented person in the country and its territories — had listed Charles Bromleighs who were either too young or much too old to be the man everyone called Chase.

A shiver eddied up her body. Jason had become the target of someone bent on revenge. Feuds between rap artists, talk show hosts, athletes, actors and spurned reality stars were headline news for televised entertainment shows, magazines and supermarket tabloids. Now CEOs had waded into the same cesspool with the others. Greer would check her computer again. This time she would search for Slow Wyne Records.

Undressing Jason proved challenging. It was easier removing his sweater than his slacks. He was all muscle and dead weight. Greer left on his boxer-briefs. She found a nightgown, several packages of brand-new panties and a couple bras with the tags still attached. The panties were her size but not her style and the bras a cup size larger than her own.

It wasn't important whether her borrowed garments would fit or not fit. Keeping her promise to Chase was.

Chapter 13

Jason woke disoriented. He knew he wasn't in his bedroom because there were no skylights. That didn't shock him as much as the soft warm body pressed against his side. Rising on an elbow, he stared at Greer. She was as lovely in sleep as in waking. His gaze moved slowly over her slightly parted lips, mussed hair clinging to her cheek and the rise and fall of firm breasts under a modest white cotton nightgown. He touched her hair, rubbing strands between his fingers. Everything about her was fresh, natural. Watching her face in repose was short-lived when she shifted onto her right side.

Sliding back to the pillows cradling his shoulders and turning on his right, Jason rested an arm over Greer's waist. He had to touch her, savor the warmth of her body and adore her openly.

Greer had accused him of wanting her for her voice, but he'd want her even if she sounded like a croaking frog. Jason admired not only her talent but also her strength, femininity and loyalty to her uncle. There was also her humility. She'd rejected the recording contract certain to bring her untold wealth and fame, and he'd engaged in an exercise of mental calisthenics as he had tried to come up with a plausible rationale as to why she wouldn't accept his offer.

Jason knew his wanting to sign her up had everything to do with his ego. His father had established Serenity with the raison d'état of signing only new talent, and forty years later, he and Ana had continued the tradition.

He also didn't want to believe he had slept with this woman and not made love to her. Unlike some of his college buddies and those with whom he'd maintained friendship from childhood, Jason had always been overly cautious as to whom he bedded. He had never engaged in one-night stands or slept with a woman until they'd dated for what he considered enough time to feel comfortable and/or to get to know her better. However, there was now one exception: Greer.

There was something inherently innate that told him she was the *one*. The one woman who could get him to consider changing his marital status to share his life *and* their future. He'd watched his twin sister with her new husband, and he saw something that hadn't been apparent before. Ana was calmer, more reflective, as if she'd rid herself of the impulsivity that had been so much a part of her aggressive personality. If Ana was fire, then Jason was water. He would become her voice of reason — whenever she got into a snit while negotiating with a client's agent, suggesting she step back and look at the deal from another angle. She'd accused him of being too soft and laid-back but Jason was quick to remind his sister and business partner that, although she'd earned a law degree, he was more than versed with the ins and outs of business. Degrees in music and an MBA had served him well when he'd taken over the reins of Serenity after she had gone into self-exile to escape the sniper who'd accidentally shot Tyler. He'd resented taking off his creative hat to replace it with the business one. Yet once he found himself holding staff meetings and making decisions that changed the business model for the company, the transition went smooth and the result was very effective. Even Ana had admitted he'd done a better job running Serenity than she had in the past.

A soft sigh came from Greer, her eyelids fluttering as she came awake. She felt a crushing weight over her belly before realizing Jason's arm was holding her down. "Good morning," she mumbled, yawning.

"Is it?" asked the deep drawling voice behind her.

She smiled. "It would be even better if you moved your arm. You're a lot heavier than you look."

He withdrew his arm from her waist, splaying his hand over her hip. "How much do you think I weigh?"

"You're at least two hundred."

"Close. I'm two-ten."

"How tall are you?"

"Six-three." Jason pressed his mouth to her hair. "How tall are you?"

"Five-seven. And you better not ask me how much I weigh because I'm not going to tell you." There was a hint of laugher in her voice.

"What's up with *you* women not telling your weight as if it's top secret?"

"*You* men don't need to know unless they're going to buy a woman something to wear. Then they should know her height, weight, dress, shoe and ring size."

Jason chuckled softly. "That's a lot."

"That's because there's a lot to us. I thought you would've known that."

"Why would I know that?"

"Haven't you ever bought clothes and jewelry for your mother, sisters or girl-friends?"

"No. I'd tell them to let me know what they want and the price, and I'd give them the money."

"That's no fun. You take out the element of surprise."

"I don't like shopping."

Greer turned to face Jason, her thigh brushing against his groin with the motion. Her breath stopped in her throat when she registered the look of desire in his eyes matching the growing hardness in his groin. "I'm sorry about that."

Cupping her hip in his hand, Jason pulled her closer. "I'm not."

"Jason?"

"Hush, baby. I'm not going to do anything to you. Especially not in someone else's house. Plus I don't have protection with me."

Greer rested her hand on his furred chest. She wasn't an ingenue when it came to men, but she also wasn't so worldly that she'd slept with more than she could count or remember. "It's been a long time for me."

Jason kissed her forehead. "Don't you think I know that?"

She closed her eyes, shutting out his intense stare. "I want you to make love to me, but when you hear my reason, you may change your mind."

"Nothing you say will make me change my mind."

"I know it may sound selfish . . ." Greer couldn't finish because she cared for Jason, and she didn't want to hurt him. She didn't want to use him just for sex. He deserved more than that.

"You want to know how it feels again, don't you?" he asked, smiling.

Her eyes flew open. He'd read her mind. "How did you know?"

"I don't have to be a rocket scientist to know you haven't slept with anyone since your divorce."

A nervous smile trembled over her lips. "Am I that transparent?"

"No, baby. It has nothing to do with transparency. You had a tumultuous marriage and a hellish divorce. It would stand to reason you probably wouldn't want to deal with another man for the rest of your life."

"You're right about that. But then you

came along."

"No, Greer. *You* came along, and I didn't know which end of my life was up or down. I told myself I didn't want you, that I didn't need you, but I was lying to myself. If not for you, I'd be more than content to spend the next three months holed up in the studio writing and occasionally sitting in with Doug and his band. But when you're not at the house, I find myself wishing I had magical powers so I can conjure you up."

Greer realized Jason had given her the opening she needed to fulfill Chase's directive that she should remain close to Jason. As close as she could without arousing his suspicions. "What if I fulfill your wish?"

An expectant expression crossed Jason's features. "What?"

"If you want, I can move in with you."

He went completely still. "What did you say?"

Greer knew it was too late to retract her words. "You heard what I said, Jason."

"Say it again?"

"What do I get if I say it again?"

He smiled, dimples deepening in the stubble. "Just say it," he crooned.

"Would you like for me to move in with you?" Rapid Spanish rolled off his tongue and Greer only caught a few words. "You're going to have to translate that for me."

"I said I'd love for you to live with me but on one condition."

It was Greer's turn to hesitate. "What is that?"

"That if everything turns out well, then we should think about making it a permanent arrangement."

Her eyes narrowed as she groaned inwardly. Greer thought he would've welcomed her suggestion without conditions. "How permanent? And what's the time frame?"

"I think after three months we should know more or less whether we should get married."

She shook her head. "No! No marriage!"

"I am not your ex."

Greer glanced over his shoulder so she wouldn't see the rage darkening his eyes. "I know you're not."

"Then stop treating me like him. I told you before, people don't hurt those they love." Pulling her closer, Jason buried his face in her hair. "I've denied it more than once when asked if I love you."

"Who asked you?"

"First Chase, then Pepper. Last night he told me that he knew I was in love with you."

"You love me." Greer didn't recognize her own voice. It was soft, childlike and barely audible.

Moving over Greer, Jason straddled her body. "Yes, I love you. Why is that so hard for you to accept?"

"We haven't dated. We . . . we haven't even made love. What if we turn out to be totally incompatible in bed?" She wanted to ask him about his declaration for her to take all the time she needed because he wasn't going anywhere and neither was she. But that was before she'd asked him to make love to her and before she had made the overture to live with him.

Jason pressed her body down to the mattress. "What makes you think it's not going to be good? Because you say so? Well there's only way to find out. We're going to get up and go to your place where you'll pack enough to last you at least a week. Then we're going out on a date and, when we come back to *our* place, we're going to make love over and over until we get right. It may take only one time or it may take all night. But there will be one thing for certain and that is we'll know whether you want to continue to live with me as my future fiancée or whether you'll continue to live in your uncle's house. Cole men are raised not to shack up with women unless they're willing to commit."

He rolled off her body and the bed, landing lightly on his feet and extending his hand. "Let's go, princess. Destiny's calling."

Greer slipped out of bed, her arms going around his waist. "You've outlined the rules without asking my input, so I'm going to set down a few of my own."

"What are they?"

Tilting her chin, she met a pair of eyes so much like her own. "I want you to start taking care of yourself. No more staying up all night and trying to get by on three or four hours of sleep. My uncle is cutting back his hours, so that means I'll probably spend more time at the restaurant. Because I won't be home to distract you, you should use that time to write. Don't worry about going out to shop for groceries because, whatever we need, I'll bring home from the restaurant. I also want you to take at least one day off during the week to relax completely. I can't have my man breaking down on me.

"I have a standing appointment on Mondays at a full-service salon to get my hair and nails done. I want you to come with me so you can take advantage of their services for men. They also offer mani-pedis, facials and massages. Not only will you look incredibly handsome, but you'll also feel wonderful. How does that sound to you?"

"What are you trying to do? Turn me into a metrosexual?"

She patted his chest. "You're already one. You just haven't acknowledged it. What do you think of my plan?"

Jason stared down at the woman who'd turned his predictable world upside down. She was the first woman who'd offered to take care of him and his needs and not the other way around. "Why are you doing this?"

Going on tiptoe, Greer touched her mouth to his. "You're not the only one who's falling in love."

His smiled was dazzling. "Don't tell me the love bug bit you, too?"

She nodded. "Big time."

Bending slightly, Jason swept her up in his arms. "Let's get out of here so we can put *our* plans into motion."

Greer giggled like a little girl when he carried her to the bathroom. She was still laughing to herself when they stopped at her place where she filled an oversize quilted duffel with enough clothes to last more than a week. Jason had mentioned marriage and the mere mention of the word frightened her more than staring down the bore of a loaded gun. The man who'd held her to his heart appeared too good to be true. It had been the same with Larry before she had exchanged vows and took his name. However, things would be different with her and Jason because they would live together first, and if it didn't work out, then they would go their separate ways to live separate lives.

Greer was surprised when their date began with a visit to a local nondenominational Christian church. She'd been raised to attend services every Sunday with her mother, brother and grandmother, and her father whenever he wasn't working, but lately she'd been what her late grandmother would've called a backslider. Jason told her that he'd been raised Catholic, had taken all the sacraments, had been an altar server and that old habits were hard to break. Even if he'd stayed out Saturday nights, arriving home at sunrise, he'd always stopped by a church to hear mass or say a prayer. Both of them complained of hunger by the time the service ended, although there were sweet rolls, bagels, coffee and tea for the church-goers to enjoy before and after the service.

The rain that had tapered off started again as everyone raced to their cars. Greer sat beside Jason staring at the torrents slashing the windshield. She shivered noticeably until Jason turned up the heat inside the vehicle.

Resting his arm over the back her chair, Jason's eyes made love to Greer's profile. "Where do you want to eat?"

"I wanted to go into Portland and eat at this café with outdoor dining, but that's not going to happen with this weather." She turned to meet his stare. "Why don't we go home and fix something together before I start Sunday dinner?"

Jason ran the back of his hand over her cheekbone. "Are you certain that's what you want to do?"

She gave him a tender smile. "Yes. I like lazing around in the house whenever it's raining."

Jason removed his arm, shifting into Reverse as he backed out of the parking space. "Home it is."

Within minutes of walking into Serenity West, Greer changed out of a pair of navy-blue tailored slacks, red jacket, a white silk blouse and black patent leather kitten heels and into yoga pants, a loose-fitting T-shirt and flip-flops. When Jason joined her in the kitchen, he'd exchanged his slacks and sweater for a pair of paint-spattered walking shorts, T-shirt and leather sandals. She glanced at his hair, noticing the ends were beginning to curl over his ears.

"What do you feel like eating?" she asked, opening the refrigerator's French doors and checking bins filled with fruits and vegetables.

He stood at the coffeemaker, grinding beans. "It all depends on what you're making for Sunday dinner."

Greer peered over her shoulder. "What do you want for dinner?"

"Anything, baby."

She glared at him. "That's not telling me what you want."

"Chicken or fish. It's your call."

Opening the freezer drawer, Greer found plastic bags labeled with their contents and wrapped in butcher paper. She picked up a package of chicken cutlets. "I'll make chicken marsala, roasted vegetables and linguine with garlic and oil." The double wine rack on the countertop was stocked with wines ranging from whites to full-bodied burgundies.

"That sounds good."

They'd settled on dinner but now she had to decide what to prepare for brunch. "Do you eat grits?" she asked Jason as the aroma of brewing coffee filled the kitchen.

Folding his arms over his chest, Jason

found himself awed by the sight of a woman moving around his kitchen. The scene of domesticity would be imprinted in his memory forever. It was definitely something he could very quickly get used to.

"Does a cat lick its whiskers?"

She smiled, scrunching up her nose. "I take it that's an affirmative."

"Can I help you with anything?"

"I could use your help dicing an onion and green pepper."

"Are you making shrimp and grits?"

"No. I'm going to make red gravy with sausage. Once the pork is cooked, I'll remove it from the casing and add it to the sautéed onion and pepper."

Jason pumped his fist. "Da-yum!" he crowed. "What have I done to deserve someone like you?"

"If you don't know, then I can't tell you," she teased.

Greer couldn't explain, even though she'd agreed to live with Jason, why she felt more married to him than she had in the two years she was married to Larry. She rarely cooked because Larry utilized the services of a cook that had prepared his meals before they were married. He had a very sensitive stomach and required a bland diet. Greer had found herself adding condiments to what she considered barely palatable dishes. It had been another reason why she'd been so thin. After several bites, she found it impossible to finish even the smallest portion.

The coffee finished its brewing cycle, and Jason topped it off with steamed milk drizzled with pure Mexican cocoa syrup. He gave the first cup to Greer, kissing her forehead. "Enjoy."

She took a sip, her eyebrows lifting a fraction. "Nice. Why does your coffee always taste so good?"

Jason brewed another cup for himself. "The beans are Jamaica Blue Mountain."

"It's no wonder. It's the most expensive coffee in the world."

"Yes. But I get a family discount because Cole-Diz International Ltd. has coffee plantations in Jamaica, Puerto Rico and Mexico. A couple years ago they bought a large share of Regina's husband's coffee plantation in Bahia, Brazil."

"I thought Aaron was a pediatrician."

Turning slowly, complete shock freezing his features, Jason stared at Greer. "Do you remember everything I say to you?"

She lifted her shoulders under the oversize white T-shirt. "I told you before, I'm a good listener."

Jason shook his head. "No, Greer, it's more than that."

"What do you think it is?"

"I have an uncle who remembers everything he sees and hears."

"What are you trying to say?" Greer knew she sounded defensive because she preferred Jason to be direct rather than evasive.

"I'm saying, like my uncle Joshua, you have the ability of total recall. He attended West Point, and after graduating, he was recruited for army intelligence because of his special gift and the fact he was fluent in five languages other than English. Tell me now. Am I living with an intelligence agent?"

Greer rolled her eyes. "You're either addicted to *Homeland* or you've seen too many James Bond movies."

"Why are you avoiding the question?"

"I'm not avoiding it, Jason. And, no, I'm not an intelligence agent. Does that answer your question?"

The tightness around Jason's mouth deepened. "No, it doesn't. You told me you took French in high school and college, yet you claim you can remember only a few words."

Greer cursed Jason for his perceptiveness. He may not have total recall, but it was apparent he did have above-average intelligence. This was evident when he was able to play any piece without sheet music. "I hated French. I used to tune out the lessons. I learned enough to pass, and I didn't care if it lowered my GPA."

"Why didn't you take another language?"

"I had a choice between Spanish, Italian and German, and by the time I wanted to change my schedule, it was too late. The other classes were filled, so I was stuck with French. Can you please take out an onion and a green pepper and dice them?" she asked, deftly steering the topic away from her.

Jason gave her a snappy salute. "Yes, ma'am." Picking up the remote, he turned on the receiver with the iPod programmed with more than a thousand of his favorite music selections. He sang under his breath to Marvin Gaye's "Ain't That Peculiar" as he peeled the onion and diced it.

"You must like old-school," Greer remarked as she filled a saucepan with water for the grits.

"I do," he confirmed. "I grew up listening to the music from my father's generation, and I loved it. That's when record companies used live studio musicians and not prerecorded tracks. After I finish composing a piece, I record it using all the instruments, then I merge them into a single track."

Greer sang along with Jason to the songs she was familiar with, their voices blending harmoniously. He was one of those songwriters who had a very good voice, but when she complimented him, he claimed his brother's voice was superior to his. He was unable to disguise the pride in his voice when he bragged that Gabriel had won three Grammy awards and an Oscar for a soundtrack before he'd celebrated his thirtieth birthday.

They worked well together and, within the span of an hour, they'd become a couple in and out of bed. Jason startled Greer when he took her arm and pulled her close. "Dance with me, baby."

Wide-eyed, she stared up at him. "I can't, Jason. The food is going to burn."

He swung her around, turning off the stove top. "Satisfied?" he whispered. The harmonious voices of The Dells singing "Oh, What a Night" pulled him into a spell from which Jason never wanted to escape. He hadn't made love to Greer because that wasn't a priority. Getting her to trust him not to hurt her was.

Greer wondered if Jason knew what he was doing to her as she sunk into the contours of his hard body. He was a constant reminder of what she'd been denied for years. She was a normal woman with passions she'd repressed until desire had become a stranger. And she knew her feelings for him had nothing to do with being rational or even close to logical. A former Navy SEAL operative had asked her to protect someone for which assignment he'd been paid an enormous sum, and she'd agreed, in exchange for his ghosts assisting in identifying her unsub. She checked in electronically with her supervisor every ten days, and so far she had nothing to report. Her supervisor had advised her to take her time; once warrants were issued, the agency wanted to make certain, beyond the shadow of doubt, that the names and locations targeted in the raid were accurate and able to stand up in a court of law.

Anchoring her arms under his shoulders, she rested her head on his chest. They danced in place, their hips swaying and dipping in unison; she smiled. "I remember my grandmother, God bless the dead, warning me about grinding with boys."

Jason chuckled. "That's because she knew, after grinding with a girl, boys could tell if they would let them go a little further and perhaps cop a feel. And if they were truly lucky, then they would get into those sweet drawers."

"Nana said no man was getting into her panties unless she was his wife. But on the other hand, my mother warned me about buying a pig in a poke. She claimed no woman should ever buy a pair of shoes without trying them on."

"I like your mother's perspective much better than your Nana's."

"Different times, different mores."

"Thank goodness for that."

"I thought you were old-school, Jason," Greer said accusingly.

The song ended and Jason eased back slightly. "I am when it comes to music and relationships. You'll never have to concern yourself with me cheating on you."

"If you did take leave of your senses, then you wouldn't have to worry about cheating with another woman because I'd hurt you real bad."

Throwing back his head, Jason roared in laughter. "Yeah, right. What are you? A buck twenty? And you talk about taking me out."

Lowering her arms, Greer took a step backward. "I'm still not telling you how much I weigh."

"It really doesn't matter. The only way you could take me would be with a gun, sweetheart. And you'd better not get too close before you get the chance to squeeze off a round because I'd have you on your cute ass in about two seconds."

Her eyes narrowed. "Have you had marital arts training?"

Jason crossed his arms over his chest, the muscles in his biceps bulging from the motion. "MMA."

"No! You do mixed marital arts fighting?"

He gave her a smug grin. "Yep."

"Do you compete?"

"I did a few times. The last time I competed, I almost broke my hand."

Greer's grin matched his. "So my man can kick some ass."

"If I have to."

"Then we share something more in common than just music."

"What's that?"

"I have a black belt in tae kwon do."

Jason blinked. "You're kidding."

"No, I'm not. After Gramps passed away, Nana came to live with us. She volunteered to chauffeur me and my brother to piano, ballet, karate and soccer practice. Cooper hated piano and of course he wouldn't take ballet, so we took karate together. And before you ask, yes, Larry knew I was trained in karate. That's why he attacked me when my back was turned."

Jason reached out to place his fingers over

her parted lips. "I want this to be the last time you ever mention his name."

Wrapping her fingers around Jason's wrist, Greer held his hand in place while she pressed a kiss to his palm. He'd rubbed a lemon over his palms to eradicate the smell of onions. Her tongue flicked over his fingers before she took the middle one into her mouth. Time stood still as they were locked in a trance, their gazes meeting and fusing as she suckled his finger.

A groan came somewhere deep in Jason's chest, and he hardened so quickly he felt slightly light-headed. He managed to extricate his finger, his hands going around Greer's waist. Wordlessly they communicated what each wanted, and he picked her up, taking long strides that carried them out of the kitchen and across the living room to the staircase. He prayed he wouldn't ejaculate until he joined his body with Greer's.

Taking the stairs two at a time, he walked through the anteroom and into the bedroom. The sound of rain lashing the windows and skylights had become the accompaniment to a yet-to-be-written symphony of love.

He placed her on the bed with a gentleness he hadn't known he possessed, his body following hers down. Greer was beyond special; she was extraordinary and unique. She was the woman with whom he'd fallen in love; the woman he wanted as his wife and the mother of his children.

They'd talked about marriage but not about children or where they would live. He had two homes and Florida was closer to her parents in Virginia than Oregon was. But then he had to consider her relationship with her uncle. Burying his face between her neck and shoulder, Jason breathed a kiss there.

"Are you using protection?"

Greer closed her eyes. "No."

She'd stopped taking an oral contraceptive once she was assigned to desk duty. A female agent going undercover always faced the risk of being raped, and/or becoming pregnant if she were to engage in a physical relationship with a perp. Fortunately for her, she hadn't been faced with either dilemma.

Raising his head, Jason cradled Greer's face. He was buying time to slow down the rush of desire in his loins. He'd promised her long, leisurely lovemaking and if his heart didn't fail, then that was what he would offer her. "Do you want children?"

Greer laid her hand alongside his clean-shaven jaw. "Eventually I would like to have one or two babies."

He smiled. She'd given him the answer he wanted. "So would I."

CHAPTER 14

Removing the pins from Greer's hair one by one, Jason began the intro to their dance of desire. She'd shampooed her hair, and instead of blowing it dry, she had braided the damp strands and pinned them into a twist. A wealth of coconut-scented corkscrew curls lay over his pillow. He'd had erotic dreams where Greer was in his bed, and he was making the most exquisite love to her. However, his dreams were about to become a reality. He'd fantasized about her from the first moment he saw her, and knowing that fantasy was to be fulfilled was mind-boggling. This encounter wasn't about taking pleasure but giving it. Twentysomething Greer Hill's life had been filled with deceit, duplicity and crazy, and now it was time for Greer Evans to experience the full range of trust, love and passion.

Jason dropped the fistful of pins on the bedside table. "You're not going to need those." Resting a hand on her flat belly, he gathered the hem of her shirt. "And you're not going to need this." Sitting back on his heels, Jason divested her of the T-shirt in one smooth motion.

Greer, staring up at her soon-to-be lover, resisted the urge to cover the bra with her hands. She was certain Jason could see her rapidly beating heart through the lacy fabric. She was a mass of nerves. Why, she thought, was she reacting like a virgin, curious and yet fearful of what was to come?

"I'm going to do things to you that you may not like or be familiar with," Jason continued in a tone that sought to put Greer at ease when she bit on her lower lip to stop its trembling. "And if you don't like it or if I inadvertently hurt you, I want you to tell me. If you can't go all the way, I want you to tell me to stop, and I will." Sliding a hand under her hips, he pulled the pants down her hips and off her legs and feet.

Greer released her lip and nodded. "Okay."

He unhooked her bra, slipped it off and held it between his thumb and forefinger. "Pretty, but totally unnecessary. You have perfect breasts."

She covered her breasts with her hands. "I can't go out without a bra."

"When we're together, you don't have to wear one." Jason hadn't lied. Greer's breasts were small, but full, firm, perched high above her rib cage. He dropped the bra on the floor beside the bed. "Let's see what other goodies you're hiding under lace and silk." Fingers that had the ability to caress keys to create music sent currents of desire racing through Greer. Flashing his wolfish grin, he removed her bikini panties, tossing them over his shoulder. "And panties are definitely optional."

Smiling, Greer breathed in deeply to rid herself of a sudden attack of nerves. She welcomed the banter because it gave her time to prepare for what was to come. "If I prance around without underwear, then you'll have to do the same."

Supporting his weight on his forearms, Jason lowered his body, the hair on his chest grazing her nipples. "I don't think so, beautiful. You can prance around without your bra and panties because nothing on you moves. I'm afraid if I prance, I'll end up spraining my package. Can you visualize me going to the doctor and asking him to give me a sling to hold my family jewels in place because they hurt like hell every time I take a step?"

Greer giggled like a little girl. "Okay.

You're exempt from going commando."

Jason's tongue traced the outline of her mouth with an agonizing slowness before it slipped through her parted lips. "Thank you for being reasonable." His tongue worked its magic, moving in and out of her mouth and precipitating a familiar throbbing between her thighs.

She'd become an instrument with Jason using it to make the most incredibly beautiful music. She was soaring, desire heating her blood. Greer couldn't get close enough to Jason as she pressed her swollen breasts to his chest. She was on fire — everywhere.

Her hands searched under his T-shirt, fingertips feathering over the solid muscles in his broad chest, fingertips leaving tracks in the thick mat of hair. The hair on his body excited her. Larry's skin had been almost as smooth as her own. She gently ran her fingernail over his chest.

"Baby. Oh, baby," Jason chanted hoarsely, his hand roaming intimately between Greer's thighs. Withdrawing his hand, his mouth replaced his fingers. He wanted a natural woman and Greer was that and more. He could touch and kiss her everywhere without restraints.

Writhing beneath him, Greer couldn't stop the moans escaping her parted lips. "I need you so much," she pleaded.

The silent, sensual energy he projected made her need Jason whenever they shared the same space. At first she'd believed it was because it'd been more than seven years since she'd been intimate with a man but she was proven wrong the night she sat on stage and sang directly to him. He'd accused her of seducing him when it'd been the reverse. She'd spent years waiting for someone like Jason to restore her faith in the opposite sex. There hadn't been time when she was undercover to establish a relationship. However, some of the agents she'd worked with had asked her out. If she did go out, it was to join a group at a favorite restaurant or bar for dinner and drinks.

Greer had celebrated her thirtieth birthday with her parents and brother and each had expressed concern that she would spend the rest of her life alone. She had wanted to tell them the lack of a man in her life was none of their concern, but smiled instead and said she was quite satisfied with her current lifestyle.

Greer needed him and Jason needed and wanted her. He halted his sensual assault long enough to undress and reach for a condom in the drawer of the bedside table. He watched her watching him as he slipped the latex sheath over his erection, smiling when she opened her arms and her legs to invite him to share their love in the most intimate way possible. He moved over her, his hands beneath her hips permitting her to feel his hard pulsing length against her belly while trailing a series of slow, shivery kisses down her neck all the while she whispered his name.

"Do you have any idea what you're doing to me, baby?"

Greer caressed the length of his back, making her aware of the unleashed power in his strong male body. "Yes. It's the same thing you're doing to me," she said breathlessly.

"You make me want you in spite of myself. And you make me need you when I know it makes me vulnerable to the pain I won't be able to bear if you left me."

The chill that washed over Greer had nothing to do with the merging of desire and passion but Jason's plaintive entreaty. He'd exposed his vulnerability as surely as he'd opened a vein, letting his blood flow unchecked. Handsome, wealthy, and talented Jason Cole had exposed himself while silently communicating his continued existence depended upon her staying with him.

The notion buoyed and chilled her at the same time, and suddenly she felt like a pregnant woman whose every action and decision she made impacted the future of her unborn child. Although flattered, Greer didn't want to carry that responsibility. They'd talked about marriage, but in the abstract. She had fallen in love with Jason, but her future wasn't as clearly defined as his. Even if Chase and his people were able to thwart those who'd targeted Jason for death, there was still the question of her tracking down the unknown subjects responsible for illegal gun sales.

Her arms went around his neck. "I'm not going to leave you." She sounded more confident than she felt.

"Thank you, my darling."

"Gracias, mi vida." He continued to thank her in English and in Spanish as he journeyed down her scented body, and then staked his claim as he buried his face between her thighs.

"J-a-son," she said, his name coming out in three instead of two syllables as his teeth gently massaged the nodule of flesh at the apex of her thighs. "I . . . I . . ."

"It's okay, baby," he mumbled, not releasing her flesh. "I'll go slowly."

He'd promised Greer long, leisurely lovemaking and Jason took his time arousing her passion until she shook from her head to her toes, holding on to the sheet in a deathlike grip. He reversed his journey, kissing her softly and allowing her to taste herself on his tongue. Taking her right hand, he pressed it to his erection. "Let's do this together."

Greer's fingers circled his tumescence, squeezing gently. Jason was larger than any man she'd slept with. Together they guided his throbbing sex into her wetness. She moaned softly when her celibate flesh opened slowly to accommodate his swollen girth.

"Am I hurting you?" Jason asked in her ear.

Greer smiled dreamily. It was the best hurt she'd ever experienced. "No."

He laughed softly. "I had no idea you'd be this small and tight."

She pressed a fist to his back. "You're talking too much."

Jason took that as his cue to stop talking. Nothing mattered. Not his music. Not Serenity Records. He forgot everything as he supported her hips in both hands and thrust into her pulsing flesh with the force of a tornado racing across a swatch of land, sweeping up everything in its path. The intensity of their lovemaking matched the rain slashing the windows as they climbed to heights of an ecstasy in an act that merged lovemaking with raw, unadulterated possession where they'd become one.

Greer felt the pulsing grow stronger and stronger, and if she didn't let it go, she would pass out from the rapture holding her captive. Desire raced through her body like a lit fuse, heating her blood to the boiling point. Jason had said he loved her but those were words uttered much too often and glibly. However, his lovemaking communicated silently that he did indeed love her.

The beginning of an orgasm seized her, and she attempted to hold it at bay. She didn't want it to end; she'd waited too long to experience the sensations that reminded her of why she'd been born female. Her orgasm was not to be denied as she surrendered to the most exquisite ecstasy she'd ever known. The first one was followed by another, this one stronger and more intense. They kept coming until she arched off the bed, screaming Jason's name followed by incoherent mumbling as tears streamed down her face.

Greer's sighs of repletion hadn't faded completely when Jason surrendered to the passion he'd withheld from every woman with whom he'd shared a bed. Growling deep in his chest, he caught the tender flesh at the base of her throat at the same time he ejaculated, the pulsing continuing until he felt as weak and helpless as a newborn.

Reversing their positions, he cradled her smooth legs between his. "Are you all right?"

"I'm wonderful," Greer crooned.

"That's because you are wonderful. I don't think we got it right this time. We're going to have to practice some more before we'll be able to take this show on the road."

She looked into the large, deep-set golden eyes peering back at her. They were dancing in amusement. Looping her arms around his neck, Greer pulled his earlobe between her teeth. "How many more practice sessions do you think we'll need?"

"Let's see. If we make love on average of at least five times a week —"

"No, you didn't say five times," she said, cutting him off.

"Okay," Jason conceded, grinning, "I'll settle for three. Three times a week times fifty-two weeks a year comes out to one hundred fifty-six. Then if we multiply that by just say fifty years and . . ." He paused doing the calculation in his head. "That adds up to seventy-eight hundred."

Greer rolled her eyes at him. "You wish. Fifty years from now you'll be lucky if you can get it up to even think of poking me with it."

"My father is in his seventies and he's still knocking boots with my mother."

"How do you know?"

"Because one day I heard her call him a randy old goat."

Throwing back her head, Greer laughed, the sound bubbling up from her throat. "You need to move out of your mama's house."

"I am."

"When, Jason?"

He blinked, all traces of levity missing in his expression. "I've decided to make Serenity West my permanent home."

Greer felt her heart stop before it started up again. "Why?"

"Are you saying you don't want to live in Oregon?" He'd answered her question with one of his own.

"No . . . no. I'm not saying that."

"When you mentioned Bobby cutting back on his hours, I assume you'd eventually take over running Stella's."

She nodded. "Once he retires, I'll own Stella's."

Jason kissed her forehead. "Do you plan on running it?"

"Of course."

"That settles it. We'll live here."

A slight frown creased Greer's forehead. "What's going to happen to your company in Florida?"

Jason kissed her again, this time over her left eye. "Don't worry about that. I have enough relatives versed in the ins and outs of running a business to step in for me." He didn't mention he would have to talk to Ana about replacing him. "I'll stay on as musical director and producer, and if I have to travel to Florida on business, then I'll schedule my visits where they don't interfere with whatever we have planned. And if I have to rehearse with an artist here on the West Coast, then I'll book time at a Portland recording studio because I don't want them coming to our home."

Her eyes grew wider. "You've planned all of it out, haven't you?"

"Yes, I have. I never do or say anything until I've thought it out." He combed his fingers through her tangled hair. "If you don't want to live here, then let me know now."

Her eyebrows lifted. "Where would we live if we move from here?"

"I don't know. Maybe you'd prefer some-place else. We could also live closer to Port-land."

"You're giving me a choice as to where we live?"

Attractive lines fanned out around Jason's eyes when he smiled. "Baby, you claim you love me, but you haven't taken the time to get to know who I am. I will always give you a choice about anything that affects our lives."

With Larry, she hadn't had choices or even a single vote. She had wanted to be the good wife; there was talk they were to become the next generation of power couples groomed for the political arena. Once Larry's father was elected to the Sen-ate, Larry had planned to run as a represen-tative from their election district. Greer had been so blinded by the political rhetoric and the promise that she and her husband could affect change that she hadn't realized she'd been manipulated until it was too late.

It was nothing more than ego that had permitted her to be swept into the frenetic pace of campaigning. In the beginning, the lights, cameras, interviews and fundraisers were heady, like a child going to an amusement-theme park for the first time. After six months Greer felt as if she was on a merry-go-round that wouldn't slow down for her to get off. And when she did get off, it was to board the highest, fastest monster roller coaster in existence. When she couldn't get off the roller coaster, she was forced to jump, injuring herself in the process. Jason had said he didn't want to hear her mention Larry's name again, and she made a conscious vow not to let Larry cross her mind again.

Closing her eyes, she rested her chin on Jason's breastbone as he massaged her scalp. "I have to talk to my uncle about his house."

"What about it?"

"He intends to will it to me."

"Do you plan to sell it?"

"I can't sell the house. It holds too many wonderful memories. It's where Cooper and I spent our summers. I learned to swim in that lake. It's also where I learned fly-fishing and boating."

"What if I buy the house from Bobby instead of you inheriting it?"

"Why?"

"Because we can use it as a guesthouse whenever we entertain our families."

She opened her eyes. Greer kissed his throat. "You'll have to talk to him about that."

Things were moving so quickly Greer didn't want to believe that, a month ago, she hadn't met Jason or could've ever imagined becoming involved with him. Now she was living with him, unofficially engaged and had just experienced the most amazing lovemaking in her life. She kissed him again. "Please let me up. I have to wash up, then finish brunch."

Jason reversed their positions once again, looming over her. "You wash and I'll finish in the kitchen." He kissed the end of her nose. "Race you to the bathroom."

She scrambled off the bed, bumping into Jason as she tried knocking him off balance. They made it to the entrance of the bathroom at the same time. Extending her hand, Greer bowed from the waist. "Ladies first."

In a move almost too quick for the eye to follow, he picked her up as if she were a football and set her down inside. "Ladies first," Jason repeated.

Backpedaling, Greer cupped her breasts. "Just for that, these are off-limits."

He stalked her like a large cat. "Your *tetas* are only a temporary detour. It's all about the kitty, sweetheart." One of her hands covered her mound, and Jason laughed so hard his sides hurt.

Turning on her heels, Greer made her way

to the shower. She switched on the faucets, adjusting the temperature, then programming it with the push of a button. "You know what they say about karma, sweetheart?" she asked over the sound of running water.

"I'm not afraid of you," he said in singsong.

"You should be."

This is the Greer he liked. Teasing *and* sexy.

Greer lay with her head in Jason's lap in the darkened anteroom, dozing lightly. The only illumination came from the candles lining the fireplace mantel. It was after eight when they'd finished dinner and nine-thirty when they had finally cleaned up the kitchen and retreated to the anteroom.

"Are you certain you don't want me to light a fire?" Jason asked Greer.

She pulled the cashmere throw up to her neck. "Very certain."

"Are you falling asleep on me, babe?"

"No. I'm just resting my eyes. I knew I shouldn't have had that second glass of wine."

Lowering his head, Jason kissed her forehead. "Why don't you go to bed?"

"It's too early."

"It's never too early, Greer. I . . ." Jason's cell chimed a familiar ring tone. "Excuse me, babe, but I have to answer that call."

Jason's horse breeder cousin was calling.

Rising slightly, he held her head in one hand while he picked up the phone with the other. "What's up, Nicholas?"

"I'm getting married next Sunday afternoon."

"Whoa, *primo!* I thought that wasn't happening until the end of the month."

"That's what we'd planned until Peyton told me this afternoon that I'm going to become a father."

Jason couldn't stop smiling. "Congratulations!"

"Thanks. I'm calling because right now the Blackstones outnumber the Coles two-to-one, and I need some backup. Can I count on you to come?"

Jason turned to look at Greer. Her eyes were open. "Sure. *¿Quién más de la familia viene?* he asked, switching to Spanish.

"Of course my mom and dad are coming. Celia will call tomorrow to let me know if she and Gavin can make it."

"What about Diego and Vivienne?" Jason asked, inquiring about Nicholas's older brother and sister-in-law.

"Vivienne and S.J. both have colds, so they'll be MIA. Diego, Ana and Jacob are coming in Friday night in order to free up the jet to come out to Oregon to pick you up Saturday."

"Tell Diego not to bother sending the jet. I'll charter my own flight."

"Are you sure?"

"Of course, *primo.*"

"Are you coming with a guest? I need to know for sleeping arrangements."

Jason paused. "Wait a minute." He placed his thumb over the mouthpiece at the same time Greer pushed into a sitting position. "I'd like you to come with me to Virginia next weekend for my cousin's wedding," he whispered.

Greer knew attending the wedding with Jason meant meeting his family, and she wasn't certain whether she was ready for that. "How important is it to you for me to come?"

"*Very* important."

Her heart turned over when she saw his expression of expectation. "Where are we going and what's the venue?"

Jason brushed his mouth over Greer's. "Virginia's horse country." She nodded.

■ ■ ■ ■

Removing his hand covering the phone's mouthpiece, he said, "There'll be two of us."

"Good. I'm going to put you guys up at my house."

"What about Michael? He and Jolene are practically in your backyard."

"McLean isn't that far, but Michael says this pregnancy will probably be Jolene's last. She's spent most of her time in bed."

"When is she due?"

"Sometime in the spring."

"How many Kirklands will that make now?" Jason asked.

"It's either four or five. I can't keep count," Nicholas said, laughing. "I've got to go, *primo*, and I can't thank you enough for coming. And, by the way, count on me and Peyton coming for Thanksgiving."

"Are you certain she'll be able to fly?"

"I checked with Tyler, and he said air travel in the first trimester is usually safe."

"Good. I'll either call or text you after I confirm my flight."

"Don't worry about ground transportation, Jason. I'll have someone here at the farm pick you up."

Jason ended the call, setting the phone on the table as Greer crawled into his lap, his arms going around her waist. "Thank you."

She rested her head on Jason's shoulder. "Is the wedding formal?"

"I don't think so. It's being held Sunday afternoon."

Greer did a mental check of the clothes in her closet and none of them were wedding appropriate. "I have to go shopping."

"When?" Jason asked.

"Probably tomorrow. I doubt if I'll have time during the week. When are we leaving?"

Reaching for his phone again, Jason scrolled through the directory for the name of a company leasing private jets. "I'll let you know in a few minutes." He activated the speaker feature.

Greer listened intently to Jason's conversation as he made arrangements for them to fly into the Shenandoah Valley Regional Airport late Saturday night and return to Portland Monday afternoon.

"Please charge my account and send me an email confirmation," he said before hanging up. Jason smiled at Greer. "As soon as I get the confirmation, I'll forward it to Nicholas so he can arrange for someone to pick us up."

She nodded numbly. It'd been that easy for Jason. All he had to do was punch a button and reserve a private jet to take them across the country and back, then glibly told the person to charge his account. Is this, she thought, how it was going to be for her and the children she and Jason planned to have? Just pick up the telephone and get whatever you want? The enormity of who she'd pledged her future to shook Greer to the core. If she married Jason, then she would become one of those Coles.

"Have you ever flown a commercial carrier?" she asked.

Jason shook his head. "Never. It's a family mandate that no Cole fly commercial because one of my cousins was kidnapped as a child and held for ransom. We usually take the corporate jet if available, and if not, then it has to be a private jet. Once we're married, you won't ever take a commercial carrier again."

Greer tried suppressing the feeling of apprehension sweeping over her like a cold wave. Was her life destined to become a rerun of what she'd had with the Hills? They, too, had their mandates, asinine mandates that proved more restrictive than practical. The only difference was she hadn't known what she was getting into until after she'd become a Hill because she hadn't known her in-laws as well as she'd believed. After all, she had dated their son in high school, yet they'd managed to hide their eccentricities well.

Attending Jason's cousin's wedding would give Greer an up-close-and-personal look at what was ahead for her. And if she didn't like what she saw, then she was offered an out. At the end of year, she would decide whether she would marry Jason or remain single.

CHAPTER 15

Monday dawned with bright sunshine and warming temperatures. Greer and Jason spent the morning in the full service salon being primped and pampered. He then drove them both to Portland where she spent more than an hour in an upscale boutique trying on dresses, shoes and selecting a purse for Nicholas's wedding. She favored a bronze sheath dress, but changed her mind when the color was too close to her own complexion. The saleswoman found the same dress in her size in a rich chocolate brown. It took a while to select shoes, and in the end, Greer decided on a brown-and-white giraffe-printed calf hair pump with a four-inch heel. It had been some time since she'd worn stilettos and the shoes made her feel incredibly sexy.

"Aren't you going to model your outfit for your boyfriend?" the obviously nipped and tucked woman asked.

Greer shook her head, the tiny curls moving around her shoulders as if they'd taken on a life of their own. "No. I want him to be surprised."

The saleswoman tried and failed to raise her eyebrows. Her face was frozen in place. "And he will. You look amazing."

"Thank you." She slipped out of the heels and unzipped the dress, stepping out of it.

"I'll wrap up everything for you. Are you taking the evening bag?"

"Yes."

Greer hadn't bothered to glance at the price tags because it'd been a long time since she'd gone shopping for clothes that weren't for casual wear. Slipping back into her jeans and blouse, she pushed her feet into a pair of sandals, peering closely at her nails to see if trying on the pumps had damaged her pedicure. If she and Jason were expected to arrive in Virginia late Saturday, then she hoped there would be a salon where she could get her hair styled before the Sunday afternoon wedding began.

She emerged from the dressing room at the same time Jason was scrawling his name on a receipt. He'd usurped her and paid for her purchases. Greer wanted to tell him that she could afford to buy her own clothes but didn't want to cause a scene.

He turned around, smiling. "I had Mrs. Marlowe add a shawl in case it gets a little chilly."

"Thank you, darling." Greer's voice was saccharine-sweet.

Putting his arm around her waist, Jason pulled Greer to his length. "I want to make one more stop before we have lunch."

She took a quick glance at her watch. It was almost two. "Okay. Where are we going?"

Jason flashed his trademark dimples and winked at her. "You'll see." He shifted his attention to the saleswoman. "Can you please hold our bags until we get back?"

Genevieve Marlowe batted her eyes at the tall, good-looking man whose single purchase exceeded her monthly commission. "Of course. I'll put it in the back with your name."

She sighed inaudibly when recalling the way her ex-husband used to look at her the same way Mr. Cole looked at his girlfriend.

It didn't take Greer long to discover what Jason was up to when he held open the door to Margulis Jewelers on SW Broadway in downtown Portland.

"I haven't seen your dress so I thought

you'd want to pick out a few accessories."

"What type of accessories are you talking about?" she asked, sotto voce.

"Earrings or necklace. What do you like?"

"Pearls." It was the first thing that sprang into her head.

A well-dressed middle-aged salesman in a navy-blue pinstriped suit, stark-white shirt, burgundy tie and matching pocket square came over to greet them. He was as elegant as the antique and original furniture in the beautifully appointed jewelry store.

"Good afternoon. I'm Hugh, and I'd be glad to help you with something."

Resting his hand at the small of Greer's back, Jason nodded. "Jason Cole and this is Miss Evans. My fiancée," he added as if an afterthought. "She would like to see some pearls."

"Freshwater, cultured, Tahitian or South Sea?"

Greer offered the fastidious man an open smile. "Let me see what you have."

Hugh pressed his manicured hands together. "Please follow me." He led them to a display case where strands of pearls in different hues were displayed on white velvet. Greer sat on a stool, Jason standing behind her, one arm around her waist. "All of our strands have been hand-knotted, and you can either purchase these or select a clasp separately or we do have some with clasps."

Jason pressed his mouth to Greer's ear. "I'd rather purchase the clasp separately. But it is your choice."

"Thank you, darling."

He kissed her hair. "You're welcome, darling."

Hugh took a quick glance at Greer's bare fingers. "I noticed, Mr. Cole, that you referred to Miss Evans as your fiancée. Does she have an engagement ring?"

If Jason had been more impulsive, he would've hugged the man. "No, she doesn't."

Hugh's sky-blue eyes sparkled in his much-tanned face. "Would you like see a few of our more unique rings?"

"No."

"Yes."

Greer and Jason had spoken at the same time.

"Yes or no?" Hugh asked.

Jason decided to take charge. "We hadn't planned on becoming officially engaged until Christmas, but I suppose it wouldn't hurt to get an idea of what style ring I'd like to give Greer."

Like a bloodhound catching the scent of an escaped prisoner, Hugh turned on the charm. "Please bring your beautiful lady with me, and I'll show you some rings that are certain to please the most discriminating woman."

Greer didn't know whether it was the lights shining down on the showcases — filled with diamond rings in colors ranging from blue, pink, yellow to white — or the brilliance of the stones themselves.

Hugh measured her finger. "You're a six. Let's see what we have in your size."

Again Jason stood behind Greer, looking over her shoulder. He saw a ring he couldn't take his eyes off of, but if Greer was going to select a ring, then it had to be something she'd be willing to wear for the rest of her life.

Hugh picked up one with a large emerald-cut diamond flanked by two smaller ones, slipping it on her finger. "The center diamond is a little more than three carats. The total carat weight is three point seven-five. The setting is platinum."

Greer extended her hand, shaking her head. "It's too overpowering. What do you think, Jason?"

"I agree."

Slipping off the ring, she handed it back to Hugh. She pointed to one with an octagon-shaped center diamond. "I'd like to see that one."

"Good choice," Jason said under his breath. She'd selected the ring he liked.

"This ring is one-of-a-kind," Hugh crooned, slipping it on Greer's finger. It was a perfect fit. "The center diamond is an Asscher cut surrounded by eight specialty cut trapezoid-shaped diamonds, and you also have two rectangular straight baguette-shaped diamonds. All set in platinum."

Jason moved from behind Greer to stand beside her. "Do you like it, babe?"

She spread out her fingers. The ring was exquisite. Her gaze shifted to their salesperson. "Do you mind if I talk to my fiancé a moment?"

Hugh stood up straight. "Not at all." He walked away, giving them a modicum of privacy.

Greer rested her hand on Jason's shoulder. "What are we doing?"

He blinked once. "I'm buying you an engagement ring."

"Don't you think we're moving a bit too quickly?"

He lifted an eyebrow. "That's a question you should've asked yourself before you offered to live with me."

"Touché, Jason. I suppose I deserve that one."

Pulling her into a close embrace, Jason kissed her fragrant curls. "I told you before. Cole men don't cohabitate unless they're willing to commit. I'm committed to spending the rest of my life with you. And that ring is a sign of my commitment. We don't have to marry this Christmas, if you don't want. I'm willing to wait until you're ready, but I'm not going to wait forever."

She smiled. "I thought you were a patient man."

"I am. I waited thirty-three years for you. You try spending thirty-three years behind bars. For someone who's incarcerated, that's an eternity."

Greer touched his face, smooth and silky from a professional shave and facial. "Thank you. I love the ring."

Jason signaled to Hugh. "We'll take the ring, and we still have to look at pearls."

Hugh's grin was so wide Greer could see almost all of his porcelain veneers. "I'll have the ring cleaned while you select your pearls." He slid the ring off Greer's finger. "Would you also like to see wedding bands?"

She shared a look with Jason, who nodded. "Okay."

Greer felt as if she had entered an alternative universe where she didn't recognize anything. Not even herself when she looked at her reflection staring back at her in the bathroom mirror. And it wasn't for the first time that she questioned whether she was sane.

A man to whom money was no object had placed the titanium card on the counter to pay for seven carats of diamonds for an engagement ring and eternity band and a double strand of South Sea pearls with matching earrings as Hugh whispered to one of the salespeople that he'd just waited on Jason Cole. It was then she realized she was marrying a celebrity, someone used to people pointing fingers and whispering once they recognized him as the producer for Serenity Records. Greer had made one purchase that day — Jason's platinum wedding band.

Afterward, they had stopped at a restaurant offering more than forty varieties of crepes and then returned to the boutique where they picked up her dress and accessories. Mrs. Marlowe had gushed over her ring and Greer had been unable to stop blushing.

Leaving the bathroom, she entered the bedroom and got into bed beside Jason. He sat with his back supported by a pile of pillows, waiting for her. "I have to call my parents to let them know I'm getting married," she said.

Jason glanced at the bedside clock.

Greer noted it was after eight, and that meant it was after eleven on the east coast.

"Isn't it too late to call them?"

"No. They always stay up to watch the late news, then the late night shows." Leaning over, she picked up her cell phone. The government-issued secure cell was in the tote along with her shield and handgun. Greer smiled when she heard her mother's distinctive greeting. It was as if she were singing hello.

"Hi, Mom. How are you?"

"I should be asking you the same," Esther Evans said.

"I'm good, Mom. In fact I'm very good. Is Daddy there with you?"

A hissing sound came through the earpiece. "Where else is he going to be? Now that he's retired, he sticks closer to me than white on rice. I think he believes I've been stepping out on him."

"Mama!"

"Don't worry, Greer. After spending half my life with this man, I don't have the strength or the inclination to break in another one."

"Can you please put your phone on

speaker? I have something to tell both of you."

"You're pregnant! We're going to be grandparents!"

Greer laughed. "No, I'm not pregnant. Please put the phone on speaker."

"Who's pregnant?" asked Gregory Evans.

"For the second time I'm not pregnant, and that means you're not going to be grandparents." Greer swatted at Jason when he started sniggling. "Stop it."

"Who are you talking to?" Esther asked. "We have you on speaker."

"I'm calling to let you know I'm engaged. His name is Jason Cole, and he lives in Florida."

"Is he there with you?" Gregory asked.

"Yes, he is, Daddy. Do you want to talk to him?"

"Of course I want to talk to him."

Greer handed Jason her cell, closely watching his expression as he listened to what her father was saying to him.

"I don't think that's going to be a problem, sir. I love your daughter." His expression grew hard. "Maybe you didn't hear me the first time. I said I love your daughter, and I wouldn't do anything to hurt her. Rather than continue this conversation on the phone, I'd prefer to talk to you face-to-face. Greer and I are going to Virginia this coming weekend for my cousin's wedding. Is it possible for us to meet?" He met Greer's eyes. "Yes. Maybe since my family's going to be hers, and vice versa, I'd like you to attend the wedding, too." He shook his head. "You will not be seen as a wedding crasher. Greer will give you the particulars. Thank you. I'll see you next week." He handed the phone back to Greer.

"What did you say to him, Daddy?"

"Never you mind."

"Please don't tell me *never you mind,* Daddy. I'm going to marry this man, and I don't need you fighting with him."

"Do you really love him, baby girl?"

"Of course I love him. He's nothing like that horse's behind who managed to snow all of us until it was too late." Greer hated that she had to defend Jason, but she knew why her father was so apprehensive about her marrying again.

"Greer, baby. You have to see it from my vantage point. I can't have you hurt again."

"It's not going to happen."

"Cooper came by the other day and told us you're in Mission Grove."

"Uncle Bobby's talking about retiring."

Gregory laughed softly. "That old water buffalo has been talking about retiring for

323

as long as I've known him."

"Don't you dare call my dead sister's husband a buffalo," said Esther in the background.

"I'm going to let you two fight it out about my uncle. I'll see you guys next weekend."

"We can't make it, baby girl, even though I told your fiancé we would come to the wedding. Your mama and I have plans to drive up for my brother's big six-oh, and it's a surprise. You tell your young man that I'm giving him my blessing. I have a lot of respect for a man who can stand toe-to-toe with his future father-in-law. Let him know we'll get together soon."

Greer blinked back the tears pricking the backs of her eyelids. "I'll let him know. I love you guys."

"We love you, too," the elder Evanses chorused.

She replaced the phone on the table on her side of the bed. "My father said he's giving you his blessing but can't make the wedding because of a prior engagement."

Jason eased Greer down to his pillow. "Be certain to thank him the next time you talk to him. By the way, I understand where he's coming from when it comes to you."

"You do?"

"Yes. My father tried something similar

with my oldest sister's fiancé minutes before the wedding was about to begin. He'd asked Merrick to come to the library where he and his brothers were waiting. I believe Dad had a temporary lapse in common sense when he threatened a man who'd worked for the CIA as a covert operative."

"What did he say?"

"He told Merrick he was only going to warn him once. He wanted him to protect Alexandra with his life, and if he failed, then look for her father to come after him."

"How did Merrick take this obvious threat?"

Jason chuckled softly, his fingers rubbing the soft curls grazing his shoulder. "Merrick never batted an eye when he told his future father-in-law that the minute Alex becomes his wife, he was responsible for protecting her. Then he went on to say he may not have as much money as Alex, but he could support her and the children they would have. He also said he'd signed up to go back to the CIA — when he'd promised himself he never would — because he had a wife and family to support. He wasn't going back as an operative but as a trainer. That's when everyone realized Dad was concerned about Merrick's lack of employment. We ragged him about that for days."

"So it wasn't about protection but money."

He nodded. "More or less."

Tilting her chin, Greer stared up at the man she loved and respected. She knew her father could be intimidating — on the phone *and* in person — yet Jason hadn't backed down. He'd gone so far as to demand a face-to-face sit-down. She smiled when she realized she was going to have her own personal superhero.

"Speaking of money. Are you going to want a prenuptial agreement?"

Jason's expression changed as if he were a snake shedding its skin. "If I wanted one, would you sign it?"

"Of course," Greer said without hesitating. "I don't want or need your money."

"You don't want or need money, but I want and need you. The Coles are unique wherein there's never been a prenup or a divorce once we marry."

"So you guys are known for having perfect marriages?"

"We're far from perfect, babe. My grandfather cheated on his wife, and the result was an illegitimate child that took him four decades to acknowledge. My uncle Martin acknowledged Joshua as his brother long before my dad or his sisters. They felt if they acknowledged him, then they were being disloyal to their mother."

"What happened to Joshua's mother?"

"She married my grandfather's business partner because in those days an unwed teenage mother would've been ostracized regardless of their social status. Teresa married Everett Kirkland, gave birth to my uncle, but their marriage was fraught with violence and alienation. Although Teresa had married Everett, she was still in love with Samuel."

Thoroughly engrossed in the story, Greer asked, "Was he in love with Teresa?"

"He admitted to me a part of him would always love Teresa because she needed his protection. She was the daughter of immigrant parents who had to flee Cuba because of her father's political opposition to the government at that time. They were very poor, and Teresa was studying to become a nurse when she came to work for Cole-Diz as a part-time translator. She and Samuel had a brief affair, and she found herself pregnant at the same time *Abuela* was pregnant with her third child. When Teresa flaunted the fact she was carrying her boss's baby, all hell broke loose. I'm certain my grandmother would've divorced my grandfather if divorce at that time hadn't been such a stigma. Here she was in a foreign country, married to a man who not only controlled his money but also hers. If that had occurred today, there's no doubt she would've divorced him and wound up with a tremendous settlement."

"Did she stay with him out of necessity or because she loved him?"

"I think it was both. Someone overheard her saying she would never divorce Sammy because then he and that *puta* would get together. But she also loved her husband. He'd become her rescuer and her protector. He had saved her from an arranged marriage, and his ultimate wealth elevated her to the personification of Cuban-American elegance and sophistication. Although Grandpa wasn't the perfect husband, he *was* a good father."

"How did he reconcile with Teresa's son?"

"Grandpa suffered a stroke and even his doctors didn't expect him to survive, or even if he did, that he would never speak again. But he did. Uncle Josh sat at his bedside until he came out of the coma. What happened in that hospital room had to have changed both of them. There were times when Grandpa called Joshua *son* and he in return called him *Father*."

Greer closed her eyes. "I know of family

feuds that have gone on for generations."

"Nicholas's mother and his grandmother have been at each other's throats for years. Nichola never learned to cook or speak Spanish, and Nancy reminds her of this every chance she gets."

Shifting in a more comfortable position, Greer opened her eyes. "Why didn't she take cooking lessons?"

"Why should she when she employed a live-in cook?" Nichola is a true diva. Her father and brothers spoiled her, and her husband continued the tradition. You'll get to see her at the wedding."

"What about her mother-in-law?"

"You won't get to see the entire clan until Christmas. Between my aunts and uncles, their children, grandchildren and now great-grandchildren, there have to be more than a hundred of us."

"Where does everyone stay?"

"Everywhere. There are twenty-four rooms in the house where my father grew up. My aunts open their homes to accommodate at least forty folks between them. I have cousins in Fort Lauderdale and Miami. It's less than seventy-five miles between Miami and West Palm. My parents' house in Boca Raton is even closer, so they are able to put up many of the out-of-towners."

"It must be nice having a large family."

Jason heard the wistfulness in Greer's voice. "It does have its advantages. I take it you have a small family?"

"Very small. Both my parents had only one sibling. My father lost his parents at an early age, and his grandmother raised him. I have cousins in Maryland and a few in Oklahoma, but those are the only ones I know about."

"I suggest you get in touch with them because I'd like to invite them to our wedding."

"Will they also be invited to your week-long Christmas to New Year's family reunion?"

"Of course. Your family will become my family and vice versa."

"Are the weddings usually lavish celebrity-like affairs?"

"No. They're always private. The family compound is patrolled by security around the clock, and no one will be permitted to attend unless they're invited. Their RSVP will include their name and vehicle's license plate number. So we don't have to worry about wedding crashers. Nicholas's horse farm also has what I consider extremely good security."

"Have you ever been there?"

Jason nodded. "Once. It's beautiful. He breeds Arabians, and even though I'm not into horses, I find them to be magnificent creatures."

"I love riding horses."

Reaching down, Jason pulled one of her legs over his. "You ride, boat, swim and fly-fish. What else do you do?"

"I used to go hunting with my uncle."

"Did you ever kill anything?" he asked.

"No. One time I had a buck with a full rack in my crosshairs, but I just couldn't pull the trigger. I knew the meat and hide wouldn't go to waste, but all I could think about was his head ending up on someone's wall. So I let him go."

"Good for you."

Greer gave Jason a direct stare. "Are you an animal rights' advocate?"

"No. It's just that I don't believe in killing an animal for sport."

They continued to talk about different topics until Greer felt her eyelids grow heavy. She emitted one sigh and fell asleep.

Sleep wasn't as kind for Jason. He lay with Greer cradled in his arms, feeling the warmth of her body. Why her? he mused. Why was he planning to spend the rest of his life with her and not some other woman? And how had he fallen so quickly and so hard for her when it'd never been that way before?

His brother and cousins had always teased him because, as a musician, he should've lived the rock star life, when in fact he'd shunned it. Jason had always been more comfortable remaining behind the scene than front and center. The only time he stood still long enough to pose for photographs was when he and Ana attended music award ceremonies.

A wry smile twisted his mouth. His twin and business partner was now a happily married woman who had plans to make him an uncle for the sixth time. Although he and Ana were born only minutes apart, he'd always regarded her as his little sister. His little sister was married to her U.S. marshal husband, and she had told Jason that, if she'd known being married was so wonderful, she would've tried it years before. Then Jason had to remind her it wasn't about being married. It was about who she'd chosen as her husband.

It was the same with him. He'd found himself so relaxed and comfortable around Greer that he could be himself. That's all he had wanted to be since he was lectured about the responsibility of being a Cole.

Greer stirred in her sleep, pulling out his

arms to lie on her back. His gaze was drawn to the soft swell of breasts in the revealing nightgown and Jason hardened quickly. He wanted to wake Greer and make love to her but realized that wasn't possible. Although she'd said he hadn't hurt her, he noticed she'd moved more gingerly than normally. He would wait until her tender flesh healed before they made love again. After all, he'd professed to be a patient man.

CHAPTER 16

Los Angeles

Webb sat on a director's chair in the darkened warehouse, watching the video shoot. His lip curled into a sneer when he saw three half-naked women rub their breasts and crotches suggestively against the bare-chested singer lip-synching lyrics about what he wanted them to do to him. He grabbed the head of one, holding her head to his belly as he gyrated against her face.

Webb closed his eyes because he knew, if he continued to watch, he wouldn't be able to stop the rage roiling inside him like a dust storm. If he had a daughter, and he knew he would never have one, he would beat her senseless if she became a video ho.

The cell phone in his breast pocket rang, and he opened his eyes, reaching for it. "Yes, Monk."

"Stop! Everyone stop!" the director shouted. "Whose cell is that? Didn't you read the sign about turning off your phones?" His tirade continued as he spewed a litany of curses. He stopped abruptly when Webb approached him, one hand going to his throat.

"If you don't shut up, I'll snap your neck like a pencil. In case it's slipped your mind, I'm paying for this space and everything and everyone in it. If I hear words like that coming out of your mouth again, I'll make certain you won't be able to get a job photographing a kiddie party at Chuck E. Cheese." Shaking the trembling man, he flung him aside like a rag doll.

Webb walked over to an area of the warehouse where he could continue his telephone conversation. "Sorry about that."

"No problem. I found him, but there's a slight problem. He lives in a place where it's virtually impossible to breach. In order to gain access to the residents, you have to put your name on a list, and then you have to leave your driver's license. That means we're going to try and get to him outside the fortress. I have someone asking around about him and, once we're able to pinpoint his whereabouts, you'll get what you want."

Webb smiled. "Thanks for the update."

"Just have my package ready when I call you again."

"That won't be a problem." Webb wanted to tell Monk that the balance of his payment was in his safe, but he wouldn't get it until he had absolute proof that Jason Cole was dead. Returning the phone to his pocket, he sat down in the chair he'd vacated. Then with a barely perceptible wave of his hand, he motioned for the director to begin filming again.

The song track started up again and so did the women with their staged gyrations. Didn't they know how ridiculous they looked? If he were shooting an adult movie, Webb wouldn't hire them even if they'd agree to perform for free. No one affiliated with Slow Wyne knew the clock was ticking, ticking down to the time when the label would cease to exist.

Mission Grove

Greer sat at a table in the empty restaurant with Bobby, Andrew, Danny and Pepper. Her uncle had waited for the lunch crowd to leave, then called an impromptu staff meeting. The following morning she and Bobby were scheduled to meet with the manager of Mission Grove's bank to add her name to the restaurant's business account and her uncle's personal accounts. Then she would be authorized to sign all accounts payable and payroll checks. His promise to transfer management of Stella's was about to begin.

Bobby folded his hands together on the tabletop. "I'm sure you're wondering why I want to talk to all of you together. And don't look so scared, Danny. I'm not closing Stella's."

Greer's gaze shifted to the veteran, seeing more than fright in his eyes. It was fear. What did he have to fear? That Bobby would fire him, and he'd have to give up the apartment? His eyes met hers and she gave him a smile she hoped would reassure him that nothing was going to change his current setup.

"What's up, Bobby?" Pepper asked.

"Greer will be managing Stella's, effective next week. I'm going to take some time to relax and take care of myself. Andrew gave me the name of someone who went to culinary school with him, and as soon as I check his paperwork, he'll come onboard as Andrew's assistant. I've gotten a few responses for a waitress from the ad I put in the paper, and I'll be interviewing this weekend. If anyone here knows someone who's old enough to serve alcohol, then please let me know now." He paused. "Are there any questions?" There was a beat. "I guess that's it." Danny, Pepper and Andrew stood and walked away, while Bobby sat staring at Greer. "You look like the cat that swallowed the canary. Is there something you want to tell me?"

She chewed her lower lip. "I'm . . . I'm engaged to be married. But I don't want you to say anything to anyone until we make it official."

Propping an elbow on the table, Bobby pressed his fist to his mouth. "Who is he?" he asked after a full minute.

"Jason Cole."

Bobby's arm came down seemingly in slow motion. He waved his hand. "So that thing that went on between the two of you when you were singing wasn't an act?"

"No, Uncle Bobby."

"Do your folks know?"

"Yes."

Picking up his chair, Bobby moved closer to Greer, resting an arm over her shoulders. "Congratulations, honey bunny," he whispered. "Now are you going to take my advice?"

She held on to the large hand draped over her shoulder. "What's that?"

"Stop chasing the bad guys."

"I will after this last assignment."

Bobby glared at her, the color suffusing

his face indicating his rising anger. "What if this last assignment takes two years?"

Greer chewed the inside of her lip. "That's not going to be a problem because I'm not in the line of fire. You know I'm just here as an observer. And whoever I've been sent here to ID will eventually show him- or herself. Mission Grove isn't that large, and Stella's is the local watering hole or hang-out, so it's just a matter of time before they're going to show their hand."

"And while you sit around and wait for someone to *show their hand,* you're going to keep your husband in the dark about your *real* job."

Nothing in Greer's expression revealed her annoyance at her uncle accusatory tone. "When you were on your black ops missions, did you tell the women you were involved with about your *real* job? Or did you lead them to believe you were just another soldier fighting for freedom, justice and the American way?"

A network of lines fanned out around Bobby's eyes. "You're talking about Superman, honey bunny."

"And you're not?" she shot back. "It doesn't matter whether you were a Green Beret, Army Ranger or a Navy SEAL. You all are Superman. And the same way you guys don't go around advertising what you do also applies to me. Yes, I'm sleeping with Jason and I've accepted his wedding proposal, but until I become Mrs. Jason Cole, I can't tell him what I am and who I work for."

"I'm not telling you to compromise yourself, Greer. I want you to call your field office, and tell them to send someone to replace you because you're getting married and you want out."

"What you fail to understand is that I *don't* want out. Not now."

"Why the hell are you being so pigheaded, Greer?"

"Because I want to see this to the end," she argued quietly. "I, too, want this to be the last assignment, but I'm also not a quitter. Because I'll spend the rest of my life wondering, if I'd stayed, could I have prevented that person planning to sell a stolen firearm? The one that would eventually kill a child, mother or an innocent teenage boy standing on a street corner waiting for the light to change. I don't want that on my conscience."

"You're only one ATF agent, Greer, and you alone can't stop the proliferation of stolen guns. You're not going to be able to change the world."

"Please don't preach to me about being one person, Bobby. What if Gandhi had felt that way? Or Dr. Martin Luther King Jr.? Think of the odds against President Lincoln when he tried to pass the Thirteenth Amendment to abolish slavery. Yes, I'm one person and a woman at that, but so was Rosa Parks and because she decided to confront Jim Crow face-to-face, the South was never the same. If I'm going to live in Mission Grove and raise my children here, then I want to make certain to give them a relatively safe environment. I'm not so naive that I believe we'll ever eradicate illegal guns or drugs, but before I hand in my badge, I'm going to do everything I can to put the brakes on it."

Leaning back in his chair, Bobby stared numbly at his niece. Even before she'd joined the ATF, they'd talked at length about what it meant to become a special agent — the intense physical and psychological training. The long hours spent in the field. The downside of being away from friends and family and the possibility of being reassigned thousands of miles from home. Greer had known that, and she had still submitted her application.

There were times when Bobby thought she was trying to prove to everyone that she wasn't going to allow herself to be victimized again. The Hills had done a number on her head, and she'd unknowingly fallen into their carefully laid trap. Only those close to Larry and Greer knew they were dating; their engagement was a closely held secret as was their marriage. Two weeks after his son had married Greer in a private ceremony, Lawrence Hill Sr. announced his intention to run for senator of Maryland.

Bobby knew Jason Cole was as different from Greer's first husband as night was from day. In the two years since Jason had moved in Bear Ridge Estates, Bobby had come to like the talented musician. Bobby had found him to be friendly, magnanimous and humble. Even when folks at Stella's recognized Jason, he'd sign autographs or talk to those aspiring for a career in music. It was always an added bonus when he sat in with Doug's band. Those are the nights when Stella's was crowded to capacity. Customers referred to him as Stella's Piano Man.

"Jason wants to live in Mission Grove permanently?"

Greer nodded. "Yes. I told him about you going into semiretirement, and I would eventually take over managing Stella's and —"

"You're not going to manage it. You're going to own Stella's."

"That's when he decided to live here," Greer continued as if Bobby hadn't interrupted her. "He'll probably have to travel to Florida on business several times a year."

"Have you set a date for the wedding?"

"No." Greer told him she was living with Jason and, before the end of the year, they would decide on a date.

"Did he give you a ring?" Bobby asked.

Reaching under her sweater, she pulled out the ring hanging from a gold chain. "I don't wear it when I'm working."

Bobby cradled the ring in the palm of his hand. Illumination from the hanging light reflected off the large center stone. "Damn, girl. This must have cost him a grip!"

Greer didn't want to tell her uncle that her eternity-style platinum wedding band with thirty-six baguette-shaped diamonds totaling four carats cost more than her engagement ring. "I tried on quite a few before deciding on this one."

"It's beautiful, honey bunny."

"Thank you, Uncle Bobby." She slipped the ring back under her sweater. Her uncle calling her his pet name meant his momentary fit of annoyance was over. "I'm going upstairs to use my computer to check in."

Bobby caught her wrist. "What do you think of giving the employees a raise?"

Greer halted leaving. "Can you afford it?"

"I think so. I sat and did the computations. If we're able to maintain the same number of customers on any given day, then charging the buffet's fixed price means a 150 percent profit. Folks who usually come for lunch spend between six and seven dollars, but with a price-fixed buffet lunch, just say we charge ten-fifty for adults and half that for kids under twelve, then we'll do quite nicely with the price difference. The price will include all you can eat, dessert and nonalcoholic beverages."

"How much of a raise were you thinking about?"

"Between 8 and 10 percent."

Greer smiled, nodding. "That sounds doable. I know you have an outside bookkeeper, but I'd like to see your books."

"I was just going to suggest that. You know you're going to start taking a salary."

"I'll do that once I give up my other job. Right now I'm living rent free and not spending any money for meals because I eat here. The only thing I buy is gas for Johnny B. Goode II, so I'm practically banking my paycheck."

Bobby wanted to tell Greer that, when she

married Jason, she would never want for anything because he'd been born not with a silver but a platinum spoon in his mouth. "Remember we have to go to the bank tomorrow so you can become an authorized signatory on the accounts."

"And don't you forget that I'm going to Virginia with Jason for his cousin's wedding."

Bobby patted her hand. "It's a good sign when he brings you to a family wedding. Now that you're engaged, I don't want you working to closing. You need to get home and spend some time with your man."

Her brow furrowed. "Who's going to close?"

"I will. After all, I still live upstairs, and it's no problem for me to come down and close out the registers and lock up the place."

"What about Danny?" she asked.

"What about him?"

"Does he go out after you set the alarm?"

Bobby narrowed his eyes. "No."

"How do you know?"

"Because he doesn't know the code to the system to disarm it."

"Just asking."

Bobby shook his head. "Come on, Greer. What are you thinking? The last time you were 'just asking,' it had something to do with Chase. Has that changed?"

Greer knew she couldn't repeat to her uncle the conversation she'd had with Chase without revealing what he did for a living. "Not really," she lied smoothly. "I discovered people who lived outside the law are usually loners. Chase and Danny fit that profile."

"I've seen a lot of men like Danny after they came back from Nam. They were mere shadows, almost ghosts of the men they'd been before they had to kill or be killed. And for a boy soldier, who's not old enough to drink back in the States, it is even more traumatic than for a career soldier. I've seen career soldiers break after a while. If it hadn't been for your aunt, I could've wound up a babbling idiot. I had nightmares for a long time, then one day they vanished. I'd lived with them for so long that I kept waiting for them to return."

"Why do you think they went away?"

"I believe buying this place was the cure. I used to curse whenever my dad took me with him when he had to make house repairs for his neighbors, but it paid off when I didn't have to put out for rewiring this place or replacing the plumbing. Now I'm too old and weigh too much to get up on a scaffold and repair the roof."

Greer gazed lovingly at her uncle. "Uncle Bobby, have you ever thought about getting married again?"

He ran a hand over his shaved pate. "No."

"What about a girlfriend?"

"What about one?"

"Do you want one?" Greer asked as a slight smile played at the corners of her mouth.

"Who's to say I don't have one?"

Greer was grateful to be seated or else her legs wouldn't have been able to support her. Her uncle wanting to go into semiretirement now made sense. "When am I going to meet her?"

Pushing back his chair, Bobby came to his feet. "You'll meet her when we come to your wedding."

Greer stood. "You're kidding!"

"No, I'm not, honey bunny."

"Is she good to you?"

Bobby angled his head. "She's good *for* me, Greer. She's not my Stella because no woman can replace her. What she does is fill up the lonely hours."

She kissed his cheek. "Then I'm happy for you. And I can't wait to meet her."

Greer tapped the remote device on the visor of the pickup and the garage door slid up smoothly, quickly. Jason had given her two remote devices, one for activating the gate to the private road for residents and another for his garage. She maneuvered into the space beside the Range Rover and cut off the engine. She smiled. Was that like what it was going to be once she married Jason? She would come home from the restaurant and look forward to spending the rest of the evening with him?

Opening the door leading from the garage to the mudroom, she left her shoes on a mat. The lingering scent of lemon and pine told her the cleaning crew had been there. Jason had dimmed the lights on the first floor and her bare feet were silent on the carpeted stairs as she climbed the staircase to the second floor. Then, she saw them. White flower petals shimmered on the cherrywood hallway in the diffused light coming from a table lamp. Like Gretel, Greer followed the petals through the anteroom, the bedroom, where she stored her tote in the walk-in closet Jason had given her, and into the bathroom where dozens of votive candle twinkled like stars.

Her gaze shifted to Jason as he poured a handful of bath crystals into the tub filling with water. Her breath caught in her throat.

He wore only a pair of white drawstring pajama pants. Then without warning he turned and looked at her. There was enough illumination to see the passion replace the shock in his eyes.

"I thought you wouldn't be here for another five minutes."

Reaching for the hem of her sweater, Greer pulled it over her head. "I exceeded the speed limit because I wanted to get home to my baby."

Jason approached her, helping her out of her bra, jeans and panties. He slipped the chain with her ring over her neck, placing it on the vanity. Sweeping her up in his arms, he stood her in the tub. Wrapping both arms around her waist, he kissed her gently. "You can't do that, sweetheart. The road is too narrow and winding to speed. I don't want you to end up in the lake."

Greer kissed him back. "No one has ever drowned in that lake."

"And I don't want you to become the first one." He pressed a kiss to the column of her neck. "Sit down and relax. After I bathe you, I'm going to give you a deep-muscle massage. Then we'll share a cup of *café con leche* before we go to sleep." Picking up a padded stool, he placed it next to the bathtub.

Greer sank into the Jacuzzi, letting out an audible sigh. Resting her head on a bath pillow, she closed her eyes. "Can you please cover my hair with the shower cap?"

Jason covered her head with a plastic-lined bouffant cap, sat down and picked up a bath sponge. "Tired?"

Greer opened her eyes. "A little. Is this what I can look forward to when I come home from work?"

"You bet."

She smiled. "How was your day?"

"Relaxing," Jason admitted. "Once the cleaning service left, I spent the entire day listening to music."

Greer blew him an air kiss. "Good for you. You're learning how to relax. Did you eat dinner?"

Lifting her leg, Jason kissed her ankle. "Yes, *Mama.* I had grilled salmon with steamed asparagus and wild rice." He ran his fingers over her leg. "You need a shave."

Greer lifted her left leg. "I'll shave before the weekend."

Jason released her foot. "I'll shave your legs." Plunging his hand into the swirling waters, he cupped her mound. "Do you want to shave your bikini area, too?"

She sat up straight. "No!"

"Embarrassed, sweetheart? I promise not

to cut you."

The pinpoints of heat that began in her face crept downward to Greer's chest. "That's a little too intimate, Jason."

He laughed, the sardonic sound filling the bathroom. "More intimate than me putting my face between your thighs? You're going to have to get used to me taking care of all of your needs and that includes your *personal* needs. Like buying your tampons."

"How do you know I use tampons?"

"Lucky guess," he crooned, grinning broadly. "I'm willing to bet after a while we'll know everything there is to know about the other. Likes, dislikes, allergies, phobias, etc., etc., etc."

Greer pulled her lip between her teeth. She knew trust was the cornerstone of any meaningful relationship. It was even more important than love. Couples fell in and out of love every minute. She loved Jason, she trusted him not to hurt her, yet she couldn't trust him enough to tell him she was a federal agent. *The only thing I'm going to say is to be ready for the fallout when he does find out.* Chase's warning came back in vivid clarity, and she felt confident she would be able to handle whatever fallout that would ensue.

She beckoned to Jason. "What I'd like is

for you to join me."

"Nah, babe. Tonight's your night."

"I think I'm going to like tonight. I love the flowers, candles and, most of all, I love you, Jason Cole."

He leaned down, brushing a light kiss over her mouth. "And I love you, too, Greer Evans." He kissed her again, this time harder, longer. "Just sit back and enjoy your night of pampering."

Greer took Jason's advice, closing her eyes and giving in to the sensual feel of his hands when he lathered and shaved her legs. However, she couldn't control the shivering when he shaved her bikini area.

Once he had shaved her underarms, Jason couldn't help smiling as he viewed his tonsorial handiwork. "I think I missed my calling. I should've become a barber."

"You're doing exactly what you were destined to do, Jason."

"Falling in love with you?"

She sobered, searching his expression for a hint of guile. Greer was still attempting to process what had occurred between them. She hadn't been able to ignore her interest in the talented musician the moment he had walked into Stella's. She'd found herself, like so many others in the restaurant, transfixed by his playing but also by his ability to make Doug's band take their musical prowess to the next level.

"Had you planned to fall in love?" she asked, answering his question with her own.

"Of course not." Lines of confusion creased Jason's forehead. "Why would you ask me that?"

"I don't know."

"Yes, you do, Greer. You never say anything arbitrarily."

"You're right," she admitted. "I thought maybe, since your twin is married, you feel it's time you do the same."

Jason didn't want to believe what he'd heard. Why now? Why after accepting his proposal of marriage was Greer questioning his love for her? Who had she spoken to that attributed to her doubt and/or indecision?

"Did your brother marry because you had?" he asked, successfully tamping down his rising anger.

"He'd contemplated it, but the girl he'd been dating at the time turned him down because he told her he was going into law enforcement. Unfortunately her father had been killed in the line of duty, and she didn't wanted to relive that if she lost her husband."

"Is he married now?"

"No. He's still single."

"I suppose that shoots your theory that twins do everything together to hell."

Greer studied his face. "I just don't want you to go into something you might later regret."

Reaching down and anchoring his hands under Greer's shoulders, Jason pulled her out of the tub and set her on her feet. "I don't want you to do anything that you're not ready for. I gave you a ring because I want you to know that not only do I love you, but I'm also committed to sharing your life. I can understand your reluctance because of what you went through in your first marriage. I have flaws, babe, probably more than I know or am willing to acknowledge, but if you decide this isn't what you want, then I won't try and stop you from leaving. But I want you to remember one thing."

Greer couldn't still her trembling lip or slow down her runaway heartbeat. "What's that?"

"I will always love you."

"And I you," she whispered. Greer did love Jason. More than she could've imagined loving a man. There weren't too many things that frightened her. The exception was marriage.

Jason wrapped a towel around her body,

tucking it between her breasts. "Then why are we standing here talking smack when I promised to give you a massage and a beverage that will make you sleep like a baby?"

Going on tiptoe, Greer bit down on Jason's lower lip, pulling it gently between her teeth. "And I have my own special sleep aid that's certain to put you under in one point two seconds."

"Should I be afraid?"

"Yes, my darling," she crooned, her voice lowering seductively. "You should be very, very afraid."

It was Jason's turn to capture her lip as he worried it between his teeth. "Bring it," he challenged.

"Take it."

Those were the last words they exchanged as Greer and Jason rolled around the large bed, mouths joined and struggling to get closer. Jason held her head firmly, not permitting her to escape his marauding mouth. Silvered light from the full moon coming in through the skylights bathed them in a passionate glow.

In an attempt to catch her breath, she opened her mouth wider but that permitted Jason more access as his tongue simulated making love to her. In and out, around and around, the erotic sensations shimmying down her body to her core. Greer sandwiched her hands between their writhing bodies. She searched and found his erection, holding it in her fist as she rubbed Jason until he was forced to release her head.

"No!" he bellowed.

"Yes," she replied, her hand moved faster and faster.

It was only Jason's superior strength that allowed him to escape spilling his passions on the sheets instead of inside Greer's body. He didn't remember slipping on a condom or how he lay on his back with Greer straddling him.

Both sighed in unison when he penetrated her, her hands anchored on his chest. Jason was helpless to look away or close his eyes when Greer moved up and down, around and around his hardened sex. Her firm breasts bounced above her rib cage, her stomach muscles undulated and the pulse in her throat beat a staccato rhythm as she continued to ride him as if something or someone was chasing her. He was caught up in a spell where he'd surrendered all he was to her. Swallowing back the groans, he prayed not to ejaculate. Not yet. Not when he was experiencing the most pleasurable lovemaking he'd ever had.

Without warning, she pulled up and slid

down the length of his body and took his latex-covered penis in her mouth. Jason bellowed again and again. Her mouth was as hot as a branding iron, her tongue and teeth on a mission to drive him insane.

Greer gloried in the power she yielded over Jason as he groaned and pleaded for her to stop. But there was no stopping. Not until she demonstrated wordlessly how much she did love him. Even if they were to part, he would always know that she loved him.

Jason knew he had to end the erotic torture or he would come in her mouth, and that was something he didn't want. Anchoring his hands in her hair, he managed to extricate her mouth. Flipping her over, he entered her in one smooth thrust. Her legs went around his waist, and it was his turn to ride her as if the hounds of hell were chasing him. It ended when they climaxed together, their moans and groans mingling in a sweet harmonious duet of completion. Jason collapsed heavily on her body, feeling her rapidly beating heart keeping tempo with his.

"What did you do to me?" he asked once he'd regained his breath.

Greer welcomed the weight pressing her

down. "I wanted to show you how much I love you," she said breathlessly.

Somehow Jason found the strength to pull out and roll off her body. He removed the condom, dropping it in the waste basket beside the bed. His breathing was still labored when he reached down and pulled the sheet and blankets up and over their damp bodies.

Gathering Greer to his chest, he kissed her hair. "Thank you." He closed his eyes and drifted off to sleep.

Sleep didn't come as easily for Greer. It was the first time she'd used her mouth to make love to a man, and, much to her surprise, she liked it. There was something about Jason that made her feel reckless, uninhibited, free and confident with a man. He was good for her in and out of bed.

CHAPTER 17

Greer lay dozing on the seat that had reclined into a bed on the private jet, while Jason snored lightly in a bed across the aisle. They'd boarded the plane at the Portland airstrip where eight weeks before she'd deplaned with her brother and the team of FBI agents. Jason had left his vehicle in a restricted lot and walked the short distance to a flight attendant who waited to take their garment bags and carry-on luggage. It was after 8:00 p.m. Pacific time, and when they touched down in Virginia, it would be after midnight.

Once airborne, they were served a sumptuous dinner of poached salmon with a dill sauce, steamed kale and baked acorn squash. She'd drunk one glass of wine to Jason's two, and both had passed on dessert.

Before leaving Oregon, Greer had checked in with her supervisor to let him know she was going to be away for a few days and would check in again when she returned. Although she hadn't had to go through airport security, she'd left her handgun and badge in her uncle's safe.

It felt good not to be constantly *on the job,* wondering if this was what she had to look forward to once she identified the unsub. She was going to a wedding where she would meet her fiancé's family, and she wondered what their reaction would be once they saw her with Jason and wearing an engagement ring. Had he told his parents he was engaged or had he elected to wait until he saw them? She knew if she didn't stop thinking so much she would never get to sleep. Sighing, Greer closed her eyes in the darkened cabin, and minutes later she welcomed the comforting arms of Morpheus.

"Greer, baby, wake up. We're here."

She sat up, looking around her. They were on the ground and the flight attendants had opened the cabin door. Extending her hand, Greer let Jason pull her to standing. He led her along the aisle and preceded her down the stairs to the tarmac, the attendants following with their luggage. It was a warm fall night in Virginia with a star-littered sky.

She noticed a man leaning against the bumper of a SUV, long legs crossed at the ankles. He stood up straight with their approach.

Greer watched Jason hug a man she knew with a single glance was a Cole. They kissed each other on both cheeks, surprising her with the gesture before she remembered they still held on to their Latin customs.

Jason extended his hand and Greer took it, smiling. "Greer, this is Nicholas. He's our host and the groom. Nicholas, Greer Evans, my fiancée."

She studied the man who looked enough like Jason for them to have been brothers, instead of cousins. She extended her hand. "It's a pleasure to meet you. And congratulations on your upcoming nuptials."

Nicholas stared at the tall slender woman Jason had introduced as his fiancée. Ignoring her hand, his hands circled her waist, picking her up, while kissing both her cheeks. "Welcome to the family." He set her down, then turned to Jason. "Damn, *primo,* why didn't you say something before?"

Jason picked up their luggage where the flight crew had left them, storing them in the cargo area of Nicholas's SUV. "I wanted to surprise you."

"Well, you did. Do your folks know?"

"Not yet. I'm certain they'll hear about it after this weekend."

"Ana's here with Jacob, and she didn't mention anything to me about you getting engaged."

Jason closed the hatch. "That's because I didn't tell her."

Nicholas opened the door to the second row of seats for Greer, his hand cupping her elbow to assist her getting into the truck. "I can't believe you didn't tell your shadow," he teased.

"You're the first to know."

"All I can say is, we're going to have quite a weekend," Nicholas said, his drawling cadence identifying him as growing up in the South. He slipped in behind the wheel, waiting for Jason to shut the passenger door. He started the engine and maneuvered the vehicle off the airstrip as the jet's engines shattered the quiet of the night as it prepared for liftoff.

"Who's here?" Jason asked as Nicholas followed the signs leading west.

"Mom and Dad came in with Ana, Jacob and Diego. Celia and Gavin got here yesterday afternoon. Celia was beating her gums about leaving Isabella, so I told her to bring her. Blackstone Farms has a day-care center so there will be someone to look after her."

Jason calculated quickly. "That makes at least nine Coles. That's not a bad showing."

Nicholas smiled. "It's better than just having my mom and dad."

"Are there that many Blackstones?" Jason asked.

"It's not so much the name, but everyone living on the horse farm refers to themselves as a Blackstone. If you were to ask anyone where they're from, they'd say 'Blackstone.' "

"Is it the same at Cole-Thom Farms?"

A beat passed. "I think it's getting there. You have to remember Blackstone Farms has been around for more than forty years, and I'm a newbie. Everyone is excited because when Peyton and I marry, it will be like merging the two farms."

Greer sat behind the cousins, listening to their conversation. If and when she married Jason, she would become part of a family with rituals and traditions passed down and continued with subsequent generations. Unlike family reunions that were usually held during the summer months, the Coles gathered for an entire week beginning Christmas Eve through New Year's Day. And it was always held in West Palm Beach.

This past week had been one in which

their lovemaking had become deeper, more intense. When they weren't making love, Greer and Jason had talked — about everything. He had told her about the circumstances where his father had met his mother. As CEO of Cole-Diz, David Cole had traveled to Costa Rica to negotiate the sale of a banana plantation and had found himself hostage to a madman — who had intended to use David as leverage to get the American government to release his son who'd been held on drug trafficking charges. David, who'd been injured during the abduction, was nursed back to health by Serena Morris. During his captivity Serena and David had fallen in love, and when the Coles had employed their means of rescuing David, they were forced to bring Serena with them because she was pregnant with David's child. They had named the baby Gabriel after Serena's brother who hadn't been a drug trafficker but an informant for the DEA.

Then her brother Gabriel went into the witness protection program, and the only communication Serena had had with him was a Christmas card with updated photos of his three children and six grandchildren.

Jason was forthcoming when he had told her about the contract against his sister's life and how it had all ended when Basil had died unexpectedly from a heart attack. Greer couldn't tell Jason that the threat hadn't ended with Basil Irvine's death, and that Chase had somehow uncovered that the danger had shifted from Ana to Jason. Greer hadn't asked Chase how he knew this because he never would tell her. She'd met former elite operatives who were employed by the CIA, and they would forfeit their lives rather than compromise their missions. Flying to Virginia in a private jet and attending a wedding at a horse farm secured around-the-clock by armed guards ensured Jason's safety.

For the next two days Greer planned to forget about Chase's warning and her job — trying to identify who was stealing guns and selling them to criminals unable to pass a mandatory background check with licensed gun dealers. However that wouldn't stop those from making straw man purchases at gun shows where background checks weren't required. This weekend she wasn't ATF Special Agent Evans, but just Greer.

Traffic lights disappeared as they entered horse country. They passed mile after mile of white fences and private roads and signs identifying the farms, the dates they were established and a few posted the names of winners of major horse races. She saw the sign indicating the number of miles to Blackstone Farms.

"Blackstone Farms is one of the largest horse farms in the region," Nicholas said, not taking his eyes off the dark road. "They employ more than forty people."

Greer leaned forward in her seat. "Do they all live on the farm?"

"Yes. Most farms have resident employees."

"That must be costly," she said.

Nicholas chuckled. "Running a horse farm is not for the faint of heart. It takes an incredible amount of money to take care of one horse, and when you're talking about racing thoroughbreds or breeding Arabians, the cost increases exponentially."

"How did you get into horse breeding?" she asked Nicholas.

"I've always liked horses, so when my military career ended, I indulged in what had been a boyhood fantasy."

Jason shifted in his seat, smiling over his shoulder at Greer. "Nicholas broke with family tradition when he went to Annapolis instead of West Point."

Nicholas grunted. "Only Uncle Josh had his nose out of joint because I didn't follow

366

him and Michael to West Point. I didn't know if he was serious or joking when he called me a traitor."

Jason nodded. "It's hard to tell with Uncle Josh. Greer, you'll get to meet my very scary uncle at Christmas."

"How is he scary?"

"All he has to do is look at you and —"

"Stop trying to frighten her, Jason," Nicholas interrupted. "We know he's a pussycat."

"Yeah, right," Jason snorted. "You have to decide whether he's a cheetah or a leopard. What you don't want to do is get on his wrong side."

Nicholas shook his head. "It's Matt Sterling you don't want to cross." He took a quick glance in the rearview mirror. "Matt's son married our cousin Emily. Matt's a former mercenary and he's one scary dude."

"I think I'm going to need a playbill like they give out at theaters. Then, I'll be able to identify the cast of characters as heroes or villains," Greer said jokingly.

Jason winked at Greer. "The men in the family believe they're bully badasses until they have to deal with their wives. The women always say they rule while their men are there to serve them."

"Is it true?" she asked.

"Hell, yeah!" Jason and Nicholas chorused.

Greer thought about the Cole men serving. Jason made it a point to get up early and prepare breakfast for her. It was the only meal they shared because she ate lunch and dinner at Stella's. She would've preferred sitting down to dinner with him. It was what she considered the family meal. It'd been that way with the Evanses after her father was transferred from the field to supervisor at the Baltimore-D.C. field office. Gregory Evans loved presiding over the dinner meal wherein he used his wife and children as his captive audience in his attempt to practice jokes. It took her father many years before he acknowledged he was a frustrated stand-up comedian.

Most times Greer laughed, not because her father was funny but so ridiculous, while her mother rolled her eyes in supplication. Esther didn't have the heart to tell her husband that he wasn't funny because she'd spent too many nights staring at his empty chair during prolonged periods when he'd gone undercover.

Greer knew how her mother felt about undercover work; Greer would call Esther to let her know she was working, yet could not tell her where she was working or what she was involved in. Tracking illegal gun sales hadn't been her only objective. She'd been assigned to track a group of men purchasing cigarettes in Alabama, changing the stamps from Alabama to counterfeit New York stamps and reselling them to owners of bodegas and corner stores in New York City to avoid paying the cigarette tax.

Her musings were interrupted when Nicholas turned off the local road and onto one leading to Cole-Thom Farms. Motion sensors lit up the landscape, giving her a glimpse of the gleaming white fences surrounding the horse farm. She gasped, the sound echoing inside the truck when she saw the warning sign Trespassers Will Be Shot on Sight and if Still Alive, Then Prosecuted.

Nicholas glanced up into the rearview mirror again. "This is private property and we police it ourselves."

"So I see," Greer said under her breath.

Nicholas slowed when he reached a manned gatehouse. He waved to the man inside the spacious structure and the electronic gate opened. Greer stared through the windshield at the trio of chimneys atop the three-story antebellum great house at the end of the allée of live oak trees as Nicholas maneuvered up an incline. A full-height columned porch wrapping around the front and sides of the spectacular Greek Revival mansion came into view, and she felt as if she'd stepped back in time.

Nicholas parked in front of the house, and as soon as he cut off the engine, Jason was out of the truck, opening the door for Greer, helping her down. She waited as he and Nicholas retrieved their luggage. She followed them up the porch, and after wiping her feet on a mat inside the entry hall, she walked into the living room. She stared up at the massive crystal chandelier suspended from the ceiling rising more than twenty feet above a parquet floor bordered by an intricate rosewood-inlaid pattern. Her gaze lingered on the twin curving staircases leading to the second story.

Nicholas climbed the staircase with their garment bags. "I put you in the west wing. It's the last place when the sun comes in, so that will give you a chance to sleep in a little late. Don't worry about getting up for breakfast. There will a buffet breakfast in the dining room until noon. I don't know what you plan to wear, but the wedding's going to be business-casual. Ties are optional." He opened the door to a bedroom at the end of the hallway. "Sweet dreams."

Greer noticed an elusive dimple in Nicholas's left cheek. "Thank you for your hospitality."

He winked at her. "There's no need to thank me. You're family."

Jason closed the door to the bedroom while she surveyed the space where they would sleep for the two nights they were in Virginia. A four-poster mahogany bed draped in sheer mosquito netting, a matching decoratively carved armoire, two chintz-covered armchairs with matching footstools, a padded window seat spanning the width of three tall, narrow windows all were from a bygone era. Greer didn't know if the furnishing were antiques or exquisite reproductions.

"This house is magnificent," she said reverently.

Jason placed their bags on luggage racks. "Nicholas has invested a lot of money in this house, land and horseflesh."

Slipping out of her running shoes, Greer placed them in a corner. "I can't wait to see the horses."

Crossing the room, Jason cradled her face. "You can use the bathroom first."

Going on tiptoe, she kissed him. "I won't be long."

Twenty minutes later she emerged from the bathroom in a pair of cotton pajamas.

371

Greer had packed pajamas because she was uncertain whether she would have to share a bedroom with someone other than Jason. "I left you some hot water," she teased when he patted her softly on her bottom.

"Don't wait up for me."

Greer doubted whether she would be able to keep her eyes open even if Jason had asked her to stay awake. She dimmed the lamp on Jason's side of the bed and slipped under the lace-trimmed sheet and feather quilt. Within minutes of her head touching the pillow, she was asleep.

Greer descended the staircase, slowing when she saw a petite raven-haired woman staring up at her. They were similarly dressed in jeans and flats. Greer had turned back the cuffs on her man-tailored shirt.

"Good morning," she said in greeting, continuing her descent. As she came closer, she knew intuitively the woman was Jason's twin sister. They had the same black curly hair, large golden-brown eyes and olive complexion. She extended her hand. "I'm Greer Evans."

Smiling, dimples deepening, Ana studied the woman who'd succeeded where so many had failed with her brother. She held out her arms and wasn't disappointed when Greer hugged her. "And I'm Ana Cole Jones." Easing back, she reached for Greer's left hand. *"¡Mierda!"* She clapped a hand over her mouth. "Sorry about that," she apologized. "I know my brother didn't pick this without some help."

Light from the chandelier reflected off the blue and white prisms in the diamonds. "We picked it out together."

"I knew it because Jason hates shopping. Your ring is ab-so-lute-ly gorgeous." She'd drawn the word out into four distinct syllables. Ana looped her arm through Greer's. "Come with me and I'll introduce you to my cousin Celia, and Nicholas's mother and fiancée. You'll meet the men later. They're probably sleeping in because some of them had an impromptu bachelor party over at Blackstone Farms. Nicholas said they were drinking moonshine. He decided not to join them because he knew he had to meet your flight."

Greer felt the nervous energy radiating from her future sister-in-law. She gave her a sidelong glance, marveling how much she resembled the photographs of her Cuban-born grandmother. She walked into the dining room with Ana, her gaze sweeping over

the occupants. The older woman with stylishly coiffed gray hair had to be Nicholas's
mother, and the woman sitting next to her
had to be Celia. She looked like a delicate
doll with large dark eyes, pert nose, full lips
and a mop of black hair framing her café au
lait complexion.

"Everyone," Ana announced, "this is
Greer Evans, my future sister-in-law. Greer,
the lady with the perfect hair is Nichola,
Nicholas's mother. The *chica* on her right is
her daughter Celia. And the blonde who
keeps telling everyone she's not experiencing any premarital jitters is Peyton Blackstone."

Greer found herself surrounded as the
three women complimented her on her ring
while welcoming her into the family. "Thank
you. I feel like a Cole even before I marry
Jason."

"How and where did you meet Jason?"
Celia asked.

Nichola gave her daughter a pointed look.
"Let the child get something to eat before
you begin to interrogate her."

Greer smiled at the older woman with not
only perfect hair but who was also elegantly
dressed in a pale blue raw silk suit and Fer-
ragamo pumps. "I just want some coffee
right now." A coffee urn and chafing dishes

were set up on a buffet server.

Ana took charge. "Sit down, Greer. I'll bring you a plate. How do you like your coffee?"

"Light with one sugar."

"Could you please bring me a cup, too?" Peyton asked.

"No coffee for you," Ana and Celia chorused.

A blush darkened Peyton's palomino-gold face. The added color made her large cool-gray eyes and natural ash-blonde hair appear lighter. "I usually add lots of milk."

Celia shook her head. "No coffee. I know you don't want your baby born with a caffeine addiction."

Peyton rested a hand over her flat belly. "I don't know why, but I'm craving coffee."

"The first three months of my pregnancy, I couldn't tolerate the smell of brewing coffee," Celia admitted.

Ana set a plate of scrambled eggs, home fries, turkey bacon and beef sausage in front of Greer. "If I could have a baby without experiencing cravings, morning sickness, swollen ankles or not being able to bend over to tie up my shoes, I'd have a dozen of them."

Celia met Ana's eyes. "If you eliminate salt, then you won't retain fluid."

"Thank you, Dr. Faulkner. Which one are you? Dr. Faulkner or Cole-Thomas?" Ana asked.

Celia gave her a facetious smile. "It's still Cole-Thomas. Cole-Thomas is on my medical license, so I see no need to change it. What about you, Greer? Are you going to be Greer Cole or Greer Evans Cole?"

"I'll probably drop Evans."

Nichola took a sip of tea. "It makes it a lot easier for your children if they don't have a hyphenated surname. My mother-in-law insisted on retaining her maiden name when she married, so Timothy was saddled with Cole-Thomas."

Celia glared at her mother. "Please, Mom. Don't start in on *Abuela.*"

Nichola put down her cup so hard it rattled on the saucer. "I don't understand my children. They invariably defend their grandmother at every turn."

"Mom, don't be so melodramatic," Celia said when Nichola stood up and stalked out of the dining room. Puffing out her cheeks, Celia blew out a breath. "Peyton, Greer, you've just witnessed the family drama queen in all of her spectacular glory."

Ana sat down next to Greer. "I love Nichola, but there are times when I can't deal with her theatrics."

"That's because Daddy entertains the theatrics," Celia added.

Peyton waved a hand. "Can we please drop this topic? I'm carrying Nichola's grandchild, and I'd like my son or daughter to have a positive relationship with their grandmother."

"Don't get me wrong, Peyton. My mother is a very good mother and an even better grandmother. It's just that she refuses to get along with *Abuela*."

"Greer, how did you meet my brother?" Ana asked, deftly shifting the topic of conversation.

She told them about waiting tables at Stella's and Jason asking her to make a demo tape after hearing her sing on Karaoke Night. Celia asked if she was waiting tables so she would be available to go on auditions.

"No. I'm a former schoolteacher. I'm working at the restaurant to help out my uncle."

"Do you plan to return to the classroom?" Peyton asked.

"No," she repeated. "I'm going to eventually run my uncle's restaurant."

Ana gave Greer a long, intense stare. "You and Jason are not going to have a bicoastal marriage." The question was a statement.

Greer smiled. "No. We're going to live in Oregon."

Ana smothered a curse. "I don't mean to beat up on you, Greer, but when was my brother going to tell me this?"

"Tell you what?" Jason asked, walking into the dining room. He made a beeline to Greer, leaning down and brushing a kiss over her parted lips. "Good morning, babe."

She touched his arm, smiling. "Good morning." He looked shockingly virile in a white T-shirt, relaxed jeans and running shoes. He hadn't shaved and his hair was still damp from a shower.

Jason rounded the table, kissing Celia and then Peyton. "I'm Jason," he said, introducing himself. "Congratulations on the baby and welcome to the family." He kissed Ana, ruffling her hair. "Hey, kid."

"When were you going to tell me that you plan to move to Oregon?" Ana questioned.

He stood up straight, heading for the buffet server. "I don't have to move because I already have a home there. I plan to make it my permanent base because Greer is involved with her family's business."

"What about Serenity, Jason?" Ana asked her twin.

"Nothing's going to change, Ana. I'll still be involved. What I'm going to do is ask

Diego to release Graham so he can assist you on the business end."

Ana shook her head. "I don't think he's going to go for it. I've lost count of the number of times I've asked Diego if I could hire him."

Jason filled his plate with eggs, sausage and potatoes. "Don't worry about it, Ana. I'll take care of Diego."

"How are you taking care of me?"

All eyes focused on the tall, powerfully built man with cropped gray-flecked hair, deep-set dark eyes in a lean face the color of cured tobacco.

"Buenos días, primo," Jason said, smiling. "How's the head?"

Diego held his head with both hands. "Don't ask." He made his way on shaking legs to a chair. "Cee Cee, would you please bring your big brother a cup of black coffee?"

Celia pushed back her chair. "This is a first. The almighty powerful CEO of Cole-Diz humbling himself to beg for coffee."

Diego glared at his sister. "I'm not begging. I merely asked you to bring me coffee."

Jason sat down next to Greer, their shoulders touching. "Diego, once your vision clears, I'd like to introduce you to my fiancée, Greer Evans."

Diego's gaze shifted to the woman sitting next to Jason. "You're engaged? When?"

"Last week. And do you know what I want for a wedding gift?"

"I'll give you anything you want," Diego said as he closed his eyes.

"I want you to release Graham now so he can work for Serenity."

Diego opened his eyes and gingerly shook his head. "Come on, Jason. I'd give you anyone but Graham."

Jason obviously decided to push his agenda. "Graham is the only one with a music and business background. Serenity needs him on the East Coast because I'm making Oregon my permanent home."

Diego stared at Greer for the first time, seeing why his younger cousin was so smitten. Greer was youthfully beautiful. The natural reddish highlights in her hair reminded him of Jason's mother's. It was the same with her gold-flecked eyes. It was apparent Jason was marrying a woman who looked a lot like Serena Cole.

"Does Greer have anything to do with your decision to live in Oregon?"

"Diego!" Ana and Celia admonished at the same time.

Jason and Diego engaged in what had become a staredown. "Yes, she does."

Taking a sip of the strong black coffee Celia had placed in front of him, Diego slumped back in his chair. "Okay, Jason. You can have Graham."

Ana jumped up and hugged Diego. "Thank you."

He pushed her away. "Cee Cee, can you give me something for my headache?"

"It's not a headache, brother love. It's called a hangover."

Diego stood, cursing under his breath in Spanish as he left the dining room.

Greer watched, taking everything in.

"I told him not to drink that stuff," Peyton said, struggling not to laugh. "He told me it couldn't be that bad because Ryan and Jeremy had downed a few shots."

Jason swallowed a mouthful of eggs. "What did he drink?"

"It's my cousin's so-called specially blended bourbon. It's stronger than the liniment I use on horses."

Jason angled his head. "I think I want to sample this specially blended concoction."

Greer clicked her tongue against her teeth. "If you get toasted, then don't expect me to bring you coffee." Everyone laughed as Ana,

Greer and Celia exchanged high-five hand-shakes.

She hadn't officially married Jason, yet she felt a connection with the Coles as if she'd known them for years.

When asked about her wedding, Peyton said, "I decided on a less-than-formal wedding because I know Nicholas and I have to do this again in December. By that time, I have to go through several fittings because of the baby."

"Had you and Nicky planned this baby?" Celia asked.

"No. We had what I call an 'oopsie' moment. I didn't find out I was pregnant until I was in the hospital after my crazy, druggy ex tried to gut me in front of more than a hundred people. The doctors ran several tests, and when they told me I was pregnant, I nearly fainted because, if Reggie hadn't been shot midattack, he would've been responsible for taking not one but two lives."

Greer closed her eyes for a moment. It looked as if she wasn't the only one with a crazy ex-husband bent on murdering his wife. And if Peyton's ex had succeeded, then Peyton wouldn't be here preparing to marry a man that would join not only two families but also two horse farms.

Celia smiled. "That's what you get for

sleeping with a Cole man. All they have to do is look at you and you'll find yourself *swole* up."

"Word," Ana drawled. "Look at Michael and Jolene. What is this? Their fourth or fifth?" She smiled at Greer. "I wouldn't mind another niece or nephew, but if you're relying on Jason to protect you, then you better think about taking a contraceptive."

"I agree," Celia concurred. "If you need a prescription for the pill I'll write you one."

Peyton doubled over in laughter. "Y'all ain't right."

Celia pointed a finger at her. "If we're not right, then why are you *swole*?"

Peyton wrinkled her nose. "Is *swole* a real word?"

"Yes," chorused Greer, Ana and Celia.

The women continued to trade jokes, laughing uncontrollably until Gavin Faulkner and Jacob Jones stumbled into the dining room, heading for the coffee urn. They looked worse than Diego, and if the situation wasn't so pathetic, Greer would've laughed.

She could never understand why bachelor parties translated into excess when it wasn't that way with bachelorette parties. She wondered how Jason would fare when it came time for his rite of passage from a single guy to a married man. Hopefully he would exercise more self-control and not overindulge.

She sobered inwardly when she thought about Ana and Celia warning her about an unplanned pregnancy because she didn't want to experience an oops moment with Jason. So far she'd relied on him to protect her but that couldn't continue indefinitely. Once they returned to Mission Grove, Greer planned to see an ob-gyn.

CHAPTER 18

Greer smiled when Jason gently squeezed her fingers as they sat together in the church at Blackstone Farms listening to Reverend Jimmy Merrill officiating the wedding between Peyton Blackstone and Nicholas Cole-Thomas. She knew Jason was thinking about the time when they would stand before their friends and family to exchange vows to love, cherish and protect each other.

Peyton, dressed in an off-white sweep-train sheath in four-ply silk and silk chiffon with a draped weave bodice, stared up at Nicholas as she repeated her vows. Her burnished hair was swept up in a twist and festooned with tiny red and white rosebuds. Her maid of honor wore red and her matrons of honor wore similar street-length dresses in black, the colors of the farm's silks.

Those close enough to the couple witnessed the naked love in the eyes of Nicholas as he slipped an eternity band on his bride's hand. He wore a black tailored suit with a spread collar white shirt and red silk tie. Peyton's male cousins — Jeremy, whom Nicholas had selected as his best man, Ryan and family patriarch Sheldon were the groomsmen.

The weather had cooperated with above-average temperatures. Two tents were erected, one for dining and the other for dancing. Bales of hay, carved pumpkins and cornstalks tied with black and red ribbons served as decorations.

Even though the men had taken the occasion to dress down by not wearing ties, they did wear jackets with their suit trousers. The women, on the other hand, sported dresses and suits with sexy stilettos. Living and working on a horse farm didn't lend itself to wearing four- and five-inch heels. The ceremony ended as Nicholas dipped his wife, kissing her passionately as flashbulbs flashed, capturing the scene for perpetuity. Greer, holding on to Jason's hand, followed him out of the church, blinking against the brilliant autumn sunlight.

Coming to Virginia with Jason was what she had needed to relax completely. After the wedding they were invited to tour Blackstone Farms and then join in the reception dinner. Greer got a chance to see and touch the magnificent thoroughbreds. It'd been years since she had ridden a horse, and if she'd bought the appropriate footwear, she would've gone riding with some of the younger children who lived on the farm.

Jason splayed his hand over Greer's back, leaned in close and pressed a kiss to her temple. He couldn't believe how sexy she looked in the body-hugging dress and shoes. The double strand of pearls shimmered against her skin. Her heels put the top of her head at his ear, and whenever he looked into her eyes, he felt as if he were drowning in pools of polished amber.

"How did I get so lucky?" he whispered in her ear.

She flashed a demure smile. "Whatever do you mean?"

"You don't know?"

Greer feigned innocence. "No."

She knew precisely what he was talking about only because she felt the same about Jason. If she hadn't been assigned to the town where she'd spent her childhood summers, chances are she never would've crossed paths with Jason Cole. And she'd expected him to be the quintessential self-centered celebrity with a trail of women worshipping at his feet, but he'd proved to be just the opposite. He was as private as he was solitary, shunning the spotlight when he'd chosen to build a home in a community where privacy had become an absolute rather than a privilege.

"If that's the case, then I'll have to show you when we get back to Mission Grove."

Lowering her lashes, she stared up at Jason. "Will I like it?"

"It's guaranteed to please."

The sexy banter ended when they followed the crowd to the tent from which wafted the most mouthwatering aromas. The two farms' cooks had gotten together to plan the buffet menu. Jackson Hubbard, or Jacks as he was referred to by those living at Cole-Thom, had prepared Latin-infused dishes, while the two cooks at Blackstone Farms had prepared a variety of regional dishes.

Jason led Greer to a table quickly filling up with teenagers. "Sit down and I'll bring you a plate."

She sat, placing her small purse next to her. "Hello," she said when a gangly teenage boy gawked at her. His Adam's apple bobbed up and down several times before he was able to croak his greeting. Greer glanced away rather than add to his obvious embarrassment. The bartenders at the far corner of the tent were checking the IDs of those who didn't look old enough to drink.

Watching Jason as he moved along the food line, she remembered what Nicholas had said to her the night he drove them from the airport: *The women always say they rule while their men are there to serve them.* Jason had just verified this when he had offered to bring her food. She'd noticed Nicholas, Gavin and Jacob doing the same at the buffet. Their women never got up to get anything because their men were there to serve them. It was a tradition she liked a lot.

She noticed many of the men had shed their jackets with the rising temperature, and a few of the younger children had taken off their shoes to run barefoot on the grass. Ana had revealed the weddings at the Cole family estate were informal in keeping with the celebratory atmosphere of New Year's Eve. It was also a family tradition that any male claiming Cole blood wore white ties. It was another ritual that had begun when Samuel Cole married Marguerite-Joséfina Diaz.

Greer knew of a lot of asinine family rituals, yet the Coles' made sense to her. A weeklong family reunion provided more time for family members to bond than one lasting a weekend. New Year's Eve weddings were the perfect way to celebrate a new year, and also the date for anniversaries was indelibly branded in their husbands' memories. Music blared from the neighboring tent and couples were up and dancing to the infectious R&B tune. Peyton had revealed her passion for R&B so the playlist covered old and new selections.

Jason returned with two plates, setting them down in front of Greer. "Thanks for saving me a seat. I'm going to get something to drink. What do you want?"

"Either sweet tea or lemonade."

"Are you sure you don't want anything stronger?"

She smiled. "Very sure."

They were scheduled to fly back to Portland later that night and she'd learned over the years never to drink alcohol when flying. The pressurized cabin and the altitude usually made her light-headed. She would take a sip of champagne during the champagne toast, but no more than that.

Waiting for Jason to return, Greer spread a napkin over her lap and arranged their place settings. "What's in your cup?" she asked when he sat down.

"Sweet tea."

She gave him an incredulous look. "Sweet

tea or Long Island Ice Tea?"

He handed her the cup. "Take a sip. See," he crooned when she nodded. "Alcohol and jetlag don't mix."

"Alcohol and flying are a lethal combination for me," Greer said. Picking up a fork, she stared at the contents of her plate. "What did you give me?"

Taking his fork, Jason pointed to the shredded meat. "That's *pernil* or roast pork shoulder. The black rice is known as *moro.* And that little ring of goodness is *mofongo.* It's mashed green plantains with pork, served with a garlic sauce."

Greer pointed to slices of fried plantains topped with garlic in olive oil. "What's the garlic sauce called?"

"*Mojito.* It's not the Cuban cocktail, but a garlicky, oniony, citrusy sauce you can dip or brush on all kinds of things." Jason kissed her hair. He'd watched her blow-dry her hair before flat ironing it for the wedding; then she had swept it up into a ponytail, tying it with a wide black velvet ribbon. *"Bienvenido al Caribe."*

"That I understand," Greer confirmed. "Should I assume you want me to learn to cook what's on my plate?"

"No. I can make everything that's on your plate."

Her eyes opened wider. "Why haven't you?"

"Because I didn't know whether you'd like it. Eat up, baby, and let me know what you think."

"Who taught you to cook?"

"My mother."

Greer took a forkful of *mofongo,* chewing slowly. "Sweet mother of glory! This is so good. Who made this?"

"Nicholas's cook. He used to own a restaurant in Florida. Miami's loss is Cole-Thom Farms' gain."

"These are the type of dishes we should introduce to our customers at Stella's."

"There you go," Jason said with a wide grin.

Greer didn't want to believe she'd eaten everything on her plate and yet still wanted more. The spicy food had triggered an unusual thirst and she went to the bar for water. Rousing applause went up under the tent when the wedding party returned from taking photographs, and Nicholas quickly had someone bring Peyton a plate of food. Within minutes of taking a few bites, the natural color returned to her face as she rested her head on her husband's shoulder.

Jason slipped Greer's purse into the pocket of his suit jacket. Talking long strides, he took her hand. "Come and dance with me, babe." He led her into the dance tent, pulling her close to his chest.

She smiled, recognizing the tune. "I love this song." It was John Legend's "Tonight."

"Am I the best you ever had, Greer?"

A slight frown appeared between Greer's eyes. "Are you talking about the song?"

"No. Am I?" Jason repeated.

Easing back, Greer looked at Jason as if he'd taken leave of his senses. "You have to ask?"

"Yes, I do."

"Do you know what you're asking?" she whispered angrily. "You're asking me to compare you to the other men I slept with." She tried extricating her hand only to have Jason tighten his hold on her fingers. "There were two others before you, Jason. A boy in college and Larry, and neither of them were half as good as you. Now, does that answer your question?"

"That wasn't what I was asking," Jason rasped in her ear. "I wanted to know if you felt I was worthy of you."

Humiliation washed over Greer as if she'd been knocked down from a back draft. "Why ask me that now, Jason? You claim you're committed to me. Well, it's the same for me. I'm committed to you. Committed enough to spend the rest of my life with you."

His eyes widened to where she could see the contrast of his pitch-black pupils in the center of liquid gold. "Prove it."

A nervous laugh escaped her parted lips. "I've already proven it. I'm wearing your ring. Isn't that enough?"

Jason shook his head. "No."

Greer blinked. "What more do you want?"

"Marry me tomorrow."

She stumbled, missing a step but Jason righted her. "You're kidding."

Jason stopped. "No, I'm not. We're already in Virginia where there's no waiting period, and we don't have to be a resident of the Commonwealth. We can get married the same day we get the license."

"What's the rush, Jason? I'm not going anywhere."

"I'm still conflicted about our living together."

Jason's explanation rendered Greer momentarily speechless. Her offer to live with him was akin to walking into a trap of her choosing. Greer cursed her ability of total recall when she remembered him telling her, *Cole men are raised not to shack up with women unless they're willing to commit.* That was apparent when Nicholas married Peyton within two weeks of her disclosure she was carrying his child instead of them waiting until the end of the year.

"We get married and then what?" she asked.

"We live together as husband and wife."

Greer glanced around her. The music had stopped, and only she and Jason were left on the dance floor. "Everyone is staring at us. Let's go someplace where we can talk in private." Still grasping her hand, Jason led her out of the tent and into an open meadow. "Please stop. I can't walk on the grass in heels." Hunkering down, Jason held on to her ankle as he removed one shoe, then the other. She rested a hand on his shoulder, feeling the heat from his body through the fabric of the suit jacket. "What are you doing?"

Jason gave her a sheepish grin. "I'm admiring my handiwork. Your legs look amazing." He pushed his hand up her thigh. "I need to check to see if you have any stubble on your —"

Greer slapped his hand. "Don't you dare!"

He stood up straight. "No one can see us out here."

"I don't care. I'm not going to let you feel me up out in the open."

Jason shook his head. "You are a bundle

of contradictions." He held up his hand when she opened her mouth to defend herself. "Please let me finish. Behind closed doors you are the most uninhibited sexy woman I've ever known, but whenever we're out in public, you put up an invisible wall that says don't touch. Which one are you?"

Greer closed her eyes. She wanted to tell Jason that behind closed doors she could be herself, but the moment she walked outside, she'd morphed into his protector, someone who'd promised his friend she would keep him safe in his absence.

A tentative smile trembled over her lips. "I'm the woman who loves you so much I would risk giving up my own life to protect you. I'm the woman who has pledged her future to you, and the woman who would have no hesitation having your babies. That's who I am."

"Since we're into true confessions, let me bare my soul. I never had the slightest intention of falling in love, especially with someone who looks like you. I've met so many beautiful women that I usually run in the opposite direction. But you are different because you're beautiful inside and out. You probably tagged me as a libertine, bed-hopping musician but I'm just the opposite." Jason cradled Greer's face. "I love you. But I can't continue to cohabitate with you until after we're married."

Greer wanted to ask Jason what was the difference between waiting three months or the next day? If he'd been any other man, she would've moved out and continued to date him. But he wasn't any other man. He was someone unaware he'd been targeted for death by a vengeful rival businessman.

"We've known each other eight weeks, been engaged for one week, and now you're talking about marrying tomorrow. I'm willing to bet we'll have the shortest engagement on record."

"No, we won't, Greer. My uncle Josh holds the record for the shortest. He met Vanessa on a business trip to Mexico and married her eight days later. And they're still married. My dad knew my mother six weeks before marrying her, and she was pregnant with my older brother to boot."

Greer's eyebrows lifted with his revelation. "If he was being held hostage, when did they get the time to make a baby?"

"That's something they refused to talk about."

"How long were Ana and Jacob engaged?"

Jason chuckled softly. "There was no engagement. They lived together for about a week and then decided to make it legal."

He didn't tell Greer that Diego had orchestrated their marriage of convenience when his sister had gone into hiding with Jacob as her bodyguard. The union proved a win-win for both because they'd fallen in love. "Long engagements aren't our strong suit."

Greer worried her lower lip with her teeth. Coles didn't believe in long engagements whereas her engagement to Larry had spanned eighteen months, and during that time she'd believed she'd come to know everything about him. Unfortunately she was so wrong. Jason was offering her a second chance at love and marriage, a marriage that would begin with her hiding secrets. She was a special agent *and* she'd become Jason's temporary protector. Greer had asked herself the same question over and over and the answer was always the same. Yes, she could do both, marry Jason and keep her secrets.

She smiled, her expression softening, becoming tender. "I will marry you tomorrow, but I don't want anyone to know until we repeat our vows New Year's Eve."

"Why?"

Greer's hands covered his. "We should allow Nicholas and Peyton to bask in the spotlight as the family's latest newlyweds and the exciting news that there's another

Cole on the way. Now if we go and announce to everyone that we're married, that would steal their thunder. Let them have their fifteen minutes of fame for the next few months."

Jason kissed the corners of her mouth. "I see your point. I'll have to change our flight schedule. We'll check into a hotel tonight, pick up a license and marry tomorrow, and then fly out tomorrow night."

Greer took Jason's hand as they retraced their steps. "I think we're going to have a dilemma. Which anniversary do we celebrate?"

"We'll celebrate October eighteenth as our secret wedding anniversary and December thirty-first as the open one."

"Will we ever tell anyone about our secret vows?"

"Yes. But not until Christmas," Jason said. "Everyone has secrets. There's no need for us not to have ours."

Greer didn't want to tell him how close he'd come to the truth.

After returning to the tents, Greer found herself caught up in the unrestrained frivolity as she danced nonstop. She shared a dance with Celia's husband, giggling uncontrollably when the FBI field office supervisor sang off-key to what he said was his audition song for *American Idol.* Gavin claimed he was devastated when he didn't get the golden ticket which would allow him to go to Hollywood.

Jacob was less effusive and Greer wondered if he was still suffering from the effects of the bachelor party. He did admit that he'd married the prettier twin to which she replied her twin was hotter. Jacob managed to smile when he stated that was debatable. He ended the dance, kissing her cheek and whispering he wanted her and Jason to marry New Year's Eve when he and Ana renewed their vows along with Nicholas and Peyton. She said she would talk to Jason about it. Greer couldn't tell Jacob she and Jason had already talked about it, and for the first time in the family's history, there would be a triple wedding.

The instant she came face-to-face with Diego, Greer knew dancing with him would be vastly different from her conversations with Gavin and Jacob. She moved fluidly into his outstretched arms. "Why are you glaring at me?" she asked him.

Diego's frown vanished quickly. "Sorry about that."

She angled her head. "You don't like me." The question was a statement.

"Is that important to you?"

"Of course it is. I'm marrying your cousin and that will make us family."

Diego's expression changed, softening, as if he were a snake shedding its skin, his thumb moving back and forth over the ring on her left hand. "I think of you as family because you're wearing Jason's ring. And you've succeeded where so many other women have failed, and that is to get him to fall in love with you."

"You make that sound as if I just pulled off a major coup because I managed to snag one of the country's most eligible bachelors."

"Personally I think Jason got the better of the deal. Please don't get me wrong because I'm quite fond of my little cousin."

"Jason's not so little," Greer countered, defending him.

"No, he's not."

The song ended and Diego led her into the food tent, settling her on a chair at an empty table. "Tell me about your uncle's restaurant?"

"Why? Are you looking to invest?"

The consummate businessman looked sheepish. "Not really. But if you need an infusion of cash I can write you a check as a pre-wedding gift."

Greer stared at the hands resting on his thigh when he looped one leg over the other. They were beautiful with long slender fingers and square-cut buffed nails. Her gaze moved up to this face. Looking at him was like seeing photographs of a young Samuel Cole come to life.

"We don't have a cash-flow problem." She told Diego everything about Stella's from her aunt and uncle's vision for the family-style restaurant to the newly instituted all-you-can-eat buffet. "It's become a quasi-sports bar with a pool table, mechanical bull and TVs tuned to the sports channels. Thursday is Karaoke Night with a DJ who doubles as a stand-up comic, and live music is featured on Friday and Saturday nights. When he's not busy, Jason occasionally sits in the band."

"What's going to happen when your uncle retires?"

"The restaurant will be mine."

"Will you be able to run it alone?" Diego asked.

"No. My uncle has been doing double-duty cooking and managing Stella's, but it's beginning to take its toll on him. That's why I'm helping him out."

Diego leaned closer. "Who's going to help you out when you find yourself pregnant?

Do you think you'll be able to stand on your feet for hours and not put your unborn baby at risk?"

Greer met the deep-set dark eyes that made her feel as if he could see behind her facade of indifference to know what she was thinking. Diego was asking the same questions she'd asked herself since agreeing to marry Jason.

"What aren't you telling me, Diego?"

"Get Jason to help you run Stella's. A family-owned business should be run by family not strangers. It's always been that way with Cole-Diz. It's privately held and there's a mandate all CEOs must be a direct descendant of Samuel Cole. It should be no different with Stella's. In an age where mom and pop businesses are swallowed up or are forced out of business by ever-increasing fast food chains, it's a miracle Stella's has survived."

"What about Jason's music?"

"If Jason wants to write songs, he will find the time to write. And now that he blackmailed me into giving up one of my best managers, Serenity isn't going to fall apart if Jason isn't involved. Jason's talent is identifying new talent, and that is something he can continue to do. He also has an inherent skill for running a business. When Ana took a leave of absence earlier this year, Jason stepped in and reorganized Serenity, and the results were beneficial to management, employees and their clients. If he's going to live in Oregon, then his focus must be Stella's and not Serenity."

Greer knew it was something she would have to talk to Jason about. She didn't want to assume beforehand whether he would want to help her run Stella's. "Will Graham be able to replace Jason?"

Diego smiled for the first time. "Jason has been after me to release Graham for the past two years, and I've always said no. But asking for him as a wedding gift is definitely a new low." Lowering his leg, he picked up his chair, moving it closer to Greer's. "I'm going to tell you something, and if I hear it repeated, then I'm going to disavow all knowledge. Tell Jason you want him to help you run Stella's as a wedding gift, and he won't be able to refuse you."

Greer blinked slowly. "You're not joking?"

"No. Can I count on you to keep our secret?"

"Of course." A shadow fell over the table, and Greer and Diego looked up at the same time.

Jason sat down, resting an arm over

Greer's shoulders. "We're leaving in two hours."

Diego drummed his fingers on the table. "Why don't you guys come back to Florida with us tonight? Then you can fly back late tomorrow afternoon."

"We'd love to take you up on your offer," Greer said quickly, "but I have to get back."

Cole-Diz's CEO stood up. "I guess this means we'll see you for Thanksgiving."

Greer and Jason shared a smile. "We're looking forward to it."

"What were you two talking about?" Jason asked when Diego walked.

"He was telling me that you blackmailed him into giving up Graham because there's a rule that you can't deny someone their wedding gift request."

Throwing back his head, Jason closed his eyes. "What is it you want, Greer?"

"Once my uncle retires, I would like you to help me run Stella's. But I also don't want you to give up your involvement in Serenity Records."

He opened his eyes. "That's it?"

Her smile was as bright as sunshine. "Yes, that's it. What did you think I was going to ask for?"

Lifting his shoulders, Jason slowly shook his head. "I don't know. I was thinking maybe a Ferrari or Maserati. And you know I hate going shopping."

"Duh. Why would I need those when I have Johnny B. Goode II?"

Jason rose in one fluid motion and extended his hand. "Come, darling. We have to pack."

CHAPTER 19

Greer didn't want to believe her voice sounded calm as she stood in front of the court clerk as he officiated their wedding. The driver — from the car service Jason had retained to chauffeur them from the hotel to the courthouse and then to the airport — stood in as their witness. It took less than ten minutes for her to become Mrs. Jason Eduardo Cole, and with her new marital status, she realized her new husband's cell phone was a magic lamp. All he had to do was touch a button, and he could reserve a car service, a charter jet or check into the best room in any given hotel.

"What time is liftoff?" she asked, settling on the leather seat at the rear of the limo next to her husband. Greer smiled. Jason was no longer her lover or fiancé but her lawfully married husband.

"Four-thirty. Once we're airborne, we'll eat, then I suggest you try to get some sleep or you'll be out of sorts for the next few days."

Wrapping both arms around his wife, Jason rested his chin in her hair. He could now think of her that way. Greer had voiced her reluctance to marry after they'd only known each other for a short time, yet being married to her felt as natural to Jason as breathing. He'd tried explaining his upbringing and his father's lectures, lectures he'd loathed listening to.

However, a kernel of those lectures stayed with him whenever he began a relationship with a woman. David Cole had warned his sons to treat women in the same manner they wanted a man to treat their sisters. In other words, do not mess over them. If they slept with a woman, make certain to use protection. If she was good enough to live with, then she was good enough to marry.

Greer closed her eyes, luxuriating in the warmth of Jason's body and the hauntingly sensual scent of his cologne. "I feel as if I'm dreaming and when I wake up I'll be back in Kansas."

"I don't think so," Jason said, laughing softly. "You're not Dorothy, and we are not in Oz." He kissed her hair. "We're going to have a wonderful life together."

"Promise?"

"I don't have to promise, babe. What I plan to do is spend our life together making certain you're happy."

"That's easy. Being with you makes me happy."

"Ditto here."

Greer felt herself succumbing to the smooth motion of the moving car, dozing off to sleep. She'd spent a restless night tossing and turning once she'd contemplated what she was about to do. She had asked herself over and over if she'd taken leave of her senses agreeing to marry a man who, in essence, was still a stranger to her. Then she recalled Jason telling her about his uncle who had married his wife eight days after meeting her. Their marriage was probably based on love at first sight whereas it hadn't been that way with her.

Jason had intrigued her, but it wasn't until she went to his house for the first time that she saw the man who definitely went against type. He wasn't an egotistical, spoiled, wealthy man used to getting anything he wanted. There were times when she found him to be slightly self-deprecating — a trait that didn't fit into her concept of a celebrity musician.

However, there were times when Greer

felt Jason tried much too hard to please her, and she wondered if he was trying to make up for what Larry hadn't been able to do. That's when she chided herself for revealing the details of her first marriage. If Jason hadn't known about Larry, would he have treated her the same or differently?

Jason woke her when they arrived at the airport. It was the same flight crew that had flown with them from Portland. This time they weren't the only passengers. There were two other couples onboard once they entered the cabin. Greer nodded and smiled at them as she took a seat in the rear of the aircraft. Jason sat opposite her and buckled his seat belt.

The flight attendants walked the aisle checking to see if seat belts were fastened as they prepared the cabin for takeoff. One of them informed the passengers they would liftoff as soon as the captain received the signal from the tower.

"Are you going to tell Bobby we're married?" Jason asked Greer after a comfortable silence.

Greer nodded. "Yes, only because he can keep a secret like a priest hearing confession."

"What about your parents?"

Greer shook her head. "Not yet. What

about yours?"

"No," Jason replied. "Unlike Bobby, my mother would be on the phone or emailing everyone within seconds of hearing the news. We'll stick with our decision not to tell anyone until we go to West Palm for Christmas."

A mysterious smile curved Greer's mouth. "I will tell my parents that we're getting married New Year's Eve, and give them the particulars."

There came a crackling sound throughout the cabin, then the pilot's voice. "Ladies and gentlemen, we should be moving in a few minutes. We'll be making stops in Denver and Sacramento. Portland will be our final destination. As soon as we reach cruising speed, the flight attendants will serve dinner. You'll find the menu in the pocket beside your seat. If you have any dietary restrictions, please indicate it on the menu. The weather is clear from here to the west coast. Please sit back and enjoy the flight."

Jason glanced out the oval window when the jet began to taxi down the runway, picking up speed in preparation for liftoff and soon they were airborne. "Are you going to invite anyone other than your parents and brother?"

"Bobby, of course, and my father's brother and his family."

"You're going to have to let me know how many are coming so we can have a final head count to make accommodations for our out-of-town guests."

"How am I going to plan a wedding in Florida when I'm in Oregon?" Greer asked Jason.

"You'll have a personal wedding planner who will take care of the menu, flowers and seating arrangement. There are always two live bands and two DJs, so there won't be a lull in the music."

"Who selects the playlists?" Greer asked.

"We'll deal with the DJs, while the AARP crowd will give the band leaders their favorites."

Clapping a hand over her mouth, Greer smothered a laugh. "You can't say all seniors and baby boomers don't like rap and hip-hop."

"I'm sure some of them do. Just like I grew up listening to my father's music."

"And I grew up listening to my parents' R&B. Speaking of music, have you selected a song for our first dance?"

Jason rested his forefinger over his top lip. "I'm kind of partial to 'Bump N' Grind.' "

Greer narrowed one eye. "I'm serious, Jason. We can't dance to that."

"Why not?"

"Because it's inappropriate."

Jason rolled his eyes upward and blew out his breath. "What about 'Your Body's Callin' Me' instead?"

"Jason!" Greer admonished through clenched teeth. "What's up with you and R. Kelly?"

"You have to give it to him. The man's a genius when it comes to singing baby-making songs."

Greer rested her hands on his knees. "Either you pick the song or I will. And nothing with baby-making lyrics."

He covered her hands with his. "Do you want to make a baby?"

"Yes, but whenever we decide to make a baby, it will definitely not be on a dance floor." She paused. "Speaking of babies, I've decided to go on the pill."

Jason's eyes froze on her lips. "How long do you want to wait before starting a family?"

"A year."

"A year?" he repeated.

"I want us to enjoy being newlyweds for that long. After we have children, we're not going to be able to make love wherever we want or chase each other around the house naked as the day we came into the world."

Jason flashed his dimples. "Nice," he drawled. "Back to songs for our first dance. I'm partial to Tyrese's 'Best of Me.' "

She scrunched up her nose. "I don't know if I've heard of that one."

"I have it on my iPhone playlist. Do you have a song in mind?"

Greer reversed their hands, pressing a kiss to his palms. "I have two. One is Keith Sweat's 'Make It Last Forever,' and the other is Sade's 'Nothing Can Come Between Us.' "

"I like them both. That's it. We'll have a first, second and third first dance."

"We can't do that," Greer said in protest. "What if, every year, we pick a song we can dance to on our anniversary?"

"Baby, we can do anything you want." He'd enunciated each word.

All talk of planning a wedding stopped when the attendants came down the aisle to pick up their menu selections.

Greer parked Johnny B. Goode II in the garage at Stella's, got out and pulled the rope attached to the rollup garage door. Not only did the restaurant need surveillance cameras but also an automatic garage door and a new coat of red paint. She likened the restaurant to an aging beauty in need of a face-lift.

She'd wanted to sleep in late yet knew that wasn't possible. When they'd taken off from the regional airport in the Shenandoah Valley, they had encountered blue skies and fair weather until touching down in Denver. High wind warnings with gusts reaching forty miles an hour had grounded all flights. They'd sat on the ground for three hours before they were cleared to continue on to Sacramento. It was after two in the morning when she and Jason shared a shower, crawled into bed and slept instead of consummating their union. Greer had tried to convince him not to get up, but he had insisted on making breakfast for her.

She unlocked the side entrance, deactivated the alarm and made her way into the dining room, heading for the kitchen. Bobby sat on a stool at the preparation table, peeling potatoes. "Good morning, handsome."

Bobby put down the paring knife and wiped his hands on the towel slung over his shoulder. "Welcome home."

Smiling, Greer set her tote on the floor. "It's good to be home."

He gave her a bear hug. "Missed you, honey bunny."

"I was only gone three days."

Bobby held her at arm's length. "That's three days too long. Did you have a good time?"

"Yes. It was quite an adventure. The bride was beautiful, the groom handsome and the food incredible." Greer suggested they offer a few Latin and Caribbean-infused dishes when the new chef came onboard. She told him about the horse farm and the magnificent Arabians, thoroughbreds and Lipizzans, the fallout from Nicholas's bachelor party wherein the men had foolishly sampled a specially blended bourbon that made them see double.

"That's because they're a bunch of wussies. Did Jason drink it?"

"No. They had the party Friday night and we didn't arrive until Saturday morning. I have something to tell you, but you must promise me it will go no farther than this kitchen."

A muscle quivered at Bobby's jaw. "Please don't tell me you and Jason broke up."

"Quite the opposite." A beat passed. "We got married."

The beginnings of a smile tipped the corners of Bobby's mouth before he threw back his head and laughed, while holding his belly. "Yes! Your secret is safe with me."

"Let me check in and put my bag away,

then I'll help you peel potatoes."

"By the way," Bobby said, stopping her retreat, "the new cook is coming in today. You can talk to him as to what you want to add to our selections. I also hired a waitress over the weekend. She's young but has had a lot of experience waitressing while awaiting her big break in Hollywood. Unfortunately it never came. Her name is Stephanie Williamson, but she calls herself Stefi. I must say she did real good Saturday night. I'll need you to put her payroll information into the computer."

"What's the cook's name?"

"Omar Warren."

Greer filed away the two names as she unlocked the door leading to the second story, the soles of her running shoes silent on the worn rug covering the staircase. She made a mental note to replace the rug. There had been a time when nothing at the restaurant needed to be replaced or repaired because her aunt Stella fussed over the building as if it were her child.

It'd taken her some time but she had warmed to the idea of managing Stella's. It took her back to a period when everything about her life was blissful and carefree. Bobby's promise to give her his most prized possession meant he trusted her to continue his late-wife's dream to establish a restaurant offering home-cooked dishes made from scratch.

She unlocked the door to Bobby's apartment and was met with a blast of cool air. Bobby slept with the windows open year-round. Everything was neat, in its place, a reminder of his days in the military.

Greer opened the safe and removed the laptop. A sound coming from outside caught her attention as she booted up the computer. Walking over to the window, she stared through the screened-in window. The carting company had come to empty the Dumpsters. Her mouth dropped open when she saw Danny hand the garbage man something wrapped in a black plastic bag. She felt as if the breath had been siphoned from her lungs when she saw what had been in the bag. It was a MAC-10 machine pistol. The man her uncle had hired, had taken into his home, was using Stella's for an illegal gun sale operation.

Greer took her Smartphone from the tote and videotaped the garbage man inspecting the rapid-fire handgun. All along she'd suspected Chase when it had been Danny. She uploaded the video to her computer and then deleted it from her phone. She couldn't risk losing her phone with the damaging evidence.

"The Looney Tunes — playacting SOB," she said through her teeth. The Iraqi war veteran had faked PTSD, while playing on Bobby's sympathies. Going back to her laptop, Greer logged on to the ATF field office's secure site, typing in an instant message.

Identified Unsub: Daniel Poe, ex-USMC. See attached video. Please advise. Agent Evans.

Now all she had to do was wait for further instructions. Greer knew she couldn't tell Bobby what she'd witnessed because she didn't want him involved in a situation that was certain to put him in the line of fire. She would never forgive herself if anything happened to him.

She returned the laptop and tote to the safe, spinning the dial. Greer had just walked out of Bobby's apartment, closing and locking the door behind her when she heard footsteps. Turning slowly, she smiled at Danny as he came up the stairs.

"Good morning."

He nodded. "Good morning."

Her smile didn't falter when she said, "How are you?"

"Good." The single word was a monotone.

"I'll see you later," Greer said over her

shoulder as she passed him on the staircase. Nothing in her expression revealed her revulsion for a man who sold stolen guns to criminals, guns used to kill innocent adults and children. Stolen guns used by those with real mental illnesses and unable to pass the background check. He'd dishonored the uniform he wore in the service of his country and made light of an emotional condition where returning soldiers experienced feelings of helplessness and anxiety. They felt sad, frightened and disconnected. Many were stuck with a constant sense of danger coupled with haunting, painful memories. Greer knew Danny couldn't be the mastermind behind the operation, merely a link in a network spanning illegal gun sales in several states.

Greer returned to the kitchen, washed her hands and slipped a bibbed apron over her blouse and jeans. She sat next to Bobby, telling him about the weeklong reunion the Coles had celebrated for years, and he was expected to join them because he was now considered a part of their extended family.

Bobby gave her skeptical look. "How do you think the regulars will react when we close Stella's for a week?"

"They'll have to deal with it, Uncle Bobby. Maybe the reason you're so tired is because you don't close for vacation. You close for Thanksgiving, Christmas and the Fourth of July. What happened to your putting the Gone Fishing sign on the door?"

Bobby's hands stilled. "Everything changed when I lost Stella."

"My aunt's gone and I know she would want you to be not only happy, but she would've wanted you to take care of yourself. And keeping this restaurant open 362 days a year is ludicrous. You claim you want me to manage Stella's, and I'm going to do that starting today. You've instituted some wonderful changes by going completely buffet-style and eliminating Sunday dinner. Now we have to decide what other days we're going to close."

Bobby went back to peeling potatoes. "That decision will have to be yours, Miss Manager."

Greer hid a smile. She hadn't expected Bobby to acquiesce so quickly. "We're going to close between Christmas Eve and New Year's Day. When I checked your books, I realized revenue is down during that week because most of the college students go home on break. Mother's Day is another below-average revenue day. Most folks would rather go to a fancy restaurant with sit-down service." She chewed her lower lip as she tried to come up with another day to close. "Beginning today I'm going to set up a graph by days of the year and chart what we take in on any given day. Next year at this time, we'll see our peak and low periods."

Bobby dropped a potato in a large aluminum bowl. "What if you're a mother next year this time? What are you going to do? Strap your baby to your back —"

"No," Greer interrupted. "Jason has agreed to help me."

"He's a musician, Greer."

"He's more than a musician, Uncle Bobby. He has an MBA," she said when Bobby gave her skeptical look.

"It's obvious he's a man with many talents," Bobby said under his breath. The sound of the entrance bell echoed in the kitchen. He glanced up at the wall clock. "I'll get the door."

Greer was on her feet when Bobby returned with Andrew and another man. Andrew made the introductions as she welcomed Omar Warren to Stella's, wondering how many people remarked about his uncanny resemblance to Green Day's lead singer, Billie Joe Armstrong.

"Andrew, after lunch Bobby and I would like to meet with you and Omar to discuss possible changes in the dinner choices."

Andrew lifted his sandy eyebrows. "Can you give us an idea of what you want?"

"I'd like a dedicated night for Italian, Asian-fusion, Mexican, Caribbean, Southern and Cajun cuisine."

Omar and Andrew smiled. "I love the idea," Andrew remarked. "O and I will create a mock-up menu for your approval."

Bobby winked at Greer as the two cooks shed their jackets and shirts for a white smock. It was apparent they were receptive to modifying the obvious dishes that had become favorites. With theme night she was certain it would appeal to loyal regulars and attract new customers.

Greer stood at the entrance to the studio, watching Jason as he played George Gershwin's "Rhapsody in Blue." His head kept time with the bluesy rhythm. Listening to the tonality, she realized Diego was wrong, very wrong to compare Jason to his brother. For Greer it wasn't about the number of awards he'd win or lose, but recognizing the genius in others. And Jason had done exactly that when he had composed the songs for Justin Glover, whose albums had gone double platinum within seven months of its release. She applauded when Jason finished the composition.

"Bravo!"

Jason spun around on the piano bench. "How long have you been standing there?"

She smiled. "Long enough."

Jason stood, closed the distance between them and cradled her face. "You're going to have to make some noise the next time."

Her arms went around his waist. "I didn't want to spoil the mood."

Bending slightly, he swept her up in his arms. "You'd never spoil anything. How was your day?"

"It was very good."

Greer held on to his neck, sniffing his throat. "You smell like soap."

"I just took a shower. What made your day very good?"

Resting her head on his shoulder, Greer told him about diversifying the menu. She also raved about their new hires. "It's nice when you don't have to train someone."

"Who trained you to wait tables?"

"My aunt. How was your day?"

Jason let out a sigh. "Boring." He said *boring* whenever he found himself swallowed up by a creative force field he hadn't experienced since writing the songs for Justin Glover's album. During that time, he had averaged about three hours of sleep. Justin, blessed with an unparalleled voice, was able to glide fluidly from one genre to another. He had the ability to scat, rap, sing ballads, upbeat tempo dance and club rhythms, as well as mellow, heart-wrenching breakup songs. Although most critics gave his inaugural album high marks, a few indicated Justin should select a particular genre. Was he hip-hop, pop, R&B or country? Justin's response was he's all those and more, while inviting popular vocalists to collaborate with him for his next album.

"If you worked at Stella's, you'd never be bored."

He dropped a kiss on her hair. "That's because it's a fun place to work. You get to eat free, watch television, listen to the jukebox, ride the mechanical bull or shoot pool."

Greer giggled. "It's a lot more than that, sport. We bus tables, constantly fill and run and empty the dishwasher, sweep the floor, monitor the bathrooms, put out garbage —"

"I get it, babe. You've made your point."

She kissed his stubble. "Since we have a waitress to replace me, I have time to bring Stella's into the twenty-first century."

"How?"

"I'm going to computerize the inventory."

Jason placed his foot on the first stair leading to the second story. "Do you suspect someone is stealing?"

"No. I just think it's easier to keep track of how many bottles of ketchup we have on hand before reordering. I counted sixty-five cans of crushed tomatoes. At any given time we should have only half that amount on hand."

"So my baby is an efficiency expert."

Greer blushed. "No. I just want to streamline the bottom line."

Jason carried her up the staircase. "Are you certain you don't have a degree in business?"

"Very certain."

He paused halfway. "You feel as if you're putting on some weight. Are you certain you're not pregnant?"

"Very sure. I got my period today."

"Bummer. I guess we'll have to wait a few more days before we're able to consummate our marriage."

Greer tightened her hold on her husband's neck. "Good things come to those who wait."

"You ain't lying," he drawled.

"I have an appointment to see a gynecologist next Monday."

She'd told Jason she had wanted to wait a year before starting a family because she truly wanted to enjoy being a wife before becoming a mother. And she still had a few years before she had to concern herself with being high-risk.

"Do you want me to go with you?"

"I don't need you to hold my hand, Jason. The doctor's office is a stone's throw from the restaurant."

Jason set Greer on her feet, his expression a mask of stone. "It's not about holding your hand, Greer. I'm just trying to be supportive." He waved his hand in front of his face. "Look at this face and put it in your incredible memory bank. I am not Larry Junior. Just because you allowed that twisted puppeteer to control your life, don't lump me in the same category." Turning on his heels, he walked out of the bedroom, leaving her to stare at his departing back.

That's not what I meant. Before Greer could get out her apology, Jason was gone. She wasn't comparing him to her ex. They were as different as night was from day. Jason could never be Larry, and Larry definitely couldn't be Jason even if he'd been reborn.

She wasn't yet married a week, and she and her husband had had their first confrontation. As a realist Greer knew she and Jason wouldn't be able to agree on everything.

However, she was always willing to compromise if it was within her sphere of reason. They'd promised each other they wouldn't bring up Larry's name, and Jason was the first one to break the promise.

It wasn't until she stood under the spray of the shower that Greer realized she'd left her tote on the pickup's passenger seat. She wasn't concerned about anyone breaking into the vehicle because it was in an enclosed garage. The temporary lapse was a reminder she had to find a place where she could conceal her badge and gun where Jason wouldn't find it.

She completed her shower, moisturized her body, pulled on a nightgown and slipped into bed — alone.

CHAPTER 20

Los Angeles

Webb sat on the terrace outside his bedroom staring at lights in the valley of the City of Angels. His plan to systemically dismantle Slow Wyne Records had begun. An executive from another hip-hop label had come to him asking to sign one of Slow Wyne's vocalists. What the man didn't know was that the singer had become a liability because he'd begun using crack cocaine. But what the man didn't know wouldn't hurt him when Webb agreed to release the crackhead. He accepted the generous check, depositing the money in the bank under a dummy company before wiring it to an offshore account.

At the same time he was undoing Slow Wyne, he was adding to his bank accounts on several Caribbean islands. If Basil hadn't died, Webb would've been more than content to run his own security company and hopefully live to a ripe old age. But Slow Wyne was a cancer, eating at him inside and out. There wasn't anything about the company that appealed to him. First it had been the clients, and now it was the employees. All of them were slackers, and it was the reason Basil had run the company like a despot.

The burner phone rang, and Webb stared at it for three seconds, then picked it up. "Irvine."

"Have my money ready," Monk said without a greeting.

"Is he gone?"

"No. He's as good as gone. My people are inside."

Webb squinted. "Your people may be inside but he's still alive."

"That won't be for long."

"I'm not giving you anything until I have proof that he's dead."

"Mr. Irvine, did you ever go to Sunday school?"

"What the hell does this have to do with our business arrangement?"

"Just answer the question," Monk said.

"Yes, I did."

"I want you to think of Herodias who told her daughter to ask Herod Antipas for the head of John the Baptist. Mr. Irvine, I'm

Herod and you're John. Screw with me and I'll chop your flippin' head off and put it on a stake for all of L.A. to see. I'm giving you one month to have my money ready or your mother will bury her last bastard son."

"The deal's off, Monk. Keep the money and I'll call us even."

"We're not even. You still owe me half a mil."

"I owe you your life, Monk. No man threatens me and lives to tell about it. Goodbye, whoever the hell you are." Webb stood up and threw the cell phone over the balcony. He was out five hundred thousand dollars but that no longer mattered. He would take care of Jason Cole — his way and on his terms.

Greer sat at the desk signing payroll checks in the miniscule space off the kitchen that doubled as Bobby's office. It was large enough for the desk, chair, two-drawer file cabinet and the tiny bathroom with just enough space in which to turn around. When she'd come in earlier that morning, Bobby hadn't come down yet from his apartment. It was nearly one in the after-noon when he finally did, then abruptly turned around to go back upstairs. Greer didn't want to believe she was that obtuse

— that she'd forgotten today was the anniversary of her aunt's death. Bobby was in mourning.

She'd found herself spending more time at Stella's since Jason was summoned to Florida for a family emergency. Their tiff, which now seemed eons ago, had lasted mere hours. Greer woke to find Jason pressed against her back, his arm holding her captive. Five days later they consummated their marriage with lovemaking that left both fighting to breathe. After a month of marriage, the sex between them was like a drug. They were addicted to each other.

Their plan to host Thanksgiving was postponed to the following year. Nancy Cole-Thomas — *Tía* Nancy — had been the victim of a hit-and-run where she'd sustained severe head trauma, broken ribs and a collapsed lung. Fortunately the police caught the motorist when he crashed his car into a telephone pole. The driver was a seventeen-year-old strung out on ecstasy.

Jason had called her from the Palm Beach hospital where his father, aunt and uncles maintained an around-the-clock vigil at Nancy's bedside, and Greer felt it would be in poor taste to celebrate given his aunt's medical condition. He called her every morning and at night to give her updates, and she tried to lift his dark mood with stories about the quirky characters that came to Stella's first annual Halloween costume party.

Her own moods vacillated from elation to frustration with the feedback from the regional office that she should not interfere with Danny's continued activities, and to Greer that meant her future with the agency was in limbo. She was still an observer, nothing more than a civilian informant. Some agents preferred surveillance while, for Greer, her preference was going under-cover. There was always the risk of her cover being blown, but at least she wasn't sitting around snooping.

A soft knock on the door caught her attention. Her head popped up. Jason stood in the doorway, flashing his sexy wolfish grin. Her heart pounded in her chest like a trip hammer as her jaw dropped. Her shock was replaced by joy when she returned his smile. He appeared dark and dangerous, dressed entirely in black: pullover sweater, leather jacket, jeans and boots. His bearded jaw was evidence he hadn't shaved in more than a week.

"Hey, you. What are you doing here?"

"What, babe? No welcome home?"

Greer sprang from the chair and into his

arms. "You told me you wouldn't be back until Sunday."

Jason took her mouth in a punishing kiss. "I missed you too much to stay away."

Going on tiptoe, she pressed her breasts to his hard chest. "Not as much as I missed you."

His tongue slipped between her parted lips, simulating making love to her. His mouth moved to her throat, the column of her neck, breathing a kiss under her ear. "Now that's debatable."

Anchoring her arms under his shoulders, Greer tried to absorb his warmth and smell. "How's your aunt?"

"She's home, but not at her home. She's convalescing at Timothy and Nichola's house."

"Sweet heaven. Are you certain they're not going to start a nuclear war?"

Jason ran his hand over Greer's hair. "My aunt has changed. She claims she saw her dead husband in a dream, and he told her she has to make peace with her daughter-in-law or she wouldn't see him in heaven."

Greer stared at Jason, her eyes making love to him. "Was she dreaming or hallucinating?"

"Whatever it was, it worked. Even though Timothy hired a private nurse to take care of his mother, Nancy will only allow Nichola to help her, and in return my aunt is teaching her daughter-in-law how to cook."

"That's worth us having to cancel Thanksgiving."

"I agree. Now what do I have to do to convince you to have dinner with me?" Jason asked.

"All you have to do is ask."

"Mrs. Cole," he whispered in her ear, "will you do me the honor of going out to dinner with me?"

Going on tiptoe, Greer pressed her mouth to his ear. "Mr. Cole, I'd love to go to dinner with you, but it will have to be here. This is the anniversary of my aunt's passing, and Bobby's sort of out of it."

Pulling back, Jason offered Greer his arm. "Then Stella's it is."

"Please let me print out these checks, and I'll be right with you. Why don't you go out and get us a table because, as soon as karaoke begins, it will be standing room only."

He didn't want to leave her, not even for five minutes. Spending almost two weeks away from Greer had permitted Jason time to reassess his relationship with her. He'd professed to be in love with her but those were just words. During their separation, he'd experienced a profound loss of companionship, and he now knew but a glimpse of what his grandmother had spoken of when she had buried her husband after seventy-five years of marriage.

Many years ago, M.J. had taken him aside after he'd been kidded mercilessly by his cousins, the male ones in particular, about not bringing a girl with him to family functions. M.J. had told him in softly spoken Spanish that he shouldn't worry about what others said about him, and when he met the woman with whom he would spend his life, he would know it immediately. She had related how Samuel Cole had come to Cuba to purchase a sugar plantation, but anti-American sentiment was very strong and he went away without closing the deal. But she found something about the young, brash handsome American she couldn't resist. Samuel was very formal with her while she shamelessly flirted with him. She managed to exact a promise from him to return to Cuba. No one was more surprised than she when Samuel did come back.

Her voice had dropped, becoming a whisper when she had admitted to seducing her future husband. M.J. did not sleep with him until their wedding night, but she had used whatever feminine wiles she'd learned from her libertine *Titi* Gloria to get the man who'd rescued her from an arranged loveless marriage. Even in her advanced years, M.J. had not forgotten the date she saw Samuel Claridge Cole for the first time: October 21, 1924. Two months later nineteen-year-old Marguerite-Joséfina Diaz married twenty-six-year-old Samuel on December 27, 1924.

M.J. was reflective when she had admitted to Jason that Samuel was a better father than he'd been a husband, but she took the blame that she may have contributed to Samuel seeking out another woman. Anything and everything she'd wanted, her husband gave her, while Teresa had never asked for anything from him but himself. M.J. had punished her husband for his infidelity when she had banished him from her bed for two years, something she had regretted all of her life. There were two things his *abuela* told him which he never forgot: marry a woman who wanted him for himself, and never go to bed angry.

Jason knew he wasn't perfect, but he did want to be a good husband to Greer and a good father to the children he hoped they would have. He walked out of the office, scanning the dining room for an empty table. He spied Chase sitting at his usual table with a man who'd rested a bike helmet on an empty chair. It was apparent his friend had returned to Mission Grove while Jason had been in Florida.

Chase's head came around as Jason approached the table. He managed to give the biker a barely perceptible nod before the leather-clad man stood up and walked away. Rising to his feet, he extended his hand to Jason.

"Welcome back."

Jason shook the proffered hand. Chase's deeply tanned face indicated he'd spent a lot of time outdoors. "I should say the same thing to you. How was Idaho?"

Chase indicated the chair the biker had just vacated. "Sit down. The fishing was phenomenal."

"When did you get back?"

"A couple days ago. I came by your place, and Greer told me you were away. She invited me in and I must say your woman can really burn some pots."

"She cooked for you?" Jason's voice, although soft, held a thread of hostility. Greer had acknowledged Chase wasn't her type, so he couldn't understand why she would invite him into their home.

"No. She was cooking for herself, and when I mentioned how good everything smelled, she said she'd made too much for one person, so she offered to share her dinner with me." There came a beat as Chase met Jason's eyes. "I hope you're not thinking I was trying to come on to your woman?"

Jason sat up straight. "It did cross my mind."

Chase splayed the fingers of his right hand over his heart. "I have a lot of sins to atone for, but going after another man's woman isn't one of them. I know how committed Greer is to you because she must have mentioned your name a dozen times. You're a lucky man, Cole. You hit the jackpot because your woman is beautiful *and* talented."

Slumping back in his chair, Jason stretched out his legs. "That's what I keep telling myself. I'm no choirboy, but finding someone like her is like owning a Triple Crown winner."

Chase stood up. "Here she comes."

Jason rose to his feet as Greer approached the table. His gaze swept over her hair pulled back in a ponytail. She appeared no older than some of the coeds who came to Stella's. He pulled out a chair for her, curbing the urge to kiss her. "What do you want to eat?"

Greer smiled at Chase as she sat down opposite him. It was Asian-fusion night. "I'll have a few pot stickers, chicken and broccoli, and vegetable-fried rice."

Jason glanced at Chase's half-empty plate. "Do you want me to bring you anything?"

Chase waved his hand. "I'm good here. I'll go back for something later."

Five minutes later Jason returned with Greer's order and his plate filled with Thai chicken wings, shrimp rolls with Thai dipping sauce and curry chicken. He set Greer's plate in front of her, along with a place setting.

"Do you want anything to drink?" he asked her.

Picking up a napkin, Greer spread it over her lap. "I'll have one of the waiters bring us something. What do you want?"

"Perrier."

Greer knew Jason never drank any alcohol before or after flying. "Chase?"

"I'll have a tonic with lime."

Raising her hand, she caught Stefi's eye. The petite waitress had the nickname Miss Goth because of her natural inky-black short hair, translucent complexion and sky-blue eyes. Black mascara and kohl intensified the lightness of her eyes.

She came over to the table, smiling and

exhibiting a beautiful set of white teeth. Her smile slipped momentarily when she saw Jason, but she recovered quickly. "Yes, Greer."

"Could you please bring us one Perrier, a tonic water with lime and a club soda with a twist of lemon." Greer watched Chase's eyes follow Stefi. He was still staring when she returned from the bar with their drink order. It was the first time she'd noticed that he'd shown any interest in a woman.

Reaching into his pocket, Chase pulled out a large bill, pressing it into Stefi's hand. "Keep the change."

Stefi stared at the fifty as if it were a venomous reptile. Her eyes were wide with indecision. "Do you realize what you gave me?"

Deep lines fanned out around Chase's hoary-gray eyes when he smiled. "There's nothing wrong with my eyes, and I happen to count very well."

Stefi blushed an attractive pink. "Thank you, Mister . . ."

"It's Chase."

Her flush deepened. "Thank you, Chase."

Greer and Jason exchanged a knowing glance. It was obvious Chase was attracted to the pretty waitress. "Would you like a more formal introduction?" she asked him when Stefi walked over to the bar.

Picking up his fork, Chase twirled a portion of vegetable lo mein around the tines. "No, thanks. I've never had a problem letting a woman know I'm interested in her."

Jason swallowed a mouthful of curry chicken. "Are you interested in her?"

Chase nodded. "Yeah," he said offhandedly. "But not for anything long-term."

Greer went still, her expression frozen as she glared at Chase. "Maybe I shouldn't be listening to this conversation. Is this how you view all women? By long- or short-term?"

Jason rested his hand on Greer's. "Baby, please."

She flung off his hand. "Don't try and placate me, Jason. I asked Chase, not you."

"I said let it go, Greer."

She stared at Jason as if he were a stranger. He hadn't raised his voice but the effect was the same. "Okay. I'll let it go."

"Greer has a right to ask," Chase said, hoping to diffuse an argument between his friends. "I'm too transient to commit to a woman, so I will never delude her into believing there's going to be more between us when there's not. That way there are no hard feelings or misconceptions on either side."

Greer refused to back down. "You tell a

woman up-front that she's short-term?"

Chase nodded. "I do."

"And they don't have a problem with it?" she asked incredulously.

"No, Greer. The ones who are looking for marriage walk away. Those looking for fun or just a good time tell me they enjoy their short-term tenure."

Shaking her head, Greer pointed her fork at Chase. "I'll never understand men as long as I live. If I told Jason I wanted to use him short-term, I'm certain he would call me all sorts of despicable names. Wouldn't you, darling?"

"Nope. I'd renegotiate, asking for an extension, then another extension and as many as I can get until we're long-term."

Chase chuckled. "Spoken like a true businessman."

MC Oakie was setting up his equipment for karaoke when Greer heard loud voices coming from the opposite end of the dining room. Pushing back her chair, she stood up. "Excuse me. I have to see what's going on." Jason and Chase were on their feet at the same time. "I can handle this."

Stefi rushed over, high color in her normally pale face. "There are some guys giving the hostess a problem about paying. They claim they're just here for karaoke but don't plan to eat."

"The rule is, if you come through the door, you the pay the price for the buffet whether you eat or drink," she told Stefi as she wended her way among the tables. There was a group of four men and two women milling around the podium. "Is there a problem?" she asked.

A short stocky man with a colorful tattoo of an eagle on the side of his neck stepped forward. "Yes, there's a problem. This bitch —"

"Slow your roll, mister. Either you address my employees with respect or I'm going to ask you to leave."

The man took two steps, bringing him inches from where Greer stood, hands resting at her waist. He poked her chest. "I'm not going anywhere, bitch!"

She gave him a short jab to the throat seconds before Jason elbowed him to the temple. The loud mouth crumbled like an accordion. A deafening silence descended on Stella's. She nodded to Chase. "Please call the sheriff."

Her mentioning *sheriff* galvanized the others into action. Two men picked up their fallen comrade and half dragged, half carried him out of the restaurant as one of the women cried that Greer had killed her boyfriend.

Greer clapped her hands. "It's over, good people. Karaoke Night is about to begin."

Jason wound an arm around her waist. "I'll hang out here just in case they come back."

"I doubt if they will."

He gave her a level stare. "I'll still hang out here. You don't have Bobby tonight, so I'll fill in for him."

Her eyes caressed his face, seeing signs of fatigue for the first time. There were dark circles under his eyes, and his face was thinner. The strain of not knowing whether his aunt was going to survive had taken its toll. The neurosurgeon had placed her in a drug-induced coma to reduce brain swelling. "Thanks, Batman."

Jason nodded. "We make quite the dynamic duo." She mouthed that she loved him, eliciting a tired smile from him. "Ditto," he whispered.

"Careful killer. Your skills are showing," Chase teased when she returned solo to the table as Jason checked out the parking lot to ensure that the disruptive pack had left.

She ducked her head. "Jason decked him. I just stopped him from talking."

"You guys were awesome."

"What I was trying to do is save Stella's from becoming a dive where bar fights are the norm rather than the exception. My aunt and uncle worked too hard and sacrificed much too much for the law to shut us down. Bobby goes ballistic if we serve alcohol to anyone under twenty-three, and if anyone was found selling drugs . . . well I'd better not talk about that."

"Or the other possible scenario," Chase added, sotto voce.

Greer blinked slowly. She didn't tell Chase what she'd witnessed that morning she had videotaped Danny and the garbage collector. He told her. She'd sat stunned by his revelation, wondering who Chase was. Which clandestine agency did he work for? And if he didn't, then who was feeding him the information she'd passed along to her supervisor.

Once she had confronted Chase about why he'd come to her home, he did admit he knew Jason wouldn't be there because he was in Florida. Greer invited him to stay for dinner if only to try and see if the self-proclaimed ghost would inadvertently reveal more about himself. Unfortunately he hadn't. What had begun as an uncomfortable encounter for her for the first half hour segued into an easygoing experience where she found the enigmatic man brilliant as well as entertaining.

MC Oakie took to the stage as an Elvis impersonator. The rhinestone-studded white jumpsuit glittered like stars under the spotlights. He gyrated and swiveled his hips to raucous laughter. Thunderous applause followed his announcement that he would begin Karaoke Night by spotlighting one of the restaurant's employees.

Stefi appeared genuinely shocked when her name was called. Amid chanting and hooting, Stefi made her way to the stage, conferring with the master of ceremonies as to her song choice.

Greer and everyone in Stella's seemed to hold their collective breaths when Stefi sang Barbra Streisand's "People."

Greer could not believe such a powerful voice had come from the waitress's diminutive body. It was more than apparent that the aspiring actress had years of musical theater as evidenced by her ability to effortlessly project her voice. Stefi ran off the stage smiling and blushing furiously to a standing ovation.

"Is she still short-term?" Greer teased Chase.

His eyes darkened before his lids lowered, shuttering his innermost thoughts. "She can *only* be short-term."

"Jason says you usually spend Thanksgiving with your family. If you change your mind, then you're welcome to join Jason, Bobby and me."

"He's right, but this year they're joining my sister and her family who are vacationing in San Juan, Puerto Rico."

"Does this mean Jason and I can count on you joining us?"

Chase offered her a sheepish grin. "Yes."

Greer had convinced Bobby to close Stella's after lunch Thanksgiving Eve and not reopen again until the following Tuesday. The five days would serve as a mini-vacation for all of the employees.

Her uncle finally reemerged from his self-exile, walking over to the bar to talk with Pepper as Jason locked the door behind the last customer, and she began tallying the day's receipts, a task Bobby usually performed. Greer forced herself not to watch Danny as he cleaned up the dining room, depositing half-eaten food in reinforced garbage bags. It galled her that she knew of his illegal activities and had been ordered not to arrest him because the ATF sought to cast a wider net, sweeping up more than one or two gun traffickers. They wanted the mastermind behind the operation.

She wasn't certain how much longer she would remain with the agency because, every day she woke in the bed she shared with her husband, Greer wanted to live a normal life for the first time since she had celebrated her twenty-sixth birthday. She was tired of lying to Jason, tired of monitoring everything she said in his presence for fear of compromising her position as a special agent for the ATF.

"What did you think of Stefi's performance?" she asked Jason as he sat next to her, watching as she bundled bills by denomination.

"She has an incredible voice but . . ."

Greer met his eyes. "But what?"

"It's obvious she's been trained for the stage. She just wouldn't be a good fit for . . ." His words trailed off again when his cell phone rang. Reaching into the breast pocket of his jacket, he glanced at the display. "Yes, Ana?" Jason listened intently, a slow smile softening the lines of fatigue around his mouth. "Thanks. Yes. It's wonderful news. Congratulations to you, too." His eyebrows lifted. "Yes, I'll tell her."

"Tell me what?" Greer asked when he ended the call.

"Ana said to tell you hello. And she called to let me know that Justin Glover's album is now certified triple platinum."

Greer half rose from her chair to kiss Jason, then remembered where they were. "That's fantastic news. We'll celebrate but only after you catch up on your sleep. I can't have you passing out on me."

"It depends on what you do to make me pass out."

"Even superheroes need sleep."

Jason ran a hand over his face as he attempted to smother a yawn. "I tried sleeping during the flight but I couldn't relax."

"We're going home," Greer said, pushing back her chair and coming to her feet. "Bobby can finish this." Placing the receipts and money in a canvas bag, she walked to the bar. "Uncle Bobby, I started tallying the receipts, but you need to finish. Jason's falling asleep on his feet, so I'm taking him home."

Greer gasped audibly when she stared at Bobby. His eyes were swollen, red rimmed, and she knew he'd been crying. She didn't want to acknowledge the man who'd become her second father — and who'd fearlessly face down any man or beast — had spent the day in his apartment weeping for a woman who loved him as unselfishly as he loved her.

"And I'd like you to come home with me, too."

Pepper ran a towel over the bar. "That's all right, Greer. Bobby's agreed to hang out at my place tonight."

She kissed Bobby. "I'll leave the receipts in the safe. I'll finish them in the morning."

Bobby held her in a punishing bear hug. "Take care of your man, honey bunny. He loves you a lot. And don't worry about coming in early tomorrow. Stay home and spend some time with your husband," he whispered.

Greer couldn't ignore the flutters in the pit of her stomach. "Thank you." She raced up the staircase to Bobby's apartment, leaving the receipts in the safe and retrieving her tote. She returned to find Jason asleep in the chair. Anchoring an arm under his shoulder, she managed to get him to his feet and out to the parking lot. He woke when she forced him into the Range Rover's passenger seat.

"I'll drive."

She rolled her eyes at him. "Surely you jest. You can barely keep your eyes open, and you want to drive. Not tonight, darling."

Chapter 21

Jason woke and it wasn't until he saw the skylights that he realized he was home, home with Greer. He recalled her undressing him, assisting him when he brushed his teeth and had joined him in the shower. After that he hadn't remembered anything. He wanted to linger in bed but nature compelled him to get up and use the bathroom.

He reentered the bedroom, grinning from ear to ear when he saw Greer in bed, holding a mug of coffee. She wore one of his T-shits instead of a nightgown. Jason wasn't certain whether it was only their separation that made him look at her differently. The girlish aura was missing, and in its place was a confident woman.

Greer patted the mattress. "Come join me."

Jason slipped into bed next to her, she handing him the mug. "Thank you."

Greer kissed his shoulder. She picked up her mug from the bedside table, touching it with Jason's. *"Bienvenido a casa."*

"Oh, so my baby is learning Spanish."

She rested her head on his muscled shoulder. "Your baby will *not* go through what Nicholas's mother has gone through with her mother-in-law all these years. Our children will be bi- or even trilingual."

Looping his free arm around Greer's shoulders, Jason dropped a kiss on her hair framing her delicate face. He felt a gentle peace, a different fulfillment he hadn't been able to derive from music. His *abuela* was right. When he met the woman with whom he would spend his life, he would know it immediately. Marguerite-Joséfina had known it when she had seen Samuel Cole, and Jason hadn't known or was unaware of it because of his jealous mistress until he had walked into Stella's. Jason had refused to put a woman first in his life because he felt it would interfere with his creativity when it'd become the opposite. Sitting in the solarium outside his aunt's private hospital suite, he had found himself scribbling notes like a madman. Not only had he heard music in his head but also lyrics. He wrote for an acoustic piano, guitar and organ. Once he had completed the third song, Jason knew he was chronicling Greer's journey from the dark and into the light through music. The songs were for any woman who'd found herself controlled by forces not her own.

He knew she would never record the songs because it would be akin to reopening a wound that had healed over. Instead of sleeping during the return flight to Portland, Jason had spent the time ruminating which artist signed to Serenity's label would be best suited to bring his music and lyrics to life. He thought of Justin, but it would solidify him as a country artist, something Jason wasn't certain Justin wanted to be.

Ana's telephone call about Justin's inaugural album selling more than three million copies had become a personal triumph for Justin, and he expected the freshman singer to earn a Grammy nomination for Best New Artist and Best Country Song, which reached number one on Billboard's Top Country charts.

"You're very quiet this morning."

Greer's voice broke into his musings. "I was thinking about the songs I'd written while waiting for my aunt to come out of her coma."

"Will you play them for me?"

"I will once I'm finished." He exhaled an

audible breath. "When was the last time we slept in late?"

Greer rubbed her toes over his leg. "I can't remember. I hope you don't mind that I've invited Chase to celebrate Thanksgiving with us."

"He always goes to Hawaii for Thanksgiving."

"Not this year. He came by to see you when you were in Florida. I asked him to stay for dinner, and I got to see another side of your very mysterious friend."

"Please don't tell me my very mysterious friend waited for me to darken the door to try and hit on my wife," Jason teased.

"Of course not. I hope you're not jealous."

Jason set his mug down on a glass coaster. "Put down your mug," he ordered softly. "Of course I'm jealous," he whispered in her ear when she set down her coffee. "I'm jealous of any man who looks at you. And I'll kill any man who tries to hurt you."

Greer placed her fingers over his mouth. "Please, let's not talk about other people."

"Who do you want to talk about?"

Greer stared up at Jason through her lashes. "You."

Reaching over, he eased her to lie side by side with him, sandwiching her legs between his. "What about me?"

"You're young, a musician, and yet you don't have any piercings or ink."

"I'd thought about getting my ears pierced but never got around to it."

"What about a tattoo?" Greer asked.

Jason laughed, the sound rumbling in his chest. "I plan to tattoo my kids' names on my inner thigh."

"No one will be able to see them."

"No one but you." His right hand cradled her hip under the too large T-shirt. "I've missed you so much. I've missed hearing your voice, your laugh. I've missed tasting your mouth, inhaling your perfume. And I've missed making love to you."

Greer felt her eyes fill with tears from his impassioned confession. "I can't put into words how much I've missed you, but if you let me be on top, I can show you."

Reversing their positions, Jason lay on his back. Folding his arms under his head, he stared at Greer as she pulled the T-shirt over her head. He couldn't take his gaze away from her breasts, swaying slightly when she lifted her hips to remove her panties.

Greer straddled his thighs while bracing her hands on the headboard over his head. Jason pulled himself into a sitting position, his hands circling her waist. A rush of air was expelled from his lungs as she pressed her breasts to his chest. Lowering her head, she lightly touched her lips to Jason's before devouring his mouth. Her tongue then moved slowly, tracing the outline of his full, sensuous lower lip. Her hands were as busy as her mouth, fingers biting into his scalp.

Jason couldn't stop his deep moans of passion when Greer wouldn't permit him to escape her marauding mouth. Using his superior strength, he lifted her, extricated her mouth and fastened his teeth on her nipple, applying pressure but not enough to cause injury. The gentle tugging elicited a keening from Greer that made the hair stand up on his body.

He maneuvered her slender body with one arm, lifting her high enough to guide his erection inside her and filling her with the fire which threatened to incinerate him. Greer tried pulling away but Jason held her fast.

"No, baby," he pleaded.

Greer closed her eyes and gritted her teeth. She wanted it to last, but feared she was going to climax too quickly. Her heated blood raced through her veins like molten lava. She'd fantasized about an even more intense ecstasy with Jason, and now that she was experiencing it she was frightened.

Her breath was coming faster and faster. "I can't."

Jason ignored her request to be on top when he reversed their position and did not slow his powerful thrusts in an attempt to absorb Greer into himself where they would cease to exist as separate entities. "I belong to you, darling," he whispered in Spanish. *"Tome todo mí,"* he crooned over and over in singsong, clenching his teeth and praying he would not explode. He wanted her to take all of him so she could feel the love he was unable to put into words. She was so moist, so tight, that he doubted whether he could hold back ejaculating long enough for Greer to achieve her own fulfillment.

Greer slipped her arms under Jason's shoulders as she buried her face against the column of his neck, her hot breath on his ear when he slid his hands under her hips, lifting her higher and higher. The wetness flowing from her mingled with the perspiration covering their bodies. Her sensitized nipples grazing Jason's damp chest hair sent more shocks throughout her lower body. Her fingernails sank deep into the tight muscles of his shoulders, and she tried suppressing the uncontrollable screams slipping past her parted lips.

She welcomed Jason's weight, arching her back to receive his frenzied thrusts. She was too caught up with the emotions her husband had summoned — from the part of her where sanity and insanity merged — to realize the primal forces that had taken over her mind and body; raw, savage screams exploded from the back of her throat just before an awesome climax, followed by two more, consumed her in the hottest fire of oblivion.

Jason's growl of sexual triumph echoed in Greer's ear as he quickened his movements and buried his sex deep within her soft, throbbing warmth. He lay heavily on her slight frame, eyes closed. It had only taken the last seconds of his waning passion to know he would risk giving his life to keep her safe. He loved her just that much.

A light rain pelted the skylight when Jason finally got out of bed and went into the bathroom to shave. His whiskers were beginning to itch. Greer was still asleep when he walked back into the bedroom to dress. He opened one of the doors to the walk-in closet, then realized he'd given that side of the closet to Greer. A slight frown creased his forehead when he noticed the butt of a handgun in the leather tote she always carried with her. Reaching down, he picked up the deadly looking automatic. Hunkering down, he searched through the bag and found three 10-round magazines and a pair of handcuffs. His breath congealed in his chest when he opened the small leather case to find the badge and picture ID.

His wife was an ATF special agent!

Jason didn't want to believe the woman with whom he'd fallen in love, married and planned to become the mother of their children didn't trust him enough to reveal who she was. She'd talked about her ex deceiving her, and she'd done the same with him. At least Larry Hill had had an excuse. He was mentally unstable. Now he understood why she couldn't accept a recording contract. Why she wanted to keep their marriage secret.

The thoughts assaulted Jason like missiles, coming at him from all angles. He wanted to hate Greer, but he couldn't. Not when he'd found himself in too deep. What he wanted and needed were answers.

He returned the automatic and the magazines to the tote, but not the case with her badge and ID. Jason couldn't believe he was so calm as he went about getting dressed. It was as if he'd been shot up with a powerful sedative where he could only react like an automaton.

Dressed in a rugby shirt, jeans and running shoes, he sat down on the side of the bed and stared at the woman who managed to tug at his heart even when they were apart. There was so much about her he didn't know. His gaze narrowed. What else was she hiding from him? How much of her past was the truth or just lies?

Placing his hand on her shoulder, he shook her gently. Greer moaned, her eyelids fluttering as she came awake. A smile softened her mouth. The smile faded when she stared at what Jason held in front of her face.

Sitting up quickly, she reached for the case but he pulled out of her grasp. "Where did you get that?"

Tossing it over his shoulder, it landing on the floor, Jason grasped her shoulders, pulling her up. "When were you going to tell me?"

Greer's eyes were wild with rage. "You had no right to go through my things."

"I have every right, Greer, to know that my wife is leading a double life." Jason didn't want to believe he sounded so calm when all he wanted to do was punch something to relieve the rage holding him captive; he'd been a fool, an unwilling victim of duplicity.

"I couldn't tell you."

"That's B.S. and you know it." The fragile thread on his self-control snapped. "My sisters and cousins are married to federal agents, and at least they know what they do, even if they're not privy to what they're working on. You talk about your ex deceiving you. Well you've done the same thing to me."

Greer swallowed the bile in her throat. "It's not what you think."

"What am I to think, Greer? You claim you love me, but you don't trust me. Why?"

Jason was asking questions she couldn't answer. She hadn't planned on falling in love or even marrying again. But she did love Jason, more than she could've ever imagined. "I don't know."

"You don't know?" he mimicked sarcastically.

Pulling the sheet up to her chest, Greer wound it around her body. Her nakedness wasn't just about her body but also her emotions. Jason had stripped her bare, forcing her to look inside herself for reasons why she hadn't told him what she did for a living when Chase knew.

She sat up straight, supporting her back

against several pillows. "I didn't tell you because I hadn't planned to fall in love with you. But once I did, I knew there was no turning back. I had to play it out until the end."

"When is it going to end?" Jason asked.

Greer stared over his shoulder, unable to meet his angry expression. "Hopefully soon."

"I'm not going to ask you what you're involved with —"

"I couldn't tell you even if you did," she interrupted. "The only thing I'm going to say is that this is my last assignment. Once my supervisor secures the warrants and the perpetrators are arrested, I'm handing in my resignation."

"Have you identified the perps?"

Greer smiled for the first time since Jason had shoved her badge in her face. "Yes."

Jason's anger quieted as he tried to put his confused emotions into some semblance of order. He'd been living and sleeping with a woman who carried a firearm as if it were an accessory. "Does Bobby know?"

She nodded. "Yes. He's known for years that I'm with the ATF. And my brother isn't just a cop. He's FBI."

Jason gave her an incredulous stare. "Was your father *just a cop,* too?"

"No. He was DEA. And Mother was a forensic technician for the FBI."

"What the . . ." He stopped before the curse slipped out. "How can your whole damn family be federal agents?"

"Don't you dare talk about my family! It's like the pot calling the kettle black. The Coles have their share of federal agents. At least we've never had a spy."

Jason knew she was referring to Merrick Grayslake. "Don't try and shift blame, Greer."

"And don't you try and act so damn sanctimonious, Jason. Celia told me she didn't know Gavin was with the FBI until after they'd married and she was pregnant with their daughter. And you know how she found out? By seeing him at a televised press conference," she said, answering her own question. "At least you won't have to wait that long."

He gave her a long, penetrating stare. "Will you be involved in the press conference?"

"I doubt it. I've gone undercover before, and the agency wouldn't want to risk someone recognizing me."

"Are you undercover now?"

Greer shook her head. "No. I'm what you would call an eyewitness. Or if I was a civilian, then a CI or civilian informant. On the street I would be known as a snitch."

"Snitching is dangerous."

"I can take care of myself."

Jason smiled, nodding his head. "I've witnessed that." He sobered quickly. "Is there anything else I should know about you that isn't classified?"

"I do have total recall, and I speak fluent French."

He gritted his teeth. "I knew it. You lied about that, too."

"I didn't lie when you asked if I was an intelligence agent."

Jason placed a hand over his mouth to keep from spewing curses, curses he'd learned so eloquently from his grandfather. "What am I going to do with you?"

"You can divorce me."

"Oh, no, baby girl. You're not going to get out of this that easily."

Pulling back her shoulders, Greer raised her chin while giving him what she called the *stink eye.* "What do you think you're going to do?"

"It's not what I think but what I planned to do."

"And that is?"

"Use those metal bracelets you have in your tote to cuff you to bed and make love to you for twenty-four hours straight. Of course I'll stop long enough to eat, shower and maybe watch a few games on television, but I plan to make you pay for holding out on me."

Throwing back her head, Greer laughed until tears rolled down her face. "You wish! You couldn't go twenty-four hours when you were sixteen, so what makes you think you can do it at thirty-something?" Much to her surprise he laughed with her. The tense moment was over — if only temporarily.

"I *was* randy as a goat at sixteen."

"Was, Jason. I'm sorry you had to find out like this, but I thought it was for the best."

A beat passed. "I suppose if the tables were reversed I probably would do the same thing. But I want you to promise me something."

"What?"

"No more secrets."

Going to her knees, Greer pressed her mouth to his. "No more secrets."

Greer got up early Thanksgiving morning to chop and sauté the ingredients for her cornbread-sausage stuffing, while Jason acted as her sous-chef. Bobby was coming with his girlfriend, and when Chase had called the night before, he said he was bringing Stefi.

"Jason, please check and see if the potatoes are soft."

He poked a long fork into the sweet potatoes boiling in a large pot. "They're soft enough. Do you want me to pour out the water?"

"Please. Do you want to make the sweet potato casserole or should I?" Greer asked. She and Jason worked together well in the kitchen.

"I'll fix it. You have enough to do."

He was right. She'd rolled out crusts for apple, pumpkin and pecan pies, and as soon as she stuffed the turkey, she would begin making the filling for each. Thanksgiving and Christmas were Greer's favorite holidays because the house was filled with delicious, mouthwatering aromas.

The day before, Stella's had closed after lunch and Greer had come home early to set the table in the dining room, put up several loads of laundry and see if the cleaning service had missed dusting any flat surface. It would be the first time she and Jason would entertain as a couple and she wanted everything to go off without a hitch.

She and her mother communicated via Skype to discuss her upcoming wedding.

Esther had shown her samples of invitations, and they went through a dozen before Greer approved the one that best suited her personality. She emailed her mother the names and addresses of the friends she'd maintained since graduating high school and college.

Greer and Jason videoconferenced with the wedding planner. They decided on a three-tier cake with layers of red velvet, strawberry shortcake and chocolate ganache separating a layer of mocha chip, decorated with edible roses in red, pink and white nestled between the two top tiers, which would match the flowers in her bouquet. The only thing that remained was her wedding gown and shoes.

She didn't want something ostentatious with yards of fabric trailing behind her. After all, it would be her second marriage. When she asked Jason about his wedding attire, he said he had several tuxedos in his apartment at his parents' home. He sheepishly admitted he owned duplicate wardrobes on both coasts. All of his formal clothes were made-to-order and his tailor had his exact measurements. And because of his aversion to shopping, Jason ordered many of his clothes online from upscale retailers.

Greer spoke to Jason's parents when they'd called him to introduce themselves to her, and she was astounded by how much Jason and his father's voices were similar in timbre. She liked Serena immediately when she said she couldn't wait to meet her because she had always wanted three daughters. If her in-laws were anything like the Coles she'd met at Nicholas and Peyton's wedding, then she knew there would never be a dull moment whenever they got together.

Jason's cell phone chimed softly. He picked it up, reading the text. His thumbs moved quickly as he returned it. "Ana said she and Jacob found a house they like in Fort Lauderdale. They plan to close on it in two weeks."

"Where are they living now?"

"They have a condo in Boca Raton. I told Ana I would buy it from her once she moves. Then, we'll have someplace to stay whenever we visit the family."

"How often do you plan to go to Florida?"

"At least twice a year. Once we have children, we'll probably go down to New Mexico to visit with Emily and her in-laws, and to Mississippi to see Tyler and his family several times a year. They have at least a dozen kids between them."

Greer winked at him. "You Coles are rather prolific, aren't you?"

"All we have to do is smile at a woman and she's pregnant."

She wanted to tell Jason he'd just verified what Celia and Ana had told her. "Stop grinning at me because I don't intend to get pregnant before I'm married."

Jason took a step, pressing his groin to her buttocks. "Did you forget that we're already married?"

Resting the back of her handkerchief-covered head to his shoulder, Greer smiled. "I guess it won't become a reality until we repeat our vows with all of our friends and family as witnesses. Speaking of friends. Do you want me to send Chase an invitation?"

"You can, but don't feel bad if he declines."

"I bet I can get him to come. Maybe if he meets a Cole woman, he'll stop that short-term business."

Jason kissed the side of Greer's neck. "I don't think there's a Cole woman willing to put up with a man who's a nomad."

"We'll just have to see, won't we?"

Stefi paced the floor in the small efficiency apartment, waiting for Chase to call and let her know when he was on his way to pick her up. Her cell rang and she answered on the second ring. "Hello," she crooned.

"Hey, baby. I'm stuck in line in a bakery waiting to pick up my order. I'm not sure how long I'm going to be here, so I just called a car service to pick you up and take you to Jason's house. After I hang up, I'm going to call him to let him know you'll get there before me."

"Okay. But I really don't mind waiting for you to get here."

"But I do mind one of us getting there late."

"When should I expect the driver?"

"Give him about fifteen minutes, then come downstairs. They told me they don't have any available town cars, so they're sending a SUV."

"All right," Stefi said.

"See you soon, beautiful."

Stefi ended the call, smiling. She'd dated Chase for a week, and she really liked him. Unlike some of the men she'd dated, he hadn't tried to get her to sleep with him. Initially she had thought he was gay but then dismissed that notion when she'd deliberately aroused him to where she wanted him to make love to her. But she had to be careful not to mix business with pleasure. She'd come to Mission Grove to work, and not get involved with a man — no matter how much money he had.

She waited the requisite fifteen minutes, slipped on a wool jacket and picked up her small bag with the shoulder strap. Slipping it over her body, Stefi gathered her keys. Glancing around the furnished studio apartment, she walked out, closing the self-locking door behind her. The shiny black Suburban with tinted windows was idling at the curb. A tall, slender man dressed in a black suit, white shirt and sported a military-style haircut, stepped forward and opened the rear door. Cupping her elbow, he assisted her into the rear seat.

Stefi hadn't realized she wasn't the only one in the back of the vehicle until it was too late. A hand snaked out, covering her mouth, as she struggled to free herself.

"Don't fight me or I'll break your neck."

She stopped struggling and the man loosened his grip on her jaw. "We're going on a little trip." As if on cue, the partition between the driver's seat and rear seats closed, and the truck started moving. "I know who you are, and what you've been paid to do." Tears filled her eyes. "No one would expect a tiny little thing like you to be a contract killer. Put your hands behind your back." She complied and the plastic ties looped around her wrists nearly cut off the circulation.

Stefi was trussed up like a Thanksgiving turkey when her feet were also bound. The windows in the SUV were so dark she wasn't able to see the man sitting in a corner or where she was going. "Where are you taking me?"

"Some place where you won't see the light of day for many, many years. How long did you think you could get away with sticking folks with the cute little device you hold between your fingers? They think it's just a pinprick when in reality your toy is filled with venom from the inland taipan variety, the most venomous snake in the world. Your unsuspecting targets don't realize what's happening to them until the poison blocks all of their blood vessels."

"Where are you taking me?" Stefi repeated.

"Singapore. They have the world's harshest drug laws. If you're caught with two or more grams of heroin, you're automatically presumed to be trafficking in drugs. The penalty is a fine up to twenty thousand dollars to a maximum of ten years in prison. You, Moira Byers, will have ten grams of heroin in your luggage, five grams less than the fifteen for the mandatory death penalty.

The Central Narcotics Bureau officers stationed at the Changi Airport are experts when it comes to apprehending drug smugglers."

Stefi struggled against her restraints. "You're framing me."

"And you're a murderer."

She decided to try another approach. "Look, Mister . . ."

"The name is Caleb."

"Caleb, I have a great deal of money stashed away. If you let me go, I'll give you all of it. Every last penny."

"I don't need your money. The people who hired me to protect Jason Cole paid me a lot more than what you're attempting to bribe me with."

She decided on yet another approach. "How are you getting me out of the country without going through customs? What about a passport?"

"That's all been taken care of. You're flying first class in a private jet, and we have your passport. Once we land and you go through customs, you are on your own."

"I'll scream and tell everyone I've been kidnapped."

"No one's going to believe a drug smuggler."

This can't be happening. Monk promised

this would be an easy job. Stefi curled into a fetal position and cried. Her father had been a paid enforcer for several unions, and two of her uncles were hit men for organized crime families. Their weapons of choice were knives and guns. She'd become an ophiologist, milking snakes to make anti-venom. Then something had happened and she'd followed her relatives, becoming a hired killer. Monk had selected her victims and provided her with identities that got her through airport security and customs.

But it appeared as if Jason Cole's people were one step ahead of her, and she was heading to prison in Southeast Asia. Her life was about to mirror *Brokedown Palace,* but instead of going to a prison in Thailand, she would spent the rest of her life in a hell-ish Singapore dungeon.

CHAPTER 22

The doorbell chimed throughout the house and Greer and Jason exchanged a knowing look. Their guests had arrived. They'd spent hours roasting, baking and sautéing the dishes for their initial Thanksgiving gathering. She experienced a domesticity she had never felt in her first marriage. Jason's passion for cooking surpassed hers. Greer cooked out of necessity, while Jason cooked for experimentation. He'd substitute a common ingredient for an exotic one with pleasantly surprising results.

"I'll get it," she volunteered. A smile parted her lips when she opened the door to find Chase staring at her as if seeing her for the first time. "Happy Thanksgiving. Please come in."

Chase handed Greer a decorative shopping bag. "Same to you. Here's a little something for your table." He dipped his head, kissing her cheek. "Jason is safe," he whispered.

Greer blinked as if coming out of a trance. "Are you certain?"

He nodded. "My people took care of everything."

Her expression brightened. "Thank you. Where's Stefi?"

"She called this morning to say her agent got her a part in a movie being shot in New Zealand. She told me to tell you, she's sorry to leave without giving you prior notice, but it was an offer she felt compelled to accept."

Greer reached for Chase's hand, lacing their fingers together. "You did say she was short-term."

His gray eyes darkened as he studied the woman who'd managed to enthrall his friend — enough to get him to not only include her in his life but also his future. "Yes, I did. You're going to owe me, Greer."

Her jaw dropped slightly. "What are you talking about?"

"I took care of a *problem* earlier this morning, and the result is you'll be able to wake up beside your husband tomorrow morning. Yes, I know you and Jason are married. And, no, he didn't tell me."

Greer swayed slightly when her knees buckled, but she managed to right herself as Chase tightened his hold on her hand.

"Stefi?" Chase nodded again. She didn't want to know how he got his information because some things were better if not explained.

"If she ever comes back to this country, she'll be too old and broken to harm anyone. I promised you my people were going to help you out with your problem. Ten days from now it will be over."

She closed her eyes, whispering a silent prayer. "How can I thank you?"

"Name your firstborn son after me."

"I don't even know your actual name."

He laughed softly. "I'll tell you once he's here."

Greer tugged on his hand. "Come and rest yourself. My uncle and his friend are expected at any time."

Jason walked out of the kitchen and into the living room as Chase sat on a leather chaise in front of the fireplace. "Welcome, my friend."

He stood, shaking hands and pounding Jason's back. "Thanks."

A slight frown appeared between Jason's eyes. "Where's Stefi?"

"She got an acting job in New Zealand," Chase lied smoothly.

Greer gave her husband the shopping bag. "This is from Chase."

Jason removed the bottle from the bag, reading the label and the tag attached to the neck. *"¡Mierda!"* he whispered in Spanish. His neighbor had given them a bottle of aged scotch he'd won at an auction. "This girl is more than one hundred years old. Thanks, friend." Jason knew the bottle would sit in the bar untouched because neither he nor Greer drank scotch.

The doorbell rang again and hugs, kisses and handshakes were exchanged when Bobby introduced Renata Sutcliff as his very good friend and nutritionist. Tall, slender, with stylishly coiffed salt-and-pepper hair, a clear peaches-and-cream complexion and strong, even features, Greer felt an instant kinship with the woman who'd made her uncle's health a priority.

Renata successfully hid her shock at meeting Bobby's niece behind a polite smile. She didn't know what to expect, but it certainly wasn't the tall, slender woman with the golden-brown complexion and gold-flecked brown eyes. Greer was casually dressed in a white silk blouse, black tailored wool gabardine slacks and matching ballet flats.

Greer clasped her hands. "Everything is ready, so please follow me into the dining room." She removed the place setting that would've been Stefi's, unable to believe the woman would've posed a threat to Jason. She didn't want to think of the consequences if Chase and his people hadn't uncovered her plot.

"Would you like me to help you bring out something, Greer?" Renata asked.

"Yes. Thank you."

Tiny lines fanned out around Renata's dark-brown eyes when she smiled. "I told Bobby he can eat whatever he wants today because no normal person would even consider dieting on Thanksgiving."

Greer nodded. "Thankfully it's only one day a year."

Jason carried the platter with roast turkey into the dining room, placing it in the middle of the table, while Greer and Renata rolled out a serving cart topped by various dishes: macaroni and cheese made with truffle oil, sweet-and-sour green beans, sweet potato casserole with pecan brûlée topping, fresh cranberries, cornbread-sausage stuffing, giblet gravy and a tossed salad with honey-orange vinaigrette.

The hours passed with lively conversation adding to the festive mood as everyone had second servings washed down with sparkling water, rosé or white wine. Bobby exacted a promise from Jason to give him the recipe for the mac and cheese, but when he heard the price for the truffle oil, he quickly changed his mind. Cappuccino and espresso accompanied slices of pie and homemade chocolate chip cookies.

Greer shooed the men away from the table while she and Renata cleared the table and put the food away. Jason, Bobby and Chase retreated to the media center with a large wall-mounted flat screen and audio components that were separated from the primary living space. Jason lit a fire in the massive rock-faced fireplace as they settled down to watch television.

It took Greer half the time to put the kitchen in order with Renata's assistance. They sat at the cooking island talking about everything. The licensed nutritionist admitted she had never married after losing her college fiancé in an auto accident more than thirty years ago. She liked Bobby, but knew realistically she could never replace his late wife.

"You can't replace her," Greer said, "but you can help to make him happy and healthy."

Chase was the first to leave, thanking Jason and Greer for their hospitality and promising to come to West Palm Beach for their New Year's Eve wedding. Two hours later Bobby and Renata left with shopping bags of leftovers.

Standing in the doorway with their arms around each other, Jason and Greer waved as Bobby maneuvered his car out of the driveway. Jason closed and locked the door. "You did good, Mr. Cole."

Jason dropped a kiss on her hair. "I couldn't have done it without you, Mrs. Cole." Taking her hand, he led her into the media center, pulling her down to the sofa to sit between his legs. "I spoke to Bobby about buying the house on the lake, and he said he couldn't sell it to me because he'd planned to leave it to you in his will."

Greer glanced up at him over her shoulder. "What are we going to do with three homes?"

"We'll definitely use the condo in Florida."

"But what about the house on the lake? How often will we use it?"

"One of my cousins is transferring from a college in Miami to Lewis & Clark in Portland for the spring semester. He can stay in the house instead of on campus. It would be an hour's drive each way, but at least he'd have his privacy and a quiet place to study."

"I'm okay with it as long as he doesn't turn it into a frat house."

"Nathan's a cool kid."

"He'll stay cool as long as he doesn't destroy my aunt and uncle's home."

Jason pressed a kiss on the column of Greer's neck. "You'll get to meet Nathan when we go to Florida. Speaking of Florida, both Bobby and Chase are coming to the wedding. Is Bobby bringing Renata?"

"He said he is."

"It's too bad Chase couldn't have made a go with Stefi."

"It sure is," Greer drawled facetiously. She hid a smile. If it hadn't been for Chase, she and Jason wouldn't be planning to renew their secret vows. Her smiled faded quickly. He'd promised her that in ten days her life would change forever. Ten days, and then another four weeks, and she would change forever.

The seconds became minutes and minutes a half hour as they listened to the correspondents at the all-news TV station. Jason became instantly alert with the breaking news that there was a possible gas explosion at the Los Angeles home of Webb Irvine. There was footage of the police attempting to restrain a woman unofficially identified as Irvine's mother from entering what was left of the smoldering mansion. The reporter said the woman kept repeating she'd left her son sleeping inside the house. The explosion had occurred within minutes of her leaving to drive to the store.

So, it's over, Jason thought. There were no more Irvines and probably no more Slow Wyne. Even if the L.A.-based independent record label went under, Jason knew he wouldn't pick up their most talented artist. It wasn't worth the trouble.

His cell phone vibrated. He took the phone out his back pocket, staring at the display. "Are you watching the news?"

"That's why I'm calling," Ana said. "He's gone, Jay. It's finally over."

"Yes, it is. But I feel sorry for Mrs. Irvine. No parent should have to bury their children."

"I agree, but I'm not going to cry for her. She had to have known what she'd given birth to."

Jason didn't want to argue with his twin sister — not today. "Did you get my check from the bank?"

"I did, but I shredded it."

"Why?" Ana had quoted a price she wanted for her condo, and he'd authorized his bank to cut her a check.

"Because I'm not going to take money from my brother. Consider the condo a wedding gift."

"What do you want as a gift?"

"A boat. It's not for me. It's for Jacob. He loves deep-sea fishing, and when I mentioned buying him a boat, he went ballistic. My civil-servant husband has issues because I'm worth a lot of money. You don't know what it took for me to convince him to move to Bay Colony. He claims the house in the Keys can fit into our new home four times. So if you give him the boat as a wedding gift, he'll have to accept it."

"Pick out what you think he'd like, text me the dollar amount and where to send the check."

"Thank you, Jason. I love you."

"I love you, too, Ana. I'll see you guys in four weeks."

Jason ended the call, and then looked at Greer. She hadn't overheard his conversation because she'd fallen asleep. He understood Jacob's reluctance to accept expensive gifts from his wife because a man wanted to provide for his wife and not the other way around. He'd explained to his brother-in-law that all Coles came into a five-million-dollar trust at twenty-five.

At the reading of his grandfather's will,

Jason's net worth had quadrupled. Other than building the house in Bear Ridge Estates, he hadn't purchased any other big-ticket items. He didn't draw a paycheck from Serenity Records, living instead off the interest from his investments. He had more than enough money to take care of Greer, their children and their children's children.

West Palm Beach, Florida — New Year's Eve
Greer, Ana and Peyton stood with their arms around each other's waists in one of the bedroom suites in the West Palm Beach family mansion set on twelve acres, dressed in their wedding finery. Peyton had to have her platinum satin gown taken out at the waist to accommodate her expanding waistline.

Greer smiled at her fellow brides. "I have something to tell you before we go downstairs."

"What?" Peyton and Ana chorused.

"Jason and I got married the weekend we came to Virginia."

Peyton's gray eyes grew wider. "Our anniversaries are only a day apart."

Greer dropped her arm and combed her fingers through her hair, flipping it over her bare shoulder. "Yes."

Ana's dark eyes drilled into her. "You're

already my sister-in-law?"

"Yes. Jason had given me a ring, and we decided not to have a long engagement."

"But we could've had a double wedding," Peyton said.

Greer shook her head, a wealth of lush reddish-brown waves moving over her back with the motion. "It was your day, Peyton, and it would've been selfish and disrespectful if I'd intruded."

Ana flashed a dimpled smile. "It looks as if all of us are renewing our vows."

Greer's gaze swept from Ana to Peyton. "My sisters, you look beautiful."

"So do you," Peyton countered.

Ana pressed her cheek to Greer's. "I'm honored to be your sister."

Greer rested a hand on the double strand of pearls falling over her collarbone, warmed from the heat of her skin. Chase's prediction had manifested itself when, ten days following Thanksgiving, special agents from the ATF and DEA arrested sixteen people involved in the sale of illegal drugs and firearms. Danny had infiltrated the group, documenting the delivery and transfer of the stolen weapons. She hadn't known Danny was a government informant, and he was never made aware that she was a special agent. Two days after the success of the dragnet, Greer drove to the Portland field office and filled out the documents to resign her position with the agency. It was also the same day the Grammy nominations were announced, and Justin Glover was nominated as Best New Artist, his album earned a nomination for Album of the Year, and he was nominated for Record of the Year and Best Country Song. She and Jason celebrated by having a private party followed by making endless love.

There was a knock on the door and the three women turned in that direction. "Who is it?" Ana called out.

"Your father," came David's response. "And I have the other dads with me."

Greer smiled. It was about to start. "Come in."

The three men filed into the bedroom, their expressions mirroring tenderness when they stared at their daughters. Only Alphonso Blackstone had had the honor of walking his daughter down the aisle. David Cole and Gregory Evans would be afforded that privilege in fewer than five minutes.

David, wearing the requisite white tie, offered Ana his arm. "Come, baby girl. We have to get you married before the clock strikes midnight."

Greer rested her hand on the sleeve of her father's tuxedo as he adjusted her veil before handing her Jason's wedding band. She slipped it on the thumb of her left hand. "Do you mind sharing fatherly duties with Bobby?"

Gregory Evans smiled. "Of course I don't mind. I've always trusted Bobby to look after you and Cooper. Asking him to walk you down the aisle will really make this night even more special."

She knew when she walked down the white carpet to exchange vows with Jason it would be merely symbolic. For Greer it would become more personal when she'd leave her past behind to begin anew and live openly with her husband. Gathering the skirt of her gown in one hand, she carefully descended the staircase on her father's arm, gliding across the marble floor to a door leading to the Japanese garden where the ceremony was scheduled to take place. Organza-swathed chairs were lined up in precise rows under an enormous white tent. Greer watched her father tap Bobby on his shoulder. She couldn't see her uncle's expression but she was certain he was surprised by her request. It was a warm winter Florida night, the temperatures in the low seventies and perfect for an outdoor nighttime wedding and celebration to follow.

She and Jason had flown into West Palm Beach on Christmas Eve where she was introduced to more Coles, their extended families and traditions spanning four generations. There were so many children, if it hadn't been for her ability to recall everything she saw and heard, Greer would've needed a scorecard or playbill to differentiate who was who. Peyton had become the third blonde in a family where dark hair was the norm. Joshua Kirkland had passed his flaxen hair and green eyes to his grandson, Alejandro Blackwell. Gifts were given to all children under the age of sixteen; those seventeen and older that had driver's licenses were given keys to their first cars.

They had spent the first night in Nancy's home and the next three at Jason's parents' in Boca Raton. Jason had taken her to the condo Ana had given them as a wedding gift, and Greer had been overwhelmed with the breathtaking ocean views. Ana had accompanied her to a bridal boutique in Miami's South Beach and luck was with her when she found a dress needing only a minor alteration. The week was a whirlwind of shopping and eating at a different relative's home every night. Security at the Cole compound was as rigid as it was at Bear Ridge Estates. Invitations along with photo IDs were necessary for access.

One of the wedding planners approached the brides, handing each her respective bouquet. "It's eleven-thirty and we will begin in exactly five minutes. That will give all of you time to process down the carpet and repeat your vows. At eleven fifty-five you'll each be pronounced husband and wife. At midnight there will be a display of fireworks to welcome in the New Year. Then the partying will begin."

Greer blinked back tears before they fell, ruining her makeup as her uncle closed the distance between them, dabbing his own eyes with a handkerchief. "Uncle Bobby, don't or you'll have me bawling my eyes out," she implored him.

Bobby pulled her against his solid bulk. "I love you, honey bunny."

"I love you more," she teased.

By the time the prerecorded music ended and the distinctive notes of the Wedding March echoed throughout the tent, every seat was occupied. Greer, flanked by her father and uncle, made her way up the white carpet, silently acknowledging those she recognized with a smile. Nancy Cole-Thomas sat in a wheelchair, dabbing her eyes, while Nichola attempted to console her mother-in-law.

Greer met Jason's eyes, her heart turning over in tenderness when he placed his right hand over his heart. Peyton and her father followed, and then Ana and her father. Each of the men placed the right hands of their daughters into the left of their respective grooms, then stepped back to take their seats.

An eerie silence descended on the assembly as the black-robed judge began the ceremony in a resonant voice that carried easily in the night. Greer had decided to write her own vows, taking it from Charlotte Brontë's *Jane Eyre:* "I have for the first time found what I can truly love — I have found you."

Jason gazed down into the eyes of the woman he promised he would love forever, quoting from Simone de Beauvoir to Jean-Paul Sartre: "I'm altogether immersed in the happiness I derive from seeing you. Nothing else counts."

Peyton and Nicholas had written their own vows as had Ana and Jacob. This was followed by the exchange of rings, kisses and the pronouncement they were each husband and wife. If Greer hadn't felt like a wife before, she did now. And so did her family and the world.

The three couples had gathered at the receiving line as an explosion of colorful fireworks lit up the nighttime sky, spelling out HAPPY NEW YEAR! The pyrotechnics continued for ten minutes, the young children screaming in excitement. Their excitement was short-lived when those under sixteen were escorted back to the house. Those who were fifteen would have to wait another year before they were able to join the frivolity that wouldn't end until just before dawn.

Greer extended her hands to Chase when he stood in front of her. He was wearing a tailored suit. "Thank you for coming."

Bending slightly, he kissed her cheek. "You know I couldn't miss this. You are a beautiful bride. Jason is a very lucky man."

"And I'm a very lucky woman." She took a step closer. "Which name did you use to get in?"

Chase appeared very boyish when he flashed a sheepish grin. "My government name."

"What is it?" she whispered.

He winked at her. "If I tell you, then I'd have to kill you. Save me a dance." Chase was there, then he disappeared in the throng streaming out of the garden.

Chase acknowledged Diego Cole-Thomas, who wore a dark suit, white shirt and white tie, with a nod. "Nice party."

Diego flashed a rare smile. "Wonderful party. Come with me."

The two men walked a distance away until concealed behind hedges in the boxwood garden. Diego sat on a stone bench while Chase leaned back against a hedge, slipping his hands in the pockets of his trousers and crossing his feet at the ankles. Strategically placed flood lamps ringing the property lit the area up like daylight.

"It's done, Diego," Chase said after a comfortable silence.

"How can I thank you, Simon?"

Simon Charles Leighton exhaled an audible breath. "You already did when you paid me."

"This is not about money and you know it, Simon. It's about family."

"Yep. Family."

Diego angled his head. "How old are you?"

"Why?"

"Please answer the question."

"Thirty-five."

"Don't you think it's time for you to find a woman and start a family?"

Chase shook his head. "No, my friend. What woman would put up with a man who can't tell her his real name or what he does for a living? And don't forget his disappearing acts."

"If she loves and trusts you, then there's no reason why you can't have a normal relationship."

"What's this all about, Diego?"

"I have someone I'd like you to meet."

"What's up with you playing matchmaker?"

"No more questions until you meet her. The only other thing I'm going to say is she's a Cole woman." Diego stood up. "Well, my friend. I'm going to get back because this celebration only comes once a year, and I intend to enjoy every minute of it."

CHAPTER 23

Greer sat at the bridal table with her head on her husband's shoulder, watching Ana and Jacob on the dance floor dancing to "Cha Cha Slide." Nicholas and Peyton were the first couple to leave, with her pleading extreme fatigue.

Greer had changed out of her gown and into a pale pink silk pantsuit with black satin three-inch sandals. She'd danced with Jason, her father, Bobby, Chase, her brother and every male connected to her husband's family, some as young as ten.

"What time is it?" she asked.

Jason glanced at his watch. "Two-forty." He had reserved a driver to pick them up at three to take them to Boca Raton where they would spend the next two days at their condo before flying back to the West Coast.

He knew Greer was exhausted. She'd gone for her final fitting, and then had spent hours at the salon for a complete beauty makeover. He had tried to convince her to take a nap, but that was thwarted when her brother and parents had arrived.

"It's like we're in a fairy-tale world," Greer said, watching the couples whirling about the dance floor. "Cinderella and her prince have nothing on us."

"You can't be Cinderella because she had to leave the ball before midnight."

She giggled. "But I can be Cinderella after the prince finds that she fits the glass slipper."

"True."

The music stopped and the DJ tapped the microphone. "Ladies and gentlemen. I have a special request to play Rihanna's 'We Found Love.' We will also have a special performance by the male relatives of the wedding party."

Greer sat up, watching in amusement as six of Jason's cousins, ranging in age from late teens to early twenties stepped onto the stage. Screams went up from women when they realized they were going to be treated to a scene from *Magic Mike*.

It was apparent they'd spent time choreographing their steps when they slipped out of their shoes. The screams escalated when tuxedo jackets were tossed in the air. They gyrated, swiveled their hips when removing ties, suspenders and dress shirts. A collective gasp went up from the women when the spotlight slanted across rippling muscular pectorals and defined rock-hard abs. Screams of protest went up from their mothers as they shimmied out of their trousers. Wearing boxer-briefs, the half dozen superbly conditioned men slithered sensually across the stage à la Channing Tatum.

Greer was on her feet, applauding and cheering when several young women tossed bills onto the stage. The catchy dance song ended, and the dancers picked up their discarded clothing, racing off the stage. It took a full minute before the DJ was able to continue spinning his tunes.

Holding on to Jason's arm, Greer leaned into him. "Will you become my personal Magic Mike?"

Throwing back his head, Jason laughed. "I'm sorry, babe. There's no way I can move like that."

"Did you know they were going to strip?"

Jason shook his head. "No. I just prayed they weren't wearing G-strings because that truly would've been *escandaloso* and talked about for years. Come, darling. It's time for us to leave."

■ ■ ■ ■

Greer followed Jason out of the tent, waving to her parents who were dancing to a classic Motown song. Her brother appeared entranced by a petite woman with short black hair, velvety dark skin and a full, curvy body, pressed intimately to his as they danced without moving their feet. She had invited her parents to Mission Grove for an extended visit, and they had promised to come the first week in February and stay a month.

She climbed into the rear of the town car, slipped out of her shoes and rested her head on Jason's thigh. The smooth, rolling motion lulled her into a state of total relaxation. Greer hadn't planned on falling in love or marrying again, but fate had circumvented her plan the instant she had seen Jason Cole walk into Stella's.

The threat against Jason's life ended with Stefi's mysterious disappearance and the gas explosion that killed Webb Irvine; she no longer had to go undercover, and Greer now looked forward to living her life without having to look over her shoulder.

"I love you," she whispered as sleep enveloped her in its comforting arms.

Jason closed his eyes, whispering a prayer of thanks. He had told Greer if she loved him enough to marry him, then he would spend the rest of his life making her as happy as she made him. And that was what he intended to do.

Martin and David Cole, Joshua Kirkland and Timothy Cole-Thomas slipped away from the celebrating to lock themselves in the library as they did every New Year's. Each man puffed leisurely on cigars as they eyed each other. The time of reckoning had come to see who had won the wedding wager.

"Come on, Martin," Timothy urged. "Let's not prolong the suspense. Open the doggone safe."

"Slow down, *sobrino,*" Martin warned in a soft voice. "You can't be in that much of a hurry to lose your money."

Timothy blew out a perfect smoke ring. "What makes you think I'm going to lose?"

David loosened his white silk tie. "He is going to lose."

Stretching out long legs, Joshua chuckled under his breath. "If Martin had won, he would've opened the safe the minute we walked in here. Am I not right, David?"

David smiled, the expression so much like Jason's. "I'm staying out of this, brother."

"What do you know that we don't?" Timothy drawled. "You're being awfully smug."

Sucking in a mouthful of flavorful tobacco, David squinted at his nephew. "Smug or confident?"

Standing, Martin walked over to the James Baldwin print, opening the safe concealed in the wall. He removed the envelope he'd placed there a year ago. "Josh, please hand me a letter opener." The sound of ripping paper echoed sharply as all eyes were trained on the slips of paper falling to the surface of an antique table.

Joshua picked up one slip. "Martin picked Jason, Ana, and then Nicholas to marry in that order."

Timothy picked another slip. "Joshua selected Ana, Jason and then Nicholas to marry in that order."

It was David's turn to select a betting slip. "Timothy picked Nicholas, Jason and then Ana."

Martin selected the remaining slip. "David's choice is Ana, Nicholas and then Jason."

The three men threw their slips at David who couldn't stop laughing. "I told you I know my kids. Gentlemen, I will let you know where you can send your donations."

Joshua stubbed out his cigar. "I thought we had agreed the money would go to the winner's alma mater."

"I've changed my mind," David said. "Instead of donating the money to private colleges that have sizeable endowments, I decided I want the money to go to public schools for their music programs and to public television. Does anyone have a problem with this?" The three men shook their heads. "Happy New Year, my brothers and my nephew. It feels real good to take your money. And now that all of my kids are married, you'll have to think of something else to wager on."

"How about grandchildren?" Joshua asked with a wide grin.

Martin shook his head. "Oh, hell no. I'm not touching that. You and Vanessa have two children and a tribe of grandkids. David may be the only one who'll be able to match you."

David cupped his ear. "Do I hear another wager?"

"No!" the others chorused, coming to their feet.

The four men exchanged hugs and kissed one another on both cheeks, then walked out of the library to rejoin the revelry. It was New Year's Day and the entire clan had come together to preserve a tradition that had begun in 1924.

The employees of Thorndike Press hope you have enjoyed this Large Print book. All our Thorndike, Wheeler, and Kennebec Large Print titles are designed for easy reading, and all our books are made to last. Other Thorndike Press Large Print books are available at your library, through selected bookstores, or directly from us.

For information about titles, please call:
    (800) 223-1244

or visit our Web site at:
    http://gale.cengage.com/thorndike

To share your comments, please write:
    Publisher
    Thorndike Press
    10 Water St., Suite 310
    Waterville, ME 04901